HARVEST
OF
TEARS

BETTY PELLEY SMITH

Bristol Publishing Company
Lubbock, Texas

HARVEST OF TEARS

is published by
Bristol Publishing Company

Requests for information should be addressed to:
Bristol Publishing Company, Lubbock, TX 79414-2618.
You may also visit us at our website: bristolpublish.com.

ISBN: 0-9755667-6-8

Library of Congress Control Number: 2005932910

This edition printed on acid-free paper.

This is a work of fiction. The burning of the courthouse in the book is based on the burning of the courthouse that occurred in Sherman, Texas in 1930. All the characters—especially Mayor Ansel and his son, Stony—and all events portrayed in this book, except for the courthouse burning itself, are either products of the author's imagination or are used fictitiously. Any discredit to people, places or organizations is unintentional.

Cover Art: We would like to thank Rebecca Martino, the author's niece, for the orginal art on the book cover. More of Martino's art can be viewed at smartbelles.com.

Printed in the United States of America.

HARVEST OF TEARS

This book is dedicated to

My Parents,

Jay Ernest Pelley
and
Anna Beulah Sulser Pelley,

who were among the poor, good, honest,
hard-working, genuinely real, salt-of-the-earth people
that were shamelessly and ruthlessly exploited
by the greedy affluent few of a small town.

PREFACE

Hunger stalked the land for the "Great Depression" was upon it, destroying the dignity and security of a normally productive nation, settling down like a plague of locusts devouring fields of harvest crops. One-third of the country's 122 million people were ill-fed, ill-housed and ill-clothed for approximately 12 million Americans were unemployed. After the stock market crash of 1929, banks failed alarmingly fast, factories shut down with disastrous results and mortgages on homes and farms were foreclosed at a fast-paced, sickening rate. Soup kitchens and bread lines were established in larger cities to alleviate the destitute. People formed lines everywhere to obtain relief and men were walking, always walking, looking for jobs that were nonexistent or never materialized. Unscrupulous employers lowered wages to sub-survival. Workers were forced to sleep in subways or parks because they couldn't afford to pay rent. Department stores throughout the Midwest advertised that they would exchange clothing for farm produce. A survey by a leading university revealed that, of the millions of citizens turned transient, more than a quarter of a million were under 21 and almost half of those were girls.

Poverty and frustration saturated the physical and mental well-being of the people, choking out hope, dignity and self-respect. Suicides were rampant. Respectable women capitulated to prostitution in order to feed their children. Previously sober abstaining men resorted to alcohol in a vain attempt to regain their feeling of usefulness and manhood while others, lacking the strength and will to continue the apparently hopeless struggle, gave up and merely sat, staring into space.

Unspeakable squalor prevailed in both the metropolis and the rural communities. The Depression knew no boundaries and was no respecter of race, color or creed. It reached across every line, touching the life of every person in the country. Lives interweaved with each other over every section of the nation, from the North to the South, from the East to the West; albeit the factory worker, the farmer, the rancher or the gold panner. Each was vital to the other, whether it was the "hick farmer" who brought in the harvest or those "damn yanks" who provided the market.

Incredibly sad and strange as it may seem, there was poverty amid plenty. One of the most disheartening features was that farmers were paid to plow under cotton and crops for lack of a profitable market while millions went without enough food. It was a simple matter of economics—overproduction and under-consumption at the same time. Thousands of bushels of wheat were left uncut in fields because of its low price that hardly paid for harvesting. Fruit rotted in orchards while children, through poverty, were denied it. Cattle and sheep were slaughtered by ranchers because the cost of shipping them to market was greater than their sales; yet, people fought for scraps of meat from garbage cans. Cotton lay dormant, ruining in fields because the cotton pickers could not exist on the 35 cents paid for picking a 100 pounds. And, as a result of overproduction, farmers were unable to pay the interest on their mortgages so, eventually, mortgage companies went into the hands of the receiver. Farmers lost their farms by foreclosure and mortgage companies lost their holdings by tax sales. The farmers of the South and West were pauperized by the poverty of the industrial populations of the North and East who, in turn, were wiped out by the poverty of the farmers; both were rendered incapable of buying the product of the other. Thus, poverty amid plenty.

Who can say what social aspects have evolved, even still predominate, in the overall life structure of society as a result of the devastating Depression of the 1930s? It would be impossible to take into account or to evaluate the countless ways that it has influenced the lives of those who were mired the deepest in the quicksand of poverty during that era. Their progeny remember parts and pieces of the period only dimly because of man's fortunate ability to blot the image of past unpleasantness from his mind. Even those who were unborn at that time are affected in a multitude of ways. Who can say how many sequential generations will suffer, either directly or indirectly; how and to what extent their harvests will be reaped from the wildly scattered seeds sown by it? Those who were directly involved know inwardly of the Depression's deeply personal, cataclysmic effect on their own lives while their descendents, too young to have endured that dismal season, have no comprehension of its consequence on their lives— nor will they ever. It is impossible to accurately or adequately describe the disastrously debasing subjection to the degenerate privation of that ravaged epoch. This tragic stage in history was one that had to be trodden and performed upon personally in order to be able to discover its truth and meaning, to know the "gut" feelings of hopelessness and despair. Unemployment in the United States reached its peak in 1933 with 24.9 percent of the labor force out of work. More than a quarter million of these unemployed were Texans; Texans who organized and marched in desperation past the capitol in Austin, demanding jobs—not "gilded promises" stating they could not live on "hot air" alone.

Texans, loyal and fiercely proud of their heritage, haughtily aware that their land was a nation in itself before becoming a state of the Union, did not relish having to call upon government from the outside for help with problems inside its borders. But pride could not prevent the existing conditions of the Union from invading their revered "empire." Texas ranchers, declaring that they would accept blame for dust and drought but would not take the blame for poverty resulting from low prices, indignantly ordered that prices for cattle be increased. They argued that they did not need "new deals" in Texas from the federal government but only asked for a "square deal."

Virgil's profound proverb, "someday, perhaps, it may be pleasant to remember even these things," bears no particle of truth for those who survived these catastrophic years. Though memories of the dust, drought, degradation, deprivation and the Depression have faded away for the most part; still, millions of stories could be told of those troubled days in time. This, then, is only one of those stories—about a few people in a small Texas town—one small town of this vast country.

An honest man can feel no pleasure in the exercise of power over his fellow citizens.

—*Thomas Jefferson*

CHAPTER 1

Elisabeth Lancer dropped the hoe and straightened up. Placing her hands on her hips, she swayed back and forth to ease the stiffness of her back. Now, at thirty years of age, her figure still maintained the slender gracefulness of early youth, her eyes were as startlingly green and the long brown hair that hung loosely about her shoulders retained a shining luster. Her skin had turned to creamy ivory after the long winter just passed, having lost the golden tan that she acquired each spring and summer from prolonged exposure in the outdoors.

With a critical eye, she surveyed the area that she had completed weeding on the south side of her home. The flower beds, built along the length of both sides and across the front of the house, contained only rose bushes that were planted in a neat row down the center. Of all flowers, roses were her favorite. With their deeply-rich colors and the classic shape of both bud and fully-opened bloom, they almost seemed to cast a spell over Elisabeth. She ran her fingers lightly, lovingly over several of the tightly-closed buds, the first to appear in this new spring. This was the time that she had longed for all winter. Spring would awaken the dormant plants and would, once again, herald the appearance of her beloved roses.

The gentle early morning breeze was pleasant; the

freshness of the air exhilarating. Elisabeth's face was relaxed, content. She felt that she was a fortunate woman indeed. She had been blessed with three healthy children and a husband who had a fairly steady job at Blossom's Mill. And anyone who had a job of any type, steady or not, in this Depression year of 1932 was extremely favored. Jon had been employed at the mill for six years as a truck driver, hauling flour and grain to points in west and south Texas. But with the cutbacks in employment at Blossom's during this past year, he had worked irregularly. Third in line of seniority, his truck runs had become more and more infrequent.

Finally, after a period of two weeks, he had departed early this morning on a run. *That meant there would be, at least, a small pay check this month,* Elisabeth thought, *although it won't come close to covering even the barest necessities.* She sighed. *Well, we aren't the only ones who are having a hard time these days. Everyone is in the same boat. We may be poor but I certainly don't consider ourselves unfortunate, as Jon does.*

Elisabeth, a remarkably patient woman, accepted life as it came, without questions. Reared on a farm in a family of seven children, she had always been poor. She accepted that. The one thing in life that she could not accept was Jon's alienation, his indifference toward her. Reluctantly, after all these years, she had, at last, become resigned to it. Resigned, because she could find no solution. Because Jon refused to open the door between them. *It's my fault,* she thought, *I'm to blame.* Elisabeth, lost in her thoughts, did not hear Sam's approach.

Sam Britton owned the grocery store, a fourth mile up Sam Houston Road, the one on which Elisabeth lived, at the corner adjoining David Crockett Street. Sam, 42 years old, was a tall broad-shouldered man with an open friendly face that bordered on handsomeness. The unruly shock of dark hair was fringed with gray. He possessed that special youthful quality, seemingly reserved for those with a genuine outgoing interest and concern for others.

Making his morning deliveries, Sam had parked his dilapidated, but still serviceable, pickup truck in Mrs. Parson's driveway. After depositing her order, he walked across the Daltons' yard with Elisabeth's small sack of staples. As he drew near, Sam could see the gentle, softly-curved swells of her body, outlined and accentuated by the faded but neat print dress. Suddenly an unexpected surge of emotion welled up in him, almost overwhelming in its intensity. *Oh, God,* he thought, *will the pain never leave me? Won't I ever be able to conquer it? I don't know how I've stood it all these years without telling Elisabeth the way I feel about her.* His eyes were dark with pain as his thoughts persisted. *I should have left Anseltown years ago.* Yet, he knew that as much as it tortured him to see another man married to her and fathering her children, occupying the role in her life that he coveted, the thought of never seeing her again, watching her smile or hearing her laughter, was unbearable.

Elisabeth, hearing his footsteps now, turned, "Well," she laughed, "if it isn't my favorite grocer."

Sam grinned at her, "Let's keep it that way. I wouldn't want to lose your business."

Elisabeth's smile disappeared, "I don't know why, Sam, the way our bill keeps going higher and higher."

"Now, Elisabeth, stop talking like that. I'm not concerned about your bill. I know that it's as good as gold." His face was sober as he looked at her closely. "Have you lost weight, Elisabeth?" he asked. Without waiting for an answer, he added, "You haven't been ordering much meat lately and that worries me. Everyone needs meat for their strength."

Elisabeth's face flushed slightly and Sam hurried to

say "I hope you don't think I'm being a buttinsky, Elisabeth, but I'm just worried about you." Elisabeth looked at him, frowning slightly. Sam said quickly "Well, I mean, I worry about all my friends, Elisabeth. Everyone is having a damn hard time, making ends meet!"

Elisabeth's frown changed instantly to a smile. "Good neighbor Sam!" she said, "I don't know what we'd all do without you, Honestly now, one would think you'd be mad at everybody for not paying their grocery bills, but here you are, worrying about them instead."

Her face turned serious. She put her hand lightly on his arm for a moment as she said, "Oh, Sam, you're such a good man. So kind and thoughtful. You'd have made some girl a wonderful husband." His face grew red but she didn't notice as she went on, "I'm sorry that our bill has got so high, Sam…" He opened his mouth to protest but she interrupted. "No, let me finish, Sam. I'm sorry that we can pay only a little each week on it. But you know that they've cut back an awful lot at the mill and Jon is lucky if he gets to make one run a week now on the truck. But," her voice contained a note of shame as she continued, "we will pay you just as soon as Jon can get more work." Her green eyes misted. "Your bill comes first on our list." She turned away quickly.

Sam said gruffly, "Now, Elisabeth, I don't want to hear anymore of that talk. You know I'm not worried about your bill. All I'm worried about is if you and your family are eating right. You can't just live on vegetables; don't worry about running the bill up. I want to see you ordering more meat. You hear, now?"

Elisabeth had brushed quickly at her eyes while he was talking. Then, Sam heard her lilting laugh again and she said teasingly. "There you go again, Sam! I declare, you're going to get old before your time, worrying about us. We're doing alright. I've still got some canned food from last summer's garden. By the time it's gone, I'll have this year's garden to pick from. And as far as meat goes, you know, I have my backyard full of chickens. I didn't need to buy very much from you during the winter because the Johnsons butchered hogs on their farm and we got some fresh pork from them along. So..." She looked up at him, her eyes crinkled from her smile. "Now, does that account satisfy you?"

She turned serious. "We are so fortunate, Sam. There are so many who are much worse off than we are. Some people are actually going hungry right here in Anseltown!"

"Some are even starving to death in the big cities," Sam said. "I've read stories, of men going into stores in broad daylight and stealing groceries—only they don't call it *stealing*." He reflected a minute, adding, "And I'm not sure I do either. They say that their families are starving and they are just taking enough food to feed them—that they will pay for it when they can get work. They only take the bare necessities of food—no cigarettes or booze."

Elisabeth's face was set. "I don't blame them, Sam, God knows I'd steal for my children before I'd see them go hungry. Stealing is sinful but I don't think God would consider it a sin in a case like that." She was thoughtful a moment, then added in a firm voice, "Regardless, I wouldn't let them go hungry—I'd have to steal for them."

"Well, I hope that we can get rid of Hoover this year and get this Depression over with." Sam said. "I'd like to see Roosevelt as president—but anyone will be better than Hoover."

"I pray that whoever is elected will be able to end this awful Depression and give people jobs again." Elisabeth's expression was sad but, suddenly, she smiled. "But, in the meantime, I've got so much to be thankful for. My family is disgustingly healthy and," she hesitated a moment before adding, "we're happy." Sam looked at her closely but she said nothing more.

"I'd better get back to the store," he said, then laughingly added, "People may be standing in line to pay their bills!" Elisabeth laughed.

As he walked away, she called softly, almost shyly after him, "I'm awfully thankful too, Sam, for a friend like you!" He grinned back at her.

Picking up the hoe, she moved to the front of the house. She noticed the badly peeling paint. I hope that we will be able to paint the house next year, she thought. It needs it badly. Modest though it was, she loved her home. She and Jon had bought it in the second year of their marriage, making the down payment from the small nest egg left by his mother at her death. The savings had accrued mostly from the earnings of Jon and his brother. It was said of his mother, noted for her thriftiness, that she could manage to save money from amounts on which others would starve. As a widow, alone with two sons to rear, she had been forced to improvise, stretch and survive on practically nothing.

Despite its peeling exterior, Elisabeth's home was tidily clean, inside and out. The sparsely furnished interior was orderly and neat. Most pieces of the heavy old furniture had been inherited from Jon's mother and Elisabeth's parents. The austere dark wood had been softened by the hand-knitted scarves and crocheted afghans that covered and decorated table tops and chair backs.

The Lancer home, in the northwest outskirts, was three miles from the courthouse square in the heart of Anseltown. The courthouse was the focal point from which all distances to any point in town or nearby area was determined. A tall, dignified old elm tree that stood near the curb of the Lancer's large front yard cast its gentle shade across the lawn. The yards on Sam Houston Road were spacious, as were most in Anseltown. The space behind the house was even more expansive, stretching back to the narrow dirt road that wound around the thick woods just beyond. A large pecan tree grew in the center of the backyard, shading much of it and also the screened-in back porch of the house. A wire mesh fence enclosed the back half of the yard, cooping the chickens inside that Elisabeth raised. Jon had built the small square barn-like structure that stood inside the fence in the furthest corner near the road and was used to house them.

The Lancer home faced east and, across the street at the front, lay a field filled with dandelions. It was bordered on the opposite edge by a small lazy, trickling creek. Here, neighborhood children gathered to fly kites and play baseball in the spring, wade in the creek in the summer, play football in autumn and build snowmen in winter. The lot just north of the Lancer home stood bare. The house which occupied it at one time had burned several years previously and had never been rebuilt. Zeke and Nellie Dalton resided in the house on the other side of them. A quarter of a mile on down Sam Houston Road, a railroad track, curving around the woods, crossed it and separated the houses of the white people from the tarpaper shacks of "nigger row" as it was called. Sam Britton's store sat at the opposite end of Sam Houston Road where it originated at David Crockett Street, a street that ran two and a half miles to the courthouse.

As she worked, Elisabeth's mind dwelled on the happy years that she had spent in this house, despite Jon's estrangement. Her children had given her so much happiness. Larry, now 13, had grown tall so rapidly this past year that he was somewhat awkward. His voice had begun to change, a condition for which he often seemed embarrassed. He looked uncannily like Jon except that he had inherited her green eyes. A quiet serious boy, he kept his feelings locked inside him, away from others, with the exception being Elisabeth. An understanding bond linked them closely. They knew how to communicate with each other. Even in silence, they could sense the other's thoughts and feelings. This son of hers, Elisabeth thought tenderly, was so young and so vulnerable. He possessed a great sensitivity that would allow him to be easily hurt. Deeply protective of him, she realized, reluctantly, that she wouldn't always be able to shield him with her armor against the pain that he would encounter in life.

Lisa, 7 years of age, strong spirited and with a mind of her own, had already learned to use her feminine wiles to get her way. Unlike Elisabeth who thrived on work in the outdoors, Lisa preferred to help in the house. She abhorred getting her hands and clothes dirty. Elisabeth, secretly pleased with her daughter's femininity, encouraged it by assigning outside chores to the boys with Lisa performing those inside the house. It was an arrangement that was satisfactory to all concerned.

A smile touched Elisabeth's mouth as she thought of Roscoe, her youngest son of 5. A lovable little rascal, he had yet to outgrow his baby chubbiness and his cotton head that had been a trait of all three until their hair had turned from white to brown. Roscoe had Elisabeth's open-faced look and mouth with upturned corners but, unlike Larry and Lisa who had come by their mother's green eyes, his were smoky black, like Jon's. Exasperating one minute and comically laughable the next, he was a precocious child, a mixture of confused blessing to have around.

Elisabeth dug stubbornly at each pesky weed which persisted on growing between the rocks on the perimeter of the beds. She recalled how she and the children, three years previously, had hauled the heavy stones in their large toy wagon, load after load, from the quarry at the end of the meadow near the railroad track. She had invented word games and puzzles to play with them in order to make the labor lighter. Lisa and Roscoe, still small, were more hindrance than help but she had to keep them occupied while she worked. Larry had been old enough to assist greatly. Painstakingly, they had placed the rocks in a neat row three feet from the house around the front and sides. When this was finally accomplished, the wagon trips began once more. This time the trips were across the meadow to the edge of the creek where the rich sandy dirt there was shoveled into the vehicle, then delivered and scattered inside the rocked in area. Elisabeth had been stiff and sore for days afterwards but she had no regrets. For, at long last, the time had come that she loved most—the time for planting. She had grown up in the fields of her father's farm and she liked the feeling of being a part of God's plan for nature, of being involved and sharing in His creative work. It was a cooperative venture, it seemed to her, for man planted the seeds in the ground and God gave life to them and provided proper elements in the soil, sufficient sunshine and rain to make the plants burst from the earth bringing forth the harvest.

Carefully and lovingly, she planted the cuttings that she had obtained from Mrs. Parsons' rose bushes. A widow of 70, Mrs. Parsons lived on the other side of the Daltons and her yard was the pride of the neighborhood. Her unceasing work among her flowers resulted in a showcase mass of colorful blooms from early spring until the first autumn frost. With no money for nonessentials, flower cuttings and seeds were gladly exchanged between neighbors. Mrs. Parsons, very superstitious, had strictly forbidden Elisabeth to thank her for the rose cuttings, saying that, were she to do so, they would not live. Elisabeth had not laughed for Mrs. Parsons' beliefs in the realm of the mysterious were taken seriously. She had been known to render severe tongue lashings to those who presumed the liberty of making light of her soothsaying.

Before planting the cuttings, Elisabeth had first rooted them by placing each one separately in fruit jars which she filled with water. The jars were then set on the large wooden table that occupied one corner of the screened in back porch. Under her watchful eyes, they rooted and thrived, quickly growing large enough to be transferred to the earth. Her success with them earned her the reputation of possessing a *green thumb,* of being capable of growing and cultivating even the most fragile of plants when no one else could. Many brought their cuttings to her to "get them started." Some even brought their ailing plants to be healed. Nellie Dalton once said, "I declare, Elisabeth, I do believe you sing to them."

Whereupon, Elisabeth had laughingly replied, "I do, Nellie."

Slowly, Elisabeth straightened. Her back had grown stiff from the prolonged stooping. Looking back at the weed-clear beds, she inspected the area closer. Satisfied that she hadn't missed any, she proudly examined the bushes, laden with closed latent buds which concealed the potential royal beauty of their contents. It won't be long until they open, she thought contentedly. She felt relaxed. Her face contained a peaceful expression. Her love of roses, indeed her inner need for them, was deep, vital.

She squinted up at the sun. Its rays were hot, penetrating the thin dress. She could feel the perspiration trickle down her back. Its position in the sky revealed that it was almost noon. So engrossed had she been in her work and thoughts that she had lost track of time. *I'll finish clearing the north side of the house after lunch,* she thought as she climbed the front steps and sat down in the wide wooden porch swing at one end. She swung gently back and forth to raise a breeze. She wanted to rest and cool off a few minutes before going inside.

Resting from her morning's labor, Elisabeth continued

to sit. In a reflective mood, she allowed her mind to wander back to her first meeting with Jon. She had been only 17 at the time. Nevertheless, she had fallen in love with him at first sight. First laying eyes on Jon when he stepped onto the pitcher's mound while playing in a baseball game, she had stared silently, intently at him for a long time. Finally, she turned to her best friend who was sitting beside her under the shade of a tree and stated as a matter of fact, "I'm going to marry that boy, Lou Ann."

"Well, I declare, Elisabeth," Lou Ann said in a shocked tone of voice, "How on earth can you say such a thing? Why, you don't even know him."

"I don't care!" Elisabeth retorted, tossing her long brown hair, "I'm going to marry him just the same. You just wait and see."

"Well, I know that when you make up your mind about something, Elisabeth, you usually do it but, I have my doubts this time."

"Like I said, Lou Ann, wait and see." Elisabeth laughed. Almost everyone in town had turned out that hot summer day to watch their local baseball team play the one from Westville, a farming community ten miles away. There was nothing else to do on a Sunday afternoon in Anseltown. The only entertainment afforded was the one movie house and it had been closed on Sundays by voters who viewed it as a possible source of sinfulness that would desecrate the Sabbath. Hence, the slightest diversion attracted the townspeople like flies swarming to honey.

After the game, Elisabeth casually strolled over to Walter Edwards, one of the players, and said, louder than was necessary, "It's a wonder your team won today since you weren't in church this morning, sinner."

All the while, she was casting her eyes at Jon who was seated nearby, changing his shoes. Laughing at her remark, he looked up at her saying, "I didn't think Walter even knew what a church looked like."

"Well, I was wondering if you knew what a church looks like," she replied, smiling teasingly at him. The even white teeth in the wide generous mouth made an attractive contrast in her suntanned face. "Can't say that I've ever seen you there."

"Well, now, Miss I-don't-know-who, maybe you're the one who isn't attending church. I've never seen you in mine. There is more than one church in town, you know."

Elisabeth turned imploringly to Walter, "Aren't you even going to defend me, Walt? Tell him I'm not a heathen."

Jon had walked over to them. He was still barefoot. Walter grinned and threw his arm around Jon's shoulders. "I can take a hint," he said, "so I'll introduce you two. This is Elisabeth Sanders, Jon, and don't tell me you didn't notice her during the game. That's why you struck out in that last inning—you were too busy looking at her instead of the ball." Elisabeth blushed, the color rising under her tan, as Walter continued. "This is Jon Lancer, Elisabeth, and, although I hate to say it, he's the best darned pitcher in the whole state of Texas."

Jon looked embarrassed but pleased. Walter picked his glove from the ground and turned to them. Jon and Elisabeth stood silently, gazing into each other's eyes. Walter, grinning again, said, "I know you two are going to be broken hearted to know that I've got to get going. See you Wednesday evening at practice, Jon. Good-bye, Elisabeth." There was no answer and he walked away.

Jon liked what he saw. Walter had been right. He had been very much aware of the shapely, pretty girl whom he had watched covertly during the game as she laughed and talked with a group of young people. Her vibrant personality and gay, contagious laugh with its appealing lilt made her stand out in the midst of the others. Her lithe figure, though strong, had such grace that her every move was pleasing to see. And, now, he could determine what he had been unable to from a distance. Her eyes were an emerald green, enhancing her deeply tanned face. The brown hair, cascading below her shoulders, was shiningly lustrous, rich evidence of homemade soap, rainwater and vigorous brushing. The aura of health surrounding her being called to mind nature's attributes of the sun, wind and rain.

Jon could smell the fresh essence of soap in the warmth of her nearness. Drawn like a magnet to her, he gazed hypnotically into the coolness of the limpid green eyes. Suddenly, he saw color creeping into her face again, and he realized that he had been staring. Blushing furiously, he stooped, attempting to camouflage his embarrassment, and picked up his glove, saying as he did so, "Can I walk you home?" The smile that lit her face made no answer necessary. Without another word, they turned and started walking away.

Suddenly Elisabeth stopped. Pointing to his feet, she said, "Don't you think you'd better put on your shoes?" Jon stared at his bare feet, laughed and ran back to retrieve his shoes. He sat on the grass at her feet as he put them on. She watched him, laughing.

"I like to hear you laugh, Elisabeth," he said, looking up at her, his face sober, solemn in the late evening rays of the sun.

Embarrassed slightly by the compliment, she replied, "Well, I guess it's adequate."

"It's a pretty sound and I like to hear it," he said. Rising from the ground, he offered her his arm in an exaggerated gesture. She laughed again and placed her arm through his. As they passed Lou Ann, Elisabeth turned away from Jon to give her an extravagant wink.

A month later, Jon and Elisabeth said their vows in the parlor of her parents' home.

Their first year had been full and happy. As their first

anniversary approached, they were even happier to learn
that Elisabeth was pregnant. Jon continued to play baseball
in every spare minute and, although Elisabeth was jealous
of the time that the game took him away from her, she was
also proud of him. His successful reputation as a pitcher
spread throughout the state.

Excitedly bursting into the house one day after a
game, he told her of the scout from the state baseball
league who had been observing him for some time and who,
today, offered him a contract to play for a state minor
league team. Jon whooped for joy, shouting, "This is my
chance, honey—the chance I've been waiting for." Grabbing
Elisabeth, he whirled her around the room. She had never
seen him so exuberant, an exuberance she did not share.
"Don't you see, Elisabeth?" he was saying, his eyes shining,
"this is the day that I've worked and hoped for all my life!"

Elisabeth looked into his face. She was unable to
speak. Jon was deadly serious. His face grew sober. "The
salary won't be much to start with, honey," he continued,
"but as soon as I can prove myself, it will be plenty to send
for you." His voice animatedly rushed on, "And I'll be able
to buy all the things that I've wanted to get for you."

But Elisabeth didn't hear his words, "Send for me? Are
you saying that you will go off and leave me?"

"It will only be for a little while, honey," he said,
pleadingly. "You could stay with your folks just until my
salary is increased and, believe me, I'm going to prove
myself so fast that it won't take long." He was stumbling
over words in his jubilation. "And it would be better for you
to stay here until the baby comes. By then, I'll be making
more than enough to send for you and the baby and take
care of you both the way I want to." His face lit up as he
added, "Elisabeth, we'll have money—lots of money—
more money than we ever dreamed of having!"

Elisabeth's face was stormy, "How can you talk about

going off and leaving me now that I'm pregnant with your baby?" She shook her head vigorously, stubbornly. "I don't want money. I just want us to be together. I don't want to be separated from you but you wouldn't mind at all. Just as long as you can go running off to play your beloved baseball..." Her voice broke and she flung herself across the bed, crying hysterically. Suddenly, she was very fearful for she did not know how to cope with this situation.

"Honey, don't you see?" Jon asked, his eyes begging her to understand. He tried to take her into his arms but she pushed him away.

The tears continued to flow as she sobbed, "Besides, I don't want to leave Anseltown. It's my home. And you know that Mama is in bad health." She raised her head from the bed and looked at him accusingly, adding, "So is your mother. You know they would both just die if we went away and left them!"

Jon's dark eyes flashed angrily in his set, obstinate face. "Elisabeth," he said harshly, "we're married to each other—not to each other's mothers."

Frustrated by her inability to convince him, Elisabeth cried furiously, "I won't leave Anseltown. I'm happy here!" She burst into fresh sobs.

Sitting down on the bed, Jon pulled her up roughly. "Look at me, Elisabeth." His commanding tone forced her head up so that her eyes met his. They were pleading, tortured as he searched hers. After a brief look of disbelief, they turned hard, cold. He said bitterly, "You really mean it, don't you? You won't leave Anseltown to go with me!" Harshly, he thrust her from him. Rising from the bed, he stomped from the room, slamming the door behind him.

It was the first night that they had ever gone to sleep angry with each other. Nor did they speak for several days except to argue about the contract. Jon had a week in which to make his decision. On the last day, with Elisabeth still unrelenting, he went to see his mother, hoping desperately for her support. Instead, she rallied to Elisabeth's aid, telling him bluntly that he was now a family man with responsibilities.

"You will soon have another mouth to feed and it's a man's duty to take care of his wife and children," she had admonished him. "You can't go chasing around the country playing ball." She had looked at him reprovingly. "You're past childhood now."

What childhood? Jon thought, bitterly, *I never had one.* His mother's voice went on, "Life isn't a game, Jon, it would be downright sinful to consider baseball to be a job instead of earning a living doing good, honest work. God didn't intend for man to play instead of working by the sweat of his brow." Jon didn't answer. He was already going through the door. With the two of them fighting him, he was defeated.

Elisabeth, knowing that it was the final day for Jon's decision, anxiously awaited his return. She prepared supper but it grew cold as the hours passed with no sign of him. Weary, she finally went to bed, but she did not sleep. The old grandfather clock, a family heirloom and a wedding gift from her parents, struck 2 o'clock before she heard his footsteps on the front porch. They sounded strange, uneven. She pretended to be asleep when he came into the bedroom. He stumbled and the odor of whiskey was strong. It was the first time that she had ever known Jon to drink.

After that, it was never the same between them. Jon did not play baseball again. He withdrew into himself and sat for hours, brooding, not speaking to her. He refused to discuss baseball or the contract. She wished that he would. She attempted to broach the subject several times, only to have him curtly cut her off. Finally, he exploded in rage, "I don't want to talk about it. You got your way so you should be satisfied now. Don't ever mention it to me again—not now, not ever!" The veins stood out on his forehead and his face was darkly threatening. He lifted his arm as though to strike her and his voice rose sharply, menacingly. "Do you understand?" Instinctively, Elisabeth took a step backwards. Abruptly, his arm fell to his side. Then, he turned quickly and strode out of the house. Elisabeth never spoke of it again.

From that time on, she knew in her heart that Jon would never feel toward her again as he once had. Now that it was too late, she realized just how much the contract had meant to him, how deeply he had felt about leaving Anseltown. Now, she knew full well how strong and how real this obsession of Jon's had been. To him, the contract had been his door to freedom—the way to escape the town he hated—the way that represented a better life that he had longed for. But it was too late. He had closed the door between them, shutting her out. He had never forgiven her.

Elisabeth had held herself responsible, despite her youthfulness at the time, for not possessing the sensitivity to comprehend his needs and, thereby, shattering his dreams. She had failed Jon as a wife when he had needed her most. She had been taught that a woman should honor and obey her husband, yet, she had refused to leave Anseltown with Jon. Remorseful, she had been patiently lenient with him in the ensuing years when his neglect and indifference toward her and the children only served to remind her of her guilt. Those nearest her were often puzzled by her forbearance and persevering tolerance, but they dared not speak of it. Her deeply rooted and unyielding loyalty to Jon, so plainly apparent, forbade any questions. Elisabeth, alone, knew the reasons and she neither confided nor complained to anyone.

Elisabeth stirred restlessly in the swing that was stationary now as her thoughts returned to the present.

And, even now, she found herself thinking, *if only Jon had opened the door to me years ago—if only he would open it now—if only he could forgive me.* Surprised, she tasted salt on her lips. She lifted her hand and touched her face. It was wet with tears.

Sam parked the pickup in front of his store. He switched off the ignition but continued to sit behind the wheel. The thought persisted in nagging him about Elisabeth's hesitancy when she told him that she was happy in their conversation a little while ago. He wondered if she had learned of the other women in Jon's life. He knew that her fierce loyalty to Jon would never allow her to speak of it to anyone.

Sam had been in love with Elisabeth since she was 16. Until then, she had been just one of the seven Sanders kids to him. Even now, he could still envision her that day when she came riding her horse across the fields to invite them over for homemade ice cream and soda to celebrate her 16th birthday. An only child, Sam lived with his parents on the farm next to that of Franklyn Sanders, Elisabeth's father. Her long silken hair, caught by the wind, flowed behind her as she rode and he heard her musical laughter as she waved her arm at him. For the first time, he became aware that she was no longer a child but a woman. Her body had suddenly developed from straight thin angles into soft rounded curves. The long legs, no longer gangly, were graceful and berry-brown from field work under the sun. A gleaming mane of brown hair framed dancing green eyes set in a finely chiseled face, resembling that of a Grecian sculpture.

Sam, feeling that Elisabeth was still almost a child and that the dozen years difference in their ages was yet too great, worshipped her from afar and waited for her to grow up. But he had waited too long. Shocked and dismayed, his heart ached the day that she came to their farm a year later with another invitation. Only this time, it was to her wedding the following week. He listened numbly while Elisabeth talked happily with his mother, Lila. Following her to the yard when she left, he asked her gently if she were sure, reminding her that she was still very young. Tossing her head back, she looked up at him, laughing gleefully, "Oh, Sam, is that why you've been so glum? Well, I'm not too young to know that I love Jon. So, be happy for me."

She had no way of knowing that her words stabbed him like a knife. Teasingly, she said, "Sam, you're an old fuddy-duddy for being concerned about me." Then, suddenly, she turned serious, her face softly solemn, as she added, "But I love you for it." Impulsively, she stood on tiptoe and brushed her lips against his cheek. He felt the warmth of her body briefly against his, and it was all he could do to refrain from crushing her closely in his arms. Instead, he stood statue-like, his arms by his sides, as she mounted her horse and galloped away, her body swaying gracefully. The longing for her and the pain in his heart was almost more than he could bear as he watched her ride out of his life and disappear from sight. He did not attend her wedding, nor did he see her for a long time afterward.

Sam got out of the truck and walked toward the store. He was surprised—and annoyed—by the emotions that he thought he had successfully locked securely inside him long ago but which had emerged again today, once more to haunt him.

In the store, Mrs. Hawkins wore a long-sleeved dress that reached her ankles after ballooning widely over her ample waist. Her gray hair was tucked beneath the stiffly starched sunbonnet that was made from the same material as the dress. Winter or summer, long dresses were her customary attire for Mrs. Hawkins, in her words, "wouldn't be caught dead in one of those short newfangled dresses that hardly left anything to the imagination."

"I declare, I don't see how folks can afford to buy groceries these days—what with no jobs and no money," she said, peering over the rim of her glasses at him.

"Yes, everyone is having a hard time," he agreed, then asked, "What can I help you with, Mrs. Hawkins?"

"Nothing else, Sam. I got everything I needed off the shelves," she answered, pointing to the few items on the counter. Her voice dropped as she asked, "Will you kindly put them on our account? Bill thinks he may get to work a day or two at the mill this week—then, we'll be able to give you a little something on our bill Saturday when he gets paid."

Sam, who had been going through the file for the Hawkins record, glanced up at her. Her face had a shamed expression and her eyes did not meet his. He said quickly, "It's perfectly alright, Mrs. Hawkins. Don't you worry. I'm not. I know the people who pay their bills and," he grinned at her, "you folks are on my preferred list!" She looked gratefully at him but said nothing. As he filled out her account, he asked, "How are the grandkids?"

Mr. and Mrs. Hawkins had taken their son's widow and three little ones after his death a year ago to care for even though Mr. Hawkins was hardly capable of working at his age. "They sure keep a body going, I'll tell you," she replied, "and, land sakes alive, I never saw three young 'uns eat so much. It 'pears like they got bottomless pits for stomachs."

After Mrs. Hawkins left, Sam glanced worriedly down the rows of shelves, many of which were all or partially depleted. He wondered how much longer he could go on with hardly any money coming in while everyone asked for or extended their credit. He was not concerned about being paid for his customers were honest, hard working people who gave him as much as possible on their grocery bill from any paycheck, no matter how small, which they received. He didn't know how much longer his suppliers would extend credit to him. Some had already cut back, protesting his own prolonged charge account that was the result of his customers' inability to pay him. *It's a vicious circle,* he thought, *but I'll keep the store going just as long as I can.* He could not and would not cut off credit. As long as he had one staple on the shelf, one potato in the bin or one slab of dry salt pork, he would not see these people— his friends and their children—go hungry.

Sam pulled the heavy burlap bag of potatoes from the storeroom and dragged it to the empty bin along one side of a wall. Opening the bag, he picked up several potatoes at a time, carefully inspecting each one before dropping it into the bin. He discarded an occasional bad one. His motions were deft, automatic from the countless number of times that he had performed this task. As he worked he thought of his father, Hank Britton. Sam had inherited the store when his father had died.

Hank and Lila had been married in New York where they had both been born and reared. After only one year of marriage, they were blessed with a son, Sam. They wanted more children but were not blessed with another. Being an only child, Sam was unusually close to his parents. After Sam left for the university, unexpectedly, Lila conceived a "change of life" baby. Both Hank and Lila were delighted! But when he was only 18-months old, their new baby son died suddenly. They were heartbroken. Lila, always a frail woman afflicted with asthma, lost interest in life. Hank, frantically alarmed, watched helplessly as she grew weaker, seemingly wilting away from him. Distraught and desperate, he realized that he was losing her. When the doctor advised that a change of climate and scenery might help, Hank gladly sold their house, packed and stored their belongings and headed west with Lila by train in search of a new home. It was summer and Sam, home from the university, joined them in their search for a new home.

Hank, an editor for a New York paper, was armed with recommendations from his former employer. He hoped to get a job in his chosen profession in California, their planned destination. In route, they stopped to visit old friends of the family in Dallas. Their hosts conducted them on tours of the surrounding areas, including Anseltown. Lila had fallen in love with the small village at first sight.

A smile played about Sam's mouth. Even now, after all these years, he could still remember his mother's childlike excitement on seeing Anseltown. Flowers, which she loved, grew abundantly in the spacious yards. Huge stately old trees lined the streets, their branches reaching across to clasp and embrace each other and cast their gentle shade below. The large well-kept lovely old homes were reminiscent of Southern plantations.

Lila had been especially ecstatic about one plantation type structure on the outlying edge of town. It sat well back from the road on the top of a gently rising hill that overlooked a meadow, which stretched behind it and along both sides. At the foot of the slope on one side was a small clear shimmering lake. Its cool, clear water reflected the green leafed trees on the banks and the fleecy white clouds floating through the blue sky above. Tall oaks lined the drive that ran a hundred yards from the road and curved in front of the splendid dark paneled oak door to the dignified majestic edifice. The expansive lush green lawn was meticulously manicured and bordered profusely with multi-hued flowers that exuded an exquisite mixture of fragrances.

Lila's face of twenty years ago flashed before him. Her eyes had sparkled in her excitement and she had chattered happily all the way back to Dallas that day. Hank had been so relieved. It was the first time that she had shown interest in anything since the baby died.

It hadn't been difficult for Hank to make up his mind. Without telling Lila, he had returned to Anseltown the next day and gone looking for a job at the newspaper. The *Anseltown Times* was well established as the only newspaper in town and all the jobs were filled. He then looked for a business to purchase. Sam chuckled softly to himself. Hank had purchased the small grocery market, a business he knew nothing about. But he would do any kind of work to keep Lila looking as she had the day before, after viewing Anseltown. Lila was jubilant when he told her that it was to be her new home. And, he had felt so extravagantly foolhardy in his relief about Lila's renewed interest in living, he promised her then and there that one day—he couldn't say just how or when—but, one day he would buy the house for her that she loved so well.

Hank had a Dickens of a time learning the grocery business and making ends meet. He made many changes, renovating the store from the plain square barn-like room it was when he purchased it. Partitioning off a large area at the back, he made a store room in one corner and a freezer room in the other to hold the carcasses of meat that he cut up and displayed in the glass enclosed meat counter. In addition, he built shelves and bins down the side walls. The store had become a modestly-thriving business.

When Sam finished his studies, he joined Hank and Lila in Anseltown. Following in his father's footsteps, Sam had studied journalism and got a job working as a reporter for the *Anseltown Times*. All three of them had been extremely happy in Anseltown despite the clannishness of the people and the cliquish snobbery at first toward the newcomers.

And Hank had kept his promise to Lila. True to his word, five years after their arrival in Anseltown, Hank bought the house from the family when the older generation had died off and the younger one had settled elsewhere. Their excitement on the day they moved was vivid in his memory, and Sam's eyes grew moist now as he recalled how happy Hank and Lila had been the day they moved in. Lila had chosen the second floor room with a small balcony attached and overlooking the lake for their bedroom. Each morning all these years, winter or summer, Lila had never failed, as soon as she arose, to go out on the balcony and gaze lovingly at the lake and Anseltown. Nestled softly in the valley, it could be seen, shining in the sun by day with its lights twinkling by night. She had never tired of the view.

Then during the Flu Epidemic of 1919, Hank fell ill and did not recover. Sam inherited the store but continued with his first love, the newspaper. He hired Wilbur, a conscientious, quiet man to run the grocery store and they worked together well. However, Wilbur was not people oriented and Sam loved the atmosphere at the store. It satisfied the innate curiosity that is a characteristic all good newsmen—he wanted to know everything that was going on in Anseltown: The what, who, how and why of the entire town. At the store, he kept in touch with the common people. At the newspaper, he dealt with business owners, socialites, and the attorneys and judges at the courthouse.

He paused in his work to survey the store. He was fond of it. He had set up a small desk in one corner so that he could write for the newspaper when he had a spare minute. He looked affectionately at the black potbellied stove which stood in the center of the room. He had planned to get rid of it and use gas heat instead but so many of his customers, grown accustomed to its friendly warmth that drew neighbors together around its cheerful glow on cold wintry afternoons, protested that he relented. So it had remained to serve as the meeting place for women to gather and gossip for awhile, for men to argue politics and swap stories by—a present day rendezvous reminiscent of the colonial town crier. For around its cozy girth, everyone, especially Sam, kept currently abreast of his fellow townsfolk and all the news of the town itself.

In summer, the meetings were transferred from the potbellied stove to the outside where Sam had placed several wooden benches which he had built for this purpose along the back of the store. Here, in the shade of a huge elm tree, men sat and talked lazily or animatedly, depending on the latest news, chewed tobacco and, with ever handy pocket knives, whittled incessantly on pieces of wood, the prevailing popular pastime. At the long wooden table with attached benches on each side that Sam also constructed, almost never ending contests of dominoes and checkers were in progress, sparking heated but good-natured debates. The games were carried on marathon style and the place of a participant who had to leave was quickly filled by eager bystanders, impatiently awaiting turns. The large vacant lot which lay beyond the alley served as a baseball or football field, whichever happened to be in favor at the moment. From all over town, young and old alike swarmed to the popular spot to mingle and socialize, to listen and learn. Sam was particularly pleased to note that the youth came frequently, deserting the pool hall which afforded the only place of amusement in Anseltown for them.

Sam and Lila continued to inhabit the house nearby that Lila loved so well. His mother was the only one who had been cognizant of his love for Elisabeth. Not that he had ever told her. But he supposed that, in the special way mothers seem to have of possessing inner instincts about their children, she just knew. She had spoken of it only once to him, just before Elisabeth's marriage to Jon. The pain had been so fresh and so deep that he could not bear to talk of it, and he asked her not to mention it again. She understood and never broached the subject from that time on.

Sam finished emptying the last of the potatoes into the bin. His movements were slow and heavy; his face darkly meditative, reflecting his mood. He had been contented, almost happy, with his life. The hours early in the day which he spent laboring in the store and then the late afternoons and early evenings spent at the newspaper office brought him a sense of accomplishment. Weary at night, he was at peace with himself. He could sleep. And, with his friends congregating at his store and rallied around him, he wasn't lonely. He was satisfied.

Sam frowned. At least, he had thought that he was satisfied until this morning. He shook his head, attempting to dispel his thoughts. But they were there and he had to face them whether he wanted to or not. Until this morning, he had foolishly convinced himself that he had successfully buried his feelings for Elizabeth—had put her out of his heart for good.

CHAPTER 2

From Anseltown's conception, its poor had always lived in a depression of sorts. But the national one that held the country relentlessly in its omnivorous grip in the spring of 1932 contributed even more poverty and sordid squalor, mercilessly adding the "last straw" of hardship to their already impoverished lives.

Located midway between the Panhandle and the north central part of Texas and only 25 miles from the Oklahoma border, Anseltown, a small pretty town of tree-shaded streets, large columned old homes with spacious lush green lawns generously colored with flowers, gave a promise of quiet serenity that belied the seething restlessness lying beneath its surface. The town had been named for William Ansel—by William Ansel, the first mayor, albeit self-appointed. Subsequently, it became the seat of the county which also bore Ansel's name.

Migrating west from Kentucky to be one of the first settlers in this small spot of the state, William Ansel had humble beginnings as a pioneer-farmer. But the fertile land he settled on, blessed by nature that supplied the sufficient amount of sun and rain the first few years, yielded bountiful cotton harvests and endowed him abundantly. Sagaciously recognizing the needs of the area, he established a cotton gin that served not only Ansel

County but the surrounding territory as well. Shrewdly, he purchased great expansions of land, some of which he sold in later years at great profit. Instrumental in founding the town's first bank, he held the controlling interest. His venture into a cotton garment factory proved immediately prosperous, and he opened a hosiery mill. His final project was a cottonseed-oil refinery, also handsomely profitable. Since both the land and the climate was conducive to its growth, cotton was the king crop that dominated the area and provided the Midas touch for Ansel. More than one-fourth of the population of Anseltown relied on cotton and its allied plants for its livelihood, making them dependent on William Ansel whose enterprises employed them. Infatuated by and drunk with the power that had been so abruptly thrust upon him, he became obsessed with it, using every means at his disposal to maintain his control over the people, feeling justified that his domination of the largest percentage of the town's assets and wealth qualified him as the supreme monarch. Ruling with an iron hand, he prohibited the entrance of any outside enterprises whose industry might compete with his own for the labor market of the citizenry and impede his power. And, although bitterly opposed to his policies, the "little" people were, nonetheless, impotent to fight against them because of their economic dependency on him.

Not long before he died, William Ansel relinquished the mayor ship to his son, Sol. After fiercely retaining the reins of the town in his iron grip since its inception, he was satisfied to hand them over only to his heir. In this transition of power, there were no waves, not even so much as a ripple, for the methods of command remained stoically the same. And, had he lived long enough, he would have been proud of the way his son perpetuated the same control that kept the people under his domination. William Ansel had coached his son well. Without doubt,

Sol could unerringly be called a "chip off the old block."

Two classes of people populated Anseltown: The very well-to-do which had been born, through no effort on their part, into the "right" families, and the very poor. Reigning over both, Mayor Ansel set a classic example for the elite upper class, a name self-bestowed, in the art of extracting and multiplying their wealth from the exploitation of the poor. The pawns and victims outside the vicious inner circle were ever dependent on them for the miserly wages which allowed neither security nor escape. There was no choice, only a matter of bare survival in continuing to work for the favored few—or starvation. This was the toll exacted from the destitute for the dubious privilege of living here. It was the price one paid for having been born in Anseltown.

Jon yawned as he drove through the early twilight. It was only the first day of June but already the oppressive heat of a Texas summer had begun. *It's like a damn inferno,* he thought, squirming uncomfortably in his sweat sticky clothes. He blinked, squinting to see in the oncoming darkness and switched on his headlights. The large truck with Blossom Grain and Flour Company in red letters emblazoned on both sides of the van rumbled down the narrow two lane highway with its center ribbon guiding him along the thin portion of pavement allotted his vehicle. The black snakelike line, crawling down the straight stretch of seemingly endless road, accentuated the bleak monotonous landscape. It lay desolate, sterile of any plant growth. So flat and barren was the land that it conjured up an illusion of a giant scythe slicing through it to level the countryside and leave only this trail of concrete in its wake. *Little wonder*, he thought dryly, *that the small town he was approaching was called Flatland.* It lay deep in the heart of Texas on his regular circuit route from Anseltown through Wichita Falls, Abilene and San Antonio to Houston before he returned by way of Austin, Waco, Fort Worth and Dallas.

He surveyed the inhospitable country with distaste. He hated the whole damn state of Texas. It had never meant anything but grief and hardship for him. It had even half-orphaned him, depriving him of a father before he was born.

His father, Jonathan Lancer, had brought his young bride, Cindy, to Texas from Kentucky on their honeymoon. An experienced hunter and outdoorsman, he capitulated to the charms of the great Red River surrounded by verdantly abundant woods and he stayed to make a new home. The river, luring him with lavish promises of fishing, trapping and hunting, lived up to his wildest expectations and yielded its riches bountifully to his skills. Successful in establishing a market for the pelts of animals that he trapped near the river and fish caught in lines laid across it, Jonathan Lancer was happy with his new home and planned a good life for his family. But, sadly, fate willed otherwise. Working on his beloved river in the humid Texas summer shortly before Jon's birth, he contracted malaria and died two weeks later.

Young Cindy Lancer was left alone to fend for herself and her babies, working as a domestic and barely scraping out an existence, she was compelled to put her young sons to work. Even at 5 years of age, they did odd jobs, running errands for neighbors or doing anything that would bring a few cents. When Jon was 9, his mother managed to talk Mr. Barton, owner of the Anseltown plant nursery, into hiring him. Jon could remember how Mr. Barton had looked him over and, then, apparently satisfied that he was healthy and obedient enough to perform the labor, hired him. There was too much work to be done for Willie, the Negro man that Mr. Barton employed. *Another man, rather than a boy, was needed,* Jon thought bitterly now, *but that would have meant Barton would have had to pay a*

*man's wages instead of a few pennies a day to a helpless
child.*

Jon worked at the nursery until he was 17 and Mr.
Barton died. At 9 years of age, he had to drop out of school
for he worked from early morning until dusk. Even now,
Jon could recall how he had been so young that he still
possessed a childhood fear of the dark. Enroute home
after nightfall, he had to pass a hobo jungle at the edge of
the woods that bordered a railroad track. He was frightened
of the bearded, unkempt and often times, intoxicated men
that he saw in the light of the bonfires. He would catch
himself running blindly, his heart pounding and the blood
racing in his ears, until he was securely out of range. The
only times when he wasn't afraid were the ones when
Willie went with him. He had told him of his fear and,
although Willie lived in the opposite direction, whenever
he left work at the same time as Jon, he would walk him
safely past the camp.

Jon and his brother, denied the carefree status of
childhood, had been thrust directly, almost from babies,
over the threshold of a harsh adult world. But, at 14, Jon
discovered baseball. It became the all consuming obsession
of his life. At first, it offered a little of the childhood that
had eluded him, making him forget the austere reality of
his life for awhile. Then, the realization dawned that, most
important of all, it offered escape. Young though he was,
he knew that, with his limited education, baseball was the
only road to freedom for him—the only road open to him
out of this despicable town which held him captive. Jon
possessed an overwhelming desire to be a "somebody" and
not just Widow Lancer's fatherless kid. But, more than
anything else in the world, he wanted to get away from
Anseltown—to be free of this place he hated, the place that
had robbed him of his childhood, the place that would also,
eventually, rob him of his manhood. This fierce craving

was like an unquenchable fire raging inside him.

Determinedly and methodically, Jon set about to become the best, most skillful baseball player in Anseltown. Shrewdly deciding that a pitcher would attract the greatest notoriety, he practiced relentlessly, doggedly in every spare moment. Although exhausted after a long day's work at the nursery, nevertheless, he would enlist the aid of his brother or friends and train obstinately, incessantly until they, at last fatigued, would refuse to continue. Day after day he drilled, even during the cold of winter, while waiting impatiently for spring and the baseball season to begin.

At 15, his pitching skill caught the attention of the manager for the local men's team. Elated, he accepted his offer to play for them. He would now be in the most advantageous position for recognition for this was Anseltown's best team and competed against those from other towns in the state. He was exuberant. It was that all important *first step* on his way out of Anseltown. Over and over during the long grueling hours of practice, he had told himself, *if you want something badly enough, you must do everything within your power to prepare for it—to be ready to take that first step. Then, and only then, could the others follow.* Well, he had taken the first step. Now, he was going to make the others follow. He didn't care what it took or how hard it was. He would sweat and work until he strained his guts but he was going to be ready and, when the time came, he would reach out and grab those next steps.

Jon wiped the back of his hand across his eyes. He had difficulty seeing in the rushing oncoming darkness of the night. The air, propelled by the moving vehicle, came through the window and hit against his face dry and hot, a lingering reminder of the day's seething torridity.

Damn it, Elisabeth had put an end to all that. Jon's

thoughts resumed bitterly. *She dashed the hopes and dreams that I worked so hard for. She didn't have faith in me. His long frame slumped dejectedly in the seat. His hands gripped the steering wheel so tightly that his knuckles were white, What a fool I was,* he thought angrily, *to let her stop me.*

His attention was diverted by the glow of lights ahead. He was glad to see them at last. He was hot and tired and anxious to reach the Flatland Inn, his usual stop just this side of the city limits. A cold beer was sure going to hit the spot. He hadn't had one since he left Houston. He could almost feel the cold bottle in his hand and taste the mellow smooth liquid on his tongue. He would have stopped sooner for one but Flatland was the only wet town around for 75 miles after he left Houston. People flocked to it from miles away to drink the beer which they so faithfully and consistently voted out of their own communities.

All these damn small Texas towns are alike, Jon thought wryly. *Anseltown does the same thing—its citizens inevitably vote it dry and then they keep the road hot to Oklahoma to buy booze.* Jon half-laughed, half-grunted. *Will Rogers knew the makeup of people well when he said "they would vote 'dry' as long as they could stagger to the polls."*

Jon could see in large letters *Flatland Inn* lit up brightly against the blackness of the sky. The word, *beer,* in even larger letters blinked over it and could be seen a long distance away, flashing its garish welcoming beacon to thirsty customers in their self-inflicted dry cocoons. Jon's throat, aridly parched, felt like sandpaper. His foot pressed down hard on the accelerator until he reached the point where he had to slow down to turn into the large parking area for the Inn. It was already occupied even at this early hour by a dozen or so cars. The Flatland Inn, a long low structure nesting near the edge of the highway, was a combination cafe and honky-tonk roadhouse. The entrance door opened into the darkened bar which contained a gaudy nickelodeon that blared raucously and almost constantly. A huge squared arena just beyond the bar constituted the dance floor with tables, chairs and booths at the other side, filling the rest of the expansive space.

Jon slammed the door of the truck and walked quickly toward the Inn. It would be good to see Midge again. Midge Evans ran the place. She had been sick and he hadn't seen her in over a month. He hoped she was back by now. Well, he grinned to himself, if she isn't, he could find another girl here. That was never a problem at Flatland Inn. He stopped for a minute as he stepped inside, blinking, to adjust his vision to the dim interior. The tables were covered in red and white checkered oil cloths. In the middle of each one, a candle stood in an empty beer bottle and sent out an uncertain flickering glow. The wax dripped down and overflowed onto mounds of old wax, making rainbow colored cascades down the sides of the beer bottles.

"Jon—if it isn't Jon Lancer!" he heard a voice yelling over the noisy nickelodeon and the next instant, he felt Midge's arms around his neck pulling his face down to hers as she gave him a welcoming kiss. He pulled her close, grinning down at her.

"Did you miss me?" he asked.

"You don't think I kiss everybody *hello* like that, do you?" she said, laughing up at him.

"I sure as hell hope not!" he grinned.

Protruding her lower lip slightly, she pouted at him coyly. Her generous mouth made a vivid red slash in the heavily made-up face. Although her features revealed a life that had been lived too fully and too fast, nevertheless, she was an attractive woman of 35 with a voluptuous figure and good legs. The shoulder-length bleached wavy hair fell gently about her face with a softening effect.

"Midge! Midge!" A voice, calling from the bar, interrupted them.

"Oh, damn, Jon, I gotta go," she said. "One of my waitresses didn't show up tonight and I've got to pinch-hit for her. I'll see you later."

"You can pinch-hit for me anytime," Jon called after her, his eyes running over her shapely body in the black silk uniform with its low revealing neck and short skirt that showed her curves to their best advantage.

Looking back over her shoulder, she winked at him. "Keep your motor running!" Jon laughed.

He got a beer and, leaning against the bar, surveyed the occupants of the Inn. His smoldering black eyes, camouflaged by his quiet demeanor and seemingly shy nature, were deceivingly masked as he slowly and deliberately scanned the room, searching for bait. His glance strayed past and returned to stop on a small dark girl sitting alone at the back table. He watched her while he finished his beer. *She couldn't be over 20*, he thought. She had a pretty face with long black hair.

Ordering two more beers, he walked back to the table where she was sitting. In a low voice, he asked casually, "Mind if I sit down here?" Then, without waiting for an answer, he sat down and began pouring the beer in the glasses he had brought. Leaning back in his chair, he studied her coolly, intentionally. The glossy shining hair fell straight on each side from the middle part. She had an olive completion with delicate features. The nails shone scarlet on the small graceful hands. She flushed under his scrutiny. The large eyes, dark and angry, stared balefully at him.

"You sure take a lot for granted, don't you, Mister?" she asked disdainfully. Jon was amused. He noticed how her eyes, raking over him, lingered on the broad shoulders and the muscles of his arms before returning to his face again to lock their gaze with his.

"Nope, I don't think so," he answered flippantly, confidently. "I can tell that you like what you see," he paused, his eyes wandering insinuatingly over her, then added, "and I sure as hell like what I see." A faint smile touched the corners of her wide mouth. After studying his ruggedly handsome face for a moment, she picked up her glass and saluted him with it.

"I'll drink to that!" she said in her low, husky voice. Jon raised his glass and clinked it against hers. He knew that it was clear sailing now.

She told him her story as they drank another beer and ate supper. She was running away from her husband. *Every girl has a story to tell,* Jon thought, as she talked. And he had to listen to them. He had heard so many sad, stories from the girls he picked up on his truck route that he had become totally indifferent to them. The pitiful tales of woe went in one ear and out the other. *Oh, well, the faster they get it out of their system and get the stories told, the sooner he could get them into bed. So, what the hell, he'd listen. Or, at least, pretend to. They believed he did and, after all,* he reasoned, *that's what most people needed— someone to just listen to them.* Though his mind was usually thousands of miles away, he was quiet and seemingly attentive while they unburdened themselves. *Funny how girls were so appreciative when they were convinced that he was hanging on their every word—that he was interested enough, cared enough to hear them out.*

Sally's words penetrated his thoughts, partially catching his attention. She had told him that her name was Sally something-or-another but all he could remember was Sally which he would promptly forget when she was out of sight. He never remembered any of the girls' names. Her story was no more interesting than most.

Her mother had died when she was 16, leaving her alone in the world with no other relatives. Sally had turned to a lifetime friend of her parents, a kindly old man of 65 and a widower. He lived on a rundown farm five miles down the country road that met the highway near Flatland Inn. He seemed glad enough to take her in, telling her that she could earn her keep by cooking and keeping house for him.

"No wonder the old geezer was glad," Sally said, "the very first night, he woke me up climbing into my bed, ripping at my gown and pawing at me." Clawing and scratching him, she had fought him off and broke away.

As the girl across the table from him continued to speak, Jon wondered idly how many girls had literally talked themselves right into his bed without his hardly saying a word. Preoccupied with his food, he did not look up from his plate.

She paused in her story and Jon didn't answer. Then she stopped eating and looked at Jon, waiting for him to answer. "Well?" she prodded. He stopped his fork in midair and looked at her, his face slightly puzzled. Then, realizing that she wanted a reply from him, he nodded his head negatively. Satisfied, she resumed her story and droned on.

But now she sat still, not speaking anymore, staring down at the fork that she fingered against the checkered table cloth. Jon had finished eating and lit a cigarette, silently watching her.

At last, she broke the silence. "I wish to hell he hadn't shown up. I don't know what would have happened to me but nothing could have been worse than this past three years. It's been pure hell married to that old bastard— what with his pawing me all the time." Must be quite a man at his age, Jon thought to himself.

There was another long pause. Suddenly, her eyes

glittered. "But I got even with him," she said, almost as if talking to herself. "He's almost completely deaf now and when he gets to sleep—and he's so old he goes to bed with the chickens—I slip out and come down here to the Inn to dance and talk to people." Her face contained a smug expression as she laughed in satisfaction.

Jon finally spoke. "I'm sure glad you decided to come tonight, Sally."

"Well, tonight's different," she said, smiling happily at him. "It's very special because I'm not going back tonight to that old goat—tonight or ever!"

Jon's eyebrows raised, "Where are you going?"

"With you, I hope—that is if you're going toward Dallas." She looked imploringly at him.

"You're in luck. I'm going your way, Sally!" They both laughed. He picked up her hand resting on the table and looked into her eyes as he said softly, "You were right, Sally. This is going to be a very special night!" She smiled back at him. "What the hell are we waiting for?" he asked. "Let's get out of here."

Sally rose from her chair. She stooped and retrieved a small square cardboard carton tied with a piece of heavy cord from underneath her chair. "I packed my things in here and hid them outside the house today," she explained. She walked in front of him and Jon noted that she was even smaller than he had thought. Her figure was compact and shapely with its curves molded revealingly against the seams of the too-tight cotton dress. As they passed the bar, he avoided looking at Midge. But she called out to him. "See you next trip, Jon?" He saw her glaring jealously at Sally.

He waved to her. "Next trip," he promised.

With Sally in the seat beside him, Jon drove a few miles down the highway where he turned off on a side road. Going a short distance, he turned again, this time onto a narrow dirt road that was hardly more than a lane. It wound through a small patch of woods before emerging on the other side and ending abruptly at the edge of a small lake. He knew the spot well. He should. He had been here often enough. Switching off the ignition, he leaned his head against the back of the seat. They sat in silence, gazing out over the lake that lay placidly still in the moonless night. The stars, legion in number, spread across the black backdrop of sky and gave the only visible light. Their silvery reflection shimmered faintly in the water below.

Sally stirred restlessly. Finally, she slid across the seat, close to him. Not seeming to notice, Jon continued to puff on a cigarette and stared at the stars through the windshield of the truck. A balmy breeze, blowing gently off the lake, drifted through the open cab windows. He took one last draw and flipped the cigarette stub to the ground. Then, unhurriedly, he turned toward her, confidently took her in his arms and pulled her to him. His slow deliberate movements seemed to set her on fire and drive her wild. She groaned and he felt her arms encircle his neck. She strained her body tightly against him. Running her hand through his thick wavy hair, she caught the back of his head and pulled it down until his lips could meet hers. Intentionally, he drew back against her clutching hand, coolly eluding her mouth until he heard her gasp, "Please, Jon." She moaned as he lowered his face to hers and carefully crushed her red parted mouth under his.

Hell, I wish I hadn't overslept this morning, Jon thought, as he drove out of the outskirts of Dallas and onto Highway 75. *Old Tom will sure get a kick out of riding me for being behind schedule.* Tom Snyder was one of the mill supervisors at Blossom's. He never missed an opportunity to chew someone out. Most of the men excused his verbal abuse because they felt he only threw his weight around to

impress his superiors that, even at his advanced age, he
was still able to handle the job. But Jon knew better. He
had watched him when he cussed out the men and had seen
the gleam in his small, beady eyes. He was shocked and
hated him for it when he realized that Tom actually
enjoyed using his authority to humiliate those under his
control and gloated over being able to butcher a man's
dignity, cutting it into little pieces.

Oh, well, he grinned to himself, *last night was worth
having to put up with Tom's mouth. Sally something-or-
other, whatever her name was, was some dish. She might be
little but she was dynamite. That old saying, "good things
come in small packages" sure was true in Sally's case. It fit
her to a T.* He missed her constant chatter since he let her
out near a restaurant in Dallas that had a sign in the
window, *Waitress Wanted.* Not that he usually enjoyed or
even listened to the scatterbrained nonsense of the girls
he met. But Sally talked incessantly of California. He
liked hearing about California. He had always wanted to
see it. Sally was only stopping in Dallas because she didn't
have enough money to go further. And, just the minute
that she earned enough, she would light out for California
so fast it would make your head swim. She was headed for
the promised land—the land of milk and honey. Who
knows, she might even get into the movies! Men had told
her often enough that she was pretty and ought to be in
pictures. She had read in the movie magazines how the
camera added weight to a person. Well, she was tiny and
she had a good figure and she should photograph well—
don't you think so, Jon? Yes, Jon thought so. He grinned,
remembering the pleased look on her face at his answer,
then laughed and said aloud, "Look out, California, here
she comes!"

Suddenly his thoughts turned to Elisabeth as they
always did after he had been with another woman. Not

that he felt guilty. On the contrary, he often wished that she knew about them. Maybe it would tear down that wall of complacency around her which seemed to insulate her. That complacency of hers infuriated the hell out of him. *Damn it all, didn't she ever want anything better than the kind of hand that life had dealt out? Evidently not,* he thought disgustedly. *She was happy to just go along, day after day, content with the house and kids and the way things were. Content with never having any money, any luxuries, and with no hope of ever having them in Anseltown.* The calm unruffled way she had of accepting such a small pittance from life without the slightest protest was beyond his comprehension. *How could she be satisfied with such a miserly portion? Didn't she have any desire whatever to reach out for something bigger and better?*

He moved impatiently in his seat. *Well, hell, I do.* His thoughts were bitter, galling. *I feel so damn cheated, rotting away in that two-bit town. Elisabeth never understood that. She's always loved Anseltown. She thinks it's a pretty place.* Jon flipped the butt of his cigarette through the window. His eyes grew hard as he recalled Elisabeth's hurt expression when he told her, "It's a shitty town. How in hell can you think a place so damn shitty can have anything pretty about it?"

Engrossed in his thoughts, he had forgotten to turn on the headlights. He became conscious of squinting to see through the gloomy dusk of the approaching night. He switched on the lights and their twin beams flashed brightly, relieving his eyes from straining to see the road ahead. He was approaching the edge of the small country town whose lights he had seen sparkling in the distance a few minutes before. It was 7 o'clock now and, already, the few stores on the three block long main street were closed. He slowed to a halt at the only stop sign that the town boasted. It was located at the two busiest intersections—

if they could be called "busy." One was still an unpaved road. It crossed the highway whose portion of concrete strip ran through the center of town and provided the only paved street. The town had sprung up around it after the state had mapped it across this route.

Jon glanced at the movie house on one corner of the intersection. A garish sign of lights, spelling out *Alamo Theater* flashed above its front. Pictures of Tom Mix and his horse, Tony, were displayed on either side, advertising the currently featured attraction. The theater, following the custom of small town picture shows, had no specific schedule. The manager simply watched the crowd gathering outside, biding his time, until he was sure that he had all the patrons he was likely to get, then, he started the projector.

Jon sat motionless at the stop sign and looked absently at the few people standing in front of the box office. The group consisted to two young couples, several teenaged girls, talking and giggling and glancing sideways at the three boys who had just emerged from the pool hall next door. Also, several farmers in overalls with their wives, one of whom still wore her apron and a sun bonnet. *This is Saturday night,* he thought idly, *and what a hubbub of activity. The farmers have come to town to see the picture show after a hard week's work. All next week in the fields they'll talk about the way Tom and Tony outsmarted the bad guys. The women are anxious to find out how Pauline escapes the perilous predicament she was in at the close of last week's serial.*

"Whoopee!" he shouted through the window as he shifted gears and pulled away. Startled, the group turned in unison to stare at him. Glancing back briefly once more, he saw them pointing after him. Pushing his foot against the gas pedal, he roared down the street. *That's the most exciting thing that's happened to them all year,* he thought contemptuously.

As Jon sped down the lonely deserted highway once more, his thoughts were as dark as the moonless night. *The small towns are all alike in this damn state. The few rich bastards keep the poor people down, mash them under their thumbs, tighten the screws until they're nothing more than robots. The towns are open and shut traps run by a few wealthy sons-a-bitches like the Ansels and Blossoms who rob the destitute of their sweat, their pride, their youth, dreams and, in the end, their very lives. Like vampires, they drain them dry until there is no dignity left in living.*

Physical pain twisted, like a knife, inside him as his thoughts persisted. *I've watched people I grew up with turn into zombies. They're not really living—they just go through the motions of life because they keep on breathing. In the first bloom of youth, they started life with such high hopes and dreams—hopes and dreams that turned into despair and helplessness and finally died.*

Damn them! Damn the blood suckers! Damn them for their paltry wages they dole out. Damn them for the misery they heap upon us. Damn them for refusing to let outside enterprises into Anseltown. Hell, they don't want the town to progress. Why should they? With other competition, they would have to pay decent salaries, and they're not about to do that when they can get richer every day, leeching off the peasants who slave for them. Anseltown has always been an open and shut town. It's wide open for those who already "have" and shut tightly to those who "have not." And the vultures who "have" are sure as hell going to keep it that way.

Jon, slumped dejectedly behind the wheel, drove automatically without being conscious of it or anything else, so absorbed was he in his malevolent meditations. *I'm like the rest of the poor bastards,* he mused bitterly. *Just like a bug smashed under someone's thumb. And, to think I had a chance to get out of that chicken-shit town! But, no, I turned it down because of Elisabeth. Because she didn't want to leave Anseltown.* He felt anger rising inside him as it always did when he thought about the baseball contract offer which he had refused. And he thought about it a lot. It was always eating away at him, burning his insides, gnawing at his guts. *Most never get even one chance to escape from Anseltown. I got a chance to take that first step out of it. But I didn't take it and run like hell. I got my chance—and I blew it. And all on account of Elisabeth.* In his anger and frustration, Jon smacked his hand so sharply against the steering wheel that the pain from it ran up his arm and he didn't even notice.

Why had he ever married at 19? Why hadn't he waited? But he had fallen completely in love with Elisabeth. Elisabeth with the flashing green eyes and lilting laugh that made him believe that, as long as they were together, they could go anywhere and do anything in the world they really wanted to do. He stirred impatiently in his seat. *Well, he had certainly misjudged her. And, now, he was tied down with kids. Not that he didn't love them. Elisabeth accused him of not loving them at times. He didn't know what the hell she expected. He worked hard to take care of them, didn't he? He was providing a childhood for them—something that he had been denied. Hell, I don't even know what its like to be a child,* he thought bitterly. *Elisabeth couldn't understand why he felt tied down, why he resented spending his life sacrificing himself in order to raise kids. Hell, when they're grown, they can go off and do whatever they want and, by that time, I'll be so old I won't even feel like living. Even if I did, I don't want to wait that long. I want to live now!*

Abruptly, he perked upright as a thought, like an electric shock, went through him. *I'm 34 years old. The years keep grabbing me from behind, pulling at me, making me old.* He felt drained, empty. *I don't want to get old without ever having found my "Spain."* He had read a book once about a man who was consumed with a burning desire to see the castles of Spain. He worked and struggled all his life to accomplish his dream, only to have it thwarted time and again just as his goal was almost in his grasp. Finally, he grew old and died. His last words were indelibly stamped on Jon's brain, "I'm dying and I have never seen those castles in Spain. God forgive me—I have failed myself."

To Jon, those were the saddest words he had ever read. Nausea stabbed his stomach. *Hell, I'll never forgive myself if I miss my Spain. I'll be damned if I want to be like most people whose dreams of their own personal "Spain" get lost by the wayside, I don't want to accept the theory that life is life and dreams are dreams and, for the most part, "never the twain shall meet." Maybe Elisabeth and others can accept that—but I can't.*

He grunted derisively. *If I could accept that, I might as well go all the way and buy a burial plot at Memory Lane Cemetery.* Everyone he knew in Anseltown already had his own six-foot piece of ground, bought and paid for. Seems one of the first things a couple did there when they married was to take out life insurance and make their reservations at the cemetery "on the hill." *They had no hope of going anywhere from the stinking town except to the stinking graveyard. Well,* Jon thought scornfully, *I've never bought one of the damned things and I never will. He* suddenly sat erect from his slumped position, his back determinedly stiff and ramrod straight. A look of rigid defiance crossed his face. *Hell, I'm not dead yet. I'm not about to give up—not yet—not by a long shot!*

Jon pulled the pocket watch from its small concave near his belt. It was the one possession he had of his father's. His mother, after carefully guarding it all those years, had presented it to him on the day of his wedding.

Holding it near the tip of his cigarette, he puffed to create a glow in order to see the hands. *It was almost 10 o'clock. It wouldn't be long now.*

A sprinkling of lights appeared in the distance. One, a faintly glowing streak, rose high above the rest, seemingly suspended in the sky. He could not yet make out the letters in lights but he knew all too well what they were. They spelled out Ansel's Cotton Factory and were placed on top of the building, the tallest one in Anseltown. *Old man Ansel built the loftiest structure in town as a tribute to himself and to make damn sure that everybody around knew who was in charge,* Jon thought dourly.

The letters were clearly visible now as he approached the outskirts. Looking up at them, he felt as though he were a fly trapped in a web. He had a bitter taste in his mouth. *Elisabeth had thought that the kids were the answer—that they would put an end to his "nonsense"— that he'd forget it all. Well, he hadn't forgotten. And he would have been free of this gutless place a long time ago— if only Elisabeth had had faith in him. He could never forgive her for that. No, he couldn't find it in his heart to forgive her.*

He saw the sign ahead, Anseltown City Limits, at the side of the highway which ran through the center of town. The truck rumbled past the sign and on down Texas Street. Jon gazed glumly at the familiar but now dark and abandoned main street. *What a shitty town!*

CHAPTER 3

Elisabeth, bent over the large galvanized tub that rested on a low bench in the yard outside the back porch, massaged her homemade lye soap into the heavy work uniform of Jon's. She rubbed the cumbersome material diligently back and forth against the scrub board. A pan on the ground beside her was piled high with Larry and Roscoe's overalls which she had already scrubbed. The broiling rays of the noon sun beat down on her in the airless June Monday. Perspiration trickled uncomfortably down her back. Tendrils of hair clung to the moistness of her face and neck, adding to her discomfort. The heat of the day, combined with the hot water in the tub, was almost unbearable. Her face, flushed, was almost as red as her hands. She felt weak and her back ached from the unnatural position she had assumed the past two hours doing the weekly wash. Satisfied at last with her efforts on the last piece of clothing in the tub, she raised up to wring the water from it. Dizziness overwhelmed her. She would have fallen had she not grabbed the sides of the tub for support.

"What's the matter, Mama?" she heard Larry's voice asking anxiously. It sounded strange as though coming from a long way off. It was hard for her eyes to focus in the bright sunlight. The world seemed to be dancing in front of her.

"I don't know," she said slowly, uncertainly, putting her hand to her throbbing head. "I just felt dizzy all of a sudden."

"Come on, Mama, you'd better sit down," he said, taking her arm and helping her toward the steps. Without protest, Elisabeth allowed herself to be led. She sat down with Larry beside her, watching her worriedly. After a long moment, things stopped whirling before her and she could see clearly again.

Turning to Larry, she asked, "Why are you home from school, Larry? Did you..." She stopped speaking as she looked into his face. It was very pale and he had a glint of tears in his eyes. "Why, Larry, I'm alright—it was nothing. You mustn't worry." Her voice was gentle.

"Oh, Mama," he said in a fiercely intense, almost angry voice, "when I'm grown up, I'm going to get a good job and you won't ever have to work hard again. Not ever!" Elisabeth was startled by the poignant depth of feeling in her young son's voice. Tears welled up in her eyes. Attempting to conceal them, she patted his arm, saying, "Now, you mustn't fret, son. I'm fine now. It was just the heat and..."

Larry's tone was defiant as he interrupted her, "Daddy doesn't care that you have to work so hard. If he did, he'd try to get a better job so..."

"That's enough, Larry!" Elisabeth cut in sharply. "Don't ever let me hear you speak that way about your father again! He works hard for us. He does the best he can." She paused and looked at him searchingly. "Son, you're old enough to know how bad things are right now. There are no jobs. Your father is fortunate to have any work at all."

"But..." Larry began.

Elisabeth's eyes flashed warningly. "I told you not to ever speak disrespectfully of your father again."

Avoiding her eyes, he said, "I'm going to stay home

from school this afternoon and do the rest of the washing so you can rest."

"No, son, there's no use in your missing school. I'm perfectly alright now." She rose unsteadily to her feet.

"I'd rather stay home and see that you rest," he persisted.

She smiled wanly at him. "I promise to lie down, if you promise to stop worrying."

"Alright," he grinned briefly, "but I'll finish hanging the wash before I leave."

When he had finished with it, he obtained both her promise to rest all afternoon and the history book which he had forgotten that morning and reluctantly returned to school.

Elisabeth's heart was heavy as she watched him depart. She had not suspected, until now, that Larry sensed the breach between her and Jon. But she should have known, she told herself. She should have reckoned on his keenly sensitive and deeply perceptive nature that at 13 was developing an ever increasing awareness of the adult world about him.

She ached inside for this impressionable young son of hers so susceptible, so vulnerable to pain. She had tried so hard to keep their estrangement hidden from the children. For children needed a harmonious unification of their parents. Especially now in these days when there, seemingly, was no stable solidarity anywhere in the world. They desperately needed the security of a united home, to feel a safe protective mantle of love around them as a shelter against life's harsh realities.

"Stop rocking my chair, Roscoe!" Lisa said sharply, "I can't read." She glared at him as she saw his foot reaching stealthily toward her chair. "If you do it once more, I'm going to hit you on the arm." Lisa always warned Roscoe in advance of her intentions to strike him carefully pointing out the place on his anatomy that would be the target. The target depended upon her decision of the spot which would afford the right degree of pain to justify the seriousness of the offense.

Lisa was curled up on the thick cushion of the old rocking chair on the back porch. Five-year-old Roscoe sat on the couch next to her, holding a book of pictures on his lap that he had been looking at for some time. Bored, he sought his sister's attention by pushing her back and forth at intervals.

"Well, I can't read no matter if I rock or not," he said irritably. "I'll be glad when I go to school so I can." His tone changed and he said, pleadingly, "Aw, come on, Lisa, read my book to me."

"I've read it to you already," she answered, "I want to read my own book."

"Well, read your book to me then."

"No," she replied, "I'm tired of reading out loud." Roscoe's face grew sullen. Reaching out with his foot, he gave her chair a vicious shove so hard that she almost tumbled from it as it tilted forward. Jumping up, she hit his arm with a doubled up fist. He howled in pain.

"What's happening here?" Elisabeth appeared in the kitchen door that opened onto the porch.

"Lisa hit me on the arm!" Roscoe cried, rubbing the injured spot.

"What did you do to her?" Elisabeth asked.

"Nothing," he replied innocently, "I was just sitting here."

"He did so do something," Lisa said angrily. "He almost pushed me over in the chair."

"Well, she won't read to me, Mama," Roscoe said, still rubbing his arm.

"Let's have no more quarreling," Elisabeth said. "I'll read to you for awhile." Untying the apron about her waist, she hung it on the knob of the kitchen door. Although she had rested most of the afternoon, she still felt a little weak from the dizzy spell she had had. When Larry offered to do the supper dishes, she accepted gratefully.

"Oh, goody," Roscoe said, throwing a triumphant glance at Lisa, who had settled once again in the rocker with her book. "You read a lot better than Lisa anyway." Lisa stuck her tongue out at him. He looked at her belligerently and started to retort but Elisabeth interrupted.

"I don't want to hear anymore out of either of you or I won't read." Roscoe remained silent but when his mother wasn't looking, he stuck his tongue out at Lisa.

"My, it's nice and cool out here after that hot kitchen," Elisabeth said appreciatively, as she settled in the well-worn cushions of the couch next to Roscoe. She sighed contentedly and breathed deeply as the sweet fragrance of roses and honeysuckle intermingled to waft through the early summer air. The roses were in full bloom and the honeysuckle had grown so abundantly during the spring that it almost completely covered the back fence. Its nectar attracted tiny humming birds whose bright splashes of color could often be seen flashing fleetingly about the delicate foliage. Elisabeth glanced around the large back porch, the favorite family gathering place in the summer. The coolest room of the house, it allowed any stray breeze uninhibited access through the screen that enclosed the top half of the porch which extended the full width of the house. The large paper-shell pecan tree in the center of the backyard provided shady protection from the evening sun. Freezing cold from its openness in the winter, the porch was no place to linger and was used as a storage room. Jon had built a huge closet filled with shelves at the far end for the rows of jars containing vegetables that Elisabeth canned from her garden and jellies and jams made from berries and grapes which she bought at their lowest price during the season. Here, too, pecans from their tree were stored as well as bushel baskets of apples and pears given to them by the neighbors or Irma Johnson's farm. With the children's help, Elisabeth meticulously wrapped each piece of fruit in a sheet of newspaper which was then placed carefully in the baskets obtained from Sam's store. This was the task that the children liked most to perform. Crossing the porch to smell on the way outside in the winter, they loved to smell the odor seeping from the baskets and enjoyed the mellow sweetness of the tender delicacies that had ripened richly during the months of storage. It was a happy treat to be welcomed home from school on a cold blustery day by the aroma of a hot apple pie fresh from the oven.

"Read to me, Mama!" Roscoe said impatiently, tugging at her arm. Elisabeth opened the book which Roscoe had chosen from the library. Once a week, she walked the two miles with the children to the Anseltown Library for a new supply of books, a ritual that had been performed regularly since they were old enough to toddle. Reading daily, she had instilled and bequeathed her love of books to them, a love and appreciation that bordered on the sacred and never left them. The happiest memories that each would recall later were the evenings when, entranced, they would gather around their mother while she read, revealing the fascinating treasures contained between this world's endless covers. Elisabeth's enchantment with books was conveyed through the lilting excitement of her voice that held them spellbound. Her keen sense of joy in discovering the hidden delights found on the printed pages captured the imagination of her listeners and launched them on voyages into strange new lands. And, like explorers, they reveled in each new scene and waited eagerly to plunge deeply into the next.

Elisabeth began to read. Lisa, deserting her book, got

up from her chair and moved quietly next to her. Elisabeth made room for her without interrupting her reading. When she had finished reading, the small child's book, Roscoe picked up another one beside him. "Will you read this one, Mama?"

"I've already read that one to you, Roscoe," Lisa said. "I've read all of the books that you got Saturday."

"Well, I know it," he answered impatiently. Turning to his mother, he asked "Why won't Miss Jackson let me have more than five books at a time, Mama?" He didn't wait for her answer, but continued, "I don't think it's fair. I think she's just mean!"

"That isn't nice, Roscoe," Elisabeth admonished. "She isn't being mean. That is the library rule: One person is allowed to take five books a week. After all, there are lots of people who want to read and we have to take our turn with the books so we can all share them."

"Well, Jimmy Hayes never gets books," Roscoe said. "He said he hates the library because Miss Jackson is always fussing at him to be quiet." He put his finger to his lips and made a shushing sound in imitation of Miss Jackson.

Elisabeth laughed. "Well, I can't blame her, Roscoe. I do declare that boy is the noisiest child I've ever heard."

"He's like a bull in a china closet," Lisa offered. "He's always stumbling over something."

"Wherever did you hear that expression, Lisa?" Elisabeth asked.

"I heard Mrs. Dalton tell you that her husband was like a bull in a china closet when he drinks too much," Lisa answered. "She said that he stumbled over her good lamp and broke it last Saturday."

"My, you do have big ears, Lisa. Now don't you go repeating that to anyone," Elisabeth said, then added sternly for emphasis, "you hear now?"

"Yes ma'am," Lisa murmured.

Roscoe had been frowning but, suddenly, his face brightened. "Since Jimmy doesn't get any books, can I ask Miss Jackson if I can take out five more a week, Mama?"

"Hey, there, Miz Elisabeth." They were interrupted by a voice calling from the road behind the house. It was Glo-ree, a well-built Negro woman with a lean, almost muscular body conditioned from years of toil. She held the handle on one side of a bushel basket loaded with blackberries. Her tall 17-year-old son, Daniel, supported the basket's other side. The 14-year-old twins, Mary and Ruth, trailed behind them, Glo-ree's hair, cropped closely to her head, lay in tight, curly ringlets that made a frame for her broad, friendly face. The wide-set eyes were extremely expressive and her generous mouth revealed even white teeth as she grinned now at Elisabeth who had walked out to greet her. Elisabeth had great affection for this woman that she had known since her marriage to Jon. She admired her fortitude and courage in caring for her children after her husband's death several years ago. She had proved to be, not only a faithful friend, but also an inspiration. For Glo-ree possessed an aura of strength about her that had nothing to do with her physical stamina. Her hearty laughter was infectious—and she laughed often. She had an outgoing manner with an uplifting quality that instinctively drew people to her and she directed a word of encouragement toward everyone she met. Nevertheless, she kept her troubles to herself, telling her children, "Everyone's got enough trials and tribulations of his own without listenin' to ours."

Glo-ree labored long and hard to care for her family. She cooked, cleaned and accepted any type of work the white people offered. Nothing was too difficult for her willing hands to tackle. A huge black kettle wash pot could be seen hanging over a fire in her backyard in which clothes were boiled every day of the week except Sunday. Her clothes lines were always full and she ironed for hours, heating the irons on her wood-burning stove. The leading ladies of Anseltown vied for Glo-ree's services but Mrs. Ansel, as first lady, had priority.

Elisabeth looked warmly at Glo-ree's staunch figure with the perennial white apron, stiffly starched, reaching around her waist. It was almost an overskirt, covering all but an inch in the back where it was tied, and had become Glo-ree's trademark. She was never seen without it. Made from flour sacks that she bleached snowy white, the heavy amount of starch made it stand out around her and rustle when she walked. It seemed to Elisabeth that the apron must be Glo-ree's armor against adversity, keeping it at its distance, as she carried herself proudly, her back straight, her head held high and looked the world squarely in the eye.

"What in the world have you got there, Glo-ree?" Elisabeth asked, peering through the gathering dusk. Then, drawing closer, she exclaimed, "My, what beautiful berries!"

"Yes, ma'am," Glo-ree answered proudly, "we done found us some wild blackberry bushes back in the woods. They's the biggest juiciest ones I ever saw. We brung some by for you and your family."

"Well, thank you, Glo-ree. I'm mighty glad to get them."

"I'd like to make some jam out of them," Glo-ree said, "but I don't have enough sugar and no money to buy any."

Elisabeth thought for a moment, then asked, "Are there anymore berries on the bushes, Glo-ree?"

"Lawsy, yes, Miz Elisabeth," she answered. "I done reckon them bushes are completely bustin' out with 'em."

"Well, if you will come and help me, Glo-ree, I'll furnish the sugar and we'll put them up on halves,"

Elisabeth said.

"I'd shore be happy to, Miz Elisabeth," Glo-ree said eagerly. "When you wants to do it?"

"Tomorrow," she replied, looking at the berries. "These are good and ripe—just right for canning."

"We's goin' be out there bright and early in the morning, picking," Glo-ree said, smiling. She turned to her children. "You hear that, young 'uns—we goin' rise and shine in the morning."

"But, Mama," Daniel said, "I gotta go to Mr. Johnson's farm tomorrow to work."

"You don't have to git there till 8 o'clock, Daniel, and we'll have them berries picked and forgot about long 'fore then," she said.

"But, Mama..." he started to protest but she interrupted. "Now don't give me no sass, boy, you goin' pick berries in the morning." She looked at him affectionately and said teasingly, "You won't give me no sass while's you eatin' that blackberry jam next winter."

Daniel grinned broadly at her. Glo-ree turned back to Elisabeth, saying "I'll be here early with the berries, Miz Elisabeth." Then they walked toward their home. They lived a quarter mile down the road across the railroad track which made a dividing line, separating the Negro shacks from the houses of the white people. Glo-ree's family occupied the first one across the track. A dozen of these black tarpaper huts lined the edge of the dirt road which narrowed considerably after crossing the railroad and came to a dead-end at the edge of a pasture a mile further on. Since it only accommodated the black people of "nigger row" and was leading nowhere, the city had never seen fit to widen or gravel it beyond the track. Rainy weather converted it into an impassable sea of mud. Originally built by the railroad for its workers of an earlier time, the huts had been abandoned but left standing. A larger Negro community with a school that combined both elementary and high school and a Negro church was located in the northern outskirts of town. Negroes who came to Anseltown from other parts, unable to find a place to live in that shoddy section, welcomed the shelter of these vacant shacks.

Squalor and stark poverty were glaringly evident. The doors and windows were merely openings in the structures, wide open to the elements. Cheese cloth was stretched across them in the summer in an effort to halt the flies from buzzing in at will to increase the misery of the stifling heat inside. Tin cans, hammered flat, were nailed on roofs to patch up leaks in an attempt to prevent rain from pouring in. In the winter, boards were secured across the open windows to fend off the penetrating cold. Darkness, like the cold, was an enemy to be wrestled with almost constantly during these months. For with the openings sealed, the interior was in almost total obscurity both day and night. The women made candles when they could afford to do so for use during daylight hours. Otherwise, the dim light yielded by the wood-burning stoves was the only relief from the blackness. Lamps were used only at night for kerosene was costly and was rationed cautiously.

Elisabeth watched Glo-ree and her family until they disappeared from her view in the growing gloom of twilight. She marveled at this Negro woman who, all alone, had managed to care for her family and to keep them fed and clothed in these times when it was so difficult for white people to survive. She marveled even more at her strongly independent spirit. Glo-ree wanted no handouts, no charity, no sympathy. She insisted on standing alone—like her name. For she had only one name—her Christian one.

Dotson, Glo-ree's husband, had been 25 years her senior. His parents were born into slavery and had been given the surname of the master they served. But when Dotson was old enough to understand, he refused to accept the name that had been bestowed on his family by a white man. He used only the name that his parents had given him as a baby.

"I knows what my name was before I married Dotson," Glo-ree would say. "It was Martin. But, when you gets married, you takes your husband's name. Well, Dotson didn't have no last name for me to take—so I don't have no last name neither."

She would go on to explain that the unusual solitary name which she possessed came instantly at her appearance in a family of nine sons when her mother took one look at her first daughter and cried happily, "Glo-ree be to God!" The distinctive spelling was a result of her parents' limited education. Glo-ree demanded that her name be accented properly, emphasizing the *ree* as her mother had done, saying, "I'ze only gotten one name and I wants it said rightly."

Elisabeth deeply admired the strength and courage of this woman. She remembered vividly the day five years ago when Glo-ree, unable to read or write, had brought a letter for her to read. A friend who had gone with Dotson to Chicago to look for work had sent it. It was short and to the point as though the writer was in a hurry to get it over and done with. It read:

> Glo-ree,
> Dotson is dead. He was run over by train. He fell as he was trying to jump off in the yards in Chicago before the railroad men could catch him riding the rails.
> Your friend, Johnson
>
> P. S. I wanted to let you know sooner but I couldn't find anyone to write a letter for me.

My boss is writing for me now. I'm sorry
about Dotson, Glo-ree.

Elisabeth recalled now how Glo-ree's erect figure had
slumped as she had read the words slowly, hesitantly. She
had reached out to support herself against the pecan tree
under which they stood, and Elisabeth had put her arm
around her shoulders while they remained immobile and
silent. Suddenly, Glo-ree brushed at the tears on her face
and straightened, her figure erect once again. She said
lowly but distinctly, "Thank you, Miz Elisabeth, for reading
the letter to me." Then she had turned and walked swiftly
away, her back stiffly straight and her head held high.
Elisabeth, at a loss for words to comfort her, sadly watched
her go. She had felt such empathy for her—a deep kinship.
For she understood the loneliness, the emptiness and the
loss that Glo-ree was suffering.

"Mama, can I have some berries to eat?" Roscoe's
impatient voice brought Elisabeth back to the present. "I'll
have to wash them first," she answered, picking up the box
of blackberries that Glo-ree's daughters had carried from
the woods. She took them to the kitchen and washed them
in the sink. She prepared bowls of them with milk and
sugar and placed the remainder in a large pan which she
covered with a clean white cloth.

She called Larry from his room where he had
disappeared to read and they sat around the kitchen table,
eating the berries and laughing happily. Elisabeth wished
wistfully that Jon were here, that he could share this time
with them. She looked at the children, ebullient now in
Jon's absence. When he was at home, the atmosphere was
strained. His moodiness and indifference cast a shadow
over them. The children were quiet and kept out of his way
as much as possible. This pained Elisabeth greatly—for
both their sakes—for the children who were denied a
father's understanding affection and for Jon who was

missing one of life's greatest joys, an offspring's love and companionship. She did not blame Jon entirely. Never having known his own father, he had had no example to follow. Then, at other times, Elisabeth wondered if this were the case or if he used the children through which to punish her for failing him. Were they just objects that stood in his path to freedom?

"If you do that again, I'll smack you in the face!" Elisabeth heard Lisa's angry words. Having finished his own, Roscoe had sneaked a spoonful of berries from Lisa's bowl. She had caught him in the act.

"Mama, let's go out on the porch and see the stars," Roscoe said, ignoring Lisa's threat. His face was smeared and stained.

"Alright, Roscoe," Elisabeth laughed, "but not until you go wash your face."

"Aw, shoot," he protested as he reluctantly left the table.

Elisabeth set the dishes in the sink and turned to Larry, "Are you coming out with us, son?"

"I'll be out in a few minutes, Mama," he replied, "I have just a few pages left to read in my book. He walked toward his room and she looked after him with pride. He was like her father, she thought, so quiet and serious and gentle. She hoped that they would be able to send him to college when the time came. He had his heart set on it. He needed that education if he were going to be a writer. Just recently, he had shyly confided to her that he wanted to write. He was so observant and sensitive to the needs of others already, possessing the ability to understand what they were feeling and thinking. *If that were one of the requirements for being a writer,* she thought, *her son would be a good one.*

Elisabeth went onto the porch where Lisa and Roscoe were already settled on either side of the couch, leaving

room for her between them. The warm night air smelled
sweetly of honeysuckle. Tiny darts of light from hundreds
of fireflies flashed furiously on and off in the darkness of
the yard. The lazy chirp of crickets was the only sound
disturbing the peaceful stillness.

"Look at all the stars," Lisa said, leaning her head
against the couch and pointing to the sky, "there must be
millions of them."

"Jillions of millions," Roscoe said, not to be outdone.
The moon was not visible affording the stars full display,
and the inky sky was almost a solid mass of the flickering
lights so thick they seemed to touch each other.

"I see the big dipper," Elisabeth said, "can you find it?"

"Where is it?" Lisa and Roscoe asked in unison.

"You can find it," Elisabeth replied, "just keep looking."

"I've found it," Larry said. He had walked out on the
porch and stood gazing at the sky.

"Show me, Larry," Lisa cried.

"Me too," Roscoe echoed.

"I see it," Lisa said excitedly, "but I'm not going to
show you, Roscoe."

"I can't find it," Roscoe said, on the verge of tears.

Larry sat down beside him and lifted his brother on his
lap. "Look by that tallest branch on the pecan tree," he
directed patiently. "Can you see it now? Look right at the
tip of the branch in the sky."

"I see it! I see it!" Roscoe shouted happily.

Turning to her mother, Lisa implored, "Mama, tell us
the story about the little children angels in heaven."

"You've heard it so many times, Lisa."

"We don't care, we want to hear it again, Mama,"
Roscoe chimed in.

Larry laughed, "You might as well tell it, Mama—you
know they won't give you any peace until you do. They
never get tired of hearing it."

"Well," Elisabeth began, "when I was a little girl, we used to sit out on our porch on the farm at night, too, and look at the stars—just the way we're doing now. And my mother would tell us stories, too. She used to tell us the one about how God separated heaven from earth. It seems that He decided to separate them by making a huge quilt which He spread between them and He called it the *sky*. But the little children angels weren't happy with the quilt because they could no longer see the children on earth. So, one day, when they were restless and lonely to see the earth children, one of them got an idea. He gathered them around him and said, 'We will cut holes in the quilt and then we'll be able to see the children on earth again.' They all got a pair of scissors and began cutting as fast as they could. Soon they had cut little holes all over the quilt. And they were so happy because now, anytime they wanted to, they could look down and watch all the little children playing on earth."

"Can they see me?" Roscoe repeated the question that he invariably asked after this story.

Lisa finished the story that she had heard over and over, "And the stars are really holes in the quilt and we can see the lights of heaven shining through."

"Yes, that's the way it goes," Elisabeth laughed.

"Can the little baby who died see us through the holes, Mama?" Lisa asked.

Elisabeth did not answer. She had told them about the baby when they had asked about the tiny grave near their grandmother's in the small cemetery by the country church. The baby, born when Larry was 2-years of age, had only lived a few hours.

Larry could not see his mother's face in the darkness but he knew that she was reluctant to talk about the baby. She had never spoken of him again since the day at the cemetery. He stood up, saying quickly, "Come on, you two, it's your bedtime."

Roscoe, ignoring him, asked, "Why did he die, Mama?" Larry was touched by her answer as she said softly, "God loves babies very much and he was lonely for a baby to play with."

Larry took hold of Roscoe's arm and pulled him along as he repeated firmly, "I told you—it's your bedtime."

Roscoe started to protest but Elisabeth said, "Run along now, both of you, and don't forget to brush your teeth and wash your face and hands."

"Aw, shoot, I don't know why I gotta wash when I'm going to bed," Roscoe grumbled, "can't nobody see me in bed."

"I'll get them into bed, Mama," Larry said. Elisabeth sat alone in the quiet darkness and listened to the night sounds. Larry reappeared shortly on the porch and sat down beside her. They sat silently for a long time staring at the stars.

After a while, Elisabeth reached over and patted his hand. "You're a good son, Larry."

He was embarrassed and didn't answer. Finally he said, "I don't think I've ever seen as many stars as there are tonight."

Relaxed by the peacefulness of the night surrounding them, they rested their heads on the back of the couch and gazed at the spectacle above. "You know," Elisabeth spoke at last, "the sky does look almost like a torn quilt with light shining through the holes."

Roscoe was awakened by the light shining from the kitchen. He thought it was morning at first until he realized that the light would not be on if it were. Looking through the window by his bed, he saw the stars still twinkling in the sky. He heard his mother's voice, speaking low. He got out of bed and went to the kitchen, rubbing his eyes sleepily. He saw his mother in her robe standing in the kitchen door talking to Mr. Randall in hushed tones. "I'll be there just as soon as I get dressed," she said. Mr. Randall left and she closed the door.

"What is it, Mama?" he asked.

"What are you doing up, Roscoe?" she asked, then added distractedly, "I guess we woke you." She walked hurriedly to her room with Roscoe following. She turned to him, saying, "Now you get back to bed. I've got to get dressed."

"Where are you going?"

"I'm going over to the Randalls. Grandma Randall is very sick and they need me."

"Is she going to die, Mama?"

"Oh, Roscoe," Elisabeth answered impatiently, taking him by the hand and leading him back to his room, "you're so full of questions and I've got to hurry." She helped him into bed and pulled the sheet up on him. "Is she going to die?" Roscoe persisted.

"I don't know, son," she answered, "Mr. Randall said that she's very sick and she is very old—almost 90."

"I'm scared, Mama," Roscoe said, "I don't want you to go off and leave me."

"Now, Roscoe, there is nothing to be afraid of. Lisa is right here in the room with you and so is King." The large brown and white collie that lay near the foot of the bed heard his name and acknowledged it by thumping his tail loudly against the floor. "Larry is in the next room," she continued, "and I won't be gone very long. Now, you just shut your eyes and you'll be asleep before you know it." She stooped and kissed him and left the room quickly.

She glanced sleepily at the wall clock. It was not quite midnight. She had only been asleep a short time and she was so tired. But, no matter, the Randalls needed her. She had risen early that morning to can the blackberries with Glo-ree. It had been a hot tedious job: Washing the berries, cooking them in big kettles and sterilizing glass jars. They had made some into preserves and canned the rest to be used in making pies and cobbler. They did not finish until late evening and Glo-ree, tired but jubilant with the result of their labor, departed, taking her share of the jars.

Her weariness abated somewhat when Elisabeth glimpsed the row of jars on the kitchen table whose precious contents would provide yet another addition of food for her family during the uncertain months ahead. Tomorrow, she thought, she would add them to the back porch closet whose shelves were slowly filling. Only last week, she had put up the crop of Kentucky Wonder green beans and the juicy early June peas that her garden had yielded. The cucumbers were almost ready to pick from the vines. She would use the smaller firm ones for sour pickles—Lisa's and her favorite. From the larger ones, she intended to make the crisp sweet bread-and-butter pickles that Jon and the boys loved. Visualizing full shelves of her canned products that would serve her family through the coming winter bolstered her sagging spirits and filled her weary body with increased vigor as she went down the back steps and walked swiftly toward the Randalls.

Roscoe heard her close the kitchen door behind her as she left. He shut his eyes tightly but he couldn't force himself to fall asleep. Sitting up in bed, he whispered loudly, "King!" The dog lay stretched on his side on the linoleum covered floor that provided him cool respite from the summer heat. He remained in his horizontal position but wagged his heavy tail noisily at Roscoe's greeting.

"Come on, boy," Roscoe insisted. After much coaxing, the dog rose lazily, shook himself vigorously and jumped onto the bed to settle down and lay his head on the pillow next to Roscoe's. Snuggling against him and putting his arm around the dog, Roscoe felt more secure. He closed his eyes again. He heard the mournful howl of a dog that carried through the stillness of the night from a long distance away, making the sound even more eerie. He scurried over King's body to the floor and ran the few steps to the bed where Lisa lay sleeping. Jumping in beside her, he whispered urgently, "Lisa, Lisa. Wake up!"

"What do you want, Roscoe?" she asked sleepily.

Then, as she became fully conscious, "You hurt my arm, jumping on it like that—what do you want anyway?"

"Grandma Randall is gonna die because I heard a dog howl and Mrs. Parsons says that's always a sure sign of a death." Roscoe's words rushed out in a breathless torrent.

Lisa was completely awake now. "What's the matter with you, Roscoe? Did you have a bad dream?"

Roscoe, braver now with Lisa awake, caught his breath and said impatiently, "No, I didn't have a night-horse."

Lisa, ignoring his misuse of the word, did not correct him as she usually did but said instead, "There's nothing wrong with Grandma Randall."

"Oh, yes, there is," Roscoe said. "Mama has gone to the Randalls because Mr. Randall told her that Grandma is awful sick. I heard a dog howl and that means she's gonna die."

"Mama told us not to pay attention to Mrs. Parson's spertitions." That was as near as Lisa could come to pronouncing the word. "Mama said that's all they are— they're not true at all."

"Well, Mrs. Parsons said that every time someone in her family has died, she has always been warned first by a dog howling." Roscoe's eyes were wide with fright in the dark.

"Well, Mama says it ain't so," Lisa said, but her voice sounded unconvincing.

"Lisa, do you believe in ghosts?"

"No," she answered. She pulled the sheet up to her

chin. Roscoe did likewise. "There's no such thing."

"There is too," he said emphatically. "There's the Holy Ghost. The preacher is always talking about him and I'm always scared at night in the dark that I'm going to see the Holy Ghost."

"The Holy Ghost is not the same thing as just plain old ghosts, silly," she said. "Sometimes you can see regular ghosts but you can't ever see the Holy Ghost."

Roscoe shivered. He felt goose pimples all over him, just talking about ghosts. "I thought you said there ain't no such thing as ghosts," he said accusingly. "And besides," he added, "if the Holy Ghost ain't a ghost, then why is it called *ghost*? Tell me that."

Lisa had no answer for that and remained silent. They lay with the sheet covering them to their heads, shivering and looking about the darkened room. King snored loudly in Roscoe's bed. Suddenly, they both jumped as a creaking noise sounded faintly outside their room. Their heads turned simultaneously and their eyes were riveted on the doorway. A shadowy figure drifted past. Instantly they were struggling to get underneath the sheet, emitting loud screeches. King lumbered off the bed and jumped on top of them, barking loudly and adding to the noisy confusion.

The light switched on in the next room. "What's going on here, anyway?" a voice called from the doorway. Recognizing their brother's voice, Lisa and Roscoe disengaged themselves with difficulty from the sheet and King who was entangled in it with them. They were crying and talking at the same time. "Oh, Larry," Lisa said, "we thought you were a ghost."

"I thought it was the Holy Ghost for sure!" Roscoe added.

Larry laughed, "Well, I'm not. I was just going to the bathroom."

"Larry, sleep in here with us," Lisa begged, "we're scared. Mama's gone to the Randalls."

"How come?" he asked.

"Grandma Randall is gonna die," Roscoe said.

"Stop saying that, Roscoe," Lisa said.

"What do you mean, Roscoe?" Larry asked.

Before he could answer, Lisa interrupted, "Grandma Randall is sick. Roscoe thinks she's gonna die because Mrs. Parsons is spertitious and she said if a dog howls, there will be a death. Roscoe said he heard a dog howl."

Larry snorted, "For crying out loud, Roscoe, do you really believe those silly superstitions?" He paused, then walked to the window and looked out. "Besides," he added, Mrs. Parsons says that a death occurs only if there is no moon in the sky when a dog howls. And, look," he pointed upward, "there's a half moon out."

Their fears were still not allayed and, under their persistent pleading, Larry consented to sleep in Roscoe's bed. As he settled down, Roscoe asked, "Larry, why does Mrs. Parsons tell lies?"

"She doesn't tell lies, Roscoe," he answered, puzzled.

"Well, you said it ain't true—what she said about the dog howling and somebody dying."

"Oh," Larry said, understanding Roscoe's confusion, "well, it isn't true, but she isn't exactly lying. She is just superstitious and believes these old wives' tales."

"What are old wives' tales, Larry?" Lisa queried.

"It is just another way of saying *superstition*. Some people just believe the things that others have made up and passed down over the years."

"Mrs. Parsons doesn't like black cats," Lisa said, "she always spits when one crosses in front of her. She said the cat would bring her bad luck if she didn't."

"Now, that's pretty silly, isn't it?" Larry asked. "How could a cat possibly bring you bad luck—and what difference would the color of the cat make anyway?"

"Mrs. Parsons has a dream book," Lisa said, "and she reads it to Roscoe and me sometimes."

"What's a dream book?" Larry asked. "Do you mean the Sears and Roebuck Catalog?"

"No, silly, the Sears and Roebuck Catalog doesn't have anything about dreams in it," Lisa replied.

"Well, that's what some people call it," Larry said. "They look through it and dream while they're awake."

"Mrs. Parsons' dream book tells about dreams you have when you're asleep," Lisa said. "It tells what they mean."

"Now, that's the silliest thing I've heard yet," Larry said.

There was no more talk. Roscoe lay cramped, but content and secure, between his sister and King on Lisa's narrow bed. He gazed through the window at the pale half moon drifting high in the sky. Cloud vapors sailed wispily past it. His eyelids drooped. He felt good because the moon was out and Grandma Randall wasn't going to die after all.

Grandma Randall died at noon the next day. Elisabeth came home at 6 o'clock that morning, relieved of her watch with the family by another neighbor. She prepared breakfast before awakening the children. Afterwards, she assigned the chores for the morning, Lisa to wash the dishes and make the beds while Larry fed the chickens and cleaned the barn with Roscoe's help. Larry assured her that he would keep an eye on the younger ones while she slept for a couple of hours. She was asleep almost as soon as her head touched the pillow.

She was awakened shortly after noon by Nellie Dalton who came to tell her of Grandma Randall's death. "Roy and Rachel want to know if you will prepare her and lay her out for burial," Nellie said, sitting at the kitchen table drinking a cup of coffee that Elisabeth had prepared for her.

"Of course I will," Elisabeth replied, making hurried preparations to leave for the Randall house.

"You're so good at this sort of thing, Elisabeth," Nellie said, "I'll never forget how nice Zeke's mother looked after you prepared her. You're always the first one that everybody thinks of calling when there's a death." She paused a minute, looking at Elisabeth fondly, then added. "In fact, Elisabeth, you're the first one folks think of calling when there's sickness too—what with all your homemade remedies and medicines."

"Oh, go on, Nellie," Elisabeth said, embarrassed by Nellie's unusual praise, "I'm just glad to be of help if I am. After all, that's what we're here for, isn't it?"

"Well, I don't know," Nellie said, "not everyone looks at it that way—nor does everyone have the knack to do things like you have. Take me, for instance. Why, I couldn't possibly prepare someone and lay them out for burial." She shook her head emphatically. "No sir, not if my life depended on it. To think of touching and washing a dead person..." She shuddered and her voice trailed off.

"Well, it's just something in life that has to be done and someone has to do it," Elisabeth said, matter-of-factly. She picked up her cup from the table and drained it hurriedly. "We'd better get going now."

Jon arrived home at 3 o'clock from his truck run and went immediately to the Randalls when Larry informed him of Grandma's death. Elisabeth already had her prepared to be laid in the casket that had not yet arrived from Jed Ellis' funeral home. Aided by Janie Hayes, Elisabeth had dressed her in the lavender voile dress that Rachel Randall, her daughter-in-law, had made for her the previous month to wear to church. Granny had been so pleased with it that she requested that it be her "burying dress." The casket arrived shortly after Jon did and he helped Roy lovingly place his mother's body inside it. Then the casket was gently placed in the parlor that had been swept, dusted and mopped by the women. Feeble and frail, Grandma had loved to sit in her rocking chair in this spot and watch for passing neighbors to call out to and converse with.

Afterward, the men gathered on the front porch, leaving the womenfolk to their work. They spoke in low reverent tones in deference to the dead. Grandma's funeral services were to be held the next afternoon at the Baptist Church. Hours of the watch for the night were decided upon. This was a duty that the men performed—to sit with the deceased until burial. Jon took the hours from 8 until midnight.

The women assembled in the kitchen and quietly made plans for the preparation of food for the family for the evening and the next day's meals. As was the custom, the dishes would be prepared in the neighbors' homes and brought in and served to the family to relieve them of unimportant tasks at such times and sustain them in their sorrow.

Later, as Jon and Elisabeth walked home together, Jon said, "Well, Grandma Randall lived a long life—if that means anything. But she was poor all during those 90 years. She never really had anything."

"No, she didn't have much in the way of material things," Elisabeth agreed, adding "but she was certainly rich in the love surrounding her. She had the love of her children and, until his death, the love of a good husband."

Jon looked at her sharply but said nothing and they continued home in silence.

CHAPTER 4

There seemed to be no cause for optimism, either in Anseltown or throughout the nation, as the summer of 1932 wore on. No sign of recovery from the Depression's vice-like grip that sapped the strength and spirit of the country's suffering populace was evident. A majority of the people were switching from the party of Herbert Hoover to the party of Franklin Delano Roosevelt. There was much talk of social revolution, the belief common that destitute people would rebel against a government and economic system that had led them into this pit of degradation and desperate circumstances.

In Anseltown rumors abounded that Blossom's Mill would shut down completely. The workers who had fretted earlier about their wage and hour cuts now worried frantically that their jobs would be curtailed all together. Most fought "going on relief" like the plague until it became a question of whether to bury their pride or literally bury themselves through starvation.

Link Hale, like many of the older men, had been among the first laid off from the mill. And he was the first one in the neighborhood to go on relief. Out of work for three months, he had a wife with a heart ailment that required medication. Depleting his meager savings, he was unable to go on any longer without asking for help.

Elisabeth had been visiting Mrs. Hale the day he came home from the courthouse after going, as he put it, "with my hat in my hand to ask for charity." Elisabeth had felt pity for this tall, gaunt man who no longer carried himself proudly. Instead, he slumped dejectedly and looked shamefaced at them.

"That was the hardest thing I've ever done in all my born days," he told them. "I stood outside that door for over an hour. Ever time I put my hand on the door knob, I just couldn't get up the nerve to turn it. Bet I tried it ten times before I got inside." Mrs. Hale's eyes filled with tears. He hurried to her side and put an awkward arm around her frail shoulders, patting her reassuringly, "Now, don't you worry none, Sarah. Things are going to work out and be fine before long—you just wait and see." She wiped her eyes and attempted a weak smile at him. Elisabeth felt a tug at her heart strings and looked away from the unabashed love shining in his eyes as Link gazed adoringly at the woman who had been his wife for 40 years.

As she prepared supper that night, Elisabeth told Jon about the Hales going on relief. They were alone in the kitchen. Larry was feeding the chickens and Roscoe and Lisa were in the yard, playing with Buck and Becky Dalton. She did not like to talk about their problems in front of them and had asked Jon not to after she overheard Lisa worriedly tell Buck that they might lose their home because her Daddy wasn't getting very much work. Jon did not agree with her and accused her of overprotecting them, saying that he certainly hadn't been shielded from the cold hard facts of life when he was small. She pointed out that, since he had been denied a carefree childhood, his unpleasant memories should give him even more cause to desire a happier one for his children. They should have one as free from worries as possible despite the trying circumstances in which their parents were caught. When he saw how upset she became, he finally, but reluctantly, consented to curb his conversation in their presence.

"I'll be damned if I go on relief," he exploded when she told him about the Hales. "I've never accepted charity from anyone and I'm not about to. We'll starve first!"

"Mr. Hale has no choice," Elisabeth said. "Mrs. Hale has got to have medicine for her heart condition."

"Well, maybe he can accept charity, but I can't."

Jon said with finality, dismissing the subject and turning back to the newspaper. Elisabeth went about preparing supper silently, lost in thought. She was thankful that her garden had turned out so well this year. If it hadn't been for that last rain, most of it would have burned up by now. But, she thought worriedly, it won't last too much longer and the grocery bill, even with the abundant help from her garden and the eggs from her chickens, had grown to almost fifty dollars. Jon paid faithfully on it every week, if only fifty cents, but it was impossible to stay ahead of it with scarcely any work available and such little money coming in. She was terribly ashamed, imposing on Sam as they were forced to do. Thank God for Sam. She didn't know what they would possibly do without him. Jon had only had one truck run in the past two weeks. He went to the mill every day, waiting in line with the other men in hopes of obtaining work of any kind, if only for an hour. It had been in vain, for the mill was operating with only a skeleton crew. Larry went with Jon every morning to sweep up any spilled grain on the platform. He brought it home to feed to the chickens for they could no longer afford to buy it.

"Nellie wants us to come over after supper," Elisabeth said as they were eating. "They're having a get-together. Zeke and Roy and Mr. Hale are going to make some music."

"Oh, goody!" Lisa exclaimed, clapping her hands, "I love music!" Frequently on warm summer nights, neighbors would gather on the front porches and yards to talk and listen to the music played by anyone who possessed an instrument and any semblance of ability to perform on it. Impromptu songfests were held when the mood struck someone's fancy. And, if the music was particularly lively, someone was likely to exhibit a merry jig. Occasionally, couples glided to the steps of the foxtrot and the two step. Sometimes, at the beckoning of a frantic tempo, some of the younger ones would break into a wild Charleston of the "black bottom" which was frowned upon and considered risqué by the older folk.

Elisabeth hurriedly washed the dishes with Lisa drying them. Through the kitchen window, she glimpsed the giant full moon as big as a bushel basket, Mrs. Parsons would say. She heard the strains of Zeke's banjo and Roy's guitar, tuning up from the front porch of the Dalton house. In the gathering dusk, Elisabeth could see the glow of the kerosene lamp set on the square post of the banister railing that enclosed the large porch which spanned the width of the house. And, in the dim glow of the lamp, she could see Rachel and Nellie sitting in the porch swing with Zeke and Roy occupying a banister. The Daltons had requested that the electric company shut off their electricity last week so there would be one less bill to pay. They were using oil burning lamps instead. *It's a good idea,* Elisabeth thought to herself, *we should have ours shut off. We could get by with lamps. It stays daylight so long now.* She would talk to Jon about it later when they were alone. She glanced at Lisa, so intent on drying a plate that she was frowning at it. Impulsively, Elisabeth leaned down and kissed the top of her head. She wanted so much for her daughter. Most of all, right now, she wanted her to remember these years as happy ones, free and unclouded by tension and unpleasantness, as childhood should be. Lisa looked up quickly, smiling at her mother. Elisabeth took the drying towel from her, grabbed her by the hand and called gaily to Jon and her sons, "It's party time—let's go!" The children raced out the back door ahead of them. Jon's face held puzzled expression as he looked at Elisabeth. "You sound as if we don't have a worry in the world," he said, disgruntled.

"Well, tonight we don't, Jon!" she said brightly. "We're going to forget all our troubles and just enjoy ourselves."

"I'm afraid my memory is not as short as yours," Jon said glumly. Elisabeth refused to let Jon or anyone spoil these few carefree hours for her. She was going to blot everything that was unpleasant from her mind for this one evening at least. When she and Jon arrived at the Daltons, she was relieved to find that Nellie was also cheerful and gay. They giggled like school girls at Zeke's and Roy's clowning, becoming serious only when they announced that Mr. Hale had sent word that he couldn't make it.

"Poor Mr. Hale," Elisabeth said, "he's got the blues awfully bad." She told them of his trip to the relief office.

"Well, hell, we can't let him stew like that!" Roy said. "Let's go get him, Zeke!" He set his guitar on the porch and vaulted over the banister, saying, "Sawing on the fiddle will cheer him up!"

Elisabeth laughed. Roy reminded her of a bantam rooster, cocky and self assured. A short, smally-built wiry man, he had an enormous ego but possessed a great sense of humor with which to water it down and redeem himself. Zeke, Nellie's husband, was tall with rugged features and as friendly as a new-found puppy. He and Roy shared an equally mutual passion for music and a tumbler of beer. Often referred to as Mutt and Jeff, they were inseparable friends.

In a few minutes they were back with Link, self-consciously carrying his fiddle. After tuning the instruments, Roy broke into a lively rendition of "Turkey in the Straw" with Zeke and Link following. This was Link's favorite song. The trio played it several times with everyone clapping their hands and tapping their feet in time, hesitant at first, but, as the rhythm caught them up, they broke into lusty singing as well. With the sounds of a get-together underway, other neighbors drifted down the street, taking seats on the porch steps and banisters. When it was overflowing, they spilled into the yard, sprawling on the soft carpet of grass. The warm night air was heavy with the spicy fragrance of honeysuckle and jasmine.

Link Hale, a quiet reserved man, took his music seriously. His face was taut and unsmiling, almost dour, over his fiddle. His eyes looked straight ahead with no hint of a smile in them or on his lips, set in a straight and rigid line. While in the process of playing, his expression never changed, no matter if the tune was gay or sad with only one exception. A fair man in his ways, he believed each player should take a turn in leading the melody. Roy, partly because it was his nature to commandeer and partly because of his innate sense of humor, loved to bedevil Link in order to see his frozen expression finally turn to anger. Anger which Link thought he kept hidden inside for he said nothing to Roy. But afterwards, he would explode to his wife, "Well Roy done it agin' didn't he? Hogged all the melody as usual!"

Roy would cut in time after time to take the lead as a session progressed. He would nudge Zeke to look at Link whose gray eyes would turn steely and his mouth gradually draw up until it became just a very small round sour pucker. Red color would stain his face and small beads of perspiration break out on his forehead. Zeke would duck his head to keep from laughing and each had difficulty in keeping a straight face. There were times when Link would become determined to take over the lead and it became a furious contest during a number. Roy would consistently manage to win out by jumping in and playing a note or two ahead until his opponent, not an aggressive person, would capitulate. The two would covertly watch Link's face, gleefully noting his mouth growing ever smaller and more puckish.

But, tonight, Roy did not tease Link—and Zeke was glad. He noticed Link's surprised look again and again as he began the melody and retained the lead, with Roy nonchalantly dawdling over this guitar. Link, stiff and somber at the outset, finally relaxed at the unexpected pleasure of carrying the lead consistently. He began to tap his foot to the music.

"Let's hear 'Birmingham Jail'," someone called out. Others followed suit, asking for both presently popular and the old-time favorites. Roy, Zeke and Link honored all requests if they were at all acquainted with the tunes. Sometimes they attempted only a few bars before abandoning it for lack of familiarity. But there was no hesitancy in playing the numbers most requested—the songs of the currently country music favorite, Jimmie Rodgers, known as the *singing brakeman*. His songs told of the great steam-driven monsters snaking along their trails of silver rails that sliced through forests and mountains, covering the country and carrying civilization, cargo and passengers, from the Atlantic to the Pacific. Occupying a status of supreme importance in the culture of the nation, the locomotive was inevitably associated by day with the proverbial little red caboose trailing behind and identifiable in the dark of night by the unique and hauntingly lonesome whistle, played from the cab by the oft-times equally lonesome engineer, filling the quiet towns and countryside. Stories of the colorful railroad men and their trains were related through his melodies; melodies such as "Freight Train Blues," "Waitin' For a Train,"

"Train Whistle Blues," "The Brakeman's Daughter," "Hobo's Meditation," "Travelin' Blues" and "Hobo Bill's Last Ride."

Possibly, the fascination of these songs germinated from the feeling that the perpetually wandering iron creatures symbolized escape, escape from the devastation of poverty-infested existence. Indeed, man, lured by the singing wheels and mysterious promises, sought its refuge in which to flee. Hordes of hobos, including men and women, boys and girls of all ages, rode the rails in hopes of finding better times in a better place. Yet, upon arriving at some strange destination, they futilely discovered that there was no difference. Things were just as bad, if not worse, from whence they had started.

"Betsy, you and Lisa come and pass the popcorn around," Nellie called from the porch. The girls got up from the group of children who were plopped on the soft grass, gazing at the stars and exchanging ghost stories, after tiring of chasing fireflies that darted to and fro flickering animatedly in the darkness. They passed the huge bowls of popcorn after serving Mrs. Parsons and Mrs. Hale first who were accorded this honor, along with the two cushioned rocking chairs, in deference to their being the oldest present.

Nellie had shucked the dry kernels from the corn which she had grown for the express purpose of popping and serving at these gatherings. Normally, no refreshments were offered, nor expected. But Nellie's congenial hospitality compelled her to offer her guests some repast, be it ever so humble. The popcorn, seasoned with salt and hot drippings from dry salt pork, was greeted with enthusiasm.

"Hey, Zeke," Roy said, "some of Fishy's three-two beer sure would go good with this popcorn!" Fishy Tate, the town bootlegger, had come by his nickname because of his avid inclination for fishing. It was banteringly questioned if he really loved to fish all that much, or if it was just his greater aversion for work of any type. He sold his catch along with his bootleg whiskey to his customers. Fishy was not a pleasant sight to behold. Tall and lanky, he had pale watery blue eyes and dark blonde hair that would have been shades lighter had it been washed more often. It hung in tangled curls over his ears and down the back of his neck. His perpetual attire was overalls which stood out stiffly, stained with blood and fish scales. Brown tobacco juice colored the corners of his mouth and the odoriferous combination of fish, whiskey and tobacco clung continuously to him. His unkempt figure, carrying a fishing pole and a can of worms with a flask peeking from the hip pocket, was a familiar sight walking down the narrow dirt road that led to a small inlet of Red River, a half mile from "Tate Hill." Fishy's house was a rambling tumble down shack in a dirt clearing, ringed by pecan trees, perched precariously atop a small hill across the street from and looking over the Memory Lane Cemetery. Hence, it had become known as "Tate Hill" throughout the surrounding "dry" territory which comprised an immense area west of the Oklahoma border and north of Dallas. Newcomers soon heard the humorous slogan, "If you want some good booze—go to Tate Hill."

"Sure enough would!" Zeke agreed.

"If you had any money, Roy, you sure wouldn't be spending it at Fishy Tate's!" Rachel said dryly.

"You don't reckon he would give us credit, do you, Zeke?" Roy asked, ignoring his wife's remark. Laughter greeted his question and Zeke hooted.

"You could squeeze that buffalo off a nickel before you could squeeze a nickel out of that bootlegger," Jon grunted.

"Poor little Addie," Mrs. Parsons said, "she's such a frail little thing."

"No wonder," Nellie said, "with all those little ones—just stair-steps—that she's had so fast. How many is it now? Six?"

"It makes my blood boil when I think of how that brute of a bootlegger mistreats her and beats her when he gets drunk," Rachel said.

"The monster," Nellie muttered, "she ought to hit him in the head with a bottle of his rot-gut stuff!"

"What—and let it go to waste?" Roy asked, registering mock dismay.

"Oh, Roy!" Rachel said, "I don't know what in the world I'm going to do with you." He smiled at her fondly.

"Fishy said his business has sure fell off since old Doc Garner died last year." Zeke remarked. "He said that he used them for filling prescriptions. But everybody knew that Doc wasn't wastin' that booze on no prescriptions!"

"Man, you talk about somebody drinking—that man could drink like a fish!" Roy said. "I'll never forget the time I went to see him when I thought I'd gone deaf in one ear." Roy shook his head slowly in disbelief and continued, "Old Doc was completely smashed. He finally got over to me that he wanted me to sit on one side of the room while he sat on the other. Then he tried to whisper to see if I could hear out of my bad ear while I put my hand over the other one. Well, he tried to whisper but he couldn't even talk straight—much less whisper!" He paused and looked at them, his face serious. "Now, tell me, folks, did you ever know a drunk who was able to whisper?" They laughed and he went on, "His words were slurry and he kept hiccupping the whole time. I couldn't understand a dad-gummed thing he said."

Zeke slapped his knee and roared with laughter. "Well," Roy went on, "he kept on asking me what he was saying. I couldn't make out a word and, even if I had, I knew that he wouldn't know if it was what he said anyhow. I never felt so damn stupid in all my life!" He waited for the laughter to subside before continuing. "Well, he finally told me he thought I was going deaf."

"Well, whatever happened about your ear, Roy?" Mrs. Parsons, wiping at her eyes, asked as the merriment abated.

"Oh, it got alright in a few days," he replied, "I guess I just got a cold in it. Regardless, I wouldn't have gone back to Doc Garner. Why, I wouldn't have taken my horse to him after that—if I'd had one!"

"I'll never forget the Christmas that Doc decided to play Santa Claus for the neighborhood kids," Link drawled. His lanky frame was draped on the banister rail, straddling it. A long leg dangled almost to the ground on one side. He chewed thoughtfully on a large plug of tobacco that was visible through his cheek. After a long minute of determinedly masticating the unwieldy chunk, he aimed a mouthful of spit into a nearby bush. He eyed the spot critically before continuing, "He got all decked out in the Santa Clause outfit, complete with a pillow in the front and a long white beard. He had a pack on his back with sacks of candy in it. He went from house to house, giving candy to the kids. He was having a whale of a good time— he'd already had a snoot full before he started!"

Link stopped and leaned back against the banister post, chewing his tobacco slowly. Everyone was listening attentively and remained silent, waiting for him to go on. A deliberate, slow-moving man, there was no hurrying Link, either physically or conversationally. "Well," he finally said after an interminable long pause, "Old Doc would stop between visits to take a nip from the flask he carried in his pack. The kids, of course, were all so excited when they saw Santa Claus, they all followed along behind him." Link chuckled and there was a twinkle in his eye. "Doc finally took a nip too many. He collapsed and passed out—right on the street—just laid out there flat as pretty as you please." Link paused and turned his head to spit again. Then, wiping his hand across his mouth, he resumed. "The kids almost went into hysterics. They were all gathered around him, crying and taking on and screaming, 'Santa Claus is dead!'"

When the laughter died down, Roy said, "This town ain't the same without Doc."

"He was always good for a laugh with his capers," Rachel added.

"Fishy said that on the day of Doc's funeral when the hearse passed his house, he was waiting in his yard for it," Zeke laughed. "He said he couldn't let Doc go by without paying his last tribute and respect to the best customer he'd ever had!" Slapping his knee, Zeke guffawed, "Fishy swore that when the hearse passed by him, ole' Doc raised up in his coffin and saluted him through the window!"

"Well," Roy said, "I'll bet Doc's happy being buried right across the street from Tate Hill so he can look up from his final resting place and see it! Leastways, he's buried close to his booze."

"Don't reckon as how Fishy is happy though," Link said dryly, "when he looks down on that graveyard and sees his business goin' down hill!" He looked around, grunting appreciatively, when everyone laughed which goaded him to add, "Fishy is the only one around that cemetery that don't rest in peace, looking down on all the customers he's lost there!"

"Oh, Link, hush your mouth," Mrs. Hale scolded, glaring at him disapprovingly. He looked dutifully chagrined.

"Aw, come, fellows," Nellie said, sensing storm clouds of dissent coming on, "cut it out!"

The men became silent momentarily then resumed their conversation in low tones, snickering among themselves while the women ignored them as they chatted together.

"I gave Addie one of my canary birds last month," Mrs. Hale was saying, "and, I declare, I never seen anyone make over anything like she did that canary. She said it was the prettiest yellow color she ever saw. I saw her last week and she asked me to come over and hear how it sings now." She rocked back and forth slowly. "My, she just simply fell in love with that bird!"

"When you go to see her, I'll go with you, Sarah," Mrs. Parsons said, "that is, if you go when Fishy ain't to home. I don't think he likes for Addie to have any friends. Last time I went to see her, he didn't even speak to me. He just looked right through me the whole time I was there— didn't say dog, kiss my foot or nothing!" She rocked angrily back and forth, recalling his slight. "When I howdy someone, I expect to be howdied back!" she said snappishly, adding curtly, "I didn't stay long!" After a moment, she slowed her chair to a halt and shook her head sadly, her anger forgotten. "Poor little Addie," she said, "she seems so lonesome."

"It's too bad she doesn't have a decent man," Rachel mused, "she's such a sweet little thing."

"Well, it's more the pity that she can't leave the rat but she has no place to go with all those kids." Nellie said, adding bitterly, "and no money." Elisabeth looked at her sharply as she continued. "You can go anywhere or do anything—as long as you've got money!" She had never heard Nellie talk in this manner before the past few days.

"Well, Nellie, as nice as it would seem to us to have money, it doesn't make people completely happy," Elisabeth said.

"I'd sure be more than willing to give it a try," Nellie replied.

"So would I," Rachel chimed in, "but I know that's one thing I'll never be lucky enough to get a chance at. I'll be happy if I'm lucky enough not to get pregnant anymore. It's hard enough to feed the three we have."

"Well, you know the old saying," Mrs. Parsons said, "the rich get richer and the poor get children."

A prolonged silence followed these embittered words, each lost in her own thoughts. The only sounds were the voices of the children murmuring among themselves from the far corner of the wide lawn, the distant croak of a frog and the lazy chirp of crickets in the warm night. Finally, Link picked up his fiddle that he had leaned against the banister and began to play "Turkey in the Straw" softly. Now that Roy wasn't monopolizing the lead, he was anxious to get started again.

"Have you heard the song called 'Seven Cent Cotton and Forty Cent Meat'?" Jon asked.

Roy didn't answer but started picking out the melody on the guitar with the others soon following. Zeke spoke the words more than sang them:

> Seven cent cotton and forty cent meat
> How in the world can a poor man eat?
> Flour up high and cotton down low;
> How in the world can we raise the dough?
> Clothes worn out, shoes run down,
> Old, slouch hat with a hole in the crown,
> Back nearly broken and fingers all sore,
> Cotton gone down to rise no more.

The first verse was all that Zeke knew but they continued playing the tune while participants took turns and improvised their own words, some serious, some comical, but all pertaining to their plight during these difficult days. The frame was set for songs about the times that they had hoped to erase for just a little while. But there was no escaping the reality of their everyday lives. Quickly, requests followed for "No Job Blues," "Depression

Blues," "Cotton Mill Blues." These songs served as a barometer during this Depression period, as music, throughout the ages, has indicated the winds of change in the lives and circumstances of the people. What man was unable to express in print, he poured into a music which at once brooded relentlessly on life's desperateness. Thus, the Blues songs of the day mirrored darkly the shattered mood of the nation's citizens in this turbulent era. And the Blues, wrung from the souls and hearts of unhappy people, reflected the sharpest statement possible—their dreams, wants, hurts, fears, frustrations and anger.

"Did you hear about the strike in the cotton mill in Tennessee?" Link asked in a pause between melodies. At the negative response, he went on. "Well, scabs were working in the mill, and the strikers surrounded it and wouldn't let food come in for them to eat and..."

"I hoped they starved!" Zeke interrupted.

"Well, they didn't," Link said in his slow drawl. "Some smart rascal hit on the idea of having food sent in through the mails. And there warn't no way the strikers could stop that."

"The dirty bastards!" Roy said under his breath so the women wouldn't hear.

"That's what we need to do here—get a union going." Jon said. "The working men have got to stick together."

"It's hard to buck the guys that are paying your salaries and can fire you at the drop of a hat!" Zeke said.

"What salaries!" Jon replied scornfully, adding, "Why, if the poor people ever had enough backbone, enough guts to object to the way they're treated and stand up to the rich bastards here in Anseltown, there would be one hell of an explosion!"

The instruments were laid aside and the music forgotten as a heated discussion began on Anseltown, unions and strikes.

"I guess we still have a lot to be thankful for," Elisabeth said, speaking to the women in general. "Folks seem to be even worse off in the big cities having to live in apartments and the slums. The children are going hungry and cold. The people there don't have any land at all on which to raise vegetables and chickens. At least, we can do that here and keep our kids from starving."

Link, sitting nearby, overheard her and said, "People all over this country are poor folks just like us, suffering just like us. We're all in the same boat—been caught up a creek without a paddle." He sat quietly, his face sad, recalling his experience at the relief office that morning— an experience he had momentarily tucked back inside the farthest recesses of his mind but which, once again, had rushed out to confront him and prick gallingly at his consciousness. Everyone sat quietly now, respecting Link's silence. No one had mentioned Link's ordeal in order to preserve his dignity. They possessed a poignant understanding of how uncomfortably close they themselves stood near the slippery edge of the same dreaded abyss, fighting and rebelling against the moment when they might also be desperately compelled to reach out and grasp for help. Link, his voice barely audible, finally said softly, "Abraham Lincoln was truly right when he said 'God must have loved the common people—for he made so many of them'."

The gloomy silence continued to prevail for several moments. It was finally broken by Mrs. Parsons. "Well, not changing the subject," she said as she promptly changed the subject, "but I came over to hear some good music and I'd sure like to hear some!"

Rachel called out loudly in a forced, almost defiantly gay voice, "Yes, come on fellows! Let's have some music! And none of those Depression songs either! We want to hear something happy!" She turned to the others, saying,

"Don't we, folks?" She was answered by a loud cheer. Clapping her hands, she looked at her husband. "Play something lively now, honey!" she commanded. "After all, we ain't down yet!"

It was almost midnight before the music stopped at last. Some of the children had fallen asleep on the grass. As the get-together came to an end and the people reluctantly started to leave, Zeke called out to them from the porch, "I'll play you home, folks!" The strains of his banjo as he strummed a lively "Turkey in the Straw" drifted through the stillness of the summer night after them as they walked down the street.

CHAPTER 5

The revival had been heralded well in advance by large posters mounted on telephone poles in all parts of town, reading:

Come One, Come All!
Hear Brother John Wheaton,
Outstanding Evangelist
Old Fashioned Revival
Courthouse Square
July 15 - August 15

Opening night, even though it fell on Monday, found an overflow crowd that filled the benches, facing the makeshift platform on the spacious south lawn of the courthouse. Those unable to find seats on the benches sat on the grass in back of them, presenting almost a solid mass of humanity that filled the large area stretching back to the courthouse. There were four good reasons for such an attendance breaking record: First, there were those who were genuinely concerned for their soul's salvation; second, there was nothing else to do in town; third, there was no spare money for any entertainment; and fourth, had there been extra cash for other diversion, there was still nothing else to do in town.

Elisabeth and the children had arrived early in order

to get a good seat. As they walked to town with the
Daltons, the setting sun, just barely visible above the
horizon, resembled a crimson ball of fire. Its still hot rays
penetrated their skin, making them glad to reach the
coolness of the courthouse lawn that was shaded by stately
elm and mulberry trees lining the curb-side edges of the
square on all four sides. The courthouse in Ansel was a
stately building erected in 1876 as a symbol of prosperity
of the area. Its two floors were tall with oversized open
windows. The courthouse lawn was crisscrossed with
walkways, and benches were everywhere under the
ancestral trees. More makeshift benches had been added
in rows for the revival meetings.

Now, sitting on one of the benches midway in the
audience, they looked around, nodding and chatting to
friends drifting in to find seats. Elisabeth had placed
Roscoe near to her with Lisa between him and Larry.
Nellie and Zeke sat with Betsy and Buck on the other side
of Elisabeth, deliberately separating the children to
eliminate the temptation for them to "act up" during the
service. Elisabeth wished that Jon had come with them
but he had refused.

The conversation increased along with the gathering
assemblage and the loud drone of voices resembled a hive
of buzzing bees permeating the balmy late evening air
which the heat of the sun that had filled. People stirred in
anticipation for the service to start when 7 o'clock,
designated as the hour to begin, came and passed with no
sign of the preacher. Finally, at ten minutes past the hour,
from behind the platform, the evangelist made his entrance.
He strode quickly up the steps at the side of it, holding his
Bible in his hand and walked to the pulpit stand at the
front center of the stage. Voices became hushed at his
appearance. He placed his Bible on the stand. His face was
stern as his eyes swept over the audience. A man of

medium stature, he possessed a discerning intensity which was revealed through his probing, but deeply sensitive, eyes.

Drawing himself to his full height, he stood for a full minute, gazing penetratingly at the people, giving the impression of minutely searching each upturned face. Everyone, even the children, ceased moving and grew still under his scrutiny. Complete silence prevailed. The silence began to take on a nervous quality with its lengthy continuation when, suddenly, his face broke into a broad disarming grin that lit up his countenance. There was an audible sigh of relief from the audience.

"I am Evangelist John Wheaton, Brother in Christ to all of you who are Christians. And I want to be the Brother in Christ to all of you others out there before this revival is over."

He paused and a voice called out, "Amen!"

"Now," he continued, "let's all sing number 98 in our song books, 'Give Me That Old Time Religion' and," he called out emphatically, "let's sing it like we mean it, folks."

The audience thumbed through the books they found on the benches when they had arrived. The pianist, an amply-endowed middle-aged woman sitting at one side of the platform, loudly struck up the notes of the battered piano that was slightly out of tune.

"Come on," the evangelist motioned upward with his outstretched hands, "let's stand up and put our hearts and minds into this song, folks." The audience stood and sang, hesitantly at first, then boldly and lustily under Brother Wheaton's enthusiastic conducting:

> Give me that old time religion
> Give me that old time religion
> Give me that old time religion
> It's good enough for me.

With each succeeding chorus, the voices became more exuberant, the bodies swayed in rhythm to the music, and by the time the long gamut of verses had been depleted, the participants had worked up a good sweat and sat down, exhausted. The men mopped their brows with their large red bandana handkerchiefs while the women fanned themselves with the song books.

"Now, that's what I call mighty good singing, folks!" Brother Wheaton said, smiling at the crowd, "and it tells me that we're going to have a mighty good revival!" Several loud *Amen's* seconded his statement, prompting him to say, "Everyone who knows we're going to have a Revival, shout *Amen!*" The audience rocked in answer. Pleased at their response, he smiled broadly and went on to say, "Folks, this next song is what I like to call our 'get acquainted' song. I'm from Dallas and I don't know many of you good people so while we all stand and sing this song, I want everyone to turn and shake hands with his neighbors around him." A murmur went up from the crowd as people looked at each other, smiling. Brother Wheaton continued, "I'm going to come down the aisle and shake hands with as many of you as possible. I want to get to know each and everyone of you." He lifted his hands, motioning them to stand.

"Come on now," he said, "let's all sing 'Stand Up, Stand Up For Jesus'." His voice rose as he added, "Folks, this ought to be our motto in life—to stand up for Jesus and go marching forward hand in hand together, serving Him!" He nodded to the pianist to begin.

After the first few bars, he called out over the singing, "Now, I want to see a lot of hand shaking going on folks. If there's someone you've been mad at and haven't spoken to lately, now's the time to shake hands and make things right with them." With that, he jumped deftly off the platform and moved swiftly along the aisles, shaking the proffered hands heartily and smiling warmly into each face. The people clamored to touch his hand, moving down the benches and crowding to the aisles. They turned to friends and neighbors seated near them, awkwardly shaking hands and smiling self-consciously.

Darkness had fallen by the time the long singing and get-acquainted session had ended. The night was heavily pungent with the aromatic sweetness of honeysuckle, climbing the walls of the courthouse, and jasmine bushes, bordering its steps. As the ground cooled from the heat of the day's sun, the steamy air rose from the earth, gently lifting the flowers' fragrance and wafting it forth on perfumed breath to leave it hanging, suspended in the atmosphere.

After the last song was sung, Brother Wheaton signaled to the ushers to come forward to take the collection. The collection vessels were tin pie plates and had no padding. The clinking of money, mostly pennies and nickels, being dropped in was noisy and loud as the plates were passed from one row to the next. Roscoe, craning to look past Elisabeth, saw Buck Dalton hit the plate hard with the penny that Zeke had given him to put in, making a loud brassy sound. Determined to make an even louder noise than Buck, he pulled his hand back and heaved his penny into the plate. Elisabeth, unaware of his intentions, had no chance to stop him and her face grew red with embarrassment as the coin banged noisily into the plate with such force that it bounced out immediately and landed on the ground beneath Roscoe's feet. She hurriedly attempted to pass the plate on to Larry but Roscoe cried out in a loud voice, "Hold the pie plate, Mama, I've got to put my penny in!" Elisabeth tried to shush him while he scrambled on the ground looking for the coin. The people nearby watched, smiling indulgently. Elisabeth held the plate, knowing to do otherwise would bring another

outburst from him, and tried to help him find the penny
while the usher stood impatiently in the aisle at the end of
the bench, frowning. To Elisabeth's immense relief, Roscoe
spied it quickly and triumphantly deposited it into the
plate, in addition to a handful of grass that he had picked
up along with it. Elisabeth quickly passed the plate while
Roscoe watched with a satisfied smile. The usher looked
at the grass strewn plate and then at Roscoe with distaste.

Now, it was time for the sermon to commence. The
overhead light bulbs that were strung out along wires
were turned off, leaving the audience in darkness a moment
while the small spotlight was adjusted and focused
dramatically on Brother Wheaton at the pulpit stand. The
people settled in their seats, oblivious to the rugged,
rough-hewn wooden benches with the backs attached at
uncomfortable angles that stretched down the length of
them.

Roscoe's head barely reached the back and he almost
slipped through the space between the seat and the back-
rest several times. Lisa nudged him and pointed to the
sky. He looked up and saw one huge star, shining alone.
Lisa was whispering under her breath

> Star light, star bright, first star I see tonight,
> I wish I may, I wish I might,
> I wish this wish comes true tonight.

"I wish I could go home. I'm tired of this revival,"
Roscoe said crossly in a voice that was clearly audible.
Elisabeth hurriedly placed her hand over his mouth to
stop his words but was unsuccessful before he had had his
say. Buck and Betsy giggled before being stifled by a look
from Nellie. Disapproving looks were cast their way.

Elisabeth bent down and whispered into his ears "You
musn't talk out loud, son. If you want to say something,
whisper it."

"I want to go home, Mama. I'm tired," Roscoe said in a loud whisper, his large black eyes looking at her imploringly. Elisabeth didn't answer but pulled him over against her until he was half lying down with his head resting in her lap. She patted him gently and, after a few minutes of stirring restlessly, he became still, a sure sign that he had fallen asleep. Elisabeth breathed a sigh of relief.

A quiet stillness descended over the large audience as Brother Wheaton began to speak for they were anxious to hear what he had to say. Acknowledged as one of the country's most outstanding evangelists, he had a distinct reputation for his hell-fire and damnation sermons. And they were not disappointed.

Warning them in advance that he had been accused of trying to "scare people into heaven," Brother Wheaton proclaimed, "If the only way he could help to get people into heaven was to literally 'scare the hell out of them,' then he would be glad to accommodate them." True to his words, he painted pictures so realistic of the devil and of sinners burning in the blazing fires of hell that his audience listened in trancelike fascination. His voice, with its almost hypnotic quality, combined with his intense manner, his ardent sincerity, and his piercing burning eyes, delivered his sermon in a fervid style that reached out and grasped the minds and hearts of his listeners. At the conclusion, 23 people walked down the aisle to once again shake his hand, this time to signify their acceptance of Jesus as their personal Savior and their conversion from sin.

Walking home afterwards, Zeke said solemnly, "Well, if there is a life in the hereafter and if there is a Heaven, it wouldn't have to be even half as great a place as that preacher says it is, to beat what we've got here now."

"You can say that again," Nellie said, caustically, "we are just existing; we don't really *live*."

Elisabeth spoke softly, almost dreamily, "Brother Wheaton makes God seem so real. I have always believed in Him but He always seemed so distant—so far away out there in space somewhere." She paused, gazing upwards. "All my life I've wanted to feel close—really close to God and tonight, for the first time ever, I did."

The Revival proved very successful, drawing great crowds, night after night. Word of it spread into the surrounding areas and large numbers from the small neighboring farm communities came into town to attend the meetings. Brother Wheaton's dramatic personality and his kinetic explosive delivery of his dynamic sermons drew people like a magnet. But not all came to listen.

Midway through the Thursday night service of the second week, his sermon was interrupted by loud jeers and catcalls that emanated from a car that slowly drove around the square. The evangelist ignored the disturbance until, as the car drew closer, the yells became louder and more insistent, drowning out his voice. He stopped speaking and turned to stare with the rest of the audience toward the car.

"That's Stony Ansel's car!" Nellie whispered to Elisabeth as they squinted into the dark perimeter outside the area of the spotlight. "That's his roadster."

Stony Ansel, the only son of the mayor and his wife, had been outrageously spoiled. Never having been denied anything that money could buy, he was wild and recklessly daring. He and his sister, Janet, were the first in town to possess the latest gimmicks and fads that came along. Mayor Ansel gave each a new car when they reached the age of 15. Stony, now 16, and Janet, one year older, were the pioneers of the town's affluent junior set, leading the way and flaunting their riches before the envious eyes of the less fortunate youth of Anseltown. With copper red hair crowning his head and adolescent pimples adorning his face, Stony had a tall gangly frame that would soon be filled out to propel him into a large specimen of a man.

"There's no mistaking Stony's voice," Elisabeth said. The car turned the corner and the street light at the curb fell on it. "That's Art Blossom in the front with Stony. It looks like Janet and Annie in the back." Annie and Art Blossom were the teenaged offspring of Barney Blossom, owner of Blossom's Grain and Flour Mill, and his wife, Daisy Mae. The two were close companions of Stony and Janet.

Mrs. Parsons, sitting in front of Elisabeth, squirmed on the pillow that she had brought to counteract the hard bench and turned to whisper, "I'm sure one of the girls is Annie Blossom. Every time you see Stony Ansel, you see Annie close by. Just before the meetin' started, I saw her and Stony walking around the square and, as usual, Annie had so much paint on her face that a body couldn't tell if she was a rich man's daughter or a new model-T Ford a'coming down the street!"

By this time the car had turned another corner and was hidden from view behind the opposite side of the courthouse. Turning back to the audience, Brother Wheaton, ever mindful of unexpected occurrences during services, subtly took advantage of the situation. Seemingly unperturbed and speaking in a low dramatic tone, he said, "The devil comes in many forms," he paused for effect, then his voice rose as he continued emotionally, "to mock, to jeer, to distract us in any way possible in order to take our attention, our minds, our hearts away from God!"

He got no further. The sound of tires squealing filled the air as the car turned the corner sharply. It picked up considerable speed and raced past now with the horn blaring. Brother Wheaton and the audience which sat in stunned silence at the cacophony of sound rushing by stared in amazement as the car turned the corner nearest them, its tires squealing wildly once again. The sound of breaking glass was heard as an object was hurled to the pavement. With the horn honking all the while, the vehicle raced to the next corner where it once again repeated the performance. This time, its speed was even faster and, as it turned, the car raised on one side so that it made the turn perilously on two wheels. Screams of laughter came from the occupants.

Just before the roadster disappeared from view behind the courthouse again, an object was beaten noisily against the door while a voice yelled loudly, "Give 'em hell, Preacher!"

The audience had come to life now and was buzzing angrily. Several men rose, simultaneously, and walked quickly toward the street. "I'll bet we put a stop to that when he comes around again," one man said heatedly.

"I'd like to get my hands on the little son-of-a-bitch!" another said. "Who does he think he is—disturbing a church meetin' like this?"

But they were denied the opportunity of halting the car. The occupants, anticipating some sort of intervention from their harassed victims, sped on past the courthouse and did not return. "The damn little coward!" a man muttered, disappointed. He picked up a piece of the broken glass tossed from the car, looked at it and handed it to one of the others. The piece contained the label bearing the words, *Kentucky Bourbon.*

Elisabeth was converted and baptized during the second week of the Revival. She had been drawn irrevocably by Brother Wheaton's words about the Lord, of His supreme sacrifice on the cross for the love and redemption of man. She had walked quickly down the aisle during the invitational hymn after Brother Wheaton's message. She was greeted warmly at the alter by the evangelist's smiling face and outstretched hand.

After her conversion, the void that she had felt in her life heretofore was filled. She no longer felt alienated from God. He no longer seemed distant nor faraway. She had searched for Him before but she had been unable to find Him until Brother Wheaton had pointed out the way. A new abiding happiness and deep inner peace filled her being. With God, her life was now meaningful.

Elisabeth had been surprised the night following her conversion when Lisa had asked her permission to go forward to the alter after Brother Wheaton's sermon. Thinking that her daughter was too young to comprehend the meaning of salvation, she shook her head. But Lisa had continued to tug at her hand while her solemn imploring eyes tugged simultaneously at her heart-strings. She had leaned down to whisper, "Come on." Then she led Lisa to the front. Brother Wheaton knelt and talked earnestly and quietly with her. Elisabeth, watching, thought she had never seen such love shining in a man's face. Lisa was certain that he must look just like Jesus. The moment was to remain forever vividly clear in her memory and her conception of Jesus thereafter would always contain the features of Brother Wheaton.

Lisa had been the first one to go to the alter. She was followed by a steady stream of people who walked down the aisle to designate their acceptance of Christ by shaking Brother Wheaton's welcoming hand. As he looked at the line of people approaching the alter behind Lisa, he said softly, "And a little child shall lead them!"

Now, on the last night of the Revival, Lisa was to be baptized. Elisabeth, Roscoe and Larry sat near the front in order to have a good vantage point near the baptistery. As the invitational hymn began, the candidates for baptism slipped out of the audience to dress in the small tents that had been erected behind the portable baptistery. Here, they changed into white sheetlike robes, long and flowing.

Nellie had taken Lisa to the women's tent so that Elisabeth might remain in her seat for the ceremony. The tank was filled with water from hoses that extended from faucets near the courthouse for the baptismal service, which was held each Sunday night for the preceding week's converts. This harvest of saints was the most discussed, anticipated event of the week and only the direst of circumstances prevented attendance of it.

At the close of the invitational hymn, Brother Wheaton left to change into one of the robes. In the interim, the young choir leader, a friendly gregarious fellow who swung his arms about uninhibitedly, smiling all the while, led the audience in singing. He was accompanied by a substitute pianist, taking the place of the regular one who was ill. She was a stout middle-aged lady, obviously in need of more piano lessons. Nevertheless, her performance did not diminish the enthusiasm of the crowd whose voices rang out joyously and lustily, drowning out the sour notes.

"Let's sing number 49, Brother Barnes," a voice called from the audience when the first song was over. This songfest was a time for requests and the songs most requested were those that predicted a much better life in the hereafter: "In The Sweet By And By," "Beulah Land" and "I Am Bound For The Promised Land."

Suddenly, the singing stopped when the lights were abruptly switched off, leaving the congregation in total darkness under the stars, while the spotlight was being coaxed into operation and focused on the baptistery. As its beam picked up Brother Wheaton descending into the tank, necks craned as the audience stirred, vying for better viewing positions.

Elisabeth glanced at Roscoe. He was still awake. This would be his first baptismal service to witness. He had slept through the previous ones. Elisabeth had prodded him to keep him awake so he could see his sister baptized.

His eyes were wide and his mouth was open, staring at the preparations being made. For once, he was speechless when he saw the preacher, outlined in the spotlight's beam, walk down the steps into the water with his robe billowing around him. Brother Wheaton pushed the robe downward into the water with his hands so that it would remain submerged. He wore a pair of pants underneath it. He never took chances anymore after an embarrassing incident early in his ministry when the gown refused to go down into the water as he did.

Moving slowly to the middle of the tank, he turned to the audience and said in a reverently low but clearly discernible voice that befitted the solemnness of the occasion, "We are gathered together for the Holy Baptism of those who have come, professing their faith and trust in our Lord. Baptism is symbolic of Jesus' crucifixion and burial for our sins but He was raised again in triumph, overcoming death. So, according to His commandment to be baptized, immersion by water represents His death and burial and being lifted up from the water signifies His resurrection from the dead. Through the redemption of His blood, we die to sin, cast off the old sinful self and rise to become new, born again in Christ. Thus, we are transformed in His likeness."

"Hallelujah!" a voice called from the congregation.

"Amen!" another echoed.

"When is he going to dunk Lisa?" Roscoe had found his voice at last and spoke in a loud whisper. A small stir went up as people seated nearby turned to look at him.

"S-h-h-h, Roscoe," Elisabeth admonished quickly. Brother Wheaton was moving toward the steps where a small figure stood, shrouded and almost hidden inside the much too large sheet-robe, at the top of the baptistery. Elisabeth saw her balancing herself by holding on to a limb from the mulberry tree nearby. The baptistery had been intentionally set next to the tree for this purpose as there were no railings to support those going up the steep steps to the tank.

"Mama, is that Lisa?" Roscoe asked in an alarmed voice. He had forgotten to whisper and his voice was rising in fright. Elisabeth tried to restrain him by putting her hand over his mouth but he deftly twisted his head and mouth free to continue even louder, "What is Lisa doing in that white thing, Mama? Is she a ghost? Has she already died and gone to Heaven?" He was on the verge of tears and half the congregation could hear him plainly now. A titter went up around them. Elisabeth wished fervently that she had let him sleep through this baptism also. She placed one arm around him and put her other hand firmly over his mouth to prevent any more words from escaping. She whispered lowly and soothingly to him all the while. She felt him relax but she took no chances. She kept his mouth covered and Roscoe watched, his eyes round and staring above his mother's hand, as Lisa was led gently into the water with her face barely above it.

Brother Wheaton softly instructed her to hold the clean white handkerchief that had been placed on the side of the baptistery for this reason over her nose and mouth. Then, holding both her hands in his left one, he raised his right hand upward, saying, "I baptize you, Lisa Lancer, in the name of the Father, the Son and the Holy Ghost. Amen." He placed one hand on hers which held the handkerchief over her face. With his other hand behind her head, he lowered her backward until she was completely immersed, then raised her upward again. She sputtered and gasped and he wiped the water from her face with the handkerchief. He guided her to the steps. She ascended them slowly with water dripping from her as he declared loudly, triumphantly, "And when Jesus was baptized, He went straightway up out of the water."

Elisabeth watched, moist-eyed, and wished that Jon had come to see the baptism of his daughter. He had refused to attend any of the services, telling her that he wanted no part of that "damn foolishness." The thought ran through her mind that his refusal to come with her for Lisa's baptism was just another form of revenge against her, to hurt her through their children as he so often did.

Cautiously, she removed her hand from Roscoe's mouth, but he was no longer afraid now that Lisa had safely departed the water. She watched him a moment in trepidation but he sat in silence now, gazing in fascination at the baptistery. She dabbed at her eyes and tried to thrust Jon from her mind as she attempted to concentrate on the remaining baptisms.

Jon stood near the courthouse, well back of the last bench. He had skirted the audience, keeping in the dark shadows so he would not be seen. Craning his neck, he could see the back of Elisabeth's head. She was near the front. He had arrived just as the invitational hymn ended and the evangelist went to change clothes.

He had not intended to come but, as he sat home alone and the hour approached for the baptismal service to begin, he grew restless. He blew out the lamp on the kitchen table where he had been sitting, idly reading the paper over again. Closing the door behind him, he walked quickly through the warm night to town.

Now, he listened absently to the hymns until the line, "I am bound for the promised land," agitated his mind. The words made him angry. *Hell, I want some of that promised land here and now,* he thought fiercely, *while I'm still alive and can enjoy it—not sometime in the far distant unknown future after death. Who even knows for sure if there is any life after death like the preachers are always telling people?*

He gazed quizzically at the people as they stood eagerly to sing the next requested song, This time, he listened closely to the words:

> There's a land beyond the river
> In that far off sweet forever,
> And we only reach its shores by faith's decree,
> When they ring those golden bells for you and me.
> Can't you hear those bells now ringing?
> Don't you hear the angels singing?
> 'Tis the Glory Hallelujah Jubilee;
> We shall see that sweet forever
> Just beyond the shining river
> When they ring those golden bells for you and me.

It was incredible. He just couldn't understand these people. The rapt expression on the faces, the eyes lifted skyward as they sang the words irritated him. *Hell, it was almost as if they looked forward to dying so, maybe, they could find that "sweet forever." Well,* he thought, *I, for one, sure don't look forward to dying in order to hear golden bells ringing. Who the hell knows if you'll hear anything—or see anything—or be anything?*

Jon edged nearer the back of the audience in order to get a closer view of the people singing the words with such feeling. He was amazed at the emotion showing, starkly plain, on their countenances. *Why, they actually believe the songs they're singing,* he thought, bewildered. This realization made him even angrier. He clenched his fists in frustration. He felt an almost uncontrollable urge to strike out at those enraptured complacent faces. He wanted to smash his fists into them until those transfixed elated expressions disappeared. Unconsciously, he took a step forward but, at that moment, the song ended and the people sat down in triumph, the men mopping the sweat from their brows and the women fanning themselves energetically. The lights went out for the baptismal service. Jon was glad that he couldn't see those stupid faces any longer.

He tried to focus his attention on the baptism of his daughter, the only reason that he had come here in the first place, but his mind was distracted, inflamed by the anger still boiling inside him. He left as soon as Lisa was baptized and walked home swiftly; his brain was a restless pool, churning with irate thoughts of resentment. He kicked furiously at a rock. *What the hell did they have to be so happy about anyway,* he thought, *when their only hope in life seemed to be predicated on dying in order to escape the miseries of this one?*

In the weeks following the revival, the people who had been drawn together closely by it, were cohesive in their desire and determination to organize a church. They implored Brother Wheaton to become their pastor but he refused. For he was strictly an evangelical preacher who moved from town to town, state to state, to hold revivals wherever he was convinced that sin was most prevalent. But he lingered long enough in Anseltown to lend support to this newly-formed band of disciples. They found a barn-like building near the edge of town whose owner was delighted to rent to them for a small sum. Sunday school classes were organized and church services were held immediately despite the rundown condition of the structure. Brother Wheaton aided in drawing up a creed for the church, and the participants took particular delight in designating themselves as *charter members.* The men set about repairing and restoring the building as best they could. Lumber, nails, paint and other supplies were solicited and scrounged from any and all sources available.

"God will provide a way" became the motto for this closely-knit group, bound together by the difficult times and poverty that plagued them on every hand. The common bond of Christian love manifested itself among them, overcoming such human frailties as disagreements and disputes which sometimes arose. This Christian fellowship gave each the strength that they required, strength that was not only spiritual but mental and physical as well.

A pastor was called *on faith*, faith that God would provide the means to support him. And on this blind faith and the combined efforts of all, the pitifully small donations that were given from such meager *mites* sufficed in keeping their pastor and church going, though poorly, at best. The pastor, Bob Clark, was a young man on his first church call. A dedicated shepherd, he was totally committed to his sheep and ministered to them with patience and love, a love that was reciprocated and returned twofold by the members. Life, for them, suddenly became more tolerable, more meaningful and worthwhile with someone to turn to and confide in, someone who would listen and someone who would understand.

The church became the center of their existence. The services, eagerly anticipated, were the high point of the week, a welcomed significant addition to their lives that helped ease the drab everyday monotony that engulfed them. Assembling together became, not only a time to worship God, but, also a time that provided the opportunity to draw strength, wisdom and stability from each other. For, by sharing their burdens, they became lighter and easier to bear.

Elisabeth and her children were among the faithful who attended each time the church doors opened for services.

CHAPTER 6

Summer was slowly coming to an end but the oppressive summer heat showed no sign of relenting. There had been no rain for a month in Ansel County to offer relief and hope for the endangered fall crops lying dormant in the parched earth. Neither did there seem to be any relief for recovery from the demoralizing Depression that was sapping the country's strength, crippling it. In the throes of the most disastrous economic Depression of its history, the nation's problems seemed to inevitably progress from bad to worse. Many factories and banks were closing, investments were declining, millions were out of work, hundreds of thousands of farmers and businessmen were ruined through ever shrinking markets, falling prices and foreclosures.

Doubts in the American capitalist system arose for the first time—doubts regarding its ability to survive in the face of the desperate conditions under which the people that it governed found themselves. As unemployment became higher, wages became lower and people became hungrier, talk of social revolution became more vocal throughout the land. But none so explosive came, as so many had predicted, with physical force, bloodshed and violent overthrow of the government. Instead, a peaceful transformation was taking place. With the presidential election coming up in the fall, the electorate's majority was switching its loyalty from the party led by Herbert Hoover to the opposing party's new leader, Franklin Delano Roosevelt. Weary and tired of the Depression, people were more than ready for the promise of something better— and Roosevelt was making that promise.

Elisabeth was worried, not only by the trying times belaboring her family, but also by the disturbing signs of unrest in the country. She listened uneasily to Jon's talk of the revolution that he felt was sure to come. And, from what he said, people were looking with more and more favor on the communist system for, as they reasoned, "we couldn't possibly be any worse off than we are now and it would be great to have the wealth split up so we could get a slice of it for our share." She didn't like to hear Jon speak of it with such regard, especially in front of the children, for she felt there was something ominous and sinister about communism.

But she had more immediate pressing problems. Her main concern was how she and Jon could obtain enough food for the family table, even the barest necessities each day. Their grocery bill with Sam was now almost a hundred dollars and they had been unable to pay anything at all on it, not even so much as fifty cents, for the past two weeks. Elisabeth had limited her purchases to only the basic staples of flour, sugar, lard, potatoes and beans. This was due to no reluctance on Sam's part, only her own. He made a point of showing her particularly nice cuts of meat indicating casually, so as not to puncture her pride, that he expected her to order them. But Elisabeth would decline politely, saying that she was not in need of meat that day. She was ashamed of their failure to keep abreast of their bill. She refused to increase it one penny more than was vitally necessary. Jon had not had a truck run now for over two weeks. There had been mostly cut backs at the mill, keeping pace with the work reductions at the cotton garment factory, hosiery mill and cottonseed oil refinery. The fortunate few who remained working had been cut to meager hours and lower wages. Each morning Jon went to the mill to inquire anxiously about the possibility of a truck run soon. With no prospects forthcoming or need for any more workers inside the mill, he doggedly made the rounds of the other factories to vie with the crowd of jobless men, knowing all the while that the results would prove to be the same. Yet, each morning, Jon, along with the others, would repeat the procedure to walk the streets once again, make the same rounds, hear the same answers.

Afterwards, discouraged and reluctant to return home and face their families, the men gathered in groups on the courthouse square to squat and talk of jobs that didn't materialize, of the government that was failing them, of the politicians' big talk that one had to take with a "grain of salt."

Elisabeth was sitting on the back porch, hemming a dress for Lisa. That morning, Jon and Larry had carried her old treadle sewing machine to the porch from the corner of her bedroom so that she might benefit from any breeze stirring as she sewed.

School would be starting in two weeks and all the children were in dire need of clothes. They grew out of them so fast. Roscoe would be starting school this year. It is going to be lonely without him under foot, she thought wistfully. She had finished letting the hems out of three of Lisa's last year's dresses that were still wearable. She had purposefully made large seams and hems so they could be ripped and let out later for longer wear. And, she had made two dresses last week from the print cotton sacks that had contained chicken feed. Also Mrs. Parsons had given her a dress that was still in good condition and

Elisabeth calculated that she could salvage enough material from it for a skirt for Lisa.

She had made two shirts for each of the boys from white bleached flour sacks and had inherited a couple of hand-me-down pants from Janie Hayes' youngest for Roscoe. With some careful patching, Roscoe could still get some wear from them. Larry had worked for Sam, helping Wilbur in the store as often as he needed him during the summer. He had offered the small sum that he earned to them to help out, but Jon had told him to save it for school clothes as they would be unable to buy any for him this year. By the time school starts, Elisabeth thought, he should have enough saved to get two pair of overalls.

Elisabeth's face was worried as she bent over the machine. Jon hadn't come back from his rounds yet. He was much later than usual. They had argued this morning before he left. She couldn't even remember what it had been about. It didn't matter. It seemed that lately they were constantly bickering about everything, anything. Their nerves were frayed. They were both on edge with worry about the grocery bill, the gas bill, the water bill—bills that needed to be paid—but no money to pay them with. Soon, they would have to have the electricity turned back on for the days would be growing shorter with darkness falling earlier as fall approached. The electric company had shut off the power in June at their request. They had made do with kerosene lamps when daylight faded into night late in the summer evenings. The gas bills would be higher with the advent of cold weather. Elisabeth hoped that winter would not come early this year. All three of the children needed new coats. They were frayed and too short but there was no possibility of new ones—not this year.

Elisabeth snipped the thread with the scissors. Finished with the hem on the dress, she set it aside and reached for the last one to be hemmed. The day was humid, the heat uncomfortably sticky. She could feel her dress clinging to her back. There wasn't a breath of air. She glanced at the sky. She wished it would rain and cool things off. But the sky was bright blue with no hint of a storm cloud in sight. The heat combined with the rhythmic drone of a locust resting on a branch of the pecan tree made her inert and sleepy.

She yawned, got up and walked to her bedroom to look at the clock. It was a quarter past three. Jon was usually back long before now but she knew he was in no hurry to return home after their quarrel this morning. She had no hope that he had found work just as he had had none when he left today to made the regular rounds. But he tried, just as all the men tried, knowing all the while that it was useless. But they had to keep trying each day in order to retain their self respect—to be able to look at themselves in the mirror—to be able to sleep at night.

She glanced into Roscoe's room as she passed. He was still sleeping. Lisa had roused a few minutes ago from her nap and was now sitting on the porch, reading.

"Honey, will you give the chickens some fresh water?" Elisabeth asked her as she sat down at the machine once more.

"Oh, Mama, you know I'm afraid of the chickens," Lisa objected, "they peck my toes." She held her bare feet in front of her and wiggled her toes. "Let Larry do it. That's his job."

"Larry is working for Sam and won't be home till late," Elisabeth said. "The chickens won't hurt you. Now, run along and give them a fresh bucket of water while I finish this hem; then, you can walk to the store with me. I need to go before supper."

Lisa grumbled but went, nevertheless, slamming the screen door unnecessarily hard behind her. Elisabeth opened her mouth to reprimand her, then closed it. She knew how much Lisa disliked the chickens and she usually refrained from asking her to tend them. She performed the household chores that Elisabeth assigned her without complaining. In fact, Elisabeth couldn't help smiling, Roscoe was the only one who objected strenuously to the tasks given him.

As she threaded the machine needle, the ever present problem of food again nagged her thoughts, piqued tormentingly at her mind. If Jon didn't find work soon, she didn't know how they could possibly make it through the winter. She shuddered involuntarily. Winter—she didn't like to think about it. She dreaded its approach. It was so bleak and barren with flowers and food unable to grow in its cold sterility. They couldn't ask Sam to carry them through it. He had to live, too. As things were, she didn't know how he managed to keep operating his store with everyone in debt to him. Of course, she did have her canned goods that she had put up from her spring garden. And she would have more canning to do from the fall garden that she had already planted though she was afraid that it wasn't going to produce much this year if it didn't rain soon. Even at best, there wasn't enough canned food to last until spring. She was fortunate to have the space in which to raise chickens for her family. But, if they had to eat them, she wouldn't have enough of them to last through the winter either.

She dreaded to see the summer end although she loved the Texas autumn with its brilliant colors of burnt oranges, golden yellows, crimson reds, earthy browns, multi-shades of jade and emerald greens that intermingled to splash and paint the countryside into a flaming breathtaking masterpiece.

Elisabeth sat idly now at her machine, her hands still, her eyes looking dreamily at the sky, mesmerized by the pictures of her mind. There were so many things that she loved about autumn: The feel and sound of dead leaves crunching beneath her feet as she walked through them and their acrid pungent smell as they burned in small piles by the curb-sides, the musty odor of new mown hay tied into bundles and scattered across farm fields, picnics in a meadow where one could bask gloriously under a warm but not hot hazy autumn sun, biting into a crisp sweetly-tart October apple and the brightly lit oversized harvest moon that heralded Indian summer. Next to spring, fall was her favorite time of the year. But it was always much too short—just a brief and beautiful interlude between the stifling heat of summer and bitter cold of winter.

Elisabeth sighed. Her face lost its entranced expression. She frowned as she picked up the dress to resume her sewing. It seemed to her, she thought, that winter was twice as long as any other season. And, right now, the one ahead of them loomed ominously, dangerously threatening and interminably long.

Her thoughts were abruptly interrupted by a squeal of terror. She jumped up, dropping the dress, and raced into the yard. She saw Lisa, surrounded by chickens, frantically waving the half-filled bucket of water at them. The chickens had encircled her, preventing her from reaching the water container to fill it with the fresh water. The mammoth Rhode Island red hens crowded close to her, clucking and pecking at the bucket and her feet.

"Just set the bucket on the ground, Lisa," Elisabeth called out. "They think there's food in it."

Lisa didn't hear her above the noisy cackling. She was both scared and furious. Suddenly, her anger overcame her fright. She hurled the water savagely over the chickens, sending them scattering and squawking and kicking up clouds of dust. Lisa dropped the bucket and ran to the gate. Elisabeth couldn't refrain from laughing. Lisa, her face

red, looked at her mother resentfully. "See, I told you that
they pecked my toes!" she cried. She looked at her legs,
smeared with dirt and water. "And now I'm all dirty from
those crazy chickens!" Her lip trembled and tears welled
in her eyes.

Elisabeth, instantly contrite for her laughter, hugged
her close, saying, "Come over to the faucet and I'll help you
wash off." Spraying the cool water over her legs, she soon
had Lisa giggling and happy again. "Now, we've got to get
to the store," she said, turning off the faucet, "it's almost
supper time."

Later, as they entered the store, Lisa looked around,
searching for her brother. "Where is Larry, Mr. Britton?"
she asked.

"He's making a delivery to Mrs. Hawkins," he replied.
Then, turning to Elisabeth, he added, "You've got a fine
boy there, Elisabeth!"

Elisabeth blushed with pleasure and pride. "Well,
thank you, Sam," she said then added, "and I want to thank
you too for all the help you've been to Larry. With his
father gone from home so much, why, he just looks on you
as his second father." She didn't notice Sam wince as he
turned away quickly and busied himself at the counter.
She went on, "I declare, he spends almost more time here
at the store with you than he does at home."

After a moment, Sam said, "Well, you know, he's
always good company." He looked up from the counter.
"Now, what can I get for you today?"

Elisabeth looked at the shelves hesitantly. Her face
was strained. She didn't answer for a moment. Then she
swallowed hard. "Anything that you want to let me have,"
she replied softly, almost tremulously. "Our bill is so high
and I do hate to keep imposing on you, Sam, but we just
don't have the money to..."

He interrupted her, saying almost sternly, "Elisabeth,

you just get anything you need and want. I've told you before not to worry your head one bit about your bill. I'll tell you one thing—I sure haven't lost any sleep over it." He stroked his chin, cocked his head to one side and grinned at her, "Why, if your bill was the only thing I had to worry about—well..." he hesitated, attempting to think of something comical to say to lift her sagging spirits, then added, jovially, "I'd have the world by the tail on a downhill pull!" He laughed, relieved to see the hint of a smile play at the corners of her mouth. He hadn't heard that spontaneous infectious laugh that was so much a part of her in a long time. He was worried about her. She had grown considerably thinner and was pale. He was concerned that she was not eating well for she bought practically no meat, only a slab of dry salt pork occasionally, and, in his mind, a meatless diet was not conducive in maintaining a strong healthy body.

Lisa's voice interrupted his thoughts. "Mama, can I have a chocolate Hershey bar?" she asked.

"No, Lisa," Elisabeth answered quickly, "no candy today."

Lisa eyed the candy longingly, then looked up at her mother pleadingly, "Please, Mama."

Elisabeth, seeing her daughter's imploring face, relented. Looking at the five-cent Hershey bars, she said, "Chocolate will spoil your supper, Lisa." Then, pointing to the penny peppermint candy, added, "you can have one of those peppermint sticks."

Sam reached for the Hershey bar instead and handed it to Lisa. Elisabeth started to protest but he interrupted, "This is on the house, Lisa," and grinned at her.

When Lisa, happily eating the candy, was out of hearing, Elisabeth turned to Sam, "Please don't do that again, Sam."

"But, Elisabeth, she wanted it so badly!"

"Sam," she said firmly, "I'm trying to teach my children that we just can't have everything that we happen to see and want in this world."

He started to say something, then thought better of it. He nodded his head. "Alright, Elisabeth," he said. She finished her shopping and, as she left the store, Sam stared at the door through which she had departed. "You're so right, Elisabeth," he murmured, "we can't have everything that we want in this world."

On the way home, Elisabeth scolded Lisa. "Don't ask Sam for candy or anything else—ever again, Lisa!"

"But, Mama," she protested, "I didn't ask Mr. Britton for the chocolate Hershey bar."

"It was the same thing, Lisa," Elisabeth said shortly, "you asked me in front of him so he felt you were asking him."

"But, Mama..." Lisa began.

"I don't want to hear anymore about it, Lisa." Elisabeth said in an unusually sharp voice. "We don't ask anyone for anything unless we work and pay for it. That's the only way you can have anything in this world—by working for it." She lifted her head high, almost defiantly, and said vehemently, "The Lancers don't take charity from anyone!"

Lisa was surprised and bewildered by the tone of her mother's voice. And she was startled to see her eyes glistening with tears. She had never seen her mother cry before. She did not understand. She was uneasy and a little frightened. Seeking reassurance from the person who was always so strong, she reached for her mother's hand. And, clinging to it, she said softly, "Yes, Mama."

It was the last Saturday in August. School would begin the following week. Summer would then officially be over for Anseltown. But, though summer was ending, the heat was not. It was noon and the day was already muggy and stiflingly hot. The humidity and temperature was climbing steadily by the hour.

While Wilbur was busy with the ordering, Larry had helped Sam with the grocery orders that morning, gathering together staples and meat, packing them in boxes and loading them on the truck. Then, he tended the store while Sam made the deliveries. The store was close and stuffy. An overhead fan that whirred lazily in the ceiling afforded little relief.

When Sam returned, there were no customers in the store and Sam began making a sandwich for Larry and himself. He cut two thick slices of bologna from a long roll. "Get us a cold soda pop, Larry," he instructed, "and a pickle from the barrel if you want it, but none for me. They give me indigestion." He placed the bologna between thick wedges of potato bread. Larry raised the lid and thrust his hand into the icy water that had melted from the chunks of ice in the box, searching for Sam's perennial Dr. Pepper. The coldness sent a charge like an electric shock through his arm that was immersed to the elbow. He lingered longer than necessary to prolong the pleasant sensation and relief that the cold water afforded against the store's heat. Finally, choosing a Nehi grape for himself, he pulled the dripping bottles out and reluctantly closed the lid. He removed the tops from them on the opener that was attached to the box. He drank deeply from the icy contents. He removed the lid from the wooden barrel nearby. With the tongs which were used for this purpose, he lifted a large sour pickle from the briny depths of the keg.

"Might as well go out back and be sociable while we eat," Sam said, handing Larry one of the sandwiches. "Besides, it will be a sight cooler than this hot box in here. There won't be any customers coming around in this heat for a spell." He picked up the piece of wood, half-carved and illegible at this stage, from the counter and carried it with him as they went out the back door. Sam's hands were never idle. He was always waiting on customers or writing for the newspaper. Even when he was sitting at the potbellied stove or on the bench outside the store, he was busy. He whittled and carved incessantly, making miniature figures of people, animals and toys. An extraordinarily patient man, Sam completed them with the finest, most minute detail. His work was well known. By request, he kept a collection of his figures in a glass case on a counter of the store so that his customers could see them while shopping and watch for any new additions which may have been supplemented since their previous visits. Their interest and open admiration pleased Sam. Every child among his customers boasted of having one of Sam's whistles that he had personally designed.

A domino game was in progress on the long wooden table underneath the shade of the elm tree. Sam settled at one end of the bench next to the players and watched the game in progress as he ate. Several other men kibitzed as they sat on the benches that ran the table's length on either side. Several boys were playing ball in the vacant lot behind them.

Larry, munching on the sandwich and pickle, stood near the table, alternating in watching the domino game and the boys in the field. Sam glanced up at him and, following his gaze to the game in progress, said, "Why don't you go and play ball, son?" Larry shook his head. He wouldn't feel right playing while he was supposed to be working. He wanted to be able to see any customers who might wander in. Sam said no more. He had finished eating and took his knife from his pocket. Picking up the piece of unfinished carved wood, he studied it carefully before beginning to whittle on it in an expert precise manner.

"This is undoubtedly the hottest day yet," Mr. Hawkins said, pulling at the neck of his shirt, "bet it makes a 110 degrees by 2 o'clock." He gazed in detachment at the concrete walk by the side of the store that was shimmering in the heat and said idly, "Why, I'll bet you could fry an egg on that cement."

"Well, now," said Sam, looking up from his whittling, "I've heard that said all my life. By George, let's see if it's true." He motioned to Larry, "Go get an egg, son, and we'll put that old theory to the test." Larry had finished eating. He set his soda pop bottle on the table and ran to do his bidding. Returning, he handed the egg to Sam. He heard the men making bets among themselves on whether the egg would fry or not. The bets were not made in money but rather on tangible items available—a favorite pocket knife, piece of chewing tobacco, even performing a favor.

Sam walked to the strip of sidewalk, carrying the egg, while everyone followed. The domino game was momentarily forgotten. Handing the egg back to Larry, Sam said, "You can do the honors."

Larry was pleased and slightly flustered by the attention focused on him. He fell to his knees. He could feel the hot concrete searing through the worn thinness of his overalls against his legs. He held the egg aloft, poised to crack on the sidewalk. Suddenly, a loud screech of tires interrupted the proceedings, jerking everyone's attention to the car that was careening around the corner on which they stood. It was so near that they could see the youthful face of the driver plainly wince as he struggled with the wheel, attempting to straighten the car after making the sharp turn. After a moment of difficulty, he regained control of it; then, jamming his foot on the gas pedal, he sent the small roadster swerving speedily on down the dirt street, spewing swirls of dust behind it.

"It's Stony Ansel," Larry said.

"He must be drinking!" Sam said angrily.

"Yeah, his face was red enough," Link Hale said, "and

I'd say it wasn't from the heat!"

"That was Art Blossom with him," Roy Randall said, "I'm sure he doesn't have any trouble getting a plentiful supply from his mother's collection of booze." His words were lost on the others, intent on watching the retreating car.

Suddenly, Sam exploded, "Good Lord! He's going to hit Daniel!"

Until then, they had not noticed the Negro boy walking at the edge of the street a short distance away. The driver's intentions were clearly obvious. The car swerved toward him and, at the last minute, Daniel jumped desperately aside, sprawling on his stomach in the ditch. He lay there, apparently stunned. The car screeched to a halt further down the road and began to turn around, its gears grinding wildly. When the car had reversed itself, the men heard the motor roar as Stony gunned it and headed back up the street toward them. Their eyes focused on the boy still lying inert in the ditch. They saw him lift his head and look back at the oncoming car. Then he jumped up and raced toward them, staying in the ditch as he ran. The ditch ended at the edge of Sam's lot and the car reached the end of it just as Daniel did. It swerved close to the shallow trench as Stony attempted to clip the Negro with the fender. But, once again, Daniel jumped out of the way just in time.

Through the windshield, Sam could see the faces of the two boys contorted in diabolical glee. The anger that rushed over him released him from his paralyzed state. He raced toward the car, oblivious of danger.

"Stop, you son-of-a-bitch!" he yelled, holding up his arms. The car jerked violently as Stony slammed his foot hard against the brakes. Sam saw his startled face staring at him through the windshield.

Daniel, who was still standing dazed in the ditch,

suddenly came to life. With the car halted only a short distance away, he saw his opportunity and seized it. Grabbing a rock from the ground, he threw it furiously at the vehicle. Though he was shaking from fear and anger, his aim was deadly accurate. Glass shattered as the rear window broke from the impact. Stony and Art, alarmed by the noise, turned in unison to see the gaping hole. The rock lay on the back seat.

"Get out of that car, you little punk!" Sam roared. Stony gazed up into his enraged face as he stood by the car. "Do you know who I am?" Stony asked with a false bravado that belied his expression of apprehension. Sam's outraged look did not falter and Stony, seeing that his words had had no apparent effect on him, added for emphasis, "Do you know who my daddy is?"

"Yes, I know who your daddy is," Sam exploded, "and I don't give a damn! I'm going to give you the lickin' that he ought to have given you a long time ago!" Sam reached for the door handle and jerked at it. The others had moved up close behind him.

Stony's face grew pale. He was thoroughly frightened now. Suddenly, he jammed his foot on the gas pedal of the idling car. It shot forward past Sam. The roadster spun around the corner with tires squealing, making an exit in the same manner that it had appeared. As it disappeared from view, they heard Stony's voice, screaming in hysterical rage back at Sam, "Nigger lover!"

Daniel, barefoot, his overalls covered in dust and with blood running down the side of his face from an angry gash made by a rock he had fallen on in the ditch, stood gasping for breath and stared after the car with pure unadulterated hatred in his eyes.

"Are you hurt, Daniel?" Sam asked, turning to him. Larry was amazed now at the gentleness of his voice which was in such contrast to the fury it contained a moment ago.

He had never seen Sam angry before. He hoped that he would never get angry with him. The men gathered around Daniel, talking excitedly.

"It's a damn shame he can get away with that just because he's old man Ansel's son." Roy said, furious.

"It's a nice howdy-do—a sad shape this town's in when you can't call the police and report a person like him." Link grunted.

"Sit here on the bench, Daniel," Sam said, "and I'll get some water and wash that cut." He started away but Daniel's voice stopped him.

"No, suh, Mr. Sam, that ain't necessary." He took a piece of white rag from his pocket that evidently served as a handkerchief and mopped at the blood on his face. He turned to leave but, when he saw the blood on the rag, he swayed slightly and said weakly, "I'll just rest here minute if you don' mind." He sat down on the ground under the tree, leaning his back against its trunk. The men wandered back to the benches nearby and watched him.

"I'm going to let Mayor Ansel know what his kid tried to do," Sam said determinedly.

"Hell, Sam, you know that ain't goin' to do a bit of good," Roy said, "that punk will just deny it and Ansel will believe him. Anything that anybody on this side of town says don't amount to a hill of beans to him. You'll just be wastin' your breath. And besides, that old bastard will just make things tough on you. No tellin' what he'll do when his kid tells him you tried to give him a lickin'."

I don't care what he tries to do to me, he's going to hear about his son," Sam replied.

"Well, suh, it ain't the fust time it's happened," Daniel said in a low voice.

"Do you mean he's tried to run over you before?" Sam asked, incredulous.

"No, suh," Daniel said, "he ain't tried to run over me

befo' but, a couple months back, him and that other boy came ridin' down the street and asked Lenny Washington would he care to ride on the runnin'boa'd. Lenny ain't never rode in a car befo' so he said 'yes, suh!' He jumped right on and them boys speeded up till they was goin' at a good clip. Then, they try to pry his fingers loose from where he was a-holdin' on the car. Lenny said he held on so tight that they couldn't get 'em loose till one of them lit up a cigarette and stuck it up gin' his fingers. Lenny said it smarted so he jes had to turn loose to get away from that hot cigarette on his hands. He fall off that car and cut hisself somepin' fierce."

Daniel's eyes had been downcast while he spoke. The men had watched him in silent consternation. He looked up now with a distraught look, fearful that the silence indicated that he had said something wrong to displease them. The sympathy in their faces disarmed him. He felt uncomfortable and strange, confronted by concern and pity for him showing from white faces. He got up slowly, uncertainly. Still no one spoke. Daniel mumbled, "That Lenny Washington—he's my best friend." His eyes glistened with unshed tears. He turned quickly on his heel and walked away.

Still silent, the men watched the shoeless forlorn figure in the tattered overalls walk down the hot dusty road. Shaking his head sadly, Sam muttered under his breath so low that it was audible to no one but Larry who was seated next to him. "Why?" he asked repeatedly as he rose and walked slowly, dejectedly back to the store.

CHAPTER 7

Elisabeth walked down the street toward home, talking comfortingly to Roscoe who was half sobbing, sniffling at regular intervals and wiping at his nose with the back of his hand. He had cried when they left the General Robert E. Lee Grade School where Elisabeth had taken him on the first day. The enrollment had only taken a short while to complete, after which the first grade was dismissed. "I thought I'd get to stay all day!" Roscoe protested as they departed the first grade room to which he had been assigned. He looked pleadingly at his mother through tear filled eyes. "Why can't I stay all day and learn to read like Lisa and Larry?" Elisabeth had tried to placate him but he was not to be consoled nor pacified about the situation.

She patted his head now as he scuffed his feet along, kicking crossly at a rock. She smiled to herself. He had so eagerly anticipated starting school for so long and his first brief encounter had proved to be a great disappointment for him. Since he opened his eyes this morning, he had jabbered constantly, until now, in his excitement of the long awaited day that had finally arrived for him—his first day of school.

They saw Jon sitting on the front steps as they neared their yard. Roscoe sat down dejectedly beside him. "We didn't do anything at school, Daddy," he said, placing his face in his hands and resting his elbows on his knees. "Didn't write or read or anything." Jon started to laugh but restrained himself after a quick glance from Elisabeth. Roscoe half-turned to look at him, his face still cupped in his hands. "Do you think that teacher will show me how to read tomorrow, Daddy?"

"Well, now, I'm sure you will begin to learn tomorrow, Roscoe," Jon answered, "but it is going to take more than a day."

"Why?" Roscoe asked.

"Come on, Roscoe," Elisabeth interrupted, "I'll fix some lunch for you; then, you can take your nap."

Jon rose from the steps, saying, "I'm going back to the mill and see if there might be any work this afternoon." Elisabeth looked at him without answering. She didn't ask about his morning rounds. There was no need. And, she knew, as well as he, that there would be no work this afternoon anyplace either. She watched him for a moment as he walked away dispiritedly, his head down.

Elisabeth washed the dishes after coaxing Roscoe to eat lunch. He had been grumpy and upset by his inability to remain at school all day. Afterwards, she put him to bed for a nap, promising to read to him. She had hardly begun to read, however, before he fell asleep, tired from the day's activities. She would be glad to finish the dishes. The sun shining through the window on her and the hot water made her uncomfortably warm. *This had been an unusually hot summer,* she thought, *and there was still almost another month of it.* The heat didn't usually subside until about the first of October. She longed for fall and its crisp coolness. Yet, she dreaded its briefness, its too quick capitulation to winter.

Glancing through the window, she saw Nellie coming across the yard toward the back door. She had walked to school this morning with Nellie and the children but Buck and Roscoe had been assigned different rooms. She dried her hands and hurried to the door. "What happened to you this morning, Nellie?" she asked. "I couldn't find you when I got ready to leave the school."

"Well, Buck got assigned to old Mrs. Bowman's room," Nellie replied. "She's a dear and still a good teacher, even at her age, but she's as slow as the seven-day itch. I thought I'd never get out of there."

"I was hoping Roscoe would get her," Elisabeth said, "she's so good with children. Miss Jenkins seems nice enough but she's so young."

"This is her first year at teaching," Nellie said, "she's just out of college."

"I hope she knows how to handle children." Elisabeth said, then laughed. "It's just as well that Roscoe and Buck didn't get in the same room—I'm afraid that, together, they'd have both it and the teacher turned upside down and in shambles!"

They settled themselves on the back porch. Elisabeth welcomed the relief from the heat of the kitchen. "Would you like a glass of iced tea, Nellie?"

"That would sure hit the spot," Nellie answered, Elisabeth returned from the kitchen with two glasses and the half filled pitcher that was left from lunch. She poured the tea and sat next to Nellie on the couch.

"What are you knitting?" Nellie inquired as Elisabeth picked up the needles and yarn from the arm of the couch.

"House shoes for the kids and Jon for Christmas," she replied.

"Don't even mention Christmas!" Nellie said, frowning. "It's hard enough to scrape out something to eat for the family from our gardens during the spring and summer, but in the winter..." Her voice trailed off, then she resumed, "It doesn't look like Mr. Hoover is going to do anything about providing jobs for the people." She looked at them dejectedly, "I just hope we get through another winter without starving."

Elisabeth, glancing at Nellie who was sitting a with downcast head, noted that her face was gloomy. She felt a surge of pity as she studied her usually good-natured and fun-loving friend. "I've never seen you in such low spirits, Nellie," she said.

Nellie lifted her head to look into Elisabeth's eyes for a long moment. Finally, she said dispiritedly, "I'm so tired of worrying about having enough food for the kids, Elisabeth." She looked down at her shabby, faded cotton dress. "I'm so tired of drab, old dresses." She waved her hand toward her house. "I'm so tired of worrying about whether we're going to lose our home." She gazed at the house with distaste and said bitterly, "Such as it is—just a little square cracker box." Turning back to Elisabeth, her voice quivered as she said vehemently, "I'm just so damn tired of being poor."

Nellie sat silently for a moment thinking that there isn't enough money for food, much less any to buy gifts for the kids at Christmas. Then trying to brighten the mood, she said, "Forgive me for being so glum. Your house shoes are lovely. Where did you get the yarn?"

"I bought this yarn last spring from Mrs. Parsons at half price. She had it left over from the rug she made. The kids always get colds in the winter going barefoot on the cold linoleum floors and we just can't afford to buy them any house shoes."

"It's hard enough just to keep them in regular shoes."

"That's for sure," Elisabeth said, adding, "I bought the yarn with money that I get from selling the eggs when the hens were laying good last spring. And, do you know what else I did, Nellie?" she turned to her as if about to divulge an important secret. Nellie shook her head.

"I saved eight dollars out of that egg money and hid it!

Jon doesn't even know about it. I just pretend like I don't even have it. I'm saving it so the kids will have some kind of Christmas. It won't be much but, at least, they can remember that they did have a Christmas." She gazed out at the pecan tree with a faraway look in her eyes, as if she were seeing into the future. "I want them to be able to look back on their childhood and remember that they always had a Christmas!" Her knitting had been momentarily forgotten. She picked it up from her lap. "Now, don't you mention to Jon about the eight dollars that I have hidden, Nellie," she said. "He'd be mad and say that it was just a bunch of foolishness to buy the kids something for Christmas when we need it so badly for bills. But..." she lifted her chin in defiance, "I don't care! We will always have bills with us but we won't have our children small but once in life."

Nellie was surprised by the vehemence in Elisabeth's voice and the determined expression on her face. Elisabeth refilled Nellie's glass with tea. "Well," she said, her face softening, "let's not go counting our chickens before they hatch. Christmas is quite away off yet and maybe the men will get work soon."

"If Roosevelt is elected, there will be more jobs—that is, if he keeps his promises," Nellie said. "We're going to vote for him. One thing's for sure—things can't get any worse than they already are!"

"We're voting for him, too," Elisabeth said, "and I just hope that he keeps all those good-sounding promises."

"Well, as bad as things are," Nellie mused, "I guess you can always find someone who's worse off than you are. Poor Addie Tate—with all those kids and that no account husband of hers..." Her voice trailed off before she continued. "Did you see her this morning?"

"No," Elisabeth replied, "Was she at school?"

"Yes, she enrolled one of her little ones in Mrs.

Bowman's room," Nellie answered, "and she had a black eye!" She paused and added, "everyone knows how she got it."

"Oh, my goodness!" Elisabeth exclaimed, shaking her head. "I wish someone would give that Fishy Tate the licking of his life. Any man that would beat a woman ought to be tarred and feathered and run out of town on a pole."

"It was so embarrassing," Nellie continued. "One of the women—a Mrs. Kelly, I think her name was—has just moved into town from Oklahoma and she didn't know anyone until we all introduced ourselves. Well, when Addie told her who she was, Mrs. Kelly just up and asked her how she hurt her eye!"

"Oh, poor dear!"

"Well, Addie's face turned as red as a beet and she mumbled around and finally said that she walked into a cabinet door. She looked like she was going to cry. As soon as she got her little one enrolled, she practically ran out of the room!"

"What a shame," Elisabeth said, "she's such a tiny gentle thing. How could any man be low down enough to hit her?" Her face was angry.

"He's not fit for anything!" Nellie agreed, then, going on, "I went with Mrs. Hale last week to visit her—you know she gave Addie one of her canaries. You never saw anyone take to anything like Addie took to that bird! She told us that she just loves to hear it singing all the time. My, but she dearly loves that canary!"

"We ought to go visit her, Nellie. Maybe it would cheer her up after what happened today."

"I'm sure it would," Nellie agreed. "She's so ashamed of the way they live. She keeps her house and little ones clean and makes them look as nice as they can with what little she has."

"Well, one morning next week, after we get the kids off

to school, let's walk over and visit," Elisabeth said. "And, Fishy should be gone fishing by then so we won't have to see him."

"Heaven forbid!" Nellie said. "I don't want to run into that poor excuse of a man!" She hesitated, then laughed, "unless I'm driving a truck!"

Later, after Nellie left, Elisabeth went out to feed the chickens. Larry had gone directly to Sam's from school to work at the store. Lisa and Roscoe were playing on the tire swing that Jon had attached by a rope to the pecan tree. Elisabeth had gathered the eggs and started for the house when she saw Glo-ree coming down the back road. She walked out to greet her, noting with surprise, her downcast face. That was unusual for Glo-ree for she normally kept her anxieties hidden, showing only a cheerful countenance to the world.

"Is anything wrong, Glo-ree?" she asked worriedly.

"My Daniel's gone," Glo-ree answered disconsolately. "He done left yesterday on that 5 o'clock freight."

"Oh, Glo-ree, I'm so sorry," Elisabeth said.

"Well, maybe it's for the best, Miz Elisabeth," she said resignedly. "Daniel said he jes' had to get out of here and away from that white boy, Stony. Otherwise, he was afraid of what he might be tempted to do."

"No one could blame Daniel," Elisabeth said emphatically. "That Stony is a terrible boy!" Glo-ree looked gratefully at her. "Where was Daniel going?" Elisabeth asked.

"He planned to go to Chicago," she answered, "I'ze got some cousins livin' there and he's goin' stay with them till he finds a job." She signed. "I hope he can find a real job in Chicago and not just be slavin' like I'ze doin' for the Ansels." She bravely tried to smile and continued. "Mayor Ansel done tole me today that he's goin' take the money out of my pay to fix the car window on Stony's car that Daniel broke Satiddy!"

"Oh, Glo-ree, Stony tried to run Daniel down!" Elisabeth cried, "Did you tell him that?"

"Well, I tried to, Miz Elisabeth, but he said that his son done tole' him that my boy throwed a rock and broke out his window when he passed Daniel. And he said he didn't want to hear no more about it!" She held out her hands to ask despairing. "What could I do, Miz Elisabeth? He tole' me if I wants to go on workin' for Miz Anzel that I have to pay for that window—that it was only the right thing for me to do since it was my boy done broke it!" She paused and added fervently, bitterly, "No suh, nobody tells ole' Mayor Ansel anything, Miz Elisabeth, 'specially a colored person like me!"

Elisabeth's face wore a look of distress. "Sam went to Mayor Ansel's office to tell him what Stony tried to do to Daniel. The mayor wouldn't even see Sam. He told his secretary to inform Sam that Stony had told him about Daniel breaking his window." Her voice rose angrily as she went on. "Of course, Stony didn't tell his daddy that he tried to run Daniel down with his car! Sam was furious at Mayor Ansel." She reached out to Glo-ree and, patting her arm comfortingly, said, "I'm so sorry, Glo-ree. I wish someone could do something about it."

"I don' know who," Glo-ree said, disconsolately. Dismayed, Elisabeth looked at her anguished face, not knowing what to say. Glo-ree slowly walked on, muttering softly to herself, "I don' know who."

On Saturday after school opened, Elisabeth and the children went with Mr. and Mrs. Hale to the Johnson farm to pick cotton. The Johnsons had asked Pastor Bob Clark to announce at the previous Sunday service their need for workers to harvest their cotton crop. Many, including women, had responded eagerly. Some of the women who desired to work were unable to do so, however, being hampered by their small children and with no place to leave them. Elisabeth asked the Johnsons if hers might come along and work with her. She thought they were old enough to do so and they could pool whatever they made, if only a few pennies. And every penny counted. The Johnsons had been agreeable. They needed help badly and, after hiring all white workers available first, then the Negroes were called upon to work also.

Elisabeth had been very proficient at picking cotton as a girl on her father's farm. Averaging 200 pounds a day at her best, she had challenged her brother in the fields, winning the contest as often as he. Although it was backbreaking labor, she was looking forward to the feel and smell of the soil beneath her feet. She missed life on a farm and had urged Jon to move to one when the children were small. She felt it would be good for them to be raised in the country but Jon was adamantly opposed to the idea. He had always lived in town and he did not like country life. She resigned herself to the fact that he would never change his mind about it just as she instinctively knew that he would never change in many other ways.

The children looked forward to this new adventure in eager anticipation. Lisa and Roscoe chattered incessantly on the way to the Johnson farm prompting Elisabeth to scold them for fear their noisiness would hamper Mr. Hale's driving. They had all risen before dawn in order to take advantage of the best hours to work—in the cool of the early morning before the sun had reached its scorching peak. The summer heat of Texas did not diminish with September's debut. It rarely abated before early October.

Hardly waiting for Mr. Hale to stop the car, Lisa and Roscoe spilled out and raced toward Johnny Jay and Jimmy Ray, the Preston twins. It was a custom of the day to bestow twins with rhyming names. Elisabeth walked with Larry and the Hales to the group already gathered, greeting each one warmly.

The long cotton burlap sacks, approximately six feet in length, three feet wide and open across the top, were being distributed to the workers. A long strap, attached at the top on each side of the sack, was slung over the picker's shoulders and pushed downward until it hung from the waist. As the worker walked between the rows of cotton, the bag was dragged from the waist behind him, leaving his hands free to pluck the white puffs from inside its rough outer shell. At first, being empty, the sack was easily pulled along. But, as the day progressed and the bag bulged with cotton, it became a heavy burden to be reckoned with, along with the broiling sun and an aching back that was aggravated from bending half way over to the knee-high plants as hands sought and tugged at their contents. The boll's fibrous outer layer was rough and hard. It's sharp edges bit into tender skin and pricked painfully beneath fingernails.

Elisabeth had made a sunbonnet for herself and a twin smaller one for Lisa on her old treadle sewing machine which had belonged to Jon's mother. She marveled at its indestructibility after the immeasurable mounds of clothes that it had turned out over the years. She placed the bonnet on Lisa's head and adjusted her own to shield them from the sun that was just now peeking pleasantly over the horizon, but which would, all too soon, become almost unbearably sultry. She hurried the children along to keep abreast of the others as they walked across the road to the soldier-straight rows of fruitfully bulging cotton.

"Now, be careful and don't pull the bolls," she cautioned them as she pulled the straps over their head and adjusted the sacks around their waists. She positioned Lisa and Roscoe in the row next to hers with Larry on the other side of them. This way she could keep an eye on their efforts and make sure that the cotton plants were being stripped cleanly. With her rural upbringing, she understood a farmer's adverse feeling toward careless workers who skipped and left plants full of cotton, or dishonest ones who attempted to pad the weight of their sacks by pulling the whole bolls and concealing their heavy bulk in the midst of the soft lightweight mountainous depths.

Elisabeth's experienced hands moved quickly and deftly among the plants, her fingers competently separating the petal shaped bolls, expertly extracting its snowy insides, tossing it into the sack that drug behind her. All the while, she watched Lisa and Roscoe closely, admonishing them when they missed any of the bolls on plants. She quickly spotted Roscoe when he tired and began tearing the whole boll loose to throw into his bag. Larry, old enough to realize the family's need of money as the fruits of their labor, conscientiously, though awkwardly, worked over the plants and helped his mother in policing the younger ones.

The day began to grow still and muggy as it wore on toward noon and the sun climbed to its zenith. Elisabeth's back, protesting against the unaccustomed bending, registered a dull ache of rebellion. Roscoe, who had so eagerly anticipated this new adventure that he arose at the unusually early hour without complaining, now felt hot and sticky. "I want to go home!" he said crossly. "I don't like picking cotton!" Before Elisabeth could answer, Lisa squealed in fright. A huge grasshopper had landed, from its giant leap, onto the front of her dress where it clung stubbornly despite her screams. Her face registered sheer panic as she gazed hypnotically down at the huge insect which perched placidly at her waist, seemingly gazing back at her. She couldn't bear the thought of touching it to brush it away. She stood for one instant, frozen, and, before Elisabeth could reach her, she turned and ran blindly through the plants past Larry's restraining hand. Roscoe, his mouth agape with astonishment, stared after her. She was several rows away, still running, when Carver, one of the Negro laborers, reached for her and quickly brushed the still clinging grasshopper from her dress. Lisa collapsed into his arms, heaving loud racking sobs. He held her close to his chest, soothing her gently. The tears streaked down her face as her sobs grew louder. She was unable to control them. She felt hot and dirty—a condition that was alien to her nature. There were scratches on her hands and arms. Her fingers hurt from the prickly bolls that had pierced painfully underneath her nails. Her misery which had grown by the hour had been climaxed by the encounter with the grasshopper.

Carver began to croon softly to her, rocking her slowly back and forth. He was a tail, muscular Negro with wide set eyes and a large mouth that revealed gleaming white teeth when he smiled. His parents had christened him after the great Negro scientist and former slave, George Washington Carver, who had accomplished wonders in developing new products from the lowly peanut and sweet potato. With his own family name of Washington, Carver's had ended up slightly in reverse—George Carver Washington.

He continued to sing softly to Lisa until her crying subsided. His voice was rich and deep. Though untrained, the beauty of his baritone had gained widespread recognition and he was called upon to sing, not only in the white churches but, also, at some of the town's leading functions. Finally, Carver held her away from him and grinned widely, "How would you like for us to sing together and keep those 'hoppers away?"

Lisa, her face dirt and tear stained, nodded solemnly. With her sobs diminished now, he handed her to Elisabeth, saying consolingly, "Now, don't you fret no more, Miss Lisa. We's gonna sing and keep those 'hoppers away from you!" As Elisabeth led Lisa back to their row, Carver began

to sing, "A frog, he would awooin' go, h-m-m-m h-m-m-m..."
The lilt of his voice and his comical accenting of the words
brought smiles to the faces of the workers.

"Girls are crazy," Roscoe said, looking at Lisa with
disgust, "grasshoppers never hurt anybody!"

"Come on now, Miss Lisa," Carver interrupted his
singing to call to her. "You gotta sing, too." He grinned
across the rows of cotton at her as he continued again,
moving his arm to lead her, watching until she shyly
answered him in song and followed his words. Then,
contented, he turned back to his work. Soon everyone
joined in, singing in time as they worked, swaying with the
rhythm. Carver changed the songs when he tired of one
with the others following him. His voice carried
resoundingly above the others, leading the melody in his
rich, round notes. The grueling heat that increased hourly,
the aching backs and skin that burned from the stinging
scratches were momentarily forgotten or, at least, pushed
to the back of consciousness, as the workers concentrated
on the songs. All the while, they stalked slowly, doggedly,
between the rows shoulders bent, fingers nimbly twisting
the white patches that disappeared into their bags. At last
though, the voices, one by one, fell silent as the day wore
on and the sun beat mercilessly upon them. Finally, only
one could be heard. It was Carver who continued to sing,
strongly at first, and then his voice gradually diminished
to a softness that drifted over the field as though from a
distance.

Elisabeth felt his voice wash over her soothingly, like
a breaking wave foaming gently over the sands of the
beach. She had never heard such poignant yearning
expressed before in a human voice as was revealed in
Carver's when he sang the words of the old spiritual:

I am just a wayfaring stranger
Traveling through this world of sin.

Elisabeth stood at the kitchen sink, peeling potatoes for supper. "Addie seemed so happy—and humble—that we came to call on her. She said that we were the first ladies to visit her besides Mrs. Hale in over a year." Jon was seated at the table and she was telling him of her and Nellie's visit that morning with Addie Tate. After seeing the children off to school, she and Nellie had waited until mid-morning to make sure that Fishy had already left for his daily fishing in the river.

"Honestly, I feel so sorry for her, Jon, I could cry!" Elisabeth's face was filled with pity. "Addie is so ashamed of the way Fishy makes a living. She said she knew that was why no respectable people wanted anything to do with them—and she really couldn't blame them!"

Elisabeth turned to Jon. Her eyes held a glint of tears. "She told us that she gets so lonely with no one to talk to but her little ones that sometimes she feels like she's going insane!" Jon said nothing and she went one. "That canary bird Mrs. Hale gave her was really a Godsend for Addie. You ought to see how crazy she is about it. She said that hearing it sing all the time helped her from being so lonely."

Elisabeth smiled. "Why, you just wouldn't believe how she babies that bird! She had its cage hanging on the front porch when we got there and, while we were having coffee in the kitchen, all of a sudden, she jumped up and ran out the door. Nellie and I wondered what in the world was happening. Then she came back carrying the cage and said she was afraid that the canary might be getting too warm in the sunshine."

"You'd think she had enough kids to take care of without taking on something else," Jon said dryly.

"Well, she's a wonderful little mother," Elisabeth said. "Her little ones were so well-mannered and spotless. And, so was her house..." she paused and added balefully, "what pitifully little there is to that shack."

Elisabeth fell silent, deep in thought. Finally, she said, "I guess with Fishy..." she hesitated, searching for words, then finished lamely, "well, with Fishy just being what he is—I suppose that canary bird is the only real thing of beauty, besides her children, that Addie sees around her."

CHAPTER 8

With the opening of school, the days had settled into the normal routine of fall. The day began for Elisabeth at an early hour when she arose to pack lunches for the children before preparing breakfast. When she had it underway, she roused Jon and the children. Larry dressed quickly to feed the chickens while Elisabeth helped Roscoe get ready for school, collecting his shoes and other items of clothing that he had strewn about the house the night before on his way to bed. Jon left before the children did to make the eternal pilgrimage with the other men to the mill and factories, looking for jobs that rarely materialized. Jobs were solicited to the point of begging, jobs of any kind, for any amount of pay and for any length of time: A morning, an afternoon or for just an hour. Occasionally, Jon was fortunate enough to be able to sweep and clean an office of the courthouse, to help take inventory in Mr. Roger's Shoe Store or to wash dishes in the Lone Star Cafe. The mill was barely managing to remain in operation. After six years, Jon had some semblance of seniority, being third in succession for a truck run after Bob Hardy and Lenny Harrison. But, if he got one twice a month, he considered himself lucky indeed. The threat of coming bills was a constant worry that was ever present, hanging heavily over them. And, each week the grocery bill climbed higher. For there was never enough money coming in to expand far enough to cover the necessities.

In November, Roosevelt was elected by a majority of approximately seven million votes. There was freshly revived hope that the heretofore seemingly endless Depression would, indeed, come to an end—at least for a time. But the new head of government would not take office for several months yet, so hopes fell once more when a miracle did not take place overnight after the election of the new leader who had promised to give new life to the country.

"Now that we have a new President, I wish he could take over right now," Elisabeth told Jon. "It seems like forever until next March. Why does it have to be so long between the time he's elected and the time he's inaugurated? The country needs help now—today."

Worry and anxiety nagged them both, confronting them each morning when they woke and lingered tormentingly through the day. It gave them no peace, no rest. Escape came only through the release of exhausted troubled sleep that overtook them at night. But the brief respite ended with the dawning of the new day which held no promise of relief. Thus, the days, filled with mental anguish, passed in monotonous sameness, with one dully drab day following another.

The meager amount of wages that Jon managed to bring in was totally inadequate. But, through Elisabeth's frugal thriftiness, wise planning, tireless and unceasing labor, her family did not go hungry as some did. Aware of the importance of nutrition for her family, she prepared well-balanced meals as best she could with what she had. She saw many, apparently healthy, children whose starchy diets added extra pounds, conveying a false appearance of well being while concealing the body-deteriorating malnutrition with which they were afflicted. Her chickens and eggs, spring and fall gardens supplemented necessary food for the family table. Her industriousness was the deterrent which prevented the grocery bill with Sam from mounting even higher. Nothing went to waste for she managed to stretch everything to its fullest potential, making it count when and where it was needed the most. As soon as the garden vegetables were ready, she carefully picked and prepared them, canning from morning till night, until they were safely preserved—priceless sustenance for her family. Her kitchen, redolent of vinegar, garlic, spices and fresh-picked herbs, gave off the fragrances of home.

On the day that she finished canning the last of her fall garden crops, Elisabeth, bone-weary, stood looking at the array of jars gleaming like precious jewels on display lining the shelves of the back porch closet. No artist's palette could contain more colors, she thought, than was captured in the brilliant prisms of ruby red relishes, emerald green pickles, gold summer squash, amber yellow peaches and amethyst purple berry preserves. The shelves were filled to overflowing. She viewed with pride and love the bountiful harvest she had reaped this fall from the hopes that she had sown in the new birth of last spring. She felt a contentment, a peace, a sense of well-being. She marveled at the way she measured fulfillment through these pints and quarts replenished by her own hands.

Her thoughts turned to her children. She smiled. They were her real fulfillment. They were her reason for living, her contribution to the world and its hopes for the future and, when she was gone, they would be an extension of her, living proof that she once existed. And she knew, without understanding how she knew, that her children had a better life before them than she and Jon had had. For no matter how difficult the present nor what desperate straits the world was in now, tomorrow would be better. Just as some autumns yield scantily poor harvests nevertheless, these autumns pass. The Biblical line ran through her mind, "This too shall pass." And when it does, good autumns and good springs will, just as surely, come once again.

All during the fall, Elisabeth worked secretly on the house shoes that she was knitting Jon and the children for Christmas. With the eight dollars that she had hoarded from selling the eggs in the spring, she bought blue cotton yardage, after carefully searching for the best buy on it, to make a shirt for Jon. After the purchase, she counted the money remaining, in trepidation. Elated, she found there was enough left to get a nice fountain pen for Larry, a cowboy hat with gun and scabbard for Roscoe and a small doll for Lisa. She would make a wardrobe for the doll from her sewing scraps, she thought, as she gazed in satisfaction on the pretty painted China face of the doll and its red real hair. Contemplating the surprise and pleasure that the gifts would bring her family on Christmas day brought a smile to her lips and a warm glow of happiness to her being, releasing her for a time from her cares. She hid the gifts high in her closet where no one ever looked. Anticipating the joy that they represented, she did not feel so guilty in having kept the money concealed from Jon.

Elisabeth, standing at the sink washing the breakfast dishes, gazed through the window at the lead grayness of the sky. Her heart felt as heavy and somber as the day outside. The children had left for school shortly before. Jon had left earlier on his morning ritual, looking for work. The cold December wind howled around the eves of the house, contributing a mournful lament to the darkness of Elisabeth's cheerless mood. She yearned for spring, but she knew that it would be a long time in coming. She had been disappointed once again by fall's fleeting appearance, the even shorter than usual interval that separated the scorching heat of summer from the frigid winds of winter.

But the unusually early winter had overpoweringly seduced the gentle Indian summer with its blustery breath, forcing autumn to surrender in docile submission. The first snowfall came in mid-October with several others following, predicting a long wintry season that happened infrequently in this north Texas area. The ground was slushy now from the melting snow of the last storm, caused by the customarily few mild days that usually followed a snowfall.

Elisabeth tried to free her mind of the oblique thoughts invading it, piercing at the armor of her indomitable, but sagging, spirit. It was only a week until Christmas. Things were no better but were growing steadily worse instead. Jon had had no truck run at all this month. He had only worked a few days during December at odd jobs that he had picked up here and there. They had had such high hopes that, by Christmas, the mill would be in full operation and Jon would have a steady job once more. But these hopes had been dashed as well as those of the other workers. The customarily joyous season ahead would be a bleak one for their families with no money for gifts and toys for their little ones. In fact, Elisabeth thought gloomily as she dried the last plate, parents would feel fortunate indeed if they were able to put ample food on the table Christmas day.

She heard a car stopping in front of the house. Glancing through the window, she saw Sam's pickup truck. She was surprised to see it for she had not ordered anything from the store. Moreover, she had bought nothing from the store all week. Elisabeth grimaced as she thought of the numerous meals of scrambled eggs she had prepared this past month. But, thank God, at least they had chickens to provide them. She had improvised, stretched and made-do with the meager staples that she had on hand, making biscuits and water gravy often for it was filling and went a long way. She had run out of potatoes two days ago and there was only enough rice left for supper. And she had a little meal left for cornbread. There had been no meat, not even salt pork, for the past two weeks. She sighed. She knew that she would have to ask Sam to credit more groceries to their bill soon. She deplored having the bill climb higher. Even more, she dreaded imposing on Sam, asking him to extend their credit once again.

She glimpsed Sam as he passed the window carrying a large cardboard carton. She met him at the back door, opening it for him. "I declare, that wind is freezing cold," she said, shivering and shutting the door hurriedly behind him.

"I think we'll be getting another snow by tonight," Sam said, setting the box an the kitchen table.

"I suppose so," Elisabeth said resignedly. Then, as Sam began lifting the contents from the box, her eyes grew wide with wonder and, moving closer, she gasped in surprise, exclaiming excitedly, "What in the world—oh, Sam, that's a doll house!" She clapped her hands together, watching in delight as he set the large house that was painted white with red window shutters and doors on the table. From the opening at the back, she could see two floors divided into three rooms on each floor and connected by a tiny staircase that ascended from the foyer of the lower floor to the hallway above. A small banister railing extended from the stairs to enclose the second floor hall. Speechless momentarily, Elisabeth watched in fascination as Sam deftly assembled it. From the large carton, he brought out miniature furniture and placed each small item carefully in the appropriate rooms. Elisabeth echoed her appreciation with *oh's* and *ah's* at the sight of each tiny piece. "Oh, Sam," she breathed, "that is exquisite!" He was positioning a tiny bed in one of the rooms. He grinned with pleasure at her obvious admiration.

"Well, I'm not much at sewing, Elisabeth, so you're going to have to make some curtains and bedspreads for the beds and..." he hesitated, then finished lamely, "anything else you think is necessary for a house."

"Oh, what fun that will be for me," Elisabeth said softly, looking at Sam adoringly. He turned away quickly, his smile fading and his face etched with pain, unable to bear the look that he knew came only out of gratefulness. Elisabeth, happily engrossed in the doll house before her, did not notice. She stood back, clasping her hands in front of her like a child, and gazed in rapture at the miracle on the table. "Oh, Sam, did you make it?" She stopped short, then laughed and answered her own question, looking at him, her eyes sparkling, "Of course, you did." Turning back to the doll house, she ran her hands gently over it, touching it almost reverently. "Each piece is a work of art," she whispered, "a masterpiece. Oh, Sam, it's just..." she hesitated for lack of words, then finished softly, repeating the word which she had used over and over as he had extracted each new object, "exquisite!" She turned to look solemnly into his face. "What a tremendous amount of work you must have put into this."

"Well, now, Elisabeth, it gave me something to do in my spare time," he drawled, grinning at her. He stood by, watching her as she ran around from side to side of the now completely furnished house, peering into each room, ecstatically examining each minute household furnishing. His face reflected the happiness showing on hers. After her excitement had subsided somewhat, he withdrew the last article remaining in the box he had brought. "This is for Roscoe," he said. Elisabeth was hardly able to tear her attention away from the doll house.

"What is it?" she asked, puzzled, as Sam held it out for her to see.

"A rubber-shooter gun," he answered. She examined

the long wooden gun-shaped object with a spring clothes pin attached securely to the handle.

"What is the clothes pin for?" she asked.

"That's for shooting the rubber *ammunition,*" Sam laughed. "I cut thin rubber strips from an old tire inner-tube and you stretch them on like this," he explained, pulling some from his pocket. He took one of the rubber rings and placed it around the end of the gun snout. He stretched it back to the clothes pin on the handle and fastened it firmly inside the spring. Then, pointing the gun at the wall, he released the clothes pin opening it with his thumb. The rubber ring flew from the gun, snapping sharply against the wall.

"How clever!" Elisabeth cried. "Roscoe will just love that, Sam. I'll have to be sure he doesn't take it to school and shoot his teacher with it!"

"I didn't make anything for Larry," Sam said, "I figure he's too old for toys but I do have something for him that I know he'd like to have."

"Oh, Sam, you've done enough..." Elisabeth started, but Sam interrupted her.

"I want him to have that old roll-top desk of my dad's. I know how much he'd like to have it—I've seen him eyeing it at the store."

Elisabeth gasped, "Oh, but you musn't, Sam! That's just too much. It's a beautiful desk."

Sam was determined to override her protests, "No one ever uses it, Elisabeth. It just sits in that back room, gathering dust, so why shouldn't someone have it who would use and appreciate it?"

"Oh, he would, Sam!" Elisabeth said, breathless and starry-eyed. "You know he wants to write and he has told me that one day he's going to get a roll top desk just like that one." She had been rambling on excitedly. Now, she stopped and said hesitantly, "I just don't know what to say,

Sam..." Her voice trailed off uncertainly.

"Well, then, it's all settled," he said firmly, reaching for his coat. "I figured I'd wait till Christmas eve after the kids are in bed. Then, Jon and I can get it into the house so Larry won't see it." He started for the door.

"I just don't know how to thank you, Sam..." Elisabeth began but Sam interrupted her once more.

"You don't have anything to thank me for, Elisabeth," he said, grinning sheepishly at her. "Why, I had a lot more fun making those things than they'll have playing with them!"

Elisabeth looked at him lovingly. "What a wonderful friend you are to us, Sam," her voice broke as she added, "I just don't know what to say..." She reached up and kissed him swiftly on the cheek. He saw the tears in her eyes. His own grew dark with emotion and he reached out toward her. Then, he caught himself and turned away, groping blindly for the door knob. Opening the door, he walked quickly into the coldness outside.

Elisabeth cleared the table of the dishes that she carried to the sink and placed in hot soapy water to soak while she began to set the rest of the room in order. *My goodness, this place looks like a cyclone struck it,* she thought to herself as she gazed happily around at the clutter of toys, colored paper and string that was strewn about the Christmas tree that stood in one corner. She and the children had searched in the woods until they found this tree, the most perfectly shaped and greenest of all, for their Christmas tree. Lisa and Roscoe had insisted that it be placed in the kitchen where the family spent the most time during the cold winter months. It was the sanctuary to which they hurried from the cold bedrooms in the morning, crowding around the warm oven with its lowered door to dress, and where they came after school in from the cold to bask in its warmth.

It was Christmas night. The children were finally in bed, exhausted but happy from the excitement of the day. Elisabeth heard Jon stirring in the next room, preparing for bed. The wind moaned around the house. She felt protected and secure in the coziness of her kitchen. Contentedly, she looked around the room at all the loved, familiar objects. This house was her haven, her ark of safety. She walked to the window and looked at the full silver moon illuminating the whiteness below. The snow was deep. It had begun last night and lasted all through the day with the huge flakes floating lazily down to cover the world's ugliness replacing it with a majestic, if only temporary, beauty.

How appropriate, Elisabeth thought, as she gazed in wonder on the virgin, antiseptic scene that for this one day at least, the earth seemed cleansed of all evil and wickedness. *The snow must be a sign from Heaven showing God's way of purging and blanketing all the world's transgressions.* Before moving from the window, she scanned the sky for a long moment. The line, "God's in His Heaven and all's right with the world," ran reassuringly through her mind. Then, she turned, gratified, back to her work. When she had finished washing the dishes, she sat down on the floor near the tree and began to pick up the scattered toy furniture, putting each piece carefully in its place inside the doll house. The warmth of both the room and the glow she felt within relaxed her and made her drowsy. She sat quietly, staring into the branches of the tree and daydreamed of the events and happiness of the day. She smiled as she contemplated the lingering memories it would afford. *Yes, it would be one that the children would remember as long as they lived. Despite all the hardships and privations they might endure, they would still have this Christmas to look back on. Memories were important,* she thought, *for they lasted a lifetime. The happy times were remembered most of all. And, today would be one of those happy times for her children to recall.*

Elisabeth reached out and touched one of the chains of red and green colored paper that wound through the branches. The paper chains and the large silver star that perched precariously on top were the tree's only decorations, but it was the most beautiful tree that she had ever seen. Lisa and Roscoe had made the chains, painstakingly and laboriously cutting and pasting them together. Larry had constructed an intricate design of a five pointed star from pasteboard and covered it elaborately in tin foil which he had collected all year from various discarded objects.

She picked up a small item from the floor and looked at it absently. It was one of the acorns that Larry had gathered from the woods and tediously drawn faces upon for Lisa. He had painted the small tops and glued them on for caps. She smiled, remembering Lisa's pleasure with them, calling them her *doll's children* and giving each a name. Larry made a kite for Roscoe cutting thin strips of wood and pasting them together for the body; then, he covered the wooden skeletal with newspaper. He tore narrow ribbons from cloth and knotted them together into a long tail which he attached to the finished kite. Roscoe could hardly wait for spring so he could fly it.

She glanced at the centerpiece on the table that Larry had made for her. He had chosen small evergreen boughs from the woods and intertwined them with red holly berries. He carefully glued them into a wooden base which he had sanded and varnished till it shone. It had been the focal point during their Christmas dinner and Larry beamed at her admiration of it. Under Sam's tutorage, he had whittled a small replica of a boat for Jon.

She picked up the small red book from underneath the

tree that Lisa and Roscoe had made for her. The covers, made from pasteboard and pasted over with red art paper, were slightly uneven, cut inaccurately by their inexperienced hands. Inside were several pages of poems about mothers that Lisa had copied from books in her large childish scrawl. Elisabeth, hugging it to her, closed her eyes and smiled for a long moment. As she opened them, they fell on the powder blue sweater lying in the tissue paper nearby. Jon had got Mrs. Parsons to crochet it. With all the worries and problems on his mind, she had not expected a gift from Jon—nor for him to even think of it. A warm radiance of happiness surged anew within her and enveloped her being.

She sat back and closed her eyes, reliving the special moments of the day, recalling the looks of happiness on the faces of her family. Lisa had been ecstatic with the doll house and furniture that Sam had made and Roscoe was anxious to shoot Buck Dalton with his rubber gun. Larry had been speechless when he saw the desk near the Christmas tree. She would never forget the look of pure joy on his face as he ran his hands lovingly over it. Each had been pleased with her *surprise gifts* and Jon had not been angry with her for secreting the egg money from him. Lisa's words, as she kissed her good-night, echoed again in her mind, "Oh, Mommy, it's been the very best Christmas we've ever had!"

And Roscoe had sleepily repeated the theme "the very best Christmas ever."

She jumped involuntarily as loud knocking at the back door violated the still quietness of the room, arousing her from her meditation. Still drowsy, she roused herself, almost stumbling as she hurried to the door. Nellie stood on the steps in the light that streamed forth on her from the kitchen. Her drawn white face, her eyes that were bleak with pain shocked Elisabeth from her sleepy state.

"I declare, Nellie, what in the world are you doing…" she began, all the while pulling her into the room from the cold. Nellie hadn't bothered to stamp the snow from her shoes. She was in no frame of mind to think of it. She stood numbly in the middle of the room, staring blankly at Elisabeth, while the snow melted on her shoes and ran in little rivulets onto the floor.

"What in the world is the matter, Nellie?" Elisabeth asked, searching for a clue in her face. Nellie didn't answer but stood silently, still unmoving, seemingly glued to the spot. Elisabeth grabbed her shoulders with her hands and shook her roughly, "Nellie, tell me! What is the matter?"

Nellie's face lost some of its confused expression and her eyes finally focused on Elisabeth's face. "Oh, Elisabeth, it's Addie Tate!" she managed to say before her voice shattered and she dissolved into tears.

"What about Addie Tate?" Elisabeth asked sharply as a premonition of pain stabbed her heart. Nellie tried to answer but loud sobs racked her until her whole body was shaking uncontrollably. Elisabeth put her arm around her waist and led her gently to a chair. She hurried to the stove and poured coffee from the still warm pot into a cup and brought it to Nellie, forcing her to swallow some. Nellie's sobs subsided slowly and she wiped at her eyes with the end of the apron she was still wearing. She began to speak in a low, inaudible voice but it was loud enough for Elisabeth to hear. Each word pierced her mind like sharp arrows. "Addie is dead. So is Fishy. Addie killed him and then shot herself."

Elisabeth gasped. Her hand flew to her throat and her face contained an incredulous look of disbelief and horror. "Oh, dear God! No—please no!" She spoke the words as a prayer. The room swam in front of her. She had trouble seeing Nellie. She was so dim and seemed so far away. She collapsed into a chair and gasped, "Why? What in the world..." That was as far as she got. Now that Nellie had begun to talk, she couldn't seem to stop—to get out fast enough all the dreaded horrid words that she had to say.

"Fishy came home drunk today and started to beat Addie. Bobby Joe, their oldest boy, said he never saw his daddy so drunk nor so mean. He said he stuck his hand in the bird cage and caught the canary and killed it. Bobby Joe said that his mother was fighting at him, trying to get the canary away from him the whole time. But she couldn't, and his daddy choked the canary to death." Elisabeth felt nauseated. Her stomach churned. She put her head in her hands and leaned her elbows against the table for support, as Nellie continued to talk, her voice unemotional now as though her fit of crying had completely drained her of all feeling.

Tears coursed down Elisabeth's face. "Poor dear little Addie! She loved that canary so much," she sobbed. Nellie's voice droned on. Elisabeth wanted to put her hands over her ears and close out the terrible words. "Bobby Joe said that Addie picked up the dead canary and went to the bedroom and got the pistol that his daddy kept there and came back and shot him. He said he ran to his mother but, before he could reach her, she turned the gun on herself and pulled the trigger."

"Oh, that poor little boy!" Elisabeth's voice was choked, "what a horrible thing for him to see—and remember." Her eyes were wide with pain.

"Addie still had the canary in her hand when the sheriff came and found them lying dead on the floor." Nellie said blankly.

"Oh, Nellie, we must go to those children!" Elisabeth said suddenly, urgently. Her tear stained face was distraught with anguish. "How frightened they must be!" She started to rise. Nellie reached out and took hold of her arm, detaining her.

"There's nothing we can do, Elisabeth—not now." Nellie bit her lip that had begun to quiver before adding that Lila Britton has taken them into her home until this is all over. "You know Sam always saw to it that the Tate children had toys for Christmas. They're such good people and they're wonderful with children. Addie told me only last week..." Her voice broke. She swallowed hard, then went on in a trembling tone, "She told me that, if it wasn't for Sam, her kids wouldn't have had any Christmas at all this year."

"What's going to happen to them now?" Elisabeth asked sadly. "Who's going to take care of them?"

"I don't know," Nellie said. "Addie had no folks. Otherwise, she'd have left Fishy a long time ago—if she'd had any place to go."

"Oh, dear God, how I wish she had." Elisabeth said prayerfully once again.

Elisabeth spent a sleepless night, staring wide-eyed into the darkness. She was exhausted and drained. The day that had began so joyfully had ended so tragically.

She could not erase Addie's face before her. Poor, poor Addie. What would become of those poor little ones of hers? Her heart ached for them.

She tried to force the tragic event from her mind but she couldn't bring herself to dwell any longer on her family's happiness that day after what had happened to the Tate family. She tried to think of the future, of the coming new year. But, right now, there didn't seem to be a future. There was no more future for poor dear Addie. She could not prevent her thoughts from returning to Addie. She would be glad when this year was ended, over and done with. She prayed that the coming year would prove to be better for everyone. It surely couldn't be worse than this past one. Just before dawn, she fell into a troubled and restless sleep.

CHAPTER 9

January continued cold and dreary with the temperature dropping below freezing day after day. Elisabeth's spirits were still at low ebb, following the tragedy of the Tate family. She looked forward to the coming of spring. *Oh, if only it were here,* she thought impatiently. *Maybe it would fulfill the promise of a bright new year after all.* With the inauguration in March of the new President and his pledge of a "new deal," the country would surely take a turn for the betterment of everyone. At the prospect, her hopes which had been almost buried by the past year's events slowly began to emerge once again.

After a long week of being cooped up in school, Lisa and Roscoe were overjoyed to find it snowing again when they got out of bed on Saturday morning. "Do you think Mama will let us go to the pond?" Roscoe asked Lisa anxiously as they hurried from the cold bedroom to dress by the oven's warmth. The small pond, a half mile away in the heart of the woods across the back road, drew children to it like a magnet. Its cool water enticed them to splash in its shallow depths in the summer and skate on its frozen surface in winter.

"I think she will if we get all our work done," she answered.

When breakfast was over, they lit into their designated chores with such vim and vigor that they were completely finished by noon. Elisabeth suspected that something was up when Roscoe began cleaning the chicken house without being prompted and Lisa uncomplainingly scrubbed the kitchen floor. She understood the reason during lunch when Roscoe asked, "Mama, can we go to the pond and see if it's frozen?"

"Don't talk with your mouth full, son," she said.

"Please, Mama, may we?" Lisa implored, her eyes searching her mother's face eagerly.

"Did you finish cleaning the hen house?" Elisabeth countered.

"Yes, and I also put fresh straw in the nests," Roscoe replied excitedly for he interpreted Elisabeth's tone as being one of acquiescence.

Elisabeth was a firm, but gentle, disciplinarian. Even if Jon hadn't been away from home so much, she realized that the responsibility of guiding them would still fall solely on her. Jon's temper flared when they misbehaved. His strict discipline and oft-times harsh punishment disturbed her. But she held her tongue in front of the children for fear it would undermine their respect for their father if they sensed that she failed to support him. Many times, though, when she and Jon were alone, she pleaded with him to be more understanding of them. Often, he would become angry with her. "Children have to be punished when they don't mind," he would storm, "you don't want them to grow into heathens, do you?"

It made her heart ache that he chose to take out his frustration over his lost dreams on her and the children. She had loved Jon so much when they married. She still loved him but the years of estrangement had taken their toll. They could not be breached. As time passed, her feeling for him had diminished somewhat. Yet, she unhesitatingly accepted most of the blame for their alienation. She had failed him. She could understand his bitterness toward her, though she could not understand his refusal to forgive her. But she could not accept his seeming indifference, even sporadic rejection, of their children.

So, she tried to be both a father and mother, to make life happy for the children, hoping to make up for Jon's lack of attention and affection. In an attempt to excuse his actions, she reminded them repeatedly that he had never known a father of his own. She tried to impress on them how hard their father worked to provide food, shelter and clothing. But, it was painfully apparent to Elisabeth how carefree and happy they were when Jon was away, how subdued and quiet they became in his presence. She was hurt deeply by the strained relationship but she found it impossible to reach Jon and to make him understand. With all her heart, she wished that Jon was able to give of himself to the children—even if he couldn't to her.

"Alright, I guess you can," Elisabeth finally answered, "but..."

"Hoo-ray!" Roscoe shouted, interrupting her while Lisa squealed in delight.

"But you have to finish your lunch first," Elisabeth resumed, "and that includes drinking all your milk. It's ..."

"Yes, I know," Lisa interrupted quickly and repeated the words so often proclaimed by her mother, "it's a sin to waste food."

Elisabeth looked at her sharply and, deciding that her remark was innocently made and not meant to be disrespectful, continued, "Yes, it certainly is, Lisa. Besides, you'll both need lots of nourishment to keep you warm."

"Yes, ma'am," Roscoe grinned happily.

"Don't you want to go, Larry?" Lisa asked. "It will be lots of fun to skate on the ice!"

"No, that's for kids," Larry replied, trying to sound grown-up, "besides, I got a book at the library yesterday that I want to read." Although he felt that he was too old to play with his young brother and sister any longer, nevertheless, he was very protective toward them. "You all just be sure that the ice is thick enough to skate on now," he called back as he headed for his room and his book.

Elisabeth gazed after him fondly. This oldest child of hers held a special place in her heart. There was a rare understanding between mother and son. A sensitive boy, she knew that he discerned the rift between his parents. Deeply affected by his father's coldness, he became silent and withdrawn in his presence. He had grown so fast and matured so much since he entered adolescence this past year, she thought. And, it seemed to her, he had become even more considerate of her. Also, he had begun to act in a paternal manner toward his brother and sister; perhaps, Elisabeth thought, in an effort to make up for Jon's lack of fatherly attention. Lately, more and more, she had found herself having serious discussions with him, relying strongly on his opinions. She was delighted that he had inherited her love of books. They held long dissertations on books and authors. And, she had been overjoyed when he had confided a short time back that he wanted to be a writer. His revelation explained the mystery of the long hours that he had spent alone in his room the past few months. He had begun to record his thoughts and feelings on paper. Elisabeth couldn't have been more pleased. She was conscious of her son's high susceptibility, his acute awareness, his ability to receive impressions in depth from people and events around him.

Already endowed with such perceptive qualities, he could develop into a good writer, provided he had the proper training and education. She prayed that, when the time came, they would be able to send him to college to pursue the knowledge necessary for this creative career and his budding talent. As yet, he had not offered to let her read his writing. And she did not ask to do so. She respected his reluctance to reveal his innermost self, reasoning that, when he was ready, he would unveil the secret sensitivities of his mind.

"Now, be sure you keep your scarf on, Roscoe," Elisabeth admonished for she knew how he hated to wear one. "I don't want you to get a sore throat."

"I sure don't want one either," he replied. "I hate for you to mop my throat. I'd rather it stayed sore."

"Well, then, you just don't go pulling your scarf off." she warned.

"Come on, Roscoe!" Lisa called impatiently from the open door.

Elisabeth followed Roscoe as he hurried outside. Crossing the back porch, she smelled the odor seeping from the two bushel baskets of apples that sat at the far end. The pungent aroma of the fresh fruit which she and the children had carefully wrapped individually in paper and stored in the baskets last fall spiced the air all winter. She took a deep breath, drinking in the fruity scent and made a mental note to bake an apple pie for supper. They would be hungry after playing all afternoon in the cold air. She watched as they ran quickly through the yard and crossed the ditch to the road while King leaped exuberantly, barking wildly, and ran in circles around them. Their passage wounded the new virgin snow, marring its antiseptic perfection with footprint scars left behind in their wake.

It's a beautiful world, Elisabeth thought. *A world made beautiful by the white blanket of innocence spread over it.* At this moment, she felt no yearning, no desire for spring. For winter was truly a thing of beauty—a time of rest and renewal for the earth in preparation for the bright new birth of spring, the carefree days of summer and the gratifying fulfillment of autumn.

She gazed upward at the gray skies. *From the looks of them, it's going to get even colder tonight,* she thought. She shivered in her thin cotton dress but she felt a rich contentment as she hurried back to the warmth of her kitchen.

"Do you think Mr. Hamm's house is really haunted?" Roscoe asked. He and Lisa, walking home from the pond in the gathering dusk, emerged from the woods near the railroad track that crossed the road a distance down the road from the Lancer house. King had disappeared in the dimness of the day after impatiently racing on ahead of them toward home.

"Glo-ree says it's haunted," Lisa replied, "and that Ernest's ghost is still in there!" She shivered as they stood looking at the lonely dilapidated structure in the gray twilight. This last house in the white section before crossing the tracks into the Negro quarter had remained vacant for several years. No one had desired to occupy it since its owner had hanged himself there.

"Why did Ernest hang himself?" Roscoe asked.

"How should I know, dumbbell?" Lisa replied. "Glo-ree said that her husband was the one who found Ernest hanging by the neck. She said that they hadn't seen Ernest for several days so Dotson went to his house and knocked and knocked at the door. When Ernest didn't come to the door, Dotson looked through the windows and he saw Ernest hanging from the ceiling in the kitchen. Glo-ree said that Dotson was so scared that he just turned around and ran straight home. Then, she made him go down to Mr. Britton's store and call the police. When the police came, she and Dotson went in with them and watched them cut Ernest down." She shuddered. "Glo-ree said his face was all black."

Roscoe had listened in fascination to the familiar, but ever suspenseful story. "Why was his face black, Lisa?"

"It turned black when he died, dumbbell." Lisa, at a loss for an explanation, said exasperatedly.

Roscoe frowned as he contemplated her answer. Dissatisfied and plainly puzzled by it, he said, "Well, if a white person's face turns black, does a Negro's turn white when he dies?"

Lisa was nettled because she was unable to expound further on the subject; a fact that she, being older and wiser than he, stubbornly refused to admit to him. "Oh hush up, Roscoe!" she said in irritation, throwing him a look of disgust.

Dismissing it from his mind, Roscoe said, "Well, I don't believe in ghosts anymore. Mama says there ain't no such thing."

"I don't know," Lisa said hesitantly, "Glo-ree said that lots of nights, she has seen a light through the windows, like someone was walking around with a candle—the way Ernest used to do." She shivered and added, "That's why no one will live here anymore because they're scared of his ghost."

"Well, I guess I wouldn't want to live here," Roscoe admitted grudgingly. Then, defiantly, he added, "But I don't believe in ghosts!"

"If you don't believe in 'em, then why don't you go in the house?" Lisa goaded.

They were walking slowly, staring at the house. "I'm not a scaredy cat," Roscoe bragged. He ran across the yard to the front steps, then stopped and looked back at Lisa. "Come on!" he said. He walked gingerly up the steps and across the front porch. Lisa followed him reluctantly to the edge of the porch where she stopped, watching as he pulled the torn screen door back. It squeaked on rusty hinges. Roscoe took hold of the door knob. When it failed to open, he looked back, relieved, at Lisa, "I can't get in. It's locked."

"The glass is out of the window over here," she replied, "you can go through there if you're so brave."

Roscoe looked at the window uncertainly. But, feeling that his honor was at stake, he walked over to it and gazed inside. Seeing nothing that appeared menacing in the bare room, his courage returned.

"I'm going in and show you there ain't no ghost in there," he told her as he wriggled through the small square opening. Lisa watched him disappear inside then, walking to the window, she hesitated, wishing that she had not dared him to enter. She viewed the deepening twilight. It would soon be dark.

"Come on, Roscoe," she whispered, "let's go home!"

"Come on in, 'fraidy-cat!" Roscoe's face peered out at her from the gaping hole. "There's nothing in here to be ascaird of." He grabbed her arm and helped pull her through. "Come on," he said, motioning, "let's look in here." He started toward the door that led to another room.

Lisa followed him closely, shivering from fright and the cold. The room, like the front one they had entered, was empty also. Newspapers, peeling paint from the walls and scraps of plaster that had fallen from the ceiling were scattered across the floor. Their feet made a scuffing sound scraping across the debris.

"Roscoe, I'm scared!" Lisa whimpered. "Let's get out of here!"

"I told you there ain't no ghosts!" Roscoe said triumphantly, his bravado returning. "Let's go in the kitchen."

"No!" Lisa protested sharply, drawing back. "That's where they found Ernest hanging!"

"Oh, come on, 'fraidy-cat. There ain't nothing to be ascaird of."

The house was almost in total darkness now as they groped their way down the hall toward the kitchen with Roscoe leading the way and Lisa hanging on to his coat collar from behind. A cobweb brushed across her face and she drew back, emitting a squeal.

"Don't be such a sissy! That's just a spider web—and a little old spider won't hurt you." Roscoe's voice betrayed the confidence of his words.

They could barely see in the darkness now as they entered the door of the kitchen from the hallway. Their eyes slowly became accustomed to the dimness until they could see the broken sink on one side of the room. It was underneath a window which was covered with newspapers that promoted the darkness and prevented any fading light from entering. Edging slowly into the middle of the large room, Roscoe stumbled on a loose rotted board and went sprawling onto the floor. Lisa, still holding to his collar, was almost thrown off balance but managed to catch herself when her hand touched and clung to a rope suspended in the air. She recoiled in horror as she remembered and she jerked her hand away. Her throat was so dry and tight with fear that she could hardly whisper, "Roscoe, this must be the rope that Ernest hung himself on!"

Roscoe had picked himself up quickly from the floor. He was breathing hard. He let out a sigh of relief when he saw an electric fixture at the end of the frayed cord. "It's just an ole' light wire," he said and, trying to sound convincing, added, "See, let me show you." He grasped the cord, pulling up the end with the electric fixture attached that had long ago slipped almost to floor level from the ceiling.

They stood still, examining it, feeling it more than

seeing it now in the almost total darkness. Suddenly, they were grabbed roughly from behind. Roscoe gasped. Lisa tried to cry out but her voice was quickly muffled by a hand that covered her mouth. Two strong arms shifted them harshly until both were held securely in the grasp of one muscular arm while a flashlight, appearing in the other hand, threw its beam squarely in their faces. Their eyes, wide with fear, were rolling wildly, vainly trying to see beyond the circle of light.

"What you doin' in here?" a raspy voice demanded.

Paralyzed with fear, they made no effort to struggle but kept their eyes focused on the object that loomed behind the sphere of light. Lisa, hardly able to breathe with the hand covering both her nose and mouth, felt faint. Both, weak from the terror that gripped them, were almost totally supported by the arm which bound them for their knees buckled under them. Panic stricken, they made no attempt to answer.

After a long moment, the hand relaxed its hold on Lisa's mouth as the voice said, "Now, don't make any noise or I'll have to gag you!"

Roscoe managed to find his voice at last and, in a husky whisper, stuttered, "Are you Mr. Ernest's ghost?" He, like everyone, had always referred to him by his given name but now, finding himself directly accosted by him, Roscoe felt the need to address his ghost as "Mr. Ernest."

"What you talkin' 'bout, boy?" asked the voice, "I ain't no ghost." The arm released them suddenly and they slid to the floor on their knees. Their legs refused to support them. "Now, you just sit there nice and quiet till I get a candle lit," the voice said.

Huddling on the floor together, they watched the shadowy figure grope on the cabinet next to the sink. Then making sure that the newspapers were in place over the window, he struck a match and lit a candle that was standing in its own wax in a fruit jar lid. Its small glow of light seemed to transform the room into extreme brightness after the pitch black darkness. Lisa and Roscoe, eyes wide and mouths agape, stared at the tall muscular Negro youth in tattered pants and a worn shabby jacket, outlined by the light of the candle he held. As he squatted in front of them, they saw a deep cut down one side of his wide black face. It was open and angry looking. Blood matted the top of his short wooly hair, the red contrasting sharply against the black of his head. The gaping cut on his head was deeper and more inflamed than the one on his face.

Lisa gasped, "How did you hurt yourself?"

He gave a low ugly laugh. "Now, do you think that anyone in his right mind would do a thing like this to hisself?" He peered closely at them. "Why did you kids come in here for anyways? Did somebody put you up to come lookin' for me?"

"Oh, no," they both said in unison. Roscoe added, "We wanted to see if Ernest's ghost really was in here!"

"We were just coming home from the pond," Lisa whimpered. Then, she turned to Roscoe, saying accusingly, "I told you that you ought not to come in this house."

"Now, what am I goin' to do with you kids? If I let you go, you'll tell your mama that I'm here. Then, she'll have the police come git me."

"Are the police looking for you?" Roscoe whispered.

Before he could answer, footsteps sounded on the back porch and a voice called softly at the door, "Daniel, let me in!"

"Who is it?" asked Lisa, looking in apprehension toward the door.

"Never you mind," he answered. "You kids just set and hesh your mouth and you won't get hurt." He opened the door to a shadowy figure holding a plate which was covered with a white cloth. Lisa and Roscoe recognized the familiar face in the candlelight. Instantly, they were on their feet. Running to her, they flung themselves against her, their arms twining about her waist. Their voices quavered as they cried, "Glo-ree, we're scared! Don't let him hurt us!"

"Lawsy me, chillun, nobody's goin' to hurt you!" she said. "Now, let me set this food down before you makes me spill it." She deposited the plate on the cabinet and turned to gather them in her arms. "What you two kids doin' here anyhow?" she scolded. "Don't you know your mama is goin' to be worried sick about you?"

"He wouldn't let us go," Roscoe said accusingly.

"Of course, he'll let you go home," Glo-ree said, turning to look at Daniel disapprovingly. "What you go scarin' these chillun for, Daniel? They's Miz Elisabeth's young 'uns."

"But, Mama," Daniel protested, "I'ze scared they's goin' tell the police and they'll come git me and lock me up in that jail."

"Nobody's goin' lock you up, Daniel," Glo-ree said but a worried look crossed her face. "How you feelin'?" she asked as she laid her hand against his forehead. After a moment, she said anxiously, "You still got the fever, boy."

"I don't feel good a'tall, Mama," he answered, "my head hurts somethin' fierce and my throat's awful sore. I been sleepin' most all day till these kids came in here and woke me up." He shivered in his thin faded jacket that was threadbare from wear. "I'm freezin' cold. I wish I could build a fire in the stove but I'm scared somebody will see the smoke comin' out the chimney."

"No, don't you dare do that, boy!" Glo-ree warned sternly. "The police would git you sho' nuff then for breaking in here." Her voice turned gentle. "Now, you jes' eat this food I brung you while I walk these chillun' home. If they don't get home soon, Miz Elisabeth's goin' have the police out lookin' for them!"

She turned to Roscoe and Lisa, "Come along now, chillun', let's get you two home." They did not have to be prodded. They were already out the door. She followed but stopped at the door and looked back at Daniel, saying, "Don't worry, boy, Miz Elisabeth won't turn you in to the law. She's a good woman." Then she closed the door and walked into the darkness after the children.

As Lisa and Roscoe ran up the steps of the Lancer house, the door was flung open and Elisabeth was outlined in the doorway. "Where in the world have you been?" she asked in an anxious voice as they raced to her waiting arms. "I was just fixing to go out looking for you." She peered into the blackness of the yard and her eyes made out a shadowy silhouette standing near the porch. Glo-ree had stopped there as was her custom. She never walked onto the front porch of a white person's home but entered, instead, by the back door.

"It's me—Glo-ree, Miz Elisabeth," she said.

"She brought us home from Ernest's house, Mama," Roscoe said.

"There's a man hiding in there with blood all over him!" Lisa said excitedly.

"What are you talking about?" Elisabeth demanded. "What were you doing in Ernest's house anyway?"

"*Please,* Miz Elisabeth, can I talk to you a minute?" Glo-ree interrupted. "Please, I just gotta talk to you!"

"Of course, Glo-ree," Elisabeth answered, "but come on in the house out of the cold." She opened the door wider, motioning her to come in.

Glo-ree shook her head emphatically as she looked at the open door. "I'll be comin' 'round to the back door, Miz Elisabeth," she said.

"Oh, Glo-ree," Elisabeth said, slightly exasperated. She did not insist further for she knew it was futile. Glo-ree refused to enter a white person's house except by the rear entrance. "Very well, I'll meet you at the back door," she said as Glo-ree disappeared around the side of the house. "Now, what's this all about?" Elisabeth asked as they sat down on the cane-bottom chairs at the kitchen table.

"Roscoe wanted to see if Ernest's ghost was in his house." Lisa said before Glo-ree could answer.

"Well, you dared me to go in," Roscoe said accusingly to Lisa, unwilling to take all the blame for their adventure.

"Hush, you two, and let Glo-ree explain," Elisabeth said.

"Well, Miz Elisabeth, Miss Lisa and Master Roscoe found my boy in Ernest's house." Glo-ree said.

At her words, Lisa and Roscoe looked at each other and giggled. Glo-ree's insistence on adding the strange sounding titles to their names never failed to make them laugh. A warning look from Elisabeth silenced them.

"I didn't know that Daniel was back from Chicago," Elisabeth said.

"Yes, ma'am," Glo-ree answered, "his job done played out there so he caught a freight train home."

Elisabeth had watched all Glo-ree's children grow up from tiny tots and she had marveled that Glo-ree managed to keep then from starving during these lean years without the help of a husband. Glo-ree had molded them into a close family unit and, under her protective hand and firm guidance, they were obedient and well-mannered. Daniel, now eighteen, and the fourteen year old twins, Mary and Ruth, were growing into responsible young adults. From early childhood, they helped Glo-ree with the washing and ironing that she took in. Daniel scrubbed the clothes on the wash board in the back yard and kept the fire built under the pot in which clothes boiled almost continuously. Mary and Ruth helped with the ironing. In addition, each accepted any odd jobs that were available from white people. Glo-ree had made them realize that their family stood alone and could only survive through their combined efforts.

"My boy's hurt, Miz Elisabeth," Glo-ree continued worriedly, "and he's sick."

Elisabeth, her face clouded with concern, asked, "What happened?"

"A railroad man caught him when he was jumpin' off the train in the freight yards and tole' him he was goin' turn him over to the police," Glo-ree explained. "Daniel was so scared that he tried to get away and the man hit him with his billy-club. Daniel hit him back agin' and knocked the man down. Then Daniel ran and got away. He hid out in the woods the rest of last night and started to come home this mornin' but he saw a police car by our house so he hid in the woods till it left. Then, he come on home." Her eyes rolled as she added, "Lawsy, Miz Elisabeth, I didn't even know he was aroun' anywheres close till that policeman done come to my door, axing me about him!"

"Is he in trouble some other way with the law?" Elisabeth asked.

"No, ma'am!" Glo-ree said emphatically, shaking her head vigorously. "Daniel says he wouldn't of hit that railroad man 'ceptin' he was hurtin' him so bad, hittin' him with that billy-club, and Daniel just was wantin' to make him stop hittin' him anymore. Then when the man fell down, Daniel just takes out runnin' 'cause he's so scared."

"Well, then," Elisabeth said, standing up, "let's see what we can do for him. Is he still in Ernest's house?"

"Oh, yes, Miz Elisabeth, he's scared to come home— the police could come back anytime. He's sleepin' on the floor and it's awful cold but he can't start no fire. Somebody liable to see the smoke from the chimney. He ain't got no cover 'ceptin' for a blanket and some newspapers I brung him. His head hurts awful bad from the man hittin' him with that billy-club and he's got a sore throat and a bad fever. His skin feels like it's on fire." In her anxiety, Glo-ree's words tumbled over each other.

"Now, Glo-ree," Elisabeth spoke authoritatively, "I want you to go home and start some water boiling and carry as much as you and the girls can to Ernest's house. I'll be along as soon as I can gather some things together."

"Yessum," Glo-ree said and hurried out the kitchen door. Elisabeth collected her thoughts, making mental note of things that she would need, as she simultaneously began giving orders, "Larry, get the kerosene lantern from the chicken house and be sure it's full of oil. And get that old mattress from the store room and a big stack of newspapers—as many as you can carry."

Elisabeth was thankful now that she was a "saver" as her father had called her. A smile crossed her face as she thought of his teasing, "That girl's a regular pack-rat," he'd say, looking at her fondly, "she never throws anything away!"

She had protested, saying, "I'm just practical, Papa, there always seems to be a future use for things if you hold onto them."

She frowned and hurried to the door to call after Larry's retreating figure, "Fetch a pillow too, son," she called, "I almost forgot the pillow."

Elisabeth made all the pillows for their beds. They were stuffed with feathers from the chickens which she killed for them to eat. After plunging the dead chickens into scalding hot water, she could pluck the feathers easily. These were stored in a cotton bag which she hung on the clothes line in the sun until they were thoroughly dry. Cases were made from large flour sacks that she had strongly bleached to render them snowy white and remove the lettering. These were then carefully stuffed with the dried feathers. Large chicken feed sacks in colorful prints and designs were utilized to make slip covers for the pillows. After being lightly starched and ironed, these slips complemented the completed pillows which proved to be most attractive and comfortable. When enough pillows had been made for their own use, Elisabeth's thrifty nature would not permit her to discard the surplus feathers so she made extra ones to give to those in need of them. She always had several on hand.

"Roscoe, you pull your wagon to the back steps, and, Lisa, you help me get those old blankets and quilts down from the closet," she directed.

She moved quickly from room to room, assembling articles which she thought she'd need: Clean white rags that she kept stored in a large chicken feed sack in the closet for bandages, cotton, scissors, a thermometer, iodine, alcohol and other medicines that might prove helpful. She picked up the old hot water bottle and hoped that it hadn't sprung a leak as yet. With the children's help, she carried the items to the wagon, arranging them with care so they wouldn't spill out. The newspapers were placed at one end with the supplies at the other, while the quilts and blankets were folded on top and the half mattress was laid over all.

Elisabeth shivered in the cold night air and suddenly, she realized that she had no coat. "I'll be right out," she said. She noted that they had failed to don their scarves and gloves in the flurry of activity.

Entering the kitchen, her attention was caught by the spicy aroma of the two fat apple pies, still warm from the oven. She picked one up from the table and wrapped it in a newspaper, encasing it entirely in the hope of keeping it warm. She reached inside the cabinet and brought out a package of coffee. Opening it, she poured a goodly amount in a small paper sack. Twisting the top of the sack, she placed it into the large pocket on the skirt of her dress. She got her coat from her bedroom closet and put it on. Starting out the door, she stopped to pick out the sundry scarves and gloves, including her own, that hung from the row of hooks by the kitchen door. The hooks, still at a low level on the wall, were placed there when the children were very small for a twofold purpose, to teach them to organize their belongings in an orderly fashion and to have the apparel easily accessible to encourage wear for necessary protection against winter cold and illness.

"Put your scarves and gloves on," she said, passing them out. She wound her own scarf about her head and neck and pulled her gloves on. Picking up the pie from the top step where she had placed it, she carried it in one hand and reached for the handle of the wagon with the other and walked toward the front road. She had only gone a few steps when the mattress slid off the top of the load onto the ground. She stopped, saying, "Larry, you and Roscoe carry the mattress between you and, Lisa, you walk by the side of the wagon and hold the blankets steady so they won't fall off." Then, they proceeded once more with King following on their heels, sniffing at the contents of the wagon and barking excitedly. Not desiring to attract attention, Elisabeth shushed him in a low commanding voice. He obeyed and dropped back to trail behind, his large shaggy outline forming the end of the strange procession.

Without talking, they walked swiftly, quietly. The only sounds came from the soft crunch of their footsteps and the wheels of the wagon sliding over the hard crust of snow. No moon was visible and the night was black. The stars glimmered faintly against the dark curtained backdrop of the sky. The vastness of space seemed strange and unfamiliar, even vaguely ominous somehow. Elisabeth shivered.

There was no answer when she knocked softly at the kitchen door of Ernest's house. She called in a low voice,

"Daniel, let me in. It's Mrs. Lancer."

A long silence followed; then, the door opened a crack and Daniel said in a frightened whisper, "What you wants, Miz Elisabeth?"

"I've come to help you, Daniel," she answered, "your mama will be here directly. Now, let me in. Nobody is going to hurt you." After a moment the door swung open and Elisabeth stepped inside the dark room. "Do you have any kind of light, Daniel?" she asked.

"Yessum, I'll light the candle," he answered and struck a match. He lit the candle that Glo-ree had brought. Glancing around the dimly lit room, Elisabeth noted the pile of newspapers spread in one corner. The room was bare except for the sink, cabinet and the old wooden stove nearby. The frayed light cord still hung from the ceiling almost to the floor which was littered with fallen plaster. After her quick survey, she turned to place the apple pie on the cabinet.

"You children bring in the things from the wagon and stack them in the corner," she instructed. They hurried to obey. She chose two of the largest rags from the supplies that they brought in and hung them over the two kitchen windows which were already covered by the newspapers Daniel had placed there. "There, that should keep any light from shining through to the outside," she said as she picked up the kerosene lantern and lit it. Setting it carefully on the cabinet, she blew out the candle, saying, "That won't be necessary with the lantern." Then, turning to Daniel, she added, "Now, Daniel, let me look at you." She took his arm, pulling him nearer the lantern and peered at him carefully in its flickering light. "My goodness!" she exclaimed, looking up at him towering over her, "you certainly did grow in Chicago! Why, you must be all of six foot tall now." She laughed gently. "I declare, Daniel, you're going to have to squat down so I can see the top of your head."

"Yessum," Daniel said. He knelt on the floor in front of her.

Elisabeth took his face in both her hands and looked closely at the long cut across the side of it. Daniel fixed his eyes, bright with fever and still haunted with fear, on hers. She bent his head gently toward the light and examined the deep red wound.

"H-m-m-m, you've got some nasty cuts," she said.

"Yessum," Daniel murmured, "and they sho' do hurt, Miz Elisabeth."

She could feel the heat of his forehead underneath her hands. "You've got a pretty high fever, Daniel," she said and added matter-of-factly, "you must have a sore throat."

"Yessum, it's right sore," he said.

The children, gathered around Elisabeth, were gazing at Daniel curiously. Suddenly, footsteps sounded on the porch and the door opened. Glo-ree called out, "Here we is, Miz Elisabeth, with the hot water." She was followed by Mary and Ruth. All three carried large steaming buckets of water which they set on the floor by the sink. The two girls stood apart, gazing shyly at Elisabeth and her family.

"How you feelin', son?" Glo-ree asked in concern.

"I feels awful bad, Mama," he replied.

Elisabeth was busying herself at the sink. She took the coffee from the pocket of her dress and shook some from the sack into the small pan that she had included with the supplies, along with a plate, cup and silverware. She dipped some hot water from one of the buckets and poured it over the coffee; then, she placed the pan on the flat top of the kerosene lantern.

"Now, while that comes to a boil, Daniel, let's doctor those cuts," she said. And, turning to the children, "Larry, you and Roscoe take those newspapers and spread them out in that corner." She pointed to the farthest one from the windows. "He'll be away from that drafty air coming in the cracks. When you get the papers spread thick on the floor, put the mattress on them." Looking at Lisa, she instructed, "You and Mary and Ruth unfold the blankets and quilts and cover the mattress with a blanket. Place the next two blankets on top of it and the quilts over them. He'll be warmer that way, sleeping between the blankets." While they scurried to obey, Elisabeth poured more warm water into another pan and shook a few drops of iodine into it from the medicine bottle.

"Sit over here on the floor, Daniel," she said, indicating a spot near the cabinet where the light from the lantern would fall fully on him. He sat down meekly, watching her intently. From one of the large clean white rags, she tore off a smaller piece and dipped it into the pan of warm iodine water. Squeezing out the excess water, she gently bathed the cut on his face. After cleaning it thoroughly, she washed the area around it until all the dried blood on his face disappeared. Picking up the pan, she emptied the reddened contents into the sink and refilled it with fresh hot water, once more adding several drops of iodine. She tore off another strip of clean cloth, saying, "Bend your head over this way toward the light so I can see better." Daniel had not taken his eyes from her face while she bathed his wound. He bent his head at her command but his eyes peered upward, keeping her face in his line of vision, still cautiously watching her.

Noting his wariness, Elisabeth spoke softly, soothingly, as to a young child, "I'll try not to hurt you, Daniel." Deftly, she pulled the hair away from the cut in a gentle motion. Squeezing the cloth almost dry of water, she began to wash the wound. He winced and pulled his head aside, uttering a low moan. "I'm sorry, Daniel," she said, "but I've got to clean it out thoroughly so it won't get infected—if it isn't already."

He bent his head toward her once more and didn't move again though she felt him flinch several times while she swiftly bathed it, dipping the rag in the water and wringing it out frequently. Satisfied that she had cleaned it sufficiently, she washed the dried blood from his head and, taking the bottle of iodine, she spread the medicine in the ridges of the cut. He gasped in pain. "That sho' 'nuff do hurt somethin' fierce, Miz Elisabeth!"

"I know it stings terribly, Daniel, but I've got to put iodine on those cuts," she answered, "it will disinfect them and make them heal." As she finished dabbing the medicine in the cut on his face, she said, smiling, "Now, I've got something that will feel good for a change!"

She picked up the pan of coffee that had begun to boil on top of the lantern. Using a spoon as a makeshift strainer to hold the grounds back, she poured the hot contents into the tin cup and handed it to him, saying, "This won't be the best coffee in the world but it will warm you up." Turning to Glo-ree, she said, "Will you cut a piece of that apple pie for him?" She nodded and began to unwrap the newspaper from the pie.

Daniel took a drink of the strong brew and looked at Elisabeth. "That's the best coffee I ever done tasted, Miz Elisabeth!" he grinned, revealing his large well-set white teeth. This was the first time she had seen him smile tonight.

"You're not hard to please, Daniel," she said laughingly. Glo-ree joined in the laughter and Elisabeth saw the look of relief on her face. She handed a large slab of the pie to Daniel who devoured it eagerly between gulps of hot coffee. Mary and Ruth watched him hungrily.

Noting their covetous glances, Elisabeth said, "I think you all deserve some pie—after all your work." She was rewarded by their looks of appreciation as she cut slices for all of them, large ones for Glo-ree and her girls and smaller portions for her own children. Roscoe visibly measured the different sized pieces and protested. "I want a big piece too, Mama!"

Elisabeth gave him a warning look. "We've got another pie at home, Roscoe," she said. He said nothing more but his face plainly showed his displeasure at being shortchanged.

There was much talk and laughter as everyone ate, obviously relieved after the past few hours. A sense of well-being pervaded. Elisabeth's serene nature imparted a feeling of confidence to those around her, a feeling, almost spiritual, that everything would work out well in due time.

Pouring the last of the coffee from the pan into Daniel's cup, Elisabeth rinsed the grounds into the sink and refilled the pan with water, setting it once again on top of the kerosene lantern. "Larry, go out and break several small twigs off the tree by the back door for me," she said.

"Uh-oh! Daniel's going to get his throat mopped!" Roscoe gloated, his eyes lighting up at the prospect, happy that he wasn't to be the recipient.

"What you gonna do to my throat?" Daniel asked, jerking his head around to look apprehensively at Elisabeth.

"You ain't gonna like this, Daniel!" Lisa said gleefully. She and Roscoe giggled.

"You children hush!" Elisabeth said sternly. And to Daniel, "It won't hurt, Daniel, and it's the best thing that I know of to cure a sore throat."

"Yeah, it will either cure you or kill you!" Larry said, coming in with the twigs.

Elisabeth threw him a disapproving glance to silence any further comment. Daniel watched intently, his face once again reflecting a mixture of distrust and fear, as she skinned the leaves from one of the twigs to leave a small well rounded smooth stick. She wrapped a piece of cotton tightly about one end and opened a small bottle. It contained a concoction of her own making, one that she had arrived at by studying store-bought medicine and imitating the ingredients through her own innate common sense. It was a mixture of one part iodine to three parts of alcohol. Elisabeth's reputation for curing sore throats had become well-known and she was called upon often to perform her skillful swabbing of inflamed tonsils with her homemade remedy. Nellie teased her about her "cures" giving her the title of "Dr. Lancer." Zeke Dalton often said jokingly, "Watch out for Elisabeth when she gets that gleam in her eye for you know she's coming after you with that cotton swabbed stick to dab it down your throat." Nevertheless, he, like the others, submitted to the throat swabbing when necessary for the soreness would disappear almost instantly.

"Now, Daniel, open your mouth wide, stick out your tongue and say *Ah-h-h*," she said as she dipped the cotton swabbed stick into the bottle, wiping off the excess liquid on the edges as she extricated it. Daniel looked about frantically. Elisabeth thought for a minute that he was going to make a dash for the door. He looked at Glo-ree with a pleading expression.

"Do I have to, Mama?" he asked, begging her with his eyes to permit him to refuse to let this white woman do whatever it was that she planned to do to him.

"Yes, you do, boy," Glo-ree said firmly, her face showing approval. "I'ze heard all about Miz Elisabeth's medicines and I knows theys works. Why, she's doctored more people in this town than ole' Doc Bobbins has. Lots of folks even calls her 'Doc Lancer'." She wagged a finger at him. "Now, you lets her do what she has to do, son!" Daniel looked at her as though she had betrayed him. Then, resignedly, he opened his mouth.

"You've got to stick out your tongue so I can see your throat," Elisabeth said. Reluctantly, he obeyed. Swiftly, she pushed the swab over his tongue and coated the swollen red right tonsil. Daniel immediately jerked his head back, gagging.

"Hell, that burns!" He looked accusingly at Elisabeth.

"You watch yore tongue, boy!" Glo-ree said angrily. Lisa and Roscoe, giggling in delight, danced around the room. Mary, Ruth and Larry laughed uncontrollably.

"I didn't get your tonsils covered, Daniel," Elisabeth said, "I missed getting the medicine on the left side and it should be mopped, too. Your throat's awfully red and inflamed."

Daniel did not answer her, Instead, he turned to Glo-ree and said defiantly, "I ain't lettin' her do that agin, Mama, and you can't make me!" Glo-ree started to say something but Elisabeth interrupted quickly.

"Alright, Daniel, we'll let it go. Right now, I would like for you to take these aspirins." She handed him two tablets and watched as he swallowed them with the last of his coffee. She emptied the boiling water from the pan into the hot water bottle and replaced the cap tightly. She tucked it inside the blankets of the bed on the floor. Finding the mentholatum and turpentine in her supplies, she scraped out a large glob of the mentholatum with her finger into a pan and set it on the lantern to heat. It melted quickly, sputtering over the hot flame. She removed the pan from the fire.

"Take your jacket off and open your shirt, Daniel," she ordered, "I'm going to rub your throat and chest with this mentholatum and turpentine. It should help clear up your chest of that cold." She poured a few drops of turpentine into the melted mentholatum. "Be quick now, I want to rub you with this while it's still warm so it will penetrate into your chest."

Daniel, observing her preparations closely, decided that this procedure would be harmless; indeed, nothing could be as bad as her throat swabbing so he did as she commanded. When he had opened his shirt, she dipped her hand into the pan, saturating her fingers with the mixture, and began to rub the warm liquid on his chest and over his neck. Her fingers, gently but firmly, massaged the medicine into his skin. The creeping heat of the liquid seeped into his pores. He began to feel warm for the first time since he had entered the cold house early last night. He yawned. Elisabeth reached for a large clean rag and, tearing a long piece from it, she folded it and wrapped it around his neck. She folded the remaining piece in squares of several layers. Placing this over his chest, she pulled his shirt firmly across the cloth and buttoned it. "I want you to leave this cloth on," she instructed, "it will help the medicine penetrate."

She walked over to the bed on the floor and pulled back the covers, "You've got a nice warm bed from that hot water bottle, Daniel, and it's time you got warm, too." She held the covers apart and motioned for him to get inside them. Daniel did not protest but slid quickly in between, pushing the hot water bottle downward with his cold feet, rubbing them gratefully against its warmth. Elisabeth pulled the covers up about his neck.

"How you feelin' now, boy?" Glo-ree asked but this time her voice did not sound worried. She knew that Miz Elisabeth would make him well.

"It's the first time I'ze been warm in a week," Daniel murmured sleepily, remembering the frigidity of the dark, dank boxcars of the trains that he had ridden home from Chicago.

"Lisa, help me get these things together," Elisabeth said, "and, Larry, you and Roscoe start carrying them to the wagon." Mary and Ruth hurried to help. "Glo-ree, you'd better leave that one bucket of water here." Only one remained untouched. One had been emptied and only a small amount of water remained in the second. "With his fever, he will probably be wanting some water to drink during the night and it's almost cool now."

When everything had been gathered and deposited into the wagon, Glo-ree picked up the two buckets and walked to the door, saying, "I'll be here in the morning, Daniel." Before turning out the lantern, Elisabeth turned toward Daniel and said, "I'm leaving some matches here next to the lantern if you need it during the night."

"Yessum," Daniel's muffled voice could hardly be heard from the warm cocoon of covers as he snuggled even deeper inside them. Elisabeth heard a deep contented sigh, then a soft snore before she had even closed the door and stepped into the night outside.

Glo-ree stood on the steps waiting for her with Mary and Ruth at her side. Larry was arranging the contents of the wagon to prevent them from spilling out.

Lisa and Roscoe chased each other about the yard with King, who had waited patiently outside for them, in wild pursuit, barking intermittently. "Lisa, Roscoe, come here." Elisabeth called softly. "And stop that dog from barking." The tone of her voice made them obey instantly and King, instinctively knowing that the game was over, followed meekly.

Without speaking, Elisabeth and Glo-ree walked across the yard together with the others following. As they reached the road, Glo-ree broke the comfortable silence. She said hesitantly, "Miz Elisabeth, I don't knows how to thank you for everything you done for my Daniel." She could see the outline of Elisabeth's face only dimly in the darkness. "If it hadn't been for you, I don't know what I'd done. I couldn't call on nobody else."

"No reason to thank me, Glo-ree," Elisabeth replied,

adding matter-of-factly. "You'd do the same thing for me and my kids." She reached out and patted Glo-ree's arm. "I'll meet you here in the morning to see how he is." Then, she turned and walked, with her children beside her, down the road toward home.

CHAPTER 10

A few days later Elisabeth, preparing breakfast, heard a knock at the back door. Opening it to Glo-ree, she invited her inside but Glo-ree declined, saying, "I don' have time, Miz Elisabeth. I'm on my way to Miz Ansel's to work. I just wanted to tell you that Daniel is feelin' much better and he came home this mornin' from Ernest's house. The police haven't come around anymore so he thought it would be safe now."

"Well, I'm so glad he's feeling alright now, Glo-ree," Elisabeth said. "When I doctored those cuts yesterday, they seemed to be healing nicely." She laughed, adding, "Daniel wouldn't let me swab his throat anymore but he did let me rub the mentholatun and turpentine on his chest again." She and the children had checked on Daniel each day while Glo-ree was at work.

"Yessum," Glo-ree said, "he don' cough no more and his fever's gone now. Lawsy, you sho' did wonders for him, Miz Elisabeth!"

"Oh, Glo-ree," Elisabeth said, embarrassed by Glo-ree's words of praise and the grateful look on her face.

"You is a good woman, Miz Elisabeth." Glo-ree said solemnly before turning to leave.

Elisabeth looked after her retreating figure; then, shivering in the biting January wind, she quickly returned to the kitchen, welcoming its warmth. It was a blustery raw day that held the promise of more snow. Spring would be a long time in coming this year, she thought wistfully, glancing at the dreary colorless space through the window. She yearned for its rejuvenating powers that would restore color once again to the world that winter bleached away. Jon had left at dawn. He should be well on his route by now, she thought. He would be gone for four days. He had been called for this run only because one of the men ahead of him in seniority, Lenny Harrison, was ill and unable to work.

She was grateful that he was working at all but she wished longingly that he had a job that would allow him to be home regularly. Maybe his relationship with the children would improve. When he was home between runs, Jon was tired. There was little communication between them. His prolonged absences were not conducive in promoting understanding. She did not condemn Jon totally; rather, she felt sorry for him. Never having known his own father, his lack of ability in the role of one was clearly comprehensible. It was not something that had been of his own choosing, his making, she reasoned.

Elisabeth was cognizant of the fact that, because of Jon's coldness toward her, her own need for love, understanding and companionship compelled her to turn more and more to the children. Jon's frequent absence and her dual roles of both mother and father had provided them with an extremely close relationship that was entirely independent of Jon. He resented this affinity; yet, when she tried to draw him into their circle of love, he withdrew, barricading himself inside, shutting them out. And, even though she did not desire it, it seemed that she had made a separate life with the children that, more or less, excluded him. The realization that their happiest times came when Jon, along with his moodiness and resentment, was absent deeply saddened her.

Elisabeth felt fortunate that the children's need for a man's influence had been found in her lifelong friend, Sam Britton. Not that she had ever discussed it with Sam. She had no inclination to discuss Jon's and her problems with anyone—ever. Jon was her husband and she could never speak ill of him. Sam loved children and possessed a special rapport with them. Each day, Roscoe and Lisa opened the door of the store to yell *Hi* to Sam on their way to and from school. He was never too busy to come outside and sit with them on the bench, to talk and to show them his latest wooden figures. Larry spent almost as much time at the store as he did at home. Now, maturing quickly, he asked Sam's advice and counsel. Although happy at their harmonious accord with Sam, nevertheless, Elisabeth wished fervently that it were with their father instead where it rightfully belonged.

"Come on, children," Elisabeth called as she set the plates on the table, "you'll be late for school."

"I'd rather be absent 'stead of just late," Roscoe said, sleepy-eyed, as he came into the kitchen.

"Get your shoes on, Roscoe," Elisabeth said, noticing his bare feet, "before you take cold."

"I'm going to, Mama," he said, "I brought them in here where it's warm to put them on." He pulled a chair close to the open oven door and sat down. He stretched his legs, holding his feet over the door to warm them before putting on his socks. He twisted around in his chair to look at his mother, standing at the sink, "What's the matter with your voice, Mama?"

"Why, I've just got a little cold," she said, "I felt it coming on last night and my throat is a little sore so my voice is hoarse."

Roscoe, frowning, thought for a moment. "Who is going to mop your throat?" he asked. He had never thought before of his mother being the recipient of her medicinal ministration.

Elisabeth laughed. "Don't worry, Roscoe, I've already mopped it this morning."

"Oh," his voice registered disbelief that anyone would perform this outrage on themselves.

"Do you feel very bad, Mama?" Larry asked, overhearing the conversation as he entered the kitchen.

"No, not really, but I'd better stay inside today." She pulled the curtains back from the window and looked out. "It is so cold outside."

"I'll take care of the chickens and all the chores, Mama," Larry said, "so you won't have to go out in the cold." He went out the door.

"Hurry," Elisabeth called after him, "breakfast is almost ready."

"M-m-m," Lisa said as she came in, "something smells good." She and Roscoe finished dressing under Elisabeth's prodding. Larry entered the door, his cheeks red from the cold. He carried several eggs which he deposited on the cabinet.

"Let's eat breakfast," Elisabeth said, setting a bowl of scrambled eggs and a plate of hot biscuits on the table.

"Mama, why are your biscuits fat?" Roscoe asked, helping himself to one.

"What do you mean—*fat?*" Larry asked, his face puzzled.

"Well, Buck Dalton says that his mother's biscuits aren't fat like Mama's." Roscoe answered, "but he likes Mama's fat biscuits better'n his mama's skinny ones."

"Whoever heard of 'fat' biscuits?" Larry scoffed, looking at Roscoe condescendingly. Lisa giggled. Roscoe stuck out his tongue at them.

"Is that why Buck comes over so much and spends the night with you—just so he can eat my fat biscuits?" Elisabeth asked, looking pleased. "Well, Roscoe, I guess Nellie doesn't make them like I do," she explained, "I don't roll them out and cut them with one of those little round cutters like most recipes call for. I just pinch off a big piece of the dough for each biscuit. I make them big like that because your father likes them that way." Later, as they left for school, Elisabeth handed Lisa a piece of paper with a few items listed on it. "Give this list to Sam on your way by the store," she instructed, "and ask him to deliver them this morning if he has time. I need to get the soup bone on so I can make a pot of soup." They started outside and she called after them, "You all hurry home after school, now. You hear?"

She watched them out of sight then, turning, she stood and surveyed her kitchen from the doorway. Like the rest of the house, it was sparsely furnished for she and Jon had been unable to buy much furniture since their marriage. With their family expanding steadily, money had been needed for more vital necessities. The heavy oak table and the cane bottom chairs with the high backs had been inherited from Jon's mother. Scanning the room, she saw the wall paper peeling badly in spots. She had hoped each spring to repaper it. *Well, that's one hope that won't materialize in the near future,* she thought. Elisabeth shrugged her shoulders. *No matter. It was still a cheerful room.* The colorful flowered curtains and matching tablecloth she had made from chicken feed sacks gave it a pleasant appearance. Its sunny aspect and the spicy aroma of the apple pie which she had baked before the children had risen lifted her spirits and gave her a warm feeling within.

Things could be so much worse, she thought as she cleared the table. *Oh, it would be easy to be unhappy by thinking of all the things that I don't have.* She knew many people who made themselves miserable, bemoaning their fate in life. Jon was one of these. But she would rather count her blessings and be grateful for all the things she did have. They were poor but she had her family and they were all healthy. *These are the important things, the things that really give meaning and value to life,* her thoughts continued. *So many are in much worse circumstances than we are. At least, Jon has a job even if it isn't steady nor the pay much. But we have a roof over our heads and food to eat for the present.* A part of a Biblical verse ran vaguely through her mind, *"Sufficient unto the day."* She could not remember the rest of it. She hummed contentedly as she washed the dishes.

On the way to school Roscoe saw Buck Dalton ahead and raced up the street to join him. Lisa walked alone, trailing behind them. Larry had hurried on to school in order to have some time in which to write on his English composition.

Approaching Sam's store, Lisa saw Mose, his small figure bent forward against the cold, slowly and stiffly shuffling along. Mose lived with his granddaughter and her family in the last house of the Negro section next to the open meadow. Bald down the middle of his head, Mose had thick tufts of snowy hair growing on each side, extending downward to join the matching white beard that curved in a solid line from his sideburns around his chin. The whiteness of his hair that resembled bolls of fluffy cotton contrasted dramatically with the shiny blackness of his skin. Children speculated on his age and had come to the conclusion that he must be at least a hundred years old. Marveling that anyone could be so old, they stood in reverent awe of him and his still sharply penetrating eyes which gave the appearance of being able to see right inside a person's head and read his every thought.

Mose entered Sam's store. When Lisa went inside, he was standing close to the wood stove in his thin shabby clothes, absorbing its warmth. Sam was waiting on Mrs. Abbey and Mrs. Ripley. The two elderly neighbors had come to do their shopping together. Mrs. Ripley had completed hers and was waiting while Sam filled Mrs. Abbey's order. They greeted Lisa and she walked to the stove. Mose did not speak but he looked piercingly into her eyes.

"Morning, Mose," Lisa said.

His mouth, above the white beard, broke into a wide grin. "Mornin', Miss Lisa," he answered, nodding his head vigorously to her.

Lisa held her hands near the stove, warming them through her mittens. They stood silently while Sam placed Mrs. Abbey's items on the counter. She gathered up her sack of staples and she and Mrs. Ripley turned to leave. "Now, Lisa, what can I do for you?" Sam asked.

"Mose is next, Mr. Britton." Lisa said.

The two women, halfway to the door, stopped and jerked around to stare at her, their mouths agape. Mose's eyes snapped to Lisa's face, boring into her. Lisa, embarrassed at being the object of everyone's gaze, felt her face flushing.

Mrs. Abbey finally found her voice. She exclaimed indignantly.

Mose said quickly, "That's alright, Miss Lisa, you go ahead and let Massa Britton wait on you."

"But you were here before me, Mose," she objected, "so it's your turn next."

Mose looked up into the hostile eyes of Mrs. Abbey and Mrs. Ripley. He faltered. He was confused and did not know what to do. Shrinking back, he looked pleadingly at Sam who had remained silent. Now, Sam spoke amiably, "What can I get for you, Mose?" His eyes sparkled pleasantly. Mose moved forward hesitantly, uneasily to the counter.

"H-m-m-p-h!" Mrs. Ripley snorted.

Mrs. Abbey walked back to Lisa and, glaring at her,

said sharply, "Don't ever do that again, Lisa!"

"But, Mrs. Abbey, Mose came in ahead of me," she protested. "It was his turn to be waited on next!"

"You ought to be ashamed of yourself! You should know better than that!" Mrs. Abbey angrily retorted. Lisa didn't answer but looked defiantly back at her. Mrs. Abbey continued to scowl at her before turning away.

"I declare, don't folks teach their kids anything anymore?" she said to Mrs. Ripley as they started for the door.

"My, oh my, I don't know what this world's a'comin' to!" Mrs. Ripley said.

Mose, carrying the small bag of rice that he ordered, stopped before Lisa as he started to leave. He bowed to her from the waist. "Thank you kindly, Miss Lisa," he said. She was surprised to see that the usually keen eyes were now misty with tears. He blew his nose on his handkerchief and turned away, shuffling and scraping his feet on the wooden floor as he walked toward the door.

Bewildered, Lisa watched until the door closed behind him. Then she turned to Sam. "Why did Mrs. Abbey and Mrs. Ripley get so mad at me, Mr. Britton? What did I do wrong?" Her eyes welled with tears.

Sam came quickly around the counter and, picking her up in his arms, he hugged her. "You did everything just right, Miss Lisa, and I'm very proud of you!"

"If I did everything right, Mr. Britton, why did they get so mad at me? Why did they want me to go ahead of Mose when it was his turn?"

"Well, Lisa," Sam said slowly, setting her down on the floor again and wiping her eyes with his clean handkerchief, "it's hard to explain. You see, Mose is a Negro..."

Lisa interrupted, "Is that why they didn't want him to have his turn—because he's black?"

"Yes, Lisa," Sam said solemnly.

"But why, Mr. Britton?" Lisa persisted. "It *was* his turn!"

"I don't know, Lisa," Sam said sadly. He was thoughtful a long moment before going on, "I guess some folks have just got to feel like they're better than *somebody*."

After leaving the store for school, Lisa thought about what had happened. She didn't understand what Sam had told her. She didn't understand why Mrs. Abbey and Mrs. Ripley had got mad at her for not going ahead of Mose when it was his turn. She didn't understand why Mose had thanked her. She didn't understand why some folks had to feel like they were better than other folks. She shrugged her shoulders resignedly. She supposed that she just didn't understand very much at all about grown-ups.

At mid-morning, Elisabeth heard a knock at the kitchen door and hurried to open it to Sam. A gust of cold wind, coming through the opened door, enveloped her.

"Come on in out of the cold," she welcomed.

Sam set the sack of groceries on the cabinet and looked at her, "Are you sick, Elisabeth?" he asked, worriedly, "you sound hoarse."

"Oh, it's nothing—just a little cold, Sam," she said, "Sit down and have a cup of coffee, you must be about frozen." She motioned him to a chair, continuing, "the coffee's hot. Figured you'd be here soon so I had the pot on." Retrieving cups from the shelf over the sink, she poured the coffee while Sam sat watching her. She carried the steaming cups to the table and sat down opposite him.

"Man, it smells good in here!" he said, looking around appreciatively.

"Oh, that," Elisabeth said, "that's my apple pie that I baked this morning. Let me get a piece of it for you."

"Sure don't mind if you do!" he laughed.

"I love spices," Elisabeth said as she cut a large slab from the pie and lifted it gently to a plate. She set it and a fork before Sam. "I think I like the smell they give to my kitchen more than the taste they add to food. I'm afraid I go overboard with them. I load apple pies with cinnamon, allspice and nutmeg." She looked at him anxiously. "Most folks don't like their food too spicy. I hope there isn't too much for you."

Sam took a large bite and closed his eyes. Opening them, he grinned at her. "By George, Elisabeth, nobody can make a pie like you can!"

Elisabeth blushed, her face lighting up from the compliment, "Oh, go on now, Sam, I'll bet you tell that to all your customers!" Then, teasingly, she added, "What you need is a wife, Sam, so you can have some good food. Why, I'll bet you seldom eat a square meal, working most of the day at the store and then half the night at the newspaper office!" Laughing, she continued, "How come you've never married? I declare I don't know how you've escaped the clutches of all the conniving females around here."

Sam looked down at his plate, averting his eyes and Elisabeth failed to notice his pained look. He changed the subject deftly, telling her the latest news of his customers and their mutual friends.

Sam finished the piece of pie with relish. Looking over his cup at Elisabeth, he grinned, "You know something? Larry is getting very good at whittling. He is really picking up the hang of it fast."

"Well, he's got a mighty good teacher!" Elisabeth said, smiling. "Lisa is just fascinated with the menagerie of animals that you're making, Sam. Why, she can hardly wait to go by on the way to school every morning and see which new animal you've started on." Elisabeth was silent a moment, growing thoughtful. Then, she said, "Sam, I want to tell you how much I appreciate your patience with my children." She stopped as if she wasn't sure she wanted to continue, then added hesitantly, "You just don't know how much your companionship means to them—and to me."

"Why, Elisabeth," he said in a surprised tone of voice, "you don't have to thank me. You know that I think the world of them. Why," he hesitated, then said softly, "they seem almost like my own." He did not look at her.

"Well," she said gratefully, "I do so appreciate all your attention and affection for them, Sam. You know with Jon away so much, they miss having their father around." Sam detected the wistful note in her voice. She hurried on, "Not that it is Jon's fault, you understand?" She looked at him questioningly and hastened on to assure him, "He has to make a living and this is the only job he can get." She was silent again. Finally, she said, almost defiantly, he thought, "He doesn't like being away from home."

Sam wondered if she knew of the other women in Jon's life. Even if she did, he knew that she would never say anything against nor degrade her man. He was well aware of her fierce loyalty. Sam was also cognizant of Elisabeth's tremendous amount of pride. *In fact,* he thought, *I know Elisabeth much better than she could ever imagine that I do.*

Tears suddenly glistened in Elisabeth's eyes. She rose quickly and started toward the sink. Sam instinctively jumped to his feet and followed her. Taking hold of her arm, he turned her around to face him. Her eyes were downcast and he lifted her chin with his hand, forcing her to look at him. "What's the matter, Elisabeth?" he asked gently.

She shook her head but said nothing while tears ran down her cheeks. Sam pulled her toward him, putting his arms around her shoulders. She rested her head against him and sobbed quietly. He could feel the nearness of her, the warmth of her body. Suddenly, all the pent-up desire that he had held in check, the longing and the love that he had felt for her for so long, was unleashed. His arms slipped to her waist and tightened. He pulled her to him roughly until her body was crushed against his own. Elisabeth taken aback, did not struggle until his mouth moved along her cheek, seeking her lips. She tried to withdraw from his grasp but he held her so tightly that she could hardly breathe. She turned her head, avoiding his lips. But his mouth was insistent, compelling, searching until, finding her lips, he bruised them under his own. She pushed at his chest in a futile attempt to free herself. He continued to hold her almost cruelly while his mouth clung forcefully to hers. Elisabeth fought against the surging emotion welling up in her but she was unable to conquer the overwhelming desire that she felt. Suddenly, her body became limp and she yielded under his kiss. Her arms that had been resisting savagely against his chest twined around his neck, straining him closer in response as she kissed him now in wild passionate abandon. After a long moment, she pushed at his face with both hands, fiercely, desperately, as she moaned, "No, Sam, no!"

Sam held her brutally. "I love you, Elisabeth!" His voice was ragged, tortured. "Don't you know that I've always loved you?"

Elisabeth jerked her head back to look up at him, her eyes wide. "Stop it, Sam!" she commanded. "You don't know what you're saying!" With a savage motion, she pulled herself out of his arms and collapsed into a chair. Averting her face, she did not look at him as she tried to regain her composure. She was trembling violently. Her voice shook as she said, "I don't know what came over me! Will you please go, Sam?" Her words rose, almost hysterically.

"Elisabeth..." He was breathing hard and his voice was hoarse.

Elisabeth interrupted him quickly. Her words came strongly now as she said slowly, deliberately "I'm so sorry this happened, Sam. As far as we are concerned, it never happened. I want it forgotten—as of right now." Then, looking at him for the first time since their embrace, she gazed steadily into his eyes, saying, "Do you understand, Sam?"

He searched her face. "It must have meant something to you, Elisabeth—the way you kissed me..."

Putting her hands over her face, Elisabeth turned away, uttering a loud anguished cry, "Don't Sam, please." She stood with her back to him, sobbing, her body visibly shaking. Involuntarily, he took a step toward her, reaching for her. Abruptly, he stopped remaining motionless. Then, his arms dropped slowly to his sides.

Finally, after an unbearably long silence, he said softly, "You don't have to worry, Elisabeth. It won't happen again." He paused, then added gently, "But I'm not sorry it happened—and I'll never forget it." He grabbed his coat from the back of the chair and strode swiftly through the door into the coldness outside.

Elisabeth sank weakly into a chair. She sat numbly, his words searing into her mind. When she heard his truck drive off, she laid her head on the table and sobbed wildly, loud distressed moans that engulfed her body.

An hour later Elisabeth was still sitting at the table. She was quiet now. All emotion had been drained from her. Her head throbbed and her face felt flushed. Confused and almost in a state of delusion, she felt strangely detached as if her mind were no longer a part of her being but was, instead, outside her body, observing her. She was unable to comprehend what had come over her. She had never been unfaithful to Jon, not even in thought. She recalled the way that she had kissed Sam and she felt shame, guilt and shock at the intensity of her emotions. She had felt desired, wanted. Sam had made her feel like a woman again—something that Jon had failed to do for so long.

Elisabeth shook her head angrily. *I will not blame Jon for my weakness,* she thought. She stared vacantly, disconsolately at the somber sky through the window. The wind howled at the eves of the house. She felt a lonely kinship with it. Its mournful sound reflected the pain inside her. She looked around her kitchen. It no longer appeared cheerful and bright or contain the sense of security that she had manifested from it such a short time ago. There was no serenity in her soul at this moment— only turmoil, torment, bewilderment. She was totally miserable.

Suddenly, without warning, the remainder of the Biblical verse that had occurred to her earlier ran burningly through her head, *"Sufficient unto the day is the evil thereof."* Fervently, she wished that her mind had not remembered. For the words haunted her mercilessly, stabbing relentlessly into her heart, indelibly branding her very soul, agonizingly reminding her of the evil which she had almost succumbed to. "Oh, dear God, forgive me!" she breathed beseechingly. She had come so very close to breaking one of God's commandments.

After their encounter that day in her kitchen, Elisabeth avoided Sam whenever possible. She sent the children to the store for grocery orders. Jon handled the finances and paid the debts when there was money to do so. But when confrontation was inevitable. Sam, true to his promise, never betrayed by word or look that anything had ever happened between them.

CHAPTER 11

"Mama, can I pull my shoes off and go barefooted?" Roscoe called excitedly as he ran across the back yard. He was carrying his school book and his sweater dangled from his arm, dragging on the ground. It was the first warm day of spring. *The day that seemed endlessly long in coming this year,* Elisabeth thought, before answering.

"I guess so," she smiled, but just until the sun starts down. "It will be chilly again then."

"Yippee," Roscoe yelled, throwing his sweater in the air. Before it hit the ground, he already had one shoe off and was furiously tugging at his sock. When he had pulled both shoes and socks from his feet, he raced back across the yard to meet Lisa walking down the road and announced the good news. Elisabeth watched them, smiling. It was an eventful day, one they looked forward to with delight, the first day they could go barefoot in the spring.

Is it really here, she wondered, looking up at the azure blue sky. The flash of a red breasted robin in the pecan tree caught her eye. *Is spring really here at last—the time that she had waited so impatiently for during the interminably long winter.* She shivered deliciously as she felt the warmth of the sun's rays through her thin cotton dress. She stood still, enraptured by the sprouting new leaves on the trees, at the rose bushes that were shooting forth new growth, promising to fulfill their beauty in blossoming new buds before long. *Oh, glorious spring!* She breathed the fresh astringent air in exhilaration. *Oh, happy spring that heralded the beginning of a brand new world once again,* she rejoiced, *a time for youth to sing its joy, a time for age to replenish its faith, a time for nature to exult in a world newborn! And,* Elisabeth thought, her face clouding for a brief instant, *God willing, it would mark the swinging of the pendulum for the country with promise of a brighter future.*

The nation, confronted by the most critical situation since Lincoln and in the midst of peak unemployment, had inaugurated a new President the preceding day. Declaring that "the only thing we have to fear is fear itself" and "the nation calls for action, and action now," his bold inaugural address had struck a responsive chord in the hearts of the country's people, rousing hopes that had grown dormant.

President Roosevelt, Elisabeth thought, *had resurrected buried hopes once again.* This time they would surely become reality through his pledged "New Deal" that would help the country climb from the dismal abyss of despair that had almost devoured it. She did not understand very much about politics or economics or all the things the politicians talked about but she gazed contentedly about her at the bright sunny day while words bounced buoyantly through her mind. *New world, new leader, new deal...*

"What are you doing, Mama?" Lisa asked, stopping before Elisabeth. She and Roscoe had been running in abandon across the yard, savoring their new barefoot freedom and reveling in the cool thick grass that tickled their toes.

Elisabeth was sitting on the back steps with a basket of eggs beside her. Picking one up, she gently and carefully scribbled circular markings over the egg with a pencil, covering its entire surface. "I'm going to set some eggs under that old setting hen that's been wanting to nest," she answered.

"Is it that mean chicken that tries to peck me when I go near her nest to get the eggs?" Roscoe asked as he stopped playing to see what his mother was doing to the eggs.

"Yes," Elisabeth replied.

"Why is she mean?" Lisa asked.

"She doesn't want anyone taking her eggs away from her nest," Elisabeth explained. "It's just nature's way of producing more chickens. She wants to set the eggs and have some baby chicks."

"Oh, goody!" Lisa said excitedly, clapping her hands, "I love baby chicks—they're so soft and cuddly! And," she added gratefully, "they don't try to peck your toes."

"Why are you writing all over the eggs for?" Roscoe asked, puzzled. "Won't they make baby chickens unless you write on them?"

Elisabeth laughed, "I'm just marking them so I'll know if another hen happens to lay a new egg in the nest during the time the mother hen is setting them. This way I'll know the original eggs that I put under her."

"How long does it take to make the baby chickens?" Lisa asked.

"Well, it usually takes 21 days for them to hatch out," she replied.

"How many will there be?" Roscoe asked, peering into the basket.

Elisabeth had finished marking them. She rose and picked up the eggs. Walking toward the gate to the chicken yard, she answered, "I'm setting 18 eggs under her so, with luck, we'll have 18 chicks."

Later in the week, Elisabeth was working among the rose bushes at the side of the house. On her knees, she was preoccupied in her dedicated zeal to eradicate the tiniest intruder. Suddenly, she glanced at the sky and realized that she must have lost track of the time for the sun had moved nearer the western horizon. It was long past due for Roscoe and Lisa to be home from school. Casting a worried look down the back road, she rose to her feet. At that moment, she saw them come into sight, hurrying along with their arms loaded with something she could not distinguish from the distance. They ran toward her, shouting excitedly, "Look, Mama! Look what we've got!" When they reached her, she saw that they carried numerous candy bars which were suspended from tiny parachutes made of colorful silk handkerchiefs. Traces of chocolate smeared their faces and the front of their clothes.

"Where did you get all this candy?" she asked, taking one. She read the words, *Baby Ruth*, emblazoned in red letters on the wrapper.

"We didn't ask anybody for it, Mama!" Lisa said proudly. "Charity didn't give it to us."

"Who's charity?" Roscoe's expression was puzzled as he looked at Lisa. Then, too excited to wait for an answer, he turned to his mother, his eyes big with wonder, "The candy came from an aeroplane!" Lisa started to interrupt, Roscoe hit at her, saying, "No, let me tell her!" Lisa dodged the blow and watched him in annoyance as he went on, his words tumbling over each other in his haste to get them out. "I saw the aeroplane throw out all these little umbrellas and they fell right in the school yard!" He grinned with pride. "I got more candy than Buck Dalton—I got 14 candy bars!"

Elisabeth, counting the remainder in his arms, calculated that he had already eaten five of the large pieces. "I only got eight," Lisa said, "I really got nine but Mary Jane grabbed one away from me when I had found it first and she wouldn't give it back!" Then, her face brightened as she added, "But Danny Harley didn't get any candy—not even one! He's so fat that he couldn't run fast enough and everyone beat him to them. Her eyes gleamed triumphantly as she added, "I got two candy bars before he could get to them. He was ahead of me at the start but I beat him out and grabbed them first!"

"Well, that wasn't very nice of you, Lisa," Elisabeth said. Lisa opened her mouth to reply, then closed it again, saying nothing.

"I see that your young 'uns got their share of candy!" Nellie Dalton called from her yard. Betsy and Buck were beside her, their arms filled with candy.

"What in the world is it all about?" Elisabeth asked, "I can't make heads or tails from what the kids are saying—they're so excited. Why," she laughed, "they said that it came from an aeroplane!"

"It did, Elisabeth!" Nellie replied, "Baby Ruth is a new candy bar and the company wanted to advertise it."

"Well," said Elisabeth, "they couldn't have thought of a better way to advertise it than through the kids."

"Yes, that's pretty all-fired smart, isn't it?" Nellie agreed, laughing. "I read that they are dropping the candy from aeroplanes over schools all over the state so people will sit up and take notice and buy it!"

"That will get the kids' attention all right," Elisabeth said; then, she added wryly, "now, if they would just drop some money out too—maybe people would be able to buy it!"

It came as no surprise to Elisabeth that, after all the candy they had consumed, neither Lisa nor Roscoe would eat supper. Lisa complained of a stomach ache and Roscoe was cross and irritable. Elisabeth gave them both a spoonful of castor oil. Over their protests, she told them, "You knew that you shouldn't have eaten all that candy before you got home. But, never mind now—what's done is done. Now, you must take your medicine without complaining. After all that candy gorging, you need a dose of laxative." With distaste, they watched the castor oil drip slowly, thickly into the spoon from the bottle. "Besides," Elisabeth added, "it's springtime and you need a good cleaning out every spring anyway."

Roscoe swallowed it with difficulty, grimacing. Wiping his mouth with the back of his hand, he sputtered, "I'm never going to eat another Baby Ruth as long as I live!"

Easter fell on the last Sunday of March. It was a beautiful warm day, fresh and new with flowers bursting forth, compelled into bloom by earth's annual springtime rejuvenation. The birds which had reappeared after the lengthy winter, trilled sweetly, their songs filling the air with melodic sound. March, traditionally, had come in like a lion, introduced by howling winds, but now, it was going out like a lamb exiting on a balmy breeze.

It was a significantly appropriate day for Easter, Elisabeth thought, looking about appreciatively. Resurrection signs of new life rose from the earth all around, triumphantly overcoming winter's cold deathlike dormant hibernation at last. Her senses were attuned to, what Jon called, the *wonders of nature.* She preferred to call it *God's handiwork.* She stood on the porch a minute, listening to the musical notes of the birds, then walked down the steps to drink in the sight of the early blooming roses with the morning dew still glistening on their velvety vivid red petals. She stooped, bending her head closely to the ostensibly sculptured face of a rose and breathed deeply of its delicate fragrance.

Roscoe, Lisa and Larry emerged from the house. Looking them over carefully in their Easter clothes, she smiled in proud approval. The boys had shined their shoes, covering most of the scuff marks and worn appearance. She had gone over Lisa's and her own shoes with white polish until they were spotless. The dainty yellow flowered cotton dress that Lisa wore was starched crisply so that the skirt stood out around her. It was made from chicken feed sacks, as were the blue and white checked shirts of the boys. Their pants were last year's but Elisabeth had carefully pressed them. Outside of Roscoe's being a trifle short, they were still nicely presentable. Elisabeth glanced down at her own 3-year-old navy blue Sunday dress. With the new collar and cuffs she had made from the white organdy scrap material that Nellie had given her, it appeared dressy despite its age.

"I declare, you all look pretty enough to have your picture taken!" she smiled up at them. "I just wish I had a camera."

"I don't look 'pretty,' Mama," Roscoe objected.

"You're right, Roscoe," she laughed, "but you and Larry both look very handsome!" Larry grinned down at her from the porch. *How tall he's getting,* she thought. "Come along now or we'll be late for Sunday School," she urged, adjusting the small matching cap with yellow ribbon streamers on the back of Lisa's head. She had even made the small purse from the same material that hung over Lisa's arm. Lisa held her arm so the purse would swing back and forth as she walked and she kept glancing at it out of the corner of her eye.

They were interrupted by Glo-ree calling from the street, "You all sho' 'nuff do look nice!"

"Why, thank you," Elisabeth replied, "Are you going to church, Glo-ree?"

"No, Ma'am," she answered, "I'ze goin' over to Mayor Ansel's. They're havin' a lot of guests today and Miz Ansel wants me to help her cook and serve dinner. But," she added proudly, "my chillun' is goin'!"

They proceeded down the street together with Glo-ree respectfully walking one step behind Elisabeth. She endeavored to adjust her steps to Glo-ree's so they would walk side-by-side but Glo-ree inevitably continued to drop a pace behind in deference to a white person. Elisabeth finally gave up the futile attempt.

"You know, Miz Elisabeth," Glo-ree said, "you is the cause of me and my chillun' goin' to church."

"And how in the world did I cause that, Glo-ree?" Elisabeth asked in surprise.

"Well, I sees you and your young 'uns goin' to church ever Sunday and it set me to thinkin' that I ought to get close to the Lawd agin' and teach my chillun' about Him," she said. "Oh, my mammy and pappy raised me in church and my ole' pappy would come back to haint me if he'd a knowed how I quit goin' for a long time!" She laughed. Pausing a moment, she added, "Miz Elisabeth, I reckon you know that my chillun' all have names from the Bible, names of people that I was taught about in church when I was just a little gal—Daniel and Mary and Ruth," Elisabeth nodded. Glo-ree fell silent, thoughtful for a time before going on. "When Dotson died, I guess my mind kind of went crazy and I got to thinkin' that maybe the Lawd had plumb forgot about me. I just didn't feel like goin' to church no mo'." She was silent again for a moment; then, her face broke into a grin. "But then I saw you and your young 'uns goin' to church ever Sunday and my kids got to axin' me why they didn't go too, like your kids, so I just figgered it was about time that I got in touch and be on speakin' terms with the Lawd agin'!"

Elisabeth smiled at her. "It's true the Lord doesn't desert us, Glo-ree," she said, "but lots of times we desert Him."

"That's 'zacly what I did, Miz Elisabeth," Glo-ree answered emphatically, "but no mo'!" She continued, "I reckymember what Dotson's grandpappy tole' us. He say that when he was slavin' for his white massa in Alabam' there was times he was so down and out and so low in spirits it 'peared like he was just too tired to go on—not even nary one mo' step. Then Grandmammy..." Glo-ree paused, chuckling to herself, recalling fond memories. "She was just a little mite of a woman but strong as nails! Well, Grandpappy say that Grandmammy would tell him, 'You just hesh yo' mouth and quit talkin' that-a-way. All you gots to do is trust the good Lawd above and just keep on puttin' one foot in front of the other'n!'"

They had reached the street now where Glo-ree turned in the opposite direction to go to the other side of town where the mayor lived. They parted and Elisabeth said, "I'm glad that you're going back to church again, Glo-ree."

As Elisabeth and the children neared the church, Roscoe suddenly yelled, "Hi, Miss Jackson!" And, turning to his mother, he explained as though she didn't already know, "That's Miss Jackson, my Sunday School teacher!" Stiffly decorous and staid, Miss Matilda Jackson was an old maid. She had been Anseltown's librarian for 25 years. Tall and thin, her angular face was swathed in wrinkles, making her appear much older than her fifty-odd years. Miss Jackson believed implicitly in the learning ability of children at a tender age through the process of story telling. To fulfill this belief, she conducted a Story Hour every Saturday afternoon in a partitioned corner of the town library. Her art of weaving tales, her gestures and expressions as she moved among the group, involving them in the stories that she narrated and acted out, held them spellbound. Miss Matilda Jackson respected children. Inevitably, she would rise and stand as they filed into her Story Hour or Sunday School room because, as she was careful to explain, it was just possible that she might be in the presence of a future President or first lady of the United States. Miss Jackson demanded respect and strict obedience in return—and it was granted her. But the children were also genuinely fond of her and, when they impulsively threw their arms around her, it succeeded in melting her aloofness.

"Hello, Mrs. Lancer," Miss Jackson greeted Elisabeth in a formal tone.

"Are you going to tell us some more about the little people and the giant today, Miss Jackson?" Roscoe asked, his eyes growing large in anticipation.

"Good heavens, no, Roscoe!" she answered primly. "You'll hear more of that story next Saturday at the library. Today, you'll hear about the Bible."

"Oh, shoot!" Roscoe said, frowning in disappointment. Then, spotting Buck Dalton, he ran to join him. Giving Elizabeth a quick hug and then righting her Easter hat, Lisa joined the others in her Sunday School room. And out of the corner of her eye, Elisabeth noticed Larry moving about the early arrivals until he found Alicia Johnson, the pretty 14-year-old daughter of Will and Irma Johnson who lived on a farm outside of town. He and Alicia had been pairing off the last few Sundays at church.

Elisabeth's was now free to find her own friends. The pleasant time of Sunday socializing followed by worship, the focus of the day, had begun.

"Now, Elisabeth, don't tell anyone that I told you," Nellie cautioned, "or I'll be like Sears and Roebuck—I'll take it back." She lowered her voice confidentially. "Rachel told me that Miriam is stepping out on her husband!"

"Already?" Elisabeth asked in a shocked tone. "I declare, they haven't even been married six months yet!" She was silent a moment, frowning, then added resignedly, "Well, like Mrs. Parsons says Miriam has a lot of irons in the fire!"

"Mrs. Parsons has an old saying for everything," Nellie said peevishly, momentarily forgetting the subject at hand.

"Why, I do believe that she could talk for a week and carry on a conversation the whole time in old sayings alone!"

On this last day of May, Elisabeth and Nellie were walking to the General Robert E. Lee Grade School to attend the grade school graduation program. Larry, recently turned 14, was in the class that was graduating into high school in the fall. They were moving at a leisurely pace for they had plenty of time before the commencement exercises were to begin. Elisabeth wanted to get there early to obtain the best vantage seat from which to view the proceedings.

Jon had refused to attend. Elisabeth's heartstrings had twisted at the disappointment on Larry's face last night when Jon announced that he did not intend to go. It had been evident for only an instant before he masked it and went quickly to his room. She must have looked at Jon in annoyance for he asked belligerently, "What's the big to do about anyway? There's no cause for everyone to be in such a huff. It's just a boring program that I don't care to waste my time sitting through, listening to that silly old lady principal prattle." He had pushed his chair away from the table in noisy agitation and stood up, adding, "Larry should just be glad that he's able to finish grade school! Hell, I couldn't even get past the third grade. I didn't have a father to help me." He had stalked out the back door, slamming it shut behind him. Elisabeth had stared after him sadly, wishing fervently that he weren't so remotely removed from her and the children, that he was capable of giving and expressing his love for the children as she was sure he must want to do. Even if he did not want to do so for her.

Nellie's voice brought Elisabeth back to the present. "I don't know why Miriam bothers to get married," she was saying, "she can't seem to hold a husband."

"Which one is she on now—number three or is it four?"

Elisabeth asked.

"Maybe she doesn't want to hold on to a husband," Nellie said, reflectively, absorbed in her own thoughts and ignoring Elisabeth's question. "After all," she grinned impishly at Elisabeth, "I still like to hear a train whistle even if I'm not going anywhere!"

"Oh, Nellie!" Elisabeth laughed.

"Well, don't you, Elisabeth?"

Elisabeth didn't answer but said wryly instead, "It looks like Miriam has caught plenty of trains in her time."

"Well, maybe, she just likes variety," Nellie said. Her face was thoughtful. "I sometimes wonder what it would be like to go stepping out with another man." She turned impulsively toward Elisabeth, asking teasingly, "Don't you, Elisabeth?"

"I declare, Nellie, how you do go on!" Elisabeth said, flustered.

"Well, I'll bet it has crossed your mind," Nellie answered eyeing her closely, "I've seen how Sam looks at you with those cow eyes—as if he could eat you up!" Nellie's comment shocked Elisabeth into momentary silence. Dismayed, she could feel her face growing hot as she finally answered, "Why, Nellie, what in the world are you talking about..."

Nellie interrupted her, saying, "It is really unfair with all the women in the world who can't get a man to marry— then, along comes a gal like Miriam and she has a knack of..." she hesitated, laughed and added, "and the figure to twist the men around her little finger and keeps getting married over and over again!"

Elisabeth scrutinized her friend's face. She thought it best that she did not protest nor pursue the subject of Sam any further. She wondered worriedly why she had made such a statement—had it been made in innocent banter or did Nellie suspect that something had happened between

Sam and her?

Nellie, apparently completely oblivious to Elisabeth's concern, sighed resignedly, saying, "And no matter how many times Miriam hooks a guy and goes before the justice of the peace, there always seems to be another one warming up impatiently in the bull pen!"

Elisabeth didn't answer. They had reached the school. Entering the auditorium, they found seats near the front, nodding and speaking as they passed the few already seated. Nellie chattered on and on, but Elisabeth didn't hear her words. She was absorbed in her own thoughts. Nellie's comment about Sam, innocent or not, nagged at her.

When the graduating class marched on stage and sat in the rows of chairs facing the audience, she tried to rid herself of the annoying words that persisted in fretting her mind. Instead, she forced herself to concentrate on the bright fresh faces that gazed in seeming expectancy toward the audience and the world before them. She studied her son's face, keenly aware of the sensitive eyes and mouth.

His shirt looked almost like a store-bought one, she thought proudly. She had purchased the white broadcloth material with some of the precious egg money that she had been saving all spring for his graduation. She had also bought a new pair of black pants, the first new pair of dress pants he had had in over a year. She carefully cleaned and pressed Jon's old, but still presentable, black tie. Larry had polished his black shoes till they shone and she could see the new black socks showing above them. She was so proud of him. It was a good thing, she thought, that the weather in Texas was already so hot that coats weren't required for she didn't know where he would have got one to wear. The boys in their shirt sleeves, black pants and ties, and the girls in white dresses and shoes presented a pleasant picture of youth and hope for the future.

The principal, Mrs. Milsap, her double chins protruding and shaking grotesquely above her fat, tightly-corseted figure, signaled from her seat at the piano near the corner of the stage and the class stood to lead the audience in singing the song that opened the program:

Texas, our Texas—all hail the mighty state!
Texas, our Texas, so wonderful, so great,
Largest and grandest, withstanding every test;
Oh, empire, wide and glorious, you stand
      supremely blest!
God bless you, Texas, and keep you brave and
      strong
That you may grow in power and worth
      throughout the ages long!

As they resumed their seats, Nellie tugged at Elisabeth's arm and pointed covertly. Everyone had grown silent and every eye, especially those of the men, was riveted on the petite baby-faced blonde that walked with a pronounced wiggle down the entire length of the auditorium to a seat in the first row. The timing of her entrance was perfectly calculated by Miriam Smith O'Malley, Gonzales, Weinberg to gain the desired effect for attention.

Nellie punched Elisabeth and gloated, "What theatrics! She missed her calling—she would have made a great actress." Elisabeth didn't answer and Nellie continued in a loud whisper, "Look at that face. You'd swear she was as pure and innocent as a newborn babe!"

"S-h-h-h," Elisabeth cautioned, looking toward the stage.

Mrs. Milsap had walked from the piano to the center of the stage where she had stood in silence and glared at Miriam, who was totally unperturbed, until she took her seat. Only then did Mrs. Milsap begin to speak.

Elisabeth didn't remember much about the program afterwards except the moment when Larry crossed the stage to receive his diploma and a handshake from the superintendent of schools. She reveled in the moment with motherly pride. But her mind would not let go of Nellie's words about Sam. He had told her that he had always loved her. She didn't want to think about that. After Sam had kissed her that day in her kitchen, she had forced herself to bury the memory in the recesses of her mind. Now, Nellie's words had opened this vault that she had thought was so safely locked and hidden. *Had she been so blind? Had it been obvious to everyone but her? No,* she thought, impatiently pushing away that idea. *Surely Nellie's fleeting remark had only been in jest, spoken lightheartedly in innocence without any knowledge or provocation.* Nevertheless, the doubts persisted in assailing her, harassing her conscience.

At the end of the program, when the class once again rose to lead the audience in singing the closing song, she stirred uneasily. She felt as though the scene in her kitchen with Sam on that cold January day had suddenly been exposed before the eyes of the world for everyone to see. She had the vague sensation that she was on trial before this jury of staring accusing faces while she pled guilty to the charge. Silently, she stood, light-headed and unsteady, while everyone sang about her:

The eyes of Texas are upon you all the livelong day!
The eyes of Texas are upon you—you cannot get away;
Do not think you can escape them from night till early
     in the morn
The eyes of Texas are upon you till Gabriel blows his
     horn!

CHAPTER 12

"Good-bye, good-bye, and now we're going to church!" The Sunday School class of boys and girls were singing their farewell song at the end of the Sunday School lesson as they prepared to leave.

Lisa had stopped singing to listen to Roscoe who was standing beside her. He usually sang, "Good-bye, good-bye, and now I'm going home!"

She had tried, without apparent success, to get Roscoe to sing the line as the others did. At first she cajoled, later she threatened to tell Elisabeth, then carried through the threat when her warning failed to prevail. Elisabeth had, in turn, scolded him roundly but Roscoe told her with a hint of defiance, "I 'm not going to stay for church so I would be telling a lie—and you told me not to lie! I'm going home and play. I don't want to stay for church. Sunday School is long enough!"

Elisabeth could find no fault with his logic nor his truthfulness and privately told Lisa to pay no attention to him for attention was what he was seeking. If it were not forthcoming, he would soon desist. Lisa obeyed and said no more about it to him but she noticed that he continued singing it his way, loudly and belligerently, Sunday after Sunday. She found herself listening, reluctantly but expectantly, each Sunday for his lyrics. And today, she was especially interested in hearing them.

True to form, Roscoe did not disappoint her. Changing the words to suit the occasion, he sang lustily, "Good-bye, good-bye, and now I'm going on a picnic!" Lisa stamped her foot in exasperation and glared at him fiercely. Roscoe feigned ignorance of her agitation toward him. As he left the room, he called back to her, "I'm going to sit on the running board of Pastor Clark's car until church is over and we can go on the picnic." Lisa stared balefully after his retreating back.

On this particular warm June Sunday, an afternoon-long picnic had been planned by the church to be held at Will and Irma Johnson's farm, ten miles north of Anseltown. Everyone had excitedly anticipated the event. The women had organized the food carefully, making lists so dishes would not be duplicated to the extent that dinner would not consist entirely of bowls of potato salad.

It was almost 1 o'clock before the congregation came pouring out of the church after the service. It had been a fine sermon, long and fiery. Now, everyone, feeling pious after their weekly Sunday morning confinement and chastisement by the preacher for their sins, was eagerly looking forward to the afternoon before them. Guilt for the past week's wickedness had been assuaged and laid aside.

Elisabeth and the children rode with Pastor Bob Clark and his wife. Almost a dozen cars formed the motorcade, loaded to capacity with the owners and their families and those who did not possess an automobile. With the Johnson family leading the way, the cars proceeded through town to Highway 65, their occupants honking and waving gaily to one another all the while.

Although Will and Irma Johnson were the proud parents of seven children, they had not been as hard hit by the Depression as some of their neighbors on nearby farms or most of their city friends. Will had inherited some hundred acres when his father died in 1924 and, through his and Irma's industrious labor, exceptional competence and thrift, they were able to purchase an additional hundred acres and pay it off in five years. In addition, Will had added more cattle to his herd, built a bigger barn, increased his equipment and made improvements on their home. Over the years, he had wisely taken care of his land: Rotating the crops, fertilizing and taking precautions to prevent erosion, enriching and improving the soil.

Because their farm was debt free, the Johnsons were, at least for the present, still managing to hold their own. Many of their farmer friends were not so fortunate. Several prominent landowners of the county had lost their fortunes, not resulting from their extravagance, but because of the economic conditions they were unable to foresee or forestall. Unable to meet the interest and taxes on their mortgaged land, they had been compelled to give the insurance company that was holding their mortgages, chattel mortgages for the interest debt; then, later, even larger chattel mortgages were necessary. Some farmers in the area, with the sharp drop in agricultural prices, became unable to meet the mortgage payments and met foreclosure. Hence, they became renters on the land they once owned, paying rent to the insurance company holding the mortgages which amounted to about one third of the interest and taxes they had previously been paying on the mortgages.

Not knowing, or desiring to know any other trade, these farmers did not wish to give up their independence of farm owners but clung to the land they loved, becoming reluctant renters. Unwilling to relinquish the farms, the mortgage holders were equally reluctant owners. The personal pride of ownership by the farmer was not shared by the present absentee landlord who regarded it only as a source of income. He did not desire to reinvest receipts to increase the land value and appearance, as was the custom of the farmer. It became a vicious circle with the land gradually deteriorating while the rental farmer desperately tried to salvage a living from it to pay the rent on land he once owned.

The festive car caravan slowed now and turned off Highway 65, eight miles outside Anseltown, onto a narrow country road, Farm Road 120. Lined with trees, it led past the Johnson farm two miles from the highway. The house, set well back from the road, was surrounded by shade trees and displayed a small front yard of lush green lawn. Painted white, it was a two-story house with a porch stretching across the front width of it on both upper and lower levels. A large porch swing hung suspended at one end of the lower level with two rocking chairs and several cane bottom straight-backed ones placed nearby. Its homespun appearance was enhanced by pots of flowers, evenly spaced at intervals on both porch levels. Bright splashes of color from the pots and the flower beds that ran across the front of the house informed the world that this was a house filled with love and gaiety. Hanging from the huge tree at one side of the house were two tire swings. Various homemade toys, including a large wooden wagon, were nearby, giving proof that there was a time for play here as well as for hard work in the fields.

A windmill could be seen behind the house and a brightly painted large red barn stood fifty yards away. A tractor and pieces of farm equipment dotted the landscape near it. In back of the barn was a smaller structure that housed the chickens and was enclosed by a screened fence surrounding it. Cattle and horses grazed peacefully behind the barbed wire fences further back.

Beyond this and some distance away lay a dense woods with a stream running through the middle of it. It gurgled, clear and shallow, over white smooth rocks before emptying with a foamy splash over a three-foot waterfall into a placid pond below that was deep enough to swim in. On summer days when work could be laid aside for awhile, the Johnson family gathered at this favorite spot to picnic on the verdant mossy banks and bathe in the refreshingly cool water. The younger ones would splash contentedly in the water bubbling over the white rocks. The older ones took turns diving gleefully off the board that Will had rigged at the edge of the pond or swung over it to drop from a rope knotted to an overhanging tree limb.

Will and Irma Johnson were loving parents who enjoyed their large brood. Will, looking over his progeny with the same expression that he had on his face when looking over prize livestock, would often comment proudly, "The good Lord didn't see fit to make Irma and me rich in material things but He shore done a good job of makin' us rich with our young 'uns." Their firm but understanding discipline enhanced their children's feelings of security. The work on the farm was Herculean in scope but it was made easier because the family cooperated together, working as a single unit. Theirs was a closely knit group, bound to each other, not only through family ties, but also by friendship.

Alicia, a sensitive intelligent girl, was 14 and the eldest of the Johnson clan. Kermit was 12, two years younger, with three boys and two girls following, each at two year intervals. A standing joke among Will and Irma's friends was that one could keep track easily of the even years because "the Johnsons always had another young 'un in an even year."

Alicia possessed a doll-like fragility with her cornflower blue eyes and long golden hair tumbling about her shoulders that belied her country existence. Nevertheless, she was strong in stamina as well as in spirit. The long lean coltish legs were tanned berry-brown from constant outdoor life and work in the sun. The blossoming womanhood of her lithe young body was beginning to attract attention from

boys. Aloofly aware of this interest, she was vaguely
pleased, yet, strangely afraid. Afraid because, being half-
child, half-woman, she did not understand the feelings
beginning to stir within her nor the changes taking place
in her body. Afraid because of an indistinct uneasiness
that the carefree childhood she had known with her
brothers and sisters—her delight in racing freely with the
wind, her wild abandoned love for the sweetness of the
earth, the sky, the air, the very essence of life itself—
might end somehow with the changes occurring in her.

The Johnson children attended the small country
school that was located at the junction of Highway 65
where it crossed Farm Road 120. Alicia had graduated two
weeks earlier as the honor student in her class of 15. She
was looking forward to attending the high school in
Anseltown in the fall and making new friends in the city
school; nevertheless, there was also a tinge of regret. She
had an undefinable feeling that her small safe world, as it
had existed until now, was coming to an end with her
departure from the tiny rural school.

Her thoughts lingered nostalgically on the days now
past: The days of racing her brothers and sisters the two
miles to school, the snowball fights on the way and picking
flowers along the path in the dewy freshness of spring to
take home to her mother. She recalled the occasions, after
an unusually heavy snowfall had occurred, when her father
would permit them to take the snow sleigh that they had
built together. With one of the plow horses pulling it, they
would pile into it; and, upon reaching the schoolhouse,
Alicia would turn the sleigh around, head old Dorsey
toward home and give him his rein. Then, oft-times, Irma
would return in the afternoon to pick them up in it. They
would go riding off toward home, the envy of all their
classmates. The pictures of the constantly changing scenes
as they rode through the snow-covered world, the sounds

of her family's voices, laughing and singing, were indelibly imprinted on Alicia's mind.

She tried to explain her mixed emotions, her anxieties and doubts to her mother. Irma calmed them by saying, "Yes, honey, things will be different for you now. You are changing—but the world is constantly changing. It doesn't stand still and neither must you. You are growing up. A sign of maturity is being able to accept the changes around you and change accordingly—that is, just as long as you stay within the confines of your values and the things that you believe in. There are some things that will never change—and those are God's laws for us. You're a good girl. You know right from wrong. Your father and I don't worry about you for we know that you will recognize the difference between the good and the bad that will come your way. And we know that you will reject the bad."

Mama had been able to calm her fears just as she always had since she was only a little girl, Alicia thought. She was her refuge, something she could cling to and depend on. Mama was the one thing in this world that would never change—she would always be there when she needed her.

The drivers parked the cars along the side of the road near the Johnsons' front yard. The occupants quickly spilled out, laughing and calling to one another. The men and boys carted the folding chairs which had been brought from the church in John Hayes' pickup truck and set them up on the grass. The children, led by the smaller of the Johnson clan, scurried immediately to the tractor. They climbed eagerly aboard, exploring the wonders of this giant toy.

At Alicia's invitation the group of adolescents, including Larry, followed her into the company parlor where the old Victrola record player stood in one corner. Alicia displayed the few records she owned, saying, "You can play them if you like." The ice was broken and shyness dissipated as a lively discussion ensued over which one to play first.

Larry stood quietly in the background of the group of eighteen, ten girls and eight boys, and secretly watched Alicia. He was amazed at how much she had changed in the last few months. He had known her since she was a small child. She had always been just another skinny girl to him. But she had certainly changed lately. And, today, she looked even more grown up in her Sunday church clothes, wearing hose and dressy pumps with a little heel. Her long golden hair, cascading over her shoulders, and the white dress emphasized the deep tan of her skin. Her tiny waist was accentuated by the wide sash that was tied in a large ribbon bow at the back. She was the prettiest girl he had ever seen. Alicia, sensing his scrutiny, suddenly stared directly into his eyes from across the room. Realizing that he had been gaping at her, Larry's face flushed red and he turned his head quickly, feigning interest in the grouping of family photographs that were hanging on the wall. He felt his face growing hot as he saw her, out of the corner of his eyes, move away from the group and walk toward him.

"I'll bet you didn't know that Jesse James hid out on my uncle's farm in Missouri," she said as she moved to his side, noticing that he was looking at the pictures. "That's my uncle there." She pointed to a man with dark eyes and a brush mustache who bore a faint resemblance to Will Johnson.

Larry's eyes grew wide, his face lighting up with interest as he forgot his embarrassment. "You mean your uncle actually saw Jesse James?"

"He certainty did!" Alicia said, tossing her head, feeling important at his obvious fascination with her conversation. "Why," she continued, "my uncle couldn't begin to count the times that he saw him..." she hesitated, then, couldn't resist adding dramatically, "and his gang!" She felt a little pang of remorse at her exaggeration but swiftly forgot it when she saw the look of admiration on Larry's face.

Larry emitted a low whistle, "Wasn't he scared of him?"

"My uncle isn't scared of anything or anybody," she answered proudly. "He and my daddy are just alike. Uncle Weldon is my father's brother."

"How come he didn't turn Jesse over to the law?" Larry asked, feeling bold at referring to him this way, as if he had known him personally.

"He said it wasn't any business of his," she said, "and Jesse didn't bother him any. My uncle said that all he ever did was to water his horse when he stopped by his farm. Jesse always talked real pleasant to him and Aunt Sarah."

Larry was silent a moment, thinking of the man he had read so much about. He has been fascinated by the glorified stories of Jesse James' life from the old newspapers in the library. It seemed to him that anyone who tried to help the poor couldn't be all bad. His mother had disapproved of his line of thinking. Impatiently, she informed him that Jesse James had broken one of God's ten commandments by stealing, no matter what he did with the loot afterwards. And that a "wrong" never made a "right." But he had continued to read about him, impressed with this modern Robin Hood who allegedly stole from the larders of the rich to alleviate the suffering of the poor. Secretly, he wished that he could aid all the people he knew that were poor even though he wouldn't want to steal to do so. But it just didn't seem right to him somehow that, with everyone living in the same world, so few could be so rich while so many suffered the miseries of poverty. There should be some way, he thought, to distribute the wealth so that all people could live in a better and more equal manner. This aspect troubled him and he discussed it with his father.

He had laughed and agreed with him, saying, "Son, I'll certainly drink to that! I'm all for it!"

He had become even more bewildered when his mother had frowned and said disapprovingly, "You'll teach him communism, Jon." So, he hadn't pursued the subject further. But he had wondered what *communism* meant and he planned to look it up at the library.

"You mean they actually talked to him?" Larry asked. Alicia, reveling in Larry's reaction, was feeling more important every minute. "Many times," she said. "Aunt Sarah said he seemed like a right nice young man—always so polite to her, tipping his hat and saying *ma'am* and *please* and *thank you* to her. Why, she even gave him a piece of pie once when he told her that he had smelled a fresh apple pie a mile away. Then, after he ate it, he said it tasted just like the ones his mother made!"

"Did they ever see his gun?"

"Well, he never showed it to them on purpose," Alicia answered, "but they could see it under his coat. Uncle Weldon said the sheriff and his posse came by several times looking for him. Uncle Weldon figured that Jesse was hiding out in the cave in the side of the mountain on his farm but he never told the sheriff about it. But after Jesse and his gang were caught, Uncle Weldon rode back to the cave and, sure enough, he found where they had been camping inside of it!"

Larry emitted another whistle. "Boy, wouldn't I like to see that cave!" he almost whispered.

"My uncle still lives there on that same farm."

"Someday, I'm going to travel and I'll go see that cave!" The words, spoken intensely, fiercely sounded like a promise.

"Do you really want to travel?" Alicia asked on a note of surprise. Larry shook his head absently, still lost in his imagination about Jesse James and the cave. "Why that's just what I want to do!" Alicia exclaimed.

Larry focused his attention on her words again. He found her easy to talk to. Relaxed now, he was comfortable in her presence. "Yes. I would like to travel all over the world. And I want to write about it and everything I see." He paused, then continued quietly, "I don't want to miss a single thing!" His face grew wistful. "I want to see Paris more than anyplace. I want to live where Hemingway lived, walk where he walked, eat where he ate, see what he saw, and try to find out why and how he writes as he does. Maybe—just maybe," he said, longingly, "I'll be able to learn to write a little bit like he writes!"

Alicia looked at him admiring. "I didn't know you wanted to write," she said.

He was embarrassed by her look but pleased that she was interested. Looking down at his feet, he said, "I guess it sounds crazy but I feel like I've just got to write. Why," his voice waxed enthusiastic, "I get so many thoughts crowding inside my head till I feel it will bust unless I can get them out. I've just got to write!" He repeated the last emphatically; then, aware of his intensity, his voice trailed off self-consciously. Embarrassed again, he forced a laugh, saying, "You'd be surprised at the stories I've written about people in this town."

Alicia did not laugh, her face was serious as she studied him closely. She felt a kindred spirit with him. He had revealed his innermost feelings and she felt privileged that he had wanted to share them with her. "I'd like to read them," she said in a quiet voice after a moment. Then, abruptly, she smiled, and, with a teasing look in her eyes, she asked, "Have you written a story about me?"

Suddenly, Larry was startled, abashed that he had talked so openly to her. He had never talked to anyone about his hopes and dreams before except his mother. Now, his clear green eyes gazed steadily at Alicia, searching her face. Then, satisfied that she was not making fun of him, he grinned widely and answered, "No, but I will!"

The insistent ringing of the dinner bell and Irma's voice interrupted them as she called loudly, "Everybody come along now before everything gets cold. Land sakes, where is everybody? Where's Alicia and the kids?"

"They're in the parlor, playing some records," Elisabeth answered.

"I hope they're not sneaking in some dancing," someone added.

As Mary Jane Hayes walked through the parlor door, she called out to Larry and Alicia, "Come on, you two—if you can tear yourself away from each other." Everyone turned to look at them, laughing as their faces reddened, before filing outside. Alone now, Alicia and Larry stood looking at each other in silence, suddenly at a loss for words. Then, without speaking, they followed the others to the yard where the women were busily making last minute preparations.

"Come on, kids, it's time to eat!" Nellie called out to the children who were engrossed in a game of hide and seek, racing in and out of the barn. Nellie added, saying to no one in particular, "I doubt if we ever get them to the table. Why, they've all been running around like chickens with their heads cut off ever since they got here!"

The men, who had been escorted to the barn by Will to look over the chickens and cattle, turned at the sound of the bell and walked back toward the long table on the side of the grassy lawn underneath the shade trees. Small tables, pushed together and covered by a multitude of tablecloths that clashed colorfully in their different designs and hues, comprised the one long table. It was weighted down with the dishes of food which had been prepared by the ladies the previous day, packed in John Hayes' truck and delivered to Irma's kitchen before church that morning.

The meat consisted of fried chicken in abundance with Irma and two other farm wives adding roast, ham and platters of sausage from their ready pork supplies. Bowls of potato salad, green salads, baked beans and assorted vegetables crowded each other down the length of the table. A huge mold-designed tub of butter from Irma's cows decorated the table's center to accompany the baskets of freshly baked bread. Plates of hard-boiled eggs and pitchers of cold milk, both sweet and buttermilk, were more contributions from Ira's cows and chickens.

The women had tried to outdo each other in desserts, both in eye-appeal, appearance and taste. One end of the table was spread with cakes which were topped by mounds of frosting. There were cakes of every type and description: Chocolate ones with whole pecan halves placed generously on the top and sides, coconut covered cakes with red cherries nestled against the snowy whiteness, caramel maple-nut decorated with walnut halves, spice cakes loaded with raisins, nuts and the pungent odor of allspice, cinnamon and ginger, covered in honey icing. Pies were also added to the already overladen table, pies piled high with billowy clouds of meringue that hid fat fillings of chocolate, lemon and butterscotch and fruit pies that were filled to the brim with cherries, apricots, peaches or berries whose juices and fragrance seeped through their cross-latticed crusts.

With everyone gathered around the table at last, Pastor Clark raised his hand for silence; then, he proceeded to say grace, blessing and praising God for the food. It was a lengthy prayer and, in the middle of it, Lisa, covertly eyeing the desserts that had drawn her and Roscoe like magnets, saw Roscoe raise his finger and rake at the edge of the meringue on the nearest pie.

"Why does the blessing have to be said *before* you eat? Why can't it be said *after* you eat?" he whispered loudly, impatiently to Lisa. She tugged at his arm in a vain attempt to quiet him. Jason and Ruthie Ellen Johnson, standing next to Roscoe, overheard him and giggled. They were promptly stifled by a frowning glance from Irma.

As soon as Pastor Clark said *Amen*, everyone began overloading their plates, jesting and jostling each other good-naturedly. Carrying their plates, the children sat together on the lawn, forming a circle. Roscoe, still disgruntled by Pastor Clark's long prayer, deemed it necessary to continue his dissertation on saying grace.

"I still don't see why the blessing has to be said before you eat." he protested to the group in general.

"Because everyone should thank God for the food He has given them," Lisa replied.

"Well, how do you know you're going to like the food before you eat it—especially if it's something you've never tasted," he argued, his spoon poised in midair. "And, what if you don't happen to like it? It don't seem like you ought to have to say *thanks* for something you hate!"

"Oh, shut up, Roscoe, and eat," Lisa retorted in an exasperated voice.

Roscoe, feeling that he had been challenged and must prove his point in front of the others who were listening closely, continued to badger her, "I don't care what you say. I don't think you should have to say *thanks* for something you don't like." He was shaking his head emphatically and his fine silky white hair fell across his forehead into his eyes as he added, "Or for leftovers either!"

His large black eyes were solemn, earnestly serious as he turned to the others in an attempt to gain their support. "We have leftovers a lot and we still have to say the blessing for them. It's the same as saying *thanks* twice for the same food. And, I don't think God expects us to thank Him twice for leftovers, especially, when you don't even like them. And," he said vehemently, looking around for approval, "I hate 'em!"

He got it from a couple of other boys his age who chimed in with, "So do I!" There were murmurs of assent. A few of the older ones laughed.

Lisa said angrily, "Oh, Roscoe, you're so dumb!" Then, tossing her head, she rose and moved away from him to sit by Ruthie Ellen.

Roscoe, not to be outdone, aimed his parting shot at Lisa's retreating back. "Anyway," he said crossly, "why do we thank God for it anyhow? Daddy says he's the one that buys the food for us—and we ought to thank him instead." His voice had risen in his anger and carried clearly to the adults. Pastor Clark turned to see who was talking. Elisabeth was mortified. She ducked her head and busied herself at the table, pretending she hadn't heard.

Afterwards, when everyone had gorged themselves from the bountiful table, the children returned to their play, swinging on the tire swings and exploring the barn. Some of the more daring took turns jumping into the large haystack from the loft. The men lounged on the grass contentedly, making small talk. They avoided discussing their jobs, or lack of them, or the Depression that held the country in its grip. The women were lighthearted and gay as they cleared the table and washed the dishes. An air of well-being pervaded the atmosphere, releasing them for a time from the anxiety and worry that played such a predominant part in everyday existence. At least, for this day, problems were forgotten and everyone felt almost carefree.

"Let's go to the swimming pond!" Jamey Peterson's suggestion was greeted by echoes of eager assent. There was general confusion as bathing suits and towels that had been brought were quickly gathered up. Noisily, the teenaged group trooped gaily off toward the distant woods.

Elisabeth gazed after them, noting without surprise that Larry and Alicia walked together, trailing the others. Janie Hayes, standing next to her, spoke, "It looks like Larry and Alicia have discovered each other." Elisabeth didn't answer. Her thoughts were of her son. He was so sensitive, so vulnerable. He could be easily hurt. She wondered what kind of girl Alicia really was.

The women, finished with the dishes, sat on the folding chairs and talked. Most of them were knitting or crocheting, their hands busily occupied with the needlework that was a constant companion and which had been brought along with the food. "I declare, Elisabeth, I do believe that was the best pecan pie I ever tasted!" Irma exclaimed. The others nodded assent. "Could you give me the recipe—or is it a secret old family recipe?"

Elisabeth, flushing under the compliment, appeared flustered. "Why, no," she said, "it's just a recipe that I made up and experimented with in order to use the pecans that I got from our tree. Of course you can have the recipe."

"Well, you're the clever one, Elisabeth!" Irma said, "making up your own recipes like that. What do you call it?"

Elisabeth, pleased by the praise but slightly embarrassed, said shyly, "I just call it Texas Pecan Pie, seeing how it's made from pecans from a good old Texas papershell pecan tree."

"Well, leave it to Elisabeth to call a spade a spade," Mrs. Parsons said. "She never was one to beat around the bush." Elisabeth joined in the laughter.

"Well," said Irma, rising, "I'm going to get a pencil and paper before she changes her mind." She returned from her kitchen with one of the children's school tablets and handed it to Elisabeth. She wrote out the recipe which was passed around and copied by the others.

Texas Pecan Pie

1 1/2 cups pecan halves

4 eggs

3/4 cup sugar

1 1/2 cups dark corn syrup

1/4 teaspoon salt

1 1/2 teaspoon vanilla or maple flavor

1/2 cup melted butter

Beat the eggs. Add the sugar and syrup, then the salt and vanilla, and last the melted butter. Place the pecans around the bottom of a nine-inch unbaked pie crust. Add the filling and bake slowly in a medium hot oven of 350 degrees for 50 to 60 minutes. The nuts rise to the top of the filling and form a crusted layer.

The men lay on the grass apart from them, not talking much now. Lots of them were dozing softly. The combination of the warm summer afternoon and the unaccustomed overloaded stomachs had made them lazy and dulled their senses, almost casting an hypnotic trance over then. The women were engrossed in their conversation. Thus, no one was perceptibly aware of the roadster, traveling fast and leaving swirls of dust churning behind it, as it sped down the country road past them a short distance away. Little could they know, or ever have guessed, what effects this small car's occupant would have on their lives—their town and their state.

Larry and Alicia, walking slowly, had fallen back quite a distance behind the others. They were absorbed in each other and their conversation, with Alicia doing most of the talking. Larry listened attentively to her viewpoints on their own private world, the universe and life in general. Young though he was, already, he had a writer's ear— listening, ever listening, to voices transmitting words,

words that would be stored inside his brain to be transferred later to paper. He was not yet aware of this. He only knew that he would rather listen than talk, that he learned only by listening, that he desired to hear the ideas and opinions of others. He had an unquenchable thirst for the sound and meaning of words.

The others had already reached the edge of the woods. Some of the boys, eager to be the first in the water, had raced ahead and were quickly changing in the sanctuary of the woods. Larry and Alicia, still near the road, heard a car motor behind them and paused to look back. It passed them at an accelerated burst of speed before becoming almost invisible through the thick cloud of dust that mushroomed from its wheels.

"That's Stony Ansel's new car," Alicia said, matter-of-factly. He's been hunting jackrabbits lately over on Mr. Jordon's farm." Modestly, she failed to add that, whenever she was working in the fields, he would stop and try to talk to her from the car.

The roadster, complete with rumble seat, was Stony's newest possession. It had been a gift from his father for his seventeenth birthday the month before. But, birthday or not, he would have received it for he wanted to be the first in town to own a car with a rumble seat. And Mayor Ansel saw to it that his son was the first in everything.

They continued on their way after the car roared past but their attention was abruptly arrested by the sudden squeal of brakes that rent the air. They watched, fascinated, as the car swerved back and forth across the narrow road, barely avoiding the ditch, before finally coming to a halt. The gears were noisily thrown into reverse and the car backed swiftly down the road in their direction. The two stood motionless, startled by the erratic behavior. The car braked to a stop a few feet away and they saw Stony's acne-spotted face peering at them through the window.

"What's going on here?" Stony called out. "What are all the cars doing back there?"

"We're having a church picnic," Alicia answered, "and we're going swimming." She added politely, "Would you like to come along?"

"Well, now, ain't that the berries?" Stony sneered. Then, scornfully, "I don't want any part of no damn church picnic." His eyes raked over Larry contemptuously as he asked, "Who's the punk with you?"

Alicia's face flushed crimson. "Come on, let's go!" she said to Larry and she turned to walk away. Larry hesitated, then followed slowly after her.

"You think you're too good to go out with me?" Stony yelled angrily after Alicia. The gears ground in noisy protest as he jerked them into low. The car roared off with the wheels spinning, kicking up dirt behind them.

Larry caught up with Alicia and saw tears glinting in her eyes. Angrily, he said, "I'd like to bust him one!"

Feeling that an explanation was necessary, Alicia said, "I don't know what's the matter with him. He stops and talks to me when I'm working in the field and keeps asking me to go out with him. I've told him over and over that I'm not allowed to go out with boys yet." She grimaced, adding, "Not that I' d go out with him if I could. I don't like him. He gives me the creeps!" She tossed her head, "If he says anything else to me, I'm going to tell Daddy!"

"He thinks he's smart and important because his father has a lot of money," Larry said.

Reaching the woods, they could hear the others already diving and playing in the water. "Come on in!" Skinny Andrews yelled to them as he splashed water at Shirley Jean Brown standing on the bank.

Later, tired from swimming, the group lounged by the pond and basked in the sunlight that filtered through the trees. Larry and Alicia drifted together once more, sitting apart from the others. It seemed only natural for them to be together. Again, Larry found himself confiding in Alicia, talking to her easily, comfortably about things that he had never shared with anyone. Absorbed in each other, they hardly noticed when Mary Jane called to them that the others were leaving to return to the house and play records. The group left, unnoticed by the two who continued to talk.

"I want to get away from Anseltown as soon as I possibly can," Larry said.

"Why?" Alicia asked in surprise.

"Because I can never amount to anything if I stay here," he answered. "I've just got to go to college some way and get a good education so I can be a writer." He looked into her face earnestly as he went on. "But, even if I don't get to go to college, I'll still get away from this town as soon as I can. Like my Dad says—it's an 'open and shut town'— open only to the rich and closed to the poor. The rich won't pay a decent living wage to the poor people so they can never get ahead here."

"But I like it here," Alicia protested, "it's a nice place to live, I wouldn't want to live anyplace else."

"Your father is a farmer," Larry explained patiently, "with his own land. He doesn't have to work for those people in town and depend on them for a living. Why, just look how old Mayor Ansel works people at the cotton mill for starvation wages. And there's not a thing they can do about it!"

"If they don't like it, they can just get their asses out!" a voice said angrily from behind them. They jerked around, startled. Stony Ansel stood beside a tree, holding a rifle. Larry wondered how long he had been listening, "Don't talk like that in front of Alicia," he said angrily.

"Well, who the shit's going to stop me?" Stony jeered. He walked toward Larry, menacingly. Larry got to his feet and stood his ground as he approached. His face showed no fear, although he was a good six-inches shorter, and Stony, three years his senior, had the muscle and strength advantage over him. Aware of his physical superiority, he goaded Larry, "Go ahead and stop me—punk!"

Before Larry could move, Alicia quickly caught his arm, saying, "Let's go, Larry!" She pulled at him.

Stony reached out and grabbed her arm. "You're not going anywhere yet!" He pulled her roughly against him and tried to kiss her. She jerked away but, in that brief instant, she smelled the odor of whiskey on his breath. Larry swung wildly at Stony's face, hitting him sharply on the cheek bone.

Stony had been holding the rifle in one hand all the while, and now, with rage contorting his face, he swung it, catching Larry on the side of the head with the barrel. The impact made a sharp cracking sound. He slumped to the ground and lay still with blood oozing down the side of his face. Alicia bent over him, crying, "What have you done? He's dead!" Larry moaned slightly and moved his head.

"The little punk ain't dead!" Stony said, looking down at them. "He'll be alright." In an insinuating tone, he added, "You must like him an awful lot, fooling around out here in the woods with him!" He had hardly gotten the words out before Alicia had leaped to her feet and almost knocked him down in her fury to get at him. She raked at his face with her nails and left a long red scratch down the length of it while she simultaneously kicked out at him. She was sobbing wildly, with anger now overcoming the fear that had gripped her when Larry fell.

Stony, dropping the rifle, grabbed her hands and jerked her up violently against him. "You little wildcat!" he snarled through clenched teeth, "I ought to kill you for that!" Then, he looked into her eyes, close to his. A grin spread slowly across his mouth, "Well, now," he drawled,

"I think I'd rather kiss you instead." He brought his lips down hard against her unyielding ones, Alicia, wide-eyed, gazed with horror into the hateful face with the pimples and the straggly red hair falling across it in unruly strands. She fought, trying desperately to pull away. It seemed to arouse him all the more. He held both her hands in one of his. With the other one, he grabbed a handful of her long silken hair and pulled her head sharply back. She gasped at the pain and her mouth opened. Quickly, he bent his lips once more to her parted ones while he held her in a vise like grip. She became dizzy and weak. She couldn't breathe in his crushing hold on her body. Her legs gave way beneath her as she momentarily lost consciousness. Coming to, she found herself lying on the ground. She felt Stony's hand clutch her dress at the hem and pull it up to the waist. She recoiled at his hot hands fumbling at her body. She came to life once again, clawing and fighting, lashing out at him with all her strength.

"You little bitch!" he roared in rage. Drawing his hand back, he slapped her stingingly across the face.

She cried out and he seized her hands again, holding them in one of his while he swiftly removed his belt and wrapped it around her wrists. "Now," he said, leaning over her again, "that ought to hold you!" His face was red and his breath came in short fast gasps.

In the furious melee between them, neither had noticed Larry a few feet away who had begun to stir on the ground. Suddenly, Alicia saw him standing over them with Stony's rifle raised. The look in her eyes betrayed his presence and Stony jerked around just in time to see the gun swinging, aimed at his head. He dodged sideways and the blow was deflected from his head to the back of his neck. He jumped to his feet before Larry could draw the gun back again and grabbed it away from him. Throwing it to one side, he grasped Larry's shirt collar in almost a single motion. He hit Larry squarely on the jaw, knocking him down. Then, before he could move, Stony seized his arms and drug him to the water's edge. Larry, dazed and weakened, made a feeble attempt to struggle once more. Stony hit him once again in the face. Blood spurted from his nose. His face twisted in frustrated fury. Stony pulled him into the water and pushed his head underneath it, holding it there. Larry, struggling desperately now, finally managed to clear his head above it. Sputtering and gasping, he fought for air.

Alicia strained helplessly against the belt that bound her hands. The scene before her was blurry, unreal. She had the vague sensation that she must be the victim of a nightmare from which she would surely soon awaken and find herself safely in her bed. She was still lying on the ground, too weak to get to her feet. She began crawling awkwardly, with her hands tied in front of her, sobbing loudly as she moved toward them. Her eyes were glued to Stony's face. She was unable to tear her gaze away. Never before had she seen an expression such as Stony's. It was one of sheer madness.

Larry struggled savagely, fiercely against Stony's demonic grasp, succeeding in pushing his head from the water to gulp for air, time after time. But, after each emergence, his attempts grew weaker. Horrified, Alicia saw his body finally remain still, motionless, his feet no larger kicking, when Stony thrust his head beneath the water once again.

She opened her mouth to scream out at Stony. Instead, she felt her throat closing in fear and she heard her voice crying weakly, "He's drowning! Let him go! Please let him go!" The words rose, and lingered on a long quivering note as sobs racked her body.

Suddenly, a figure flung itself upon Stony. It lashed out furiously, knocking Stony backwards into the water, away from Larry's now inert body. It seemed to Alicia, though she was only a few feet away, that she was completely detached from this reality, set far apart, and only watching. She remained immobile, almost deathlike, and was incapable of moving, seeing with unseeing eyes, as the man stalked Stony like a shadow. Stony had picked himself up from the water and was making a vain attempt to escape. Alicia saw the shadow reach out and grab Stony from behind, spin him around to hit him hard again. Stony fell once more. He flopped over on his stomach and, half-swimming, half-running, he made it to the edge where he crawled onto the bank.

Alicia finally came to life. She streaked into the water, moaning and muttering, clutching for Larry who had disappeared from sight. She located his body just beneath the water's surface. Her hands, still bound in front of her by the belt, moved swiftly along his body until they found his head. She grasped it, pulling it up so his face was clear of the water. She floundered with her burden, striving to keep his head above the water while she dragged him to the bank. Suddenly, she saw Larry being lifted upward. She looked up into the broad black face of Daniel whom she had seen working in the adjoining fields for Mr. Jordon. Daniel carried Larry quickly to the bank and laid him gently on the ground, rolling him over on his stomach. He straddled Larry and began pressing firmly and rhythmically on his back, it seemed like an eternity to Alicia before she saw Larry, water trickling from his mouth, moan and move; then, at last, he opened his eyes.

Tears ran down her cheeks as she knelt beside him and bent her head closely to him. "Oh, Larry, are you alright?" she sobbed. He didn't answer but moved his head slightly, looking at her through glazed eyes. At his movement, Alicia began to cry loudly until her voice reached an almost hysterical pitch. Her whole body jerked spasmodically, convulsively. She babbled incoherently. She felt the belt being loosened from her hands and she gazed unseeing into Daniel's face as he knelt before her. Her eyes were wide and vacant, her mouth was open, uttering loud uncontrollable noises. She felt herself being shaken roughly.

In contrast, Daniel's voice was unexpectedly gentle as he said, "Everything's alright now, Miss Alicia. You're alright and he is too." He nodded toward Larry. "So, don' you fret no mo'." The soothing compassion in his voice calmed her, stilling her fears. She went limp, relaxing completely and collapsed against his wide chest, her face resting against it with her eyes closed.

"You nigger lover!" a voice said scornfully. Alicia jerked upright. She saw Stony standing nearby, water dripping from his clothes and running in rivulets from his hair down his face. He was holding the rifle pointed at Daniel's chest. Daniel, instinctively and quickly, moved away from Alicia.

Alicia watched numbly as Daniel, with rage filled eyes, strode purposefully toward Stony. Stony, taken aback, by Daniel's fearless approach, retreated a few steps and waved the rifle menacingly, saying, "Stay away from me, you black bastard, or I'll blow your head off!" His voice rose on a note of fear as Daniel continued to walk toward him slowly, deliberately.

"I may be stupid, white boy, but I ain't that stupid!" Daniel said, visibly trying to control his anger and hatred. He had almost reached the end of the rifle that was still pointed at him when Stony pulled the trigger. It clicked against an empty barrel. Stony looked down at the gun, in surprise, then jerked the trigger back and pulled it again. Once again, the same metallic click of emptiness echoed. His eyes reflected his fear as he looked into the face of the oncoming determined figure and he drew back, cringing,

Daniel looked at him in disgust, "White boy, you don't think I left the bullets in that gun, do you?" he asked. Then added, "I took them out while you was trying to drown that boy!" Furiously, he grabbed the rifle, wrenching it from Stony's grasp. For an instant, Alicia thought he was going to bring it down over Stony's skull as he lifted it high over his head. But, at the last minute, Daniel raised his leg, with his knee extended, and brought the gun down over it. The gun split half in two with a sharp crack. Stony, thinking that Daniel was going to strike him with the gun, had sunk to his knees and covered his head with his arms, whining and groveling at Daniel's feet. Daniel, breathing heavily, looked down for a long moment at him. Finally, he spoke, "Don' you ever point a gun at me agin', white boy!"

Stony made no answer. He crawled away a short distance before jumping to his feet. He ran through the trees in the direction of the road. When he was a safe distance away, he stopped and turned around, yelling back, "I'll get you for this, Nigger!" His voice rose on a note of hysterical rage, "Believe me, if it's the last thing I ever do, I'll get you for this!" Then, he turned and ran again.

Without a word or a backward glance at them, Daniel walked into the woods toward the direction of Mr. Jordon's farm, his back straight and his head high. Alicia watched him until he disappeared from sight.

She went over to Larry. He was sitting up now and had witnessed the encounter between the two. Still groggy, he had not completely comprehended the drama that had unfolded about him. "What was Daniel doing here?" he asked, dazed.

"Do you know him?"

"He's Glo-ree's son." Larry answered. He attempted to rise but his legs refused to support him. He sunk weakly to the ground again.

"Can you walk, Larry?"

"I think so," he replied. "Let me rest for a minute."

They sat silently, reluctant to speak of what had happened. Finally, Alicia said in a low voice which was almost a whisper, "Please don't ever tell anyone what happened here today, Larry. I wouldn't want anyone to ever know what Stony Ansel tried to do!" Her voice was barely audible as she added, "I'd be so ashamed!"

Larry, though equally anxious to forget the events of today, also felt a responsibility toward Alicia. "You ought to tell your father."

"No!" she said sharply. "He would kill Stony if he knew!"

"He ought to be killed!" Larry muttered.

She started to cry again. "I don't want anyone to know—I'm so ashamed!"

Larry turned to her but she averted her eyes. "You, shouldn't be, Alicia," he spoke gently, "you have nothing to be ashamed of."

To his chagrin, she sobbed even harder, crying vehemently, "Stony is so nasty! I hate him!" Turning her tear-stained face to him, she said imploringly, "Please, Larry," she begged, "promise me that you'll never tell anyone—not ever!"

"I promise, Alicia," he said solemnly. Her look was one of relief but it changed once again to apprehension when Larry added, "But only if you promise me something in return." He waited for her affirmation but she remained silent and he went on, "Promise me that if Stony ever comes near you again—ever even tries to talk to you— promise me that you will tell your father he is bothering you."

"I promise," she answered quietly. After a moment, she rose quickly from the ground, saying in an urgent tone, "We must get home before anyone begins to worry about us." She looked at him anxiously. "Do you feel like walking now?"

He got up slowly. His legs felt stronger now, no longer rubbery. "Yes," he answered. Still wearing his bathing suit, he walked to the nearby bush where his clothes were hanging and began gathering them together. "I'll change into these at the house," he said.

"You've got to get that blood off, Larry," Alicia said, noting the bloodstains on his face. He washed himself quickly at the edge of the pond under her surveillance. "That cut is underneath your hair so it doesn't show," she told him. Then, smoothing her disarrayed clothing, she looked down at her skirt in dismay, saying, "Oh, my skirt is wet." She glanced upward at the sun whose still warm rays were now beginning to cast long lingering shadows across the landscape. "It should be almost dry by the time we reach home," she said hopefully.

They made their way through the stillness of the woods. Reticent to discuss what had happened, they did not talk. Emerging from the trees into the clearing, they heard the roar of a car motor and the screech of tires on the road. The dust flew, camouflaging the roadster from view, as it raced down the country lane to the main highway. Neither gave an acknowledging sign of it nor did they break the silence that engulfed them. Walking across the sun drenched meadow, their eyes were fixed steadily on the farm that was visible in the distance.

Alicia led the way into the back door of the house, avoiding the front yard where the others were. They could hear the Victrola playing and the laughter of voices coming from the parlor as they went quickly up the back stairs. Larry swiftly changed from his bathing suit into his clothes in the bedroom that Alicia pointed out. They had arrived in the midst of a flurry of activity as preparations were being made to depart so that everyone could get back to town in time to attend the evening church service. Dishes and belongings were gathered up, children were coaxed from their play, and pandemonium reigned in prodding everyone, reluctant to leave, to the cars. They were both relieved and grateful that, in the overall confusion, no one had noticed their tardiness or anything unusual about their appearance.

CHAPTER 13

Wayne Winslow, the Personnel Director for Blossom's Flour and Grain Company, sat in his small cubicle of an office. It was on the ground floor located just inside and to the right of the wide sliding doors that opened onto the long concrete platform. The company trucks were loaded from this platform with grain and flour for shipment. A small ceiling fan whirred noisily and not very effectively in the windowless room that had been carelessly partitioned off from the heavy machinery behind it. The noise from the machines vibrated through the thin walls, making conversation in a normal tone of voice impossible.

But Barney Blossom, the mill owner, was not concerned with the conversations or conveniences of his workers. He was not one to waste money on anything, let alone on his employees. He had gone into business for himself 25 years ago, using his small inheritance from his father to buy the mill from old man Dawson when he went bankrupt. Through many shrewd business deals, most of which were notoriously shady, and his art of frugal penny-pinching that consisted mainly of grossly underpaying the people he employed, he had amassed his fortune. The greater part had been accumulated during the past four years which had been the best ever for him as far as the labor market was concerned.

In this July of the Depression, summer of 1933, he could hire as many men as he needed, and then some, who were willing to work for any kind of starvation wages. For they were desperate men in dire circumstances. There were families to feed and work of any type was practically nonexistent. Barney Blossom told himself that he was not going to feel guilty about the peanut wages that he could get by with paying. He refused to feel guilty. *I'm in a position to call the shots now. And it sure as hell feels good! It hasn't always been that way. No sir!* Although he had bought the mill from old man Dawson at a rock bottom price, it had taken his entire inheritance and savings. And, he had worked his fingers to the bone, saving and scrimping and scratching to keep the mill going until it could begin paying off. *Yes sir, every body has to help themselves in this life,* he philosophized. *And, by George, I'm going to help myself, now that I finally have the world by the tail on a downhill pull!*

Wayne Winslow was wearing a tie and a white shirt, wet beneath the armpits with perspiration, and with the sleeves rolled to the elbow. A personable young man in appearance, Winslow was clean shaven and his short dark hair, parted on the left side, was trimmed neatly at all times. Now, visibly annoyed, he swatted a fly from his ear. He found it necessary to leave the door open to obtain what little relief the outside offered against the oppressive summer heat trapped inside. However, this gave the pesky gnats and flies free gratis to his office. Six months ago, when he began working at Blossom's, he asked Tom Cordell, the plant manager, to have a screen door installed to sift out the maddening insects that infested the mill, drawn to the grain. Cordell had given him a derisive laugh in answer. Winslow knew it was useless to say anything more. The flying dust and chaff from the grain filled the air, settling on everything. By the end of the day, he felt as though his clothes had been used as dust rags. And they looked it. The black patent leather shoes that he took great pride in spit polishing till they shone like twin mirrors could have had designs drawn in the grime gathered on them. Even worse, the tiny grain particles clogged his nose and throat and made him cough. He often wondered how the men who operated the machines, packed the sacks, then loaded them into the trucks could stand the suffocating silt.

Winslow, only 25, was two years out of college. He was aware that the older men, the plant manager and the foremen, patronized him, looking on him as still being wet behind the ears, and cracked jokes about him behind his back. He had caught phrases as he passed them grouped together: "College kid," "jackass," and "don't know his elbow from a hole in the ground." He chose to ignore the whole lot. He would do his job and do it well. He wouldn't be in this horse-and-buggy town for long. This job had been his second promotion already since he finished college— and it wouldn't be his last. He didn't care what these country hicks said. Blossom's was only a whistle stop on the map of his career. And, he was going all the way! He had set a goal for himself—to reach the top of the ladder by the time he was 35. He meant to climb it, rung by rung, one way or another, in spite of anyone or anything, till he reached it.

He glanced at the clock on the wall. He was waiting for Barney to arrive. Everyone called him *Barney* behind his back but never when talking to him. It was always *Mr. Blossom* then. Winslow took the coat that was hanging on the back of his chair and put it on after rolling down his shirt sleeves. He grimaced as his shirt stuck to him underneath the coat. The hot Texas heat had already reached 90 degrees. It's going to be another killer, he thought—at least a 105 today. It was the 20th day of July and the temperature had climbed to over 100 degrees every day so far this month. He hadn't wanted to put the coat on a minute too soon but he knew Barney would arrive at 10 o'clock sharp. He was never late.

Winslow heard the loud raucous voice of Barney preceding him, heralding his arrival. Waiting for him to reach his office, the contradictory combination of Barney Blossom's name struck Winslow as laughable. His first name, possibly calling to mind that of a prize fighter, was ludicrous when imagined in the same vein with Barney. Rolls of fat layered his middle, hanging over pants that slipped down underneath them, giving the impression that he was in precarious and imminent danger of losing them. Puffy bags under his eyes presented open-faced testimony to his consumption of large quantities of liquor over the years. The name of Blossom presented a study in extremes—a direct contrast to its possessor's uncouth, boisterous and profane nature. His misnomer was the butt of jokes by his employees. These jokes were, obviously, never made within his hearing. For, after all, Barney Blossom almost held the power of life and death over them. He controlled their jobs which, in turn, decided whether or not their families went on eating.

Winslow watched Barney, smoking the long perennial cigar, with concealed distaste as he swaggered into his office. That is, he swaggered as much as a short fat man is capable of doing. From his six foot height, Winslow looked down on Barney, thinking that his face was redder than usual because of the heat. Winter or summer Barney always looked moist; now, his bald head, except for the thin tufts of hair on each side, glistened in a sheen of wetness.

Winslow detested the man. He hadn't been able to stand the sight of him ever since that first day when he had reported to Barney's office. Barney hadn't even shook hands; in fact, he hadn't even stood up. He remained seated at his desk as Cordell introduced them. His outstanding records had preceded him and he expected a cordial reception but Barney immediately began berating him as if he had already done something wrong. He had been completely taken aback by his opening tirade.

"I'm going to be watching you every minute, young man!" Barney said as he picked up his records from his desk and waved them at him. "I don't give a damn what any paper says. I don't go by anybody else's recommendations. I want proof for myself. I go strictly by what I see with my own two eyes." His small eyes had narrowed into slits in his pudgy face and he squinted at him as he went on, "And you can better believe they'll be looking at you close! That little piece of paper you got from college don't mean a damn hill of beans to me!" He drew himself up to the full height of his short stature proudly and looked arrogantly into Winslow's startled face. "You wouldn't ever think it but I don't have a college diploma..." his voice boomed loudly, then he paused for effect, before adding, "and I own this place!"

Winslow, shocked at the unexpected harangue, remained speechless. Barney had dismissed him with, "It's what you do and what you can put out—that's all that counts with me. Just remember that!" He had turned back to his desk then. When he had remained standing for a moment, too stunned to say anything, Barney lifted his head long enough to say, "That will be all. Cordell will show you around the plant."

Even now, Winslow could still recall the humiliation he had felt that day as he turned and left Barney's office. Barney's words brought his mind back to the present. "Winslow, you'll be in charge of hiring the extra help. Cordell is needed in the plant so you can take over the hiring. He will instruct you in the procedure." He took a puff on the cigar and exhaled before going on. "You'll be hiring a man for the noon shift today." He paused, then added, "You can get him cheap." He drew himself up as tall as possible, looking up at Winslow through narrowed eyes, "And I want him cheap!"

"But, Mr. Blossom," Winslow said, "these men can't possibly live on less than 50 cents an hour!"

"Winslow, who the hell do you think you're working for—those damn peasants out there—or me?" Barney exploded. His face turned even more scarlet and a blue vein popped out on his forehead. "In case you don't know it, you're here to try to make money for this company—not to worry about every Tom, Dick and Harry out there!" The anger in his voice subsided somewhat as he went on. "If those men don't like my wages, they can go try to get a job someplace else in this town. I don't make them work for me—on the contrary, they come begging me for work!"

What a lousy son-of-a-bitch, Winslow thought.

Barney paused to light the cigar that had gone out, watching Winslow's face closely all the while, trying to size up the effect of his words on him. He wouldn't tolerate anyone working for him who was squeamish about squeezing every bit of work for the least amount of pay out of his laborers. He wasn't entirely sure about Winslow. He had to admit though that he was a good worker, conscientious and capable in his performance. *I handled him right—old Barney has always known how to handle his employees.* Barney thought smugly, complacently.

Between puffs on the cigar, Barney continued talking slowly and with emphasis. "If they want to work for four or five cents an hour, that is strictly up to them—not to me." He removed the cigar, now lit, from his mouth. Looking directly into Winslow's eyes, he added, stressing each word, "And, least of all, not up to you!"

Winslow started to say something but Barney

interrupted. "If you want to keep your job, get your ass out there and start interviewing those men!" All the while Barney had been strutting impatiently about the room with his hands thrust into his pant's pockets. He stopped now in front of Winslow to say, "And you'd damn well better get them as cheap as you can." Withdrawing a hand from his pocket, he punctuated his words by tapping a forefinger against Winslow's chest, "If the college kid can't handle it, there's plenty of men who would jump at the chance to have this job."

Winslow's hated himself for not hitting him in the face. Instead, he stood there motionless as Barney turned on his heel and strode out of the office. Cordell following behind him like a cowed puppy dog. Winslow remained standing for a long moment before collapsing into his chair. *I don't have anymore backbone than Cordell,* he thought contemptuously as his head sunk into his hands.

They scarcely looked at one another when Cordell returned at 10:30 and asked, "Are you ready?" Winslow didn't bother to answer. *I don't need Cordell's help to instruct me on this stinking procedure,* he thought. Quickly, he walked past him to the outside platform and looked down at the group of haggard faces that turned anxiously upward to him as he approached. Conversation ceased and silence fell over them. He started to speak and, as he did so, he looked slowly from one man to another, seeing traces of both hope and hopelessness in the eyes that gazed steadily at him. He could not bring himself to say that he was "interviewing" them, as Cordell did. To him, it was a mockery and he refused to strike yet another blow at the dignity of these men by insulting their intelligence. They knew, as well as he, that they were being auctioned on Barney Blossom's slave block.

"Men," he began reluctantly, "as I'm sure you know, we don't need much extra help at this time..." He paused and added hesitantly, "and we need only one man today." He braced himself against the audible groan that went up. Darting his eyes swiftly about the group, he counted 19. *Nineteen,* he thought, *and only one lousy job.* He felt a gnawing at the pit of his stomach as he saw hope fade from faces. The image of his father's weary lined countenance the last time he saw him before he died flashed suddenly before him.

Winslow stood, silent, staring over the heads of the men to avoid looking at the despair in their eyes, waiting for the bidding to begin. The men were all too familiar with the procedure that was now standard for Blossom's as it had been since the Depression began. The wages for regular employees were 50 cents an hour. Pay for extra workers was determined by pitting them against each other, forcing them to auction off their labor, with the reward of a job going to the lowest bidder. Additional workers were hired occasionally for only a day to fill in for a full-time employee who was ill or, infrequently, for several days at an unexpected large shipment of grain or flour.

"Fifty cents an hour!" one man spoke loudly, beginning the bidding hopefully. The bidding, by unspoken agreement, was always started at the highest possible level—at the same wage amount that the regular employees earned. Everyone was aware that this was only a formality, a desperate attempt, albeit, futile, to keep the sum boosted.

"I'll work for forty-five!" Mr. Hawkins spoke in a quavering voice from the outer fringe of the group where he was standing.

From his position in the center of the assemblage, Jon glanced at him. Jon had not had a truck run now in almost two months. Shipments had been drastically cut and, with two men ahead of him in seniority, there had been no haul for him to make. Like the others, he was here in hope of obtaining work for a day or even for an hour.

Mr. Hawkins shifted awkwardly, uneasy under the scrutiny of the others after making his bid. At 68, he was the oldest man present. Jon had known him as long as he could remember. When he was a boy, the Hawkins had lived a few houses from his own and he guessed that Mr. Hawkins had been the nearest thing to a father that he had ever had. He had taken the time to talk to him, to listen, when he was growing up. Jon recalled the innumerable times that he had been included when Mr. Hawkins had taken his own sons fishing or played ball with them. Now, his oldest son was dead. He had left a wife and two little ones who, out of necessity, had moved in with Mr. and Mrs. Hawkins. Carrying this added burden was a tremendous hardship on the old couple, both in failing health.

"Thirty-five!" Jon recognized the strong voice as that of Hollis Thompson, another old friend. Jon was familiar with every voice, every face, every man present. Literally growing up with most, he had played, fought and gone to school with them. Some were as close as brothers. A tall raw-boned man, Thompson's anxiety was plainly etched on his face. He had five children to feed.

"Thirty!" Jim Sanders spoke huskily, coughing. The chronic cough was aggravated by Jim's noticeable nervousness which increased the frequency of the attacks. Looking at the wan pale face, a long ago childhood scene flashed through Jon's mind. He had gotten in trouble over Jim on their very first day in the first grade at school. Jim, always small for his age, had been undernourished, thin and shy. With five brothers and sisters, he shared a ne'er-do-well father who deserted his family periodically. Folks said that, like a bad apple, he always showed up. And, show up he did after one of his lengthy absences, remaining only long enough to inevitably impregnate Jim's mother again before departing once more. The family's home was a converted barn near the edge of town. Kindly friends had made it halfway inhabitable, installing flooring and sealing openings and cracks as well as possible. The combination of this cold drafty shelter that induced perpetual colds and the lack of the right kind of food, or, at times, the lack of any at all , had taken its toll on the family's health.

Pete, the class bully, had picked mercilessly on Jim that first day. Finally, at recess, Jon could stand it no longer. Much to everyone's surprise, including his own, he had doubled his fist and let it fly straight to Pete's nose. He felt it flatten under his fist and saw the spurt of blood. Pete, howling in pain, ran to the teacher. She punished Jon by making him stand with his nose pressed against a chalk ring that she had drawn on the blackboard. He had been humiliated in front of the class but he didn't care for he had been proud of himself—proud that he had stood up to a boy bigger and stronger than he was. That had been the first moment in his young life that he had felt as though he were a man.

Jon, scrutinizing Jim's face as his mind digressed to the past, wondered if he still remembered that day in school. He sure hasn't changed much, Jon thought. He's still as pale and skinny and sickly as ever! Except now, he has a family of his own and his mother to take care of.

"Twenty-five!" Jon did not have to look. He knew the voice of Pete Jackson well, the class bully of that little drama so many years ago. As the years passed by, Pete had retained his status of being the strongest, biggest and best, towering head and shoulders over all the other boys in physical prowess. Proficiently natural at sports, he grew into the town's number-one all-accord athlete. As the high school football hero, he was granted all the accolades that Anseltown's worshipful admirers could provide. Idolized by the opposite sex, he could walk away with any girl he wanted—and he did.

When the war came along, he was the first one in
Anseltown to go. Barely 18, he enlisted in the army and
was acclaimed, with much pomp and fanfare, the day he
went off to battle the enemy. An impromptu town band was
hurriedly composed of anyone who owned an instrument
and could play a recognizable tune. With Pete in their
midst and the townsfolk following, the band marched from
the courthouse to the train depot, sending Pete off with a
patriotic flourish that made him swell with pride. Jon,
even now, could see him as he looked that day: Strong,
robustly healthy and modestly bashful at all the fuss
accorded him, but secretly pleased.

When Pete returned from the war, he was met by the
same band and townspeople who had bade him farewell
and who were now welcoming him home with open arms
and hearts. But, they were shocked to find that he was no
longer the carefree youth who had departed so eagerly
and willingly. Pale and gaunt, his uniform hanging loosely
or his body, Pete descended the steps of the train and
walked slowly toward his mother. A low, but audible, gasp
went up from the women. The men shook their heads
silently. Pete walked with a pronounced limp. Somewhere
in France, at a place with a strange sounding name, a
German bullet had found its target—a mark that not only
would make him lame in one leg but would also inflict an
invisible, though very real, scar on him and his family for
the rest of their lives. They had heard of his injury, but to
the people of Anseltown, the idea wouldn't register that
anything could happen to Pete. Nothing could hurt their
strong husky athlete. That possibility had seemed as
remote as that place in France. Yet, this cripple, this
skeleton of a man with the haunted eyes, the drawn taut
face that was no longer gay and smiling and only vaguely
resembling Pete's, stood before them.

A stunned stillness fell over the audience. The

atmosphere, strained and somber, was diametrically opposed to the lilting triumphant happiness that sparked the day of his departure. Hurriedly and self-consciously, Mayor Ansel gave his speech, declaring the town's gratitude for all that Pete had suffered and sacrificed to make the world safe for democracy. The band played a halfhearted rendition of "When Johnny Comes Marching Home Again," after which the members quietly commenced dismantling their instruments. The people stood about awkwardly. Hesitantly, they began to step forward and clasp Pete's hand respectfully, saying quietly "Welcome home, son," and "Glad to have you back" and "It' s good to see you," without quite looking him in the eye. Then, the crowd quickly dispelled and melted away until Pete and his mother stood alone. Looking about uncertainly, Pete said, "Let's go home, Mama."

After his return, girls no longer pursued him for Pete was not the same fun-loving boy they had known. He was a cripple and a stranger. Several months later, he married Mary Turner, a shy quiet girl, a girl he had not paid attention to previously. She wasn't a pretty girl but she wasn't "unpretty" either. Possessing a soft, gentle manner, she had a sweet nature that reflected appealingly in her face.

Jon, thinking back now, supposed that Mary had always been in love with Pete but had felt that she had no chance against all the competition. He wondered if she were truly happy with the prize she had won, a prize which she had, heretofore, obviously thought was beyond her reach, a prize that had been so lightly cast aside by others.

Pete had inquired about his old job at the cottonseed mill that he had before going to war. He was informed that it was no longer available. Apologetically, the plant supervisor told him that business had been slow, forcing him to let some workers go. Awkward and uncomfortable, he was noticeably relieved when Pete left. After that, Pete walked the streets, searching for work, any type of job. The excuse was always the same—no help was presently needed. Pete knew this wasn't so. For, in many cases, men were hired after he had applied. He recognized the true reason for their refusal to hire him. They were afraid to take a chance on him. They were afraid that he wouldn't be able to hold up his end of work because of his bad leg. Discouraged and despondent, he began to feel like only half a man. Finally, Mr. Rogers, who had been a lifelong friend of Pete's father, now dead, had hired him to help in his shoe store. Although hiring Pete through kindness and pity, Mr. Rogers succeeded in convincing him that he needed him. Soon, however, he was delighted to find that his generosity had been rewarded twofold. For Pete's eager willingness to work and to learn every facet of the shoe trade had increased Mr. Rogers' business and relieved him from shouldering the sole responsibility of the store. Operating it alone had necessitated long hours, a burden that had begun to take its toll lately on Mr. Rogers' advanced age.

To Pete's perplexity, his friends continued to treat him differently. He sensed the reticence, the strained attitude toward him. Outwardly, they were friendly enough, even too much so, shaking his hand too long, talking too effusively, not casually and easily as before. He noticed they never looked directly at him or his limp but gazed right past him instead, lingering only long enough to be civil before hurrying away. He missed the easy camaraderie, the jokes, the understanding he had enjoyed with these people that he knew and loved before he went away to war. Gradually, Pete became withdrawn. Reciprocating, he avoided his friends as they, in turn, shunned him. Polite, efficient and business-like to them as customers of the store, he kept to himself and to his home and family when he wasn't working.

Now, in the midst of the Depression, Mr. Rogers had been forced to close his store. Pete, out of work once again, was competing with men who had no affliction to handicap their remotely slim chances of landing a job.

Pete must be a very bitter man, Jon thought, looking at his haggard face. *Hell, I would be.* He had seen the way that people treated Pete when he came back—a cripple from the war. They hadn't wanted any part of him anymore, especially men like Barney Blossom. They felt that Pete wasn't man enough now to bust his butt slaving for them. *He could be of no use to them any longer, so just ignore him.* Jon felt his anger mounting. *The stinking, dirty bastards in this stinking dirty town! This hole doesn't deserve a man like Pete. Hell, what a waste! This whole town isn't worth a hair from anyone's head—much less a bum leg from a man like Pete Jackson.*

Jon clenched his teeth angrily. He'd like to see this excuse for a town blown off the face of the map. And he wished the first ones wiped out could be the well-to-do bastards who robbed the poor. His face darkened with fury as he thought of the irony of it—of the rich robbing the poor. *Yes, just as surely as if they held a gun to their victims' heads, the rich bastards robbed the destitute of their dignity and labor, forcing them to work for so little they could barely keep their families from starving. They know they've got us over a barrel–that there's no way out for us,* he fumed. His mind was inflamed, a turmoil of torment and indignation. He rubbed a tightly doubled-up fist furiously into the palm of his other hand in frustration, wanting to lash out at Barney Blossom—at all the Barney' Blossoms in Anseltown. Through clenched teeth, he muttered helplessly, "Damn them!"

"I'll be glad to work for twenty!" another voice spoke. The words drew Jon's thoughts back, with difficulty, to his

present surroundings and the event taking place. He had
not interjected a bid yet. He hadn't bothered. *We're just
prolonging the agony,* he thought, *just sweating out the
routine preliminaries before getting down to brass tacks—
and rock bottom. Everyone knows the bidding won't stop
until it hits rock bottom.* He had been through this so many
times this last year. The scene was all too familiar. He felt
as though he were a play actor, performing the same role
on a stage over and over like the actors he had seen in the
traveling medicine show which had come through
Anseltown several years ago. He had been fascinated by
them, dwelling on the glamour of their lives and the
excitement of traveling all over the country. He had often
wondered how it must be to give the same performance,
utter the same words, act the same scenes, night after
night. *Well , now I know,* he thought wryly, *and it's boring
as hell. Only this isn't acting. It's for real. And, there's no
glamour in this drama. No makeup to remove when it's over.
No celebration or party after the performance.*

Jon looked at the worried perspiring men surrounding
him. He smelled the heavy odor of body sweat that
permeated and hung in the hot stationary stillness.
Suddenly, he was seized with an almost overwhelming
insane desire to laugh. *When this scene is over,* he thought,
*not a damn thing's going to change. Nobody's going to look
one bit different. We're all going to look just exactly the same
as always, smell like goats, have empty bellies and be
precisely what we are—degradingly poor.*

In his scrutiny of the men, Jon's eye stopped on Tad
Sloane who had made the last bid. Tad had been the
scandalous, but lovable, town gigolo until he married six
years ago. A dark ruggedly handsome man, Tad had thick
black wavy hair, smoldering black eyes and a cleft in his
chin that had proved irresistible to the feminine gender of
Anseltown. An equally amorous and fickle Romeo, he had

quickly chased every girl in sight that he fancied and, just as quickly, dropped her after a triumphant conquest. His warm vibrant friendliness endeared Tad to all, both young and old alike. His romantic antics were jokingly tolerated and he was affectionately dubbed "Playboy." A stock question repeatedly asked of him, "When are you getting married, Tad?", was countered by his witty stock question in reply, "Why bother to buy a cow when milk is so cheap?"

Innumerable hearts were broken and the town was taken completely by surprise the day Tad announced that he had eloped the night before with Alice Long, the girl from Dallas, who had been visiting her cousin in Anseltown for a week. Driving across the state line to Oklahoma, they were married immediately without having to wait the customary three days required by law in Texas. As usual in Anseltown, tongues wagged in abasement, savoring and spreading the rumor like wildfire that theirs was a "have to" marriage; the majority believed the worst. This gossip was soon quelched, however, by no evidence of pregnancy which proved to be a cruel disappointing hoax to most. Most, then, decided to believe the former rampant rumor that Alice came from wealthy oil parents who would never have granted consent for their daughter to marry a "commoner" from Anseltown, thus, the reason for their elopement.

The incredulous disbelief of his friends and their jesting mockery that "Tad had finally got caught and hitched" soon gave way to envious admiration when they beheld his bride. For the girl who had stolen Tad's heart and charmed him into capitulation had long blonde hair, cornflower blue eyes and pale golden skin, presenting an illusion of a fragile Dresden doll. After one look at her, everyone was satisfied that their roving Romeo had not been trapped. Tad had willingly fallen, and fallen hard, for this beautiful girl-like but all woman, "Alice in

Wonderland." And Tad, in their estimation, could do no wrong so they eagerly approved and accepted her. At least, his immediate friends did. But Tad was from a poor family on the "wrong side of the tracks" so Alice was not welcomed into the affluent, better educated, more sophisticated society on the "right side of the tracks." This blatant snobbery was a bitter medicine for Alice to swallow. Accustomed to wealth, she had moved in the highest circles and mingled with the cream of society in her family's exclusive coterie of friends.

Her parents could not and would not accept their daughter's choice of husbands. Although deeply hurt, Alice was so much in love with Tad that she refused to allow their attitude to bother her, dismissing it from her mind. However, as the months passed, her heart ached to see them. And, when their baby arrived a year later, she longed to show them their first grandson. In addition, her life, heretofore, had been centered in the lap of luxury. Now the strain and hardship of living without the material advantages, taken so lightly before, was beginning to wear heavily on her.

With the baby only 3 months old, Alice found herself pregnant once again. She felt helpless, trapped. Her discontent grew, along with the mounds of endless washing of diapers and greasy uniforms that Tad wore as a mechanic. She loved Tad but, upon examining the life in Anseltown that she had made for herself, she found it sadly lacking. The excitement of first love and marriage had dimmed, giving way to day-after-day sameness, work and boredom. Also, she did not understand these people who were Tad's friends. She was alienated from her family, snubbed and ignored by the leisured class on the "right" side of town. Neither had she anything in common with these working friends of his. Isolated and alone, she felt like a prisoner in a cell whose bars were drawing closer and closer, hemming her tightly inside.

All during her second pregnancy, Alice found fault with Tad, fighting over any and everything, and over nothing at all. She would become furious at herself for hurting Tad—but she could not help it. She knew that he loved her very much; that despite his former escapades, she was the only girl he ever really loved. Worshipping the ground she walked on, Tad was made unbearably miserable by her unhappiness. Yet, he did not know what to do about it.

After their second son was born, Alice could bear it no longer. When he was 6 weeks old, she left both the babies with her cousin and took a bus to Dallas. Tad, returning home from work, was frantic to find her gone. He called her parents' home, only to be informed that she was safe and did not wish to see or speak to him. He made innumerable trips to Dallas but they ended in dismal failure. The servants, given orders not to permit him past the threshold, strictly enforced them. He never got through the front door.

For the first six months, Tad never gave up his efforts to contact Alice, longing to persuade his girl-wife to return to him and their sons. But his perseverance was all for naught. Slowly, he lost hope. Tad changed shockingly. His hair turned prematurely gray and he grew gaunt and thin. Silent and morose, he never smiled and scarcely spoke to anyone. His friendly outgoing nature was lost to the past. Moving robot-like, he went to work in the morning and promptly returned home in the evening to close the door behind him and shut the world out. Tad, seemingly, desired to blot out everything and everyone, to lose himself in the darkness now that the light of his life had been turned off.

Now, Jon saw the beads of sweat standing on Tad's forehead. His dark eyes were twin mirrors, reflecting the pain within for all the world to see. *Why would any man let*

a woman hurt him that much, Jon asked himself in disgust.
Then, a disgruntling thought flashed through his mind,
drawing him up sharply, *Elisabeth did the same thing to
me,* he told himself, *only in a different way. She deserted me
too—in an even more destructive way. She refused to leave
Anseltown with me when I could have had the baseball
contract. She had no confidence in me as a man.* His face
flushed red. Anger washed over him, enveloping him as it
always did whenever he was reminded of his lost
opportunity for rejuvenation. His one chance to find a new
and better life away from this town, a life he had craved
desperately, he had wasted.

"I'll work for ten!" The words where spoken low,
resignedly. Jon, engrossed in his own private thoughts,
had missed the intermittent bid for fifteen cents an hour.
He glanced over his right shoulder into the face of Harley
Potter standing behind him. Little streams of sweat, rolling
down his wide face, came from Harley's bald crown which
was framed on both sides by thin strands of hair that also
extended across the back of his head. A huge squarely-
structured man, his broad open face was illumined with
large soft brown eyes whose gentleness belied the strength
of his physical build. Jon studied his face in half admiration,
half pity. Harley was the kindest, best human being he had
ever known. This analysis of his character was viewed in
the same vein by all those knew Harley.

Now, 40 years of age, Harley looked much older-closer
to 50. When he was 14, his father died. He was forced to
quit school and go to work to support his mother, younger
brother and sister. Eric Warren, owner of the one drug
store in Anseltown, hired him to sweep and clean his
store. When he proved to be any extremely industrious
and conscientious worker, Warren fired the soda jerk, his
sole employee prior to Harley. Continuing to do the
janitorial work, Harley took care of the fountain duties as

well. Warren increased his salary from five to eight dollars a week, the amount he had paid the former soda jerk. Still paying the same compensation, Warren was now getting two jobs done simultaneously. Harley did not complain. He needed the work desperately. Besides, it was not in his nature to complain. *No one could truthfully say that they had ever heard him complain,* Jon thought. *And, if anyone ever had just cause for complaint, Harley did.*

Over the years, Warren reaped the rewards of Harley's efficient and tireless labor, his scrupulous honesty in dealing with both the public and his employer. More and more, he turned the operation of the store over to Harley. He was growing older and wanted to take things easy. Before hiring Harley, he had even thought of selling out, but with such a trustworthy employee, it would be more profitable to keep it. Warren recognized the bonanza he possessed in him. But he never let on to Harley. On the contrary, his manner toward him was stern and gruff. After all, Warren reasoned, you had to keep your employees on their toes. Make them toe the mark; don't let them step out of line. You have to keep these people under your thumb at all times and, above all, never let them get independent. It would just cause trouble. They wouldn't know how to handle independence, to be on their own. They should just be grateful to their mentors who provided jobs for them. They were respectful enough when they came to you, with hat in hand, asking for a job. And you had to make sure that they maintained that respect, make them know that you are the boss.

Warren had inherited the drug store from his father. This was the natural scheme of life in Anseltown. Businesses were passed from father to son, from one generation to the next. This kept the flow of wealth in the same families, perpetuating the power and influence, indeed, the life and death hammerlock hold of the few over

the helpless masses of the majority. Those unfortunate
enough to be born poor were caught as flies in a web,
powerless to escape. The spiders, whom fate had haplessly
chosen by birthright, toyed with them, exploited them,
controlled their destiny and often destroyed those not
strong enough to survive the macabre games.

Warren's wife hired Harley's mother as her
housekeeper, making him feel even more magnanimous.
He often remarked that, between the two of them, they
supported the Potter family. Louisa Warren paid Harley's
mother 80 cents a day, piously informing everyone that
she hired *white* help for "I'd rather help our *own kind*." She
failed to add that she disliked having Negroes in her house
or that she paid only five cents more a day for a white
woman.

Domestic services by the women of poor families, both
white and black, were vied for shamelessly by the wives of
the town's leading citizens. Amid the competitive
exploitation, comparisons were boastfully noted regarding
the procurement of the best laborers for the least
compensation—"why, for just *practically next to nothing!*"
Even the wife of the minister of the largest Protestant
church, attended by the prominent of Anseltown,
participated in this pecuniary game of purchasing pitiless
backbreaking drudgery for only pennies a day.

Harley, through years of labor and love, had managed
to see his younger brother through college and pay for his
sister's business course before she married and moved out
of state. After graduating from college, Harley's brother
married a former classmate and settled in Fort Worth
where he obtained a good job. In time, they had three
children. Harley continued taking care of his mother who
had been left partially paralyzed by a stroke five years
before. His brother and sister made no effort to help with
her care. But Harley held no grudge against them. He was

proud of the fact that he had helped promote them to a better life than he had known. And, finally, at 30 years of age, he was able to marry Elinor, the only girl he had ever courted and loved. Elinor had waited patiently over the years for him and, when they married, she accepted the care of Harley's mother without complaint.

Elinor and Harley, compatibly suited, complemented each other. Both, friendly, gregarious and unstingily generous, gave freely of themselves. The first ones called in time of crisis or need, they were eager and ready to lend a helping hand, for their love had no reservations. And, although loved in return, their friends unintentionally took them for granted for Harley and Elinor, the proverbial towers of strength, were always *there*.

Harley's brother had lost his job the year before as a result of his company's cutbacks in the current economic crisis. He had walked the streets day after day, month after month, searching in vain for another one. As hundreds of other college graduates like him were doing across the country, he humbly presented himself before endless, mostly indifferent, juries of interviewers before dejectedly finding himself out on the street again, walking and applying. This futile procedure was repeated day after day until it all became just the price he had to exact from himself each day in order to earn the right to rest at the end of it.

At last, he was forced to accept welfare to prevent his family's starvation. This indignity was a cruel blow to his pride, one that left him almost a mental cripple. Extremely depressed, he took to his bed for days on end, unwilling to leave it. So broken in spirit by the rejection he had encountered at every turn, he refused to subject himself to more of the same when he knew that it was useless. As a consequence, violent arguments ensued with his wife who concluded that he had simply stopped trying to find work.

To appease her, he made the rounds once again, even going so far as to request notes from interviewers verifying his applications which he could present as evidence to her.

Capitulating to welfare, to something that he had not worked for and earned on his own initiative and labor, was unbearably repulsive and degrading. He was unable to endure this final humiliation. His wife, returning from her second visit to the welfare office, found her husband dead in bed with a bullet in his brain, the gun still clutched in his hand.

She and the three children moved in with Harley and Elinor. With no family of her own, there was no alternative. They were welcomed with open, loving arms despite the heavy burden which they added. Harley had been out of work for over a month. Mr. Warren, prudently foreseeing further economic decline, had sold the drugstore. The new owner planned to use his own family in its operation and had no job for Harley. The newly increased responsibilities had quickly diminished Harley's modest savings.

"I'll work for five cents an hour!" Pete Jackson almost shouted the words. He spoke immediately after Harley gave his bid, almost interrupting him with the inevitable bid that everyone had been waiting for, indeed, had known would come from the very start.

Jon's eyes moved slowly over the faces, red from the heat, the perspiration standing in beads which gradually disintegrated into rivulets that rolled downward. Only too familiar with this experience, he knew that the sweat was as much a reaction from the strain of the bidding as it was from the temperature. His stomach muscles tightened spasmodically at the consuming fire that electrified the eyes of the men. They were glaring at each other with distrust, suspicion and something else as well, something that he did not readily identify at first. Then, suddenly, he recoiled in disbelief as he recognized hatred burning blindly in the haunted desperate eyes.

Damn it all to hell! What have we come to? Jon's mind supplied its own answer even while shrinking away in horror, trying to deny it. *These men who have known and loved each other all their lives have become just like animals now—they could actually kill each other.* Rage filled his being as his mind stormed on. *The sons-of-bitches: The Barney Blossoms, the Warrens, the Ansels and all the rest of them! Look what they've done to us—pitted us against each other, friend against friend, neighbor against neighbor, even brother against brother. They've filled us full of hate—making us fight each other for their lousy stinking jobs!* Jon's fists were clenched so tightly that his fingernails were cutting into his palms and drawing blood but he was not aware of the pain. His thoughts raced on, continuing to torment him! *Instead of hating the buzzards that are gutting us, we've turned on each other! We ought to be going after the leeches that suck our blood, drain us dry of everything they can drag out of us for nothing—so they can go on getting richer.* Jon rubbed his hand across his face, wiping blood across his cheek. *And there's not a damn thing we can do about it,* he thought hopelessly. Suddenly he felt very weak.

An uneasy, impatient quiet had fallen over the group. Not moving, they stood with eyes glued to Winslow's face, waiting for him to choose his man. Instead, the silence was broken by a voice other than Winslow's.

"I'll work for a sack of flour, Mr. Winslow!" It was Harley Potter. All heads turned in unison toward him, their eyes raking him coldly. Harley lowered his head momentarily to avoid looking at them; then, raising it, he mumbled apologetically, "I'm sorry, fellows, but we ran out of flour this morning and the kids are hungry. They've only had biscuits and gravy to eat the last two days."

An angry mutter went up from the group. They did not

want to hear excuses. This was a precedent. It was the first time anyone had ever offered to work for less than five cents an hour—for no money at all—for only a sack of flour instead.

Winslow saw the men move menacingly toward Harley. Sensing the angry threatening mood, he said quickly, "You've got the job, Potter—come on up!"

Barney would be proud of me today, Winslow thought scornfully. The contempt that he felt for himself galled him. He watched apprehensively as Harley quickly came forward, the men closing in behind him. Harley, electing not to go up the steps at one side, jumped instead onto the middle part of the five-foot high platform. He elevated himself to it just as several hands, reaching out toward him, grasped at him from behind. As he slipped through them, eluding their clutches, the men remained with their hands outstretched, suspended in midair toward him for several seconds before letting them fall slowly to their sides. Harley looked down from the platform at their upturned faces, wrought with despair. They stared back at him through hate-filled eyes. He had became the object upon which they could focus and heap their frustrated hostility, for he had won the coveted award. Harley had deprived them of their prize—the chance to continue to exist for yet one more day.

Harley gazed searchingly, longingly from one man to another but he saw no understanding, found no solace. Then, quickly, he turned away to escape the animosity and malice in the smoldering eyes that were burning into his very soul. He reeled blindly his back to them and, as he walked unsteadily into the mill, tears ran down his cheeks.

Winslow had observed the drama unfolding before him from an almost trancelike state. He felt detached, a separate entity from the event taking place. It all seemed unreal.

He did not want to be a part of it for he did not want
to remember his father, to visualize him again, bowed and
stooping under the weight of endless work in order to care
for his family. A farmer, he had known no respite from
toiling the ground, coaxing an existence from the earth
despite drought, dust storms, too much rain or too many
pests that plagued the crops. But, watching the men,
Winslow unwillingly began to see his father's face etched
and reflected in each one of theirs, as they sweated and
struggled against each other. He blinked his eyes, hoping
to erase his father's image. But it was to no avail. Fate
forever seemed destined to haunt his mind that his father
had died before he could make it up to him—to make his
life worry-free for the first time. He had wanted to give
him, at long last, a justly earned reprieve from the bitter
strife, heartaches and labor that he had so patiently endured
for his family. *It isn't fair,* Winslow thought, and he asked
himself the same question now that he had tormentedly
asked himself over and over again! *Why wasn't he allowed
to live long enough so that I could have made things easy for
him—for just a little while at least?*

And, until today, when he saw the violent desperation
that had been unmasked so revealingly in these men
before him, he had never before sensed its existence in his
father. Winslow shook his head hard as though to clear
cobwebs from his mind. *No,* he thought, *he just hadn't
wanted to admit it to himself before. His father had just
never been volatile. He had tranquilized his despair,
suppressed, silenced and concealed it.* Now, Winslow
realized, and recoiled from the realization, *his father had
learned to live with the quiet desperation inside him.*

Winslow's tortured thoughts reverted to the present
when he saw the men angrily grasping at Harley from
behind as he jumped to the platform. Feeling revulsion,
Winslow knew that, had he not slipped through their

hands quickly, in another moment they would have attacked him. He stared, in stunned disbelief, at the open hatred glaring from their faces. He glanced at Harley who was now going into the mill. His glance froze and became riveted to the tears of anguish on his face. Winslow felt as though he had been hit hard in the pit of his stomach. His insides churned and sweat poured down his face. He felt dizzy. He heard Cordell call to him. Brushing roughly past his restraining hand, he rushed quickly into the mill, running the last few steps into the latrine where he vomited violently.

Jon had been jostled to one side by the men who walked after Harley as he proceeded to the platform. He looked in loathing at the hate-distorted faces with disbelief registered on his own. *Damn them! They're going to hit Harley. These crazed animals are going to beat him up! Harley—the man everybody loves—the man who has been a friend to every single one of them, the man who loaned them money when they needed it, who even helped some of them build their homes, has always been available and needy to help those of us who needed him. Now, these mad men—Harley's friends—are ready to kill him. And, all because he was willing to work for a stinking sack of flour.*

Repulsed at the sight, he stared angrily at the men clutching at Harley. Clenching his fists tightly, he moved swiftly and purposely forward. His brain clicked wrathfully. *These mad dogs may have lost their senses but, if one of them lays a hand on Harley, the bastard will have me to deal with.* Then, seeing Harley safely on the platform, free of those behind him, Jon breathed a ragged sigh of relief. And he, unlike the others blinded by hate, saw the tears in Harley's eyes as he turned away from them. Jon felt nauseated. The murderous helpless rage that enveloped him was overpowering in its intensity. Loudly and venomously, he spat out, "The sons-a-bitches who run this son-of-a-bitchin' town!"

Later that evening, Wayne Winslow sat in his living room, staring sightlessly through the window at the gathering darkness. When his wife called him to dinner, he never moved. Lost in thought, he heard nothing. She came to the door and started to say something then decided against it when she saw his face. She sat down quietly beside him and put her hand on his arm. "What's the matter, honey?" she asked gently. He looked into her face a long time before answering.

Beth had been his wife for five years, since their first year in college. She had dropped out of school and took a job in order for Wayne to continue. She was fiercely ambitious for her husband. He had recognized this drive of hers and accepted it as only natural that she should feel this way about her husband's career. After all, she had abandoned her own to promote his. Young and in love, she wanted so much out of life for them. Lately, however, the thought had crossed his mind that she was permitting her forceful aspirations to interfere and control their lives to an abnormal, unhealthy degree.

He had wanted a baby now but Beth had objected, saying that it was too soon for them to be saddled with a baby. There was plenty of time for children, she argued, after they gained the objectives for which they had struggled so long. She obviously thought she had convinced him that her way was the right way when he finally stopped bringing up the subject. Small traces of bitterness and resentment toward her rancored him despite his attempt to quell these feelings, for he loved her.

But, Winslow thought now, he couldn't help feeling that Beth had changed. She was not the same unselfish girl that he had married. Now it seemed more important to her to collect prominence and social status than to please her husband. He studied Beth closely as she sat beside him.

He saw the taut lines that were beginning to show on her pinched, pretty face. Since they had come to Anseltown, she had grown thin, thinner than she had ever been. He attributed her nervousness and loss of weight to her obsessive desire to succeed here and to impress the people that mattered in Anseltown, to have them accept this personable and brilliant young couple into their hallowed circle. Beth had seen to it that she met the right people, moved in the right groups, even went to the right church. She insisted that they join the country club although it was way beyond their means at this point.

He realized that a certain amount of "joining" and socializing was necessary for them to "get ahead" as Beth so often reminded him, but he felt that she greatly overdid it, going overboard in her aspiring endeavors. He was often embarrassed by the obviousness of her fawning eagerness, her society ladder efforts, the strain and pressure of the social climbing. The ever present social climbing was taking its toll on her health and placing an uneasy cloud over their lives.

"What's the matter, Wayne?" Beth repeated the question again, but, this time, her voice held a sharp irritable edge that he had become familiar with lately. "And why are you looking at me like that?" Secretly, she hoped that he was not going to harp about their starting a family again.

"I'm awfully tired, Beth" he said, leaning back against the cushions. Then, he related the day's events at the mill: His encounter with Barney Blossom, the bidding for the job and Harley Potter winning out by working for a sack of flour to feed his family. He told her of the hostile feelings, the hatred and resentment of the men toward Potter which almost caused them to attack him. He did not tell her of seeing the image of his father's face in those bidding for work nor of his sickness afterwards.

When he had finished, Beth seemed relieved. She dismissed the incident lightly, saying, "Don't take it so seriously, Wayne. Remember our English course in college and the aphorism by Voltaire—'Let each man tend his own garden'." She rose abruptly and went back to the kitchen.

He didn't answer. His eyes followed her as she left the room; his lips compressed to a narrow line. Exasperated, he shook his head saying aloud, "She missed the whole point."

He continued to sit in the deepening gloom, alone with his thoughts. He sighed deeply, wearily, recalling another line by another man, Edmund Burke, "The only thing necessary for the triumph of evil is that good men do nothing."

CHAPTER 14

"Yonder comes old Mayor Ansel asslin' down the street," Jon remarked. He and Lonnie Rogers stood in front of Roger's Shoe Shop across from the courthouse. It was 10 o'clock of another sultry July morning and Jon had already made the rounds—the mill, factories, cafes, even offering to clean the offices of the courthouse, searching for any kind of work. It was the same as yesterday and the day before and the day before that. There were no jobs to be found. He hadn't had a truck run since May when he had been laid off indefinitely. He didn't want to go home in failure once again. He didn't want to face Elisabeth and see the worry in her eyes with the unasked question that echoed through his own mind. *How much longer are we going to be able to feed the children?*

To avoid this cheerless prospect, Jon wandered to town to meet with the other men who gathered there to sit on the benches around the square and discuss their plight. Essentially, though, they wished to postpone the inevitable dismal confrontation at home. Too, there was always the faint hope of picking up some hint or sign of work that might be available somewhere, anywhere in town. For it was here on the courthouse lawn that gossip, miscellaneous tidbits of information and news were passed along. By the time the small daily newspaper came off the press in the afternoon, it was only an official confirmation of the news that everyone already knew about the events of the town and its citizens.

"You can set your watch by Sol," Mr. Rogers said, glancing at the mayor's approaching figure and slowly pulling out his gold pocket watch from its resting place near his belt. It hung suspended from its connecting gold chain that was attached in the button hole of his vest. Slightly stooped from age, Lonnie Rogers was, nevertheless, a distinguished man with a sheen of silver hair that framed a face devoid of lines despite his advanced years. Upon meeting him for the first time, one was surprised to find his eyes still brightly blue, youthfully clear and possessing such an electric element that they almost seemed to give off sparks. They made a contradictory, but striking, contrast to his shining white hair. "Yep," he continued, "it's 5 minutes after 8. He's right on the dot."

Mayor Ansel's daily schedule was well-known to the town after his 25 year rule over it. Promptly at 8 o'clock each morning, five days a week, he arrived at the bank building where his office was located and parked in the space reserved for him. From there, he walked two blocks down Texas Street, the main street running through the heart of town to the Lone Star Cafe where he had his morning coffee and held court with his city officials. It was here that he heard his councilmen's pros and cons on the town's operation and the discussions on the state of their business affairs. Only the business owners comprised the city council. Mayor Ansel listened carefully, sifting through the trivia, tempering and testing the attitude of his subjects. And, it was also here that the mayor conducted his first priority, issuing his orders and instructions for the management of Anseltown.

Mayor Ansel moved slowly along the sidewalk, nodding and speaking to the merchants as they came to their doorways to pay their respects. They would give him time to get settled in his usual chair at his usual table in the cafe before following him for the customary session. The manner of the mayor's greeting made it clearly apparent to the recipients, as well as the onlookers, which ones were in current esteem and which ones had fallen from grace. For anyone who dared to oppose the mayor's actions or views was shunned and ignored until he had properly redeemed himself.

Few had the fortitude to oppose Mayor Ansel. Those who were bold enough to do so soon learned the danger and futility of their recklessness. According to the degree of his folly, the foolish offender was brought back into line or banished from town through financial strangulation. For, like his father before him, the mayor did not hesitate to punish the defiant through his influence and power. Bank loans could be withheld at his command. His nod could ostracize or destroy the wayward transgressor. Mayor Ansel was both hated and feared. But the ill-will of others mattered not to him. Money and power were his idols. He had both. He felt no need of anyone's good will.

A cantankerous old man, Mayor Ansel was referred to by most, out of hearing distance, of course, as "that cranky old bastard." Now, almost 70, he was even more contentious following a light stroke three years ago. It had left his right leg slightly weak and he used a pearl topped cane, leaning lightly on it when he walked. Many maintained that he did not need the cane for support but used it only to push anyone firmly aside and clear the way ahead of him, just as he had always manipulated others with his money and power along his pathway in life. Sol had not married until he was 45. Old-timers contended there had been a reason for this, asserting that Sol, as a young man of 20, had fallen deeply in love with the daughter of a worker in his father's clothing factory. His parents were violently opposed to his choice. She was the offspring of a common laborer, not from an elite family; therefore, she was not "right" for their son. The girl suddenly disappeared from town and her family reported that she had gone to reside with relatives in Kansas City. Thereafter, it was rumored that a mysterious and generous check was sent each month to a Kansas City post office box by old William Ansel.

Finally, Sol, apparently having found a proper and suitable mate that met the requirements of his parents, married a rich socialite widow from Dallas. Although, according to rumor, no love was lost in the union, it did not prevent the begetting of offspring in due time—a daughter, Janet, the first born, with a son, Sol, Jr., arriving one year later. He was immediately dubbed "Stony" by the mayor because, he would say proudly, "He's a chip off the old block."

"Howdy-do, Sol," Mr. Rogers said. He was one of the few who called the mayor by his first name, laying claim to this honor by his length of acquaintance with him.

Mayor Ansel disdained this familiarity with rare exception. The mayor was fond of relating a story regarding his name. Born to aged parents who realized that he would be their one and only offspring, they called him "Sol" for, he would say vainly, they maintained that he was their own private sun that rose and set just for them alone. But, privately, and unbeknownst to the mayor, his oft-quoted anecdote was parodied loosely by others—that after his parents took one good look at him, they promptly named him Sol for "Solitude" because they sure as hell didn't intend to have another one like him.

Mayor Ansel shook Mr. Roger's pro-offered hand heartily. "Hey there, Lon, how's ever' little thing goin' now?" he asked genially, giving the semblance of a grin. Jon noticed that the smile did not extend to his eyes. They remained cold under the gray bushy brows that matched the heavy thatch of gray hair.

He glanced at Jon, the traces of the smile disappearing from his face. He inclined his head ever so slightly, just barely nodding in acknowledgment of his presence, before turning back immediately to Mr. Rogers. Jon started to speak but he caught himself and stopped short. A wave of anger washed over him and his face turned crimson. He was relieved that he hadn't spoken or nodded.

The old son-of-a-bitch, he thought, *he's too good to speak to me. I'm a nobody—just one of the peasants.* He stood stiffly and stared hostilely at the mayor while he talked with Mr. Rogers, ignoring Jon's presence. Then he turned and walked down the street without ever looking at Jon again.

"Who does that old bastard think he is anyhow?" Jon muttered angrily.

Mr. Rogers, startled at his anger, answered somewhat testily, "Just the mayor of this town."

With an equally sharp edge to his voice and a look of disgust plainly evident on his face, Jon said, "I don't see how in hell you can stand to kowtow to him!"

Mr. Rogers sighed and said patiently, almost as if he were speaking to a small child, "Ah, Jon you're too sensitive."

"Bull-crap!" Jon spat out. "If it wasn't for that son-of-a-bitch, this town would be a good town to live in instead of the shitty place it is. It could have grown and become a very progressive city if the mayor hadn't sewed it up and prevented outside companies from coming in to start new businesses. Everyone knows that he even stopped the Southwestern States Railroad from coming through Anseltown!" Jon's eyes were twin points of anger as he stared after the mayor's retreating figure. "No sir! He wasn't about to let anyone else come in and share his wealth. With competition, he couldn't have kept all us peasants under his thumb like he has. With other jobs available to us, we wouldn't have been dependent on his alone. He'd have had to pay a decent living wage to us. And, he sure as hell wasn't about to have that happen!"

Mr. Rogers listened quietly to Jon's irate tirade. He understood his anguish. He had known Jon since he was born, as well as most everyone else of Jon's generation in Anseltown. He sympathized with their plight. He knew what it was like to be poor. The son of indigent immigrant parents, he was fortunate to have served as an apprentice of his father's and learned the art of shoe making while still a child. Old William Ansel had been pleased with his father's old world workmanship with leather and endorsed his opening a store in the early days of Anseltown. Lonnie Rogers had inherited the shop and, through his industriousness and quality of work, it had grown and prospered until he had become comfortably well-off.

Now, for the first time since his father had opened the shop 33 years ago, it was closed. Seemingly, in the Depression, shoes were a luxury. He had come to the shop each morning since its closing, simply from years of habit. He had finished taking inventory of its stock over a week ago, but still he came each morning at the usual hour, lingering to talk to passing friends, before attending the meeting at the Lone Star Cafe.

He was well aware of the poverty and conditions in Anseltown. Long ago, he had recognized the lack of human compassion in Sol Ansel. He loathed his disdainful treatment of the poor and his unfeeling regard toward them as if they weren't human beings but only instruments to be used for his own selfish purposes—merely a means to increase his own wealth and power.

Now, hearing Jon's bitterness, thoughts which he did not care to voice to Jon ran through his mind. *I wish that it would have been within my power to have changed things in Anseltown,* he fretted, *but I couldn't fight Sol Ansel alone.* A small consoling thought crossed his mind. *But, I was able to help one person—Pete Jackson—when no one else in town wanted him after the war because of his crippled leg.*

He sighed, thinking of Pete. He regretted closing the store even more for Pete's sake than for his own. *I've got enough to get by on,* he thought sadly, *but Pete doesn't and no one wants to hire him. But,* he argued with himself, *what else could I do?* Then, trying to free himself of the guilt that persisted in nagging him, he shook his head helplessly while his mind repeated *I was only one man—I couldn't fight Sol Ansel alone.*

Mr. Rogers' thoughts were interrupted by a squeal of tires. He saw the police car come around the nearby corner, braking suddenly from an accelerated speed in order to make the turn. The driver wheeled sharply to maneuver into the parking space reserved for the Chief of Police in front of the courthouse. Disengaging himself from behind the wheel of the car, a young, handsome man strutted up the walk to the courthouse. The police uniform emphasized Jess Chalker's broad-shouldered lean masculine figure.

He puffed arrogantly on a long cigar, a habit he had only recently acquired since becoming the new Chief of Police. "I hear the mayor is not too happy with his new police chief," Mr. Rogers remarked, grateful for the opportunity to change the subject.

"Well, that's just tough." Jon answered. "He's got no one but himself to blame for that, being he's the one who appointed him."

Walter Anderson, owner of the department store next to Mr. Rogers' shoe shop, walked by on his way to the Lone Star Cafe. Overhearing their conversation, he stopped and said, "That was a pretty nice wedding present for the mayor to give to his new son-in-law."

"No question about that," Jon said wryly. "He never wanted his precious daughter to marry a policeman in the first place. But, he didn't have much choice in the matter, seeing as how there was a kid on the way. And, you can bet on one thing for sure—the mayor will bring Jess up in the world. Why, he'll probably be a judge before you know it!"

Mayor Ansel and his wife had announced the marriage of their 18-year-old daughter, Janet, last Christmas day, reporting that the young couple had eloped in September. Suspicions were confirmed when it soon became evident that Janet was pregnant. There were many smug, knowing looks and "I-told-you-sos" when she gave birth to a son in the middle of April.

In January, Mayor Ansel appointed Jess as the new Chief of Police when Chief Wade Hughes had died suddenly of a heart attack after 27 years of service. Until Jess's marriage to Janet, it had been an accepted fact that old Dad Patton was next in line for the job. At the top of the list in seniority and with 16 years of unblemished service behind him, he was the logical heir. But, no one, least of all Dad Patton, was taken by surprise by the mayor's choice.

Suddenly, Jon chuckled as he watched Jess Chalker's figure disappear into the courthouse. "It sure tickles me."

"What does?" Anderson asked idly.

"Well," Jon answered, "it tickles me just thinking about how it must gall old man Ansel to have a peasant in the family." He laughed aloud, continuing, "For the first time in his life, he had to cater to a poor guy from the wrong side of the tracks! How it must have stuck in his craw to have to make Jess the Chief of Police."

Jon's voice grew derisive, "Old Jess is a good old boy but he isn't from one of the town's elite families and the mayor wouldn't so much as give him the time of day if Jess hadn't got his only daughter pregnant. Everyone knows he hates Jess but, now that he's his son-in-law, the mayor has to bring him up in the world and make him important." Jon was quiet for a minute, relishing his thoughts. Then, he chuckled once more. "Yeah, Jess is sure squattin' in tall cotton now. He wasn't so dumb. He knew how to get ahead in life."

Anderson didn't make any reply. Mr. Rogers was staring into space, not listening. Instead, his mind was obviously reflecting on the past. "I wonder whatever became of little Mae Belle Stephens?" he said.

"Who?" Jon asked.

Continuing to stare into space, Mr. Rogers was oblivious to Jon's question and did not answer. Anderson finally spoke. "Mae Belle was the girl that Sol wanted to marry years ago only his papa wouldn't let him and had her sent away." He paused, then added, "More than likely, Sol has another kid somewhere."

"She sure was a pretty little thing," Mr. Rogers said. He sighed, adding, "I guess old Sol isn't as bad as his papa was, after all. At least, he didn't send his daughter away." He remained silent for a long moment, silently reminiscing. Then, seemingly reluctant to do so, he forced his mind back to the present, sighed again and slowly pulled his watch from his pocket. Looking at it, he said, "We'd best be getting on down to the Lone Star, Walter. We're going to be late."

As they walked away, Jon called sarcastically after them, "No, by all means, gentlemen, don't keep the good mayor waiting."

"Now, what in the hell is Jess doing?" Mayor Ansel asked in an exasperated voice. He and Art Jensen, the president of the First National Bank of Anseltown, were sitting in the mayor's office conversing before going to lunch. It was their custom to lunch together each Friday, a custom that had grown to be a habit over the years. Today they procrastinated, reluctant to leave the pleasant coolness of the office and step into the sizzling August heat that baked the concrete walks outside. They dreaded the two-block long walk down Texas Street to the Lone Star Cafe that would leave them drenched with perspiration before reaching their destination.

In the midst of their conversation, they had been interrupted by the loud wail of a siren coming from the police car that was speeding down the street. Mayor Ansel rose and walked to the window. His aged steps were slow and, by the time he looked out, the car had already disappeared from view. He walked back to his desk, sat down and picked up the phone.

"Operator, get me the police station," he commanded into the instrument. Impatiently, he rapped his fingers against the desk top as he waited. "Never saw a boy who could do so damn many things wrong," he muttered to himself.

A voice answered at the other end of the line. "Let me speak to the Chief," the mayor barked. And, a moment later, "What the hell is going on, Jess?" he asked querulously. Not waiting for an answer, he went on, "If I've told you once, I know I've told you a hundred times not to use the siren in town unless it is absolutely necessary. I can't stand that noise at my age."

"Well, I'm afraid it was necessary, Mayor," Jess Chalker answered sharply. "We just threw a nigger in jail for raping and killing a white girl."

Mayor Ansel sucked in his breath. He tried to speak but no sound came. He gulped noisily and finally found his voice. "What in the hell..." he began but his voice failed him again. There was another pause during which he swallowed hard several times, his throat muscles working noticeably. His face was ashen. Art Jensen had risen from his chair, watching the mayor closely and listening intently.

Finally, the mayor rasped harshly, "Who was the girl?"

"It was the daughter—the oldest kid of the Johnsons that live on a farm about ten miles east of town."

"Will Johnson's daughter?" the mayor asked, incredulous. There was silence again before he asked, "How old was she?"

"I'm not sure," Jess answered, "about 14 or 15, I think."

"Where did it happen—how did it happen? Who was the nigger?" Mayor Ansel was beginning to recover from the initial shock and collect his thoughts.

"Her father found her by the pond on his farm about two hours ago," Chalker said. "From the marks on her throat, it looks like she was strangled."

"Who is the nigger?" the mayor asked again.

"His name is Daniel," Chalker said. "He lives over on Sam Houston Road in one of those shacks by the railroad."

"Daniel?" Ansel repeated the name then, as recognition came, he said hoarsely, "Why, that's Glo-ree's boy!"

"Is Glo-ree that nigger woman who works for you?"

"Yes," the mayor replied, then asked, "Are you sure Daniel done it?"

"It sure as hell looks that way." Stony said he saw him come out of the woods on the Johnson farm and go into Mr. Jordon's field. And..."

"What do you mean—*Stony said*? He's in school," the mayor interrupted.

"Well, Mayor, it seems like he played hooky this morning to go hunting for squirrels. You know how he likes to hunt—especially with that new gun you gave him to replace the one he broke a couple of months back."

"Why, that young whippersnapper!" Mayor Ansel sputtered, his attention, momentarily diverted and focused on his son. "I'll tan his hide if he's been lying to me and laying out of summer school! He promised me faithfully to study hard in this summer session and pass that English course he failed in the spring." He paused, then went on angrily, "When I get home, I'm going to have a long talk with that boy."

His attention turned back again to Daniel. "You sure the nigger is Daniel—Glo-ree's boy?"

"He says his name is Daniel, Mayor," Chalker said impatiently.

"I wouldn't have believed it," the mayor said. Then added through clenched teeth, "You can't trust any of those black bastards!"

"Mr. Jordon has the farm next to the Johnsons and that's who Daniel's been working for. Mr. Jordon told me that he hired him to plow and repair the equipment or anything he needs done. He couldn't believe that Daniel would do such a thing but he said he came into town this morning so Daniel could have slipped away from the farm while he was gone. His wife was in the house and didn't pay any attention to him."

"The black son-of-a-bitch!" The impact of the crime began to sink into the mayor's brain.

"Well, this black son-of-a-bitch has got one hell of a busted nose and two black eyes." Chalker said, "I'm sure it's broken but we ain't had time to have the Doc look at it yet. And, as far as I'm concerned, it can stay broke. That nigger's lucky to still be alive. Mr. Johnson would have killed him if we hadn't got the bastard in the car when we did and got out of there."

"What happened?"

"Johnson followed us over to Jordon's place. The nigger was in the field when he saw us jump out of the car and start toward him and he made a run for the barn.

"Jordon and Stony stayed outside in case he got out and Officer Johnny Payne and I went in. We didn't have much trouble finding him. We flushed him out of the loft where he was hiding under some hay. Johnson got there just as we brought him out of the barn. He piled into him. Man, I never saw a man pile into anyone like Johnson did that nigger." Chalker gloated, recalling the scene with relish. "I hated to but I knew I had to stop Johnson if I didn't want a dead coon on our hands. Johnny and I had one hell of a time getting him away from Johnson. He was plumb crazy." He paused, then added, "'Course, I can't blame him none."

"That filthy coon!" the Mayor rasped. "You can't trust any of 'em farther than you can throw a bull by the tail." Chalker grunted assent. The mayor asked, "Is there anything I can do, Jess? What have you done so far?"

"Sheriff Hardy and Jones, the county attorney, have already sworn out the warrant. I got Judge Wheelus at home—caught him just in time too. He was almost ready to leave for Dallas for the weekend. He's called a special grand jury to meet tomorrow. He said that, under the circumstances, he didn't want to wait until Monday—it warrants calling a special meeting on Saturday."

"When did Bob say it can go to trial?"

"He said that after the grand jury meets and an indictment is secured, it takes five days, under the law, between the dates of an indictment for a felony and the day of the trial," Chalker replied, "so that would set the trial to start next Thursday."

"The sooner the better," the mayor grunted.

"I've got to go now, Mayor," Chalker said. "I've got to get over to the county attorney's office and talk to Jones."

"I'll meet you there, Jess," the Mayor replied to Chalker's disgust. "And, look, I'd like for you to get the sheriff on the phone for me. Tell Hack to get on over to Sandy's office and meet us there. We've got a lot to discuss." Mayor Ansel hesitated then, his voice dropping to a low confidential note, he continued, "Now, son..."

At the other end of the line, Chalker's face was set in

a look of agitation. *Yes, we've got a lot to discuss but we don't need you, Mayor,* he thought to himself. He hated to hear the Mayor's voice take on that tone. He knew from experience what it meant. Mayor Ansel was going to start telling him—again—how to run his business. He covered the mouthpiece with his hand and muttered profanely under his breath while the mayor went on.

"You know, son," the mayor said, "I've been around this place a lot longer than you—and everyone else. I know this town better than anybody—from *A* to *Z*—so I can give you a lot of tips, from facts to folks. If you want to know anything or need any help, well, you just call me, son. You hear now?"

"I'll sure do that, Mayor," Chalker said dryly and hung the receiver up with a bang before exploding angrily, "that damn, meddling old man!"

"Where's Stony?" Mayor Ansel barked at his wife that evening as he entered the door. Stella Ansel, a large buxom woman who still, despite her age, had dyed blond hair which was carefully styled into tightly curled ringlets that made a cap-like covering over her head.

Looking up from the flowers that she was arranging in the vase on the table of the vestibule, she gave him a sharply probing look, but answered dutifully, "He's in his room, dear." She hesitated, then said anxiously, "I do hope you're not going to get on him for playing hooky after what's happened. He told me all about how that nigger killed that poor girl. Stony's awfully upset. Isn't it terrible? I just can't believe it. Why, who would have thought such a thing could happen right here..." She paused, agitated, then added on a tremulous rising note, "Right here in our town." Perturbed, she turned to him. She laid her hand on his arm and said imploringly, "Please, Sol, don't..."

Moving aside, he brushed her hand from his arm and interrupted her before she could finish. "Don't keep bothering me, woman," he said sharply. "Give me a little respite, will you? I just want to talk to the boy." And, with that, he hung his cane on the wall rack and walked toward the stairs.

Entering the upstairs room without knocking, he looked at his son sprawled an the bed. Stony ignored his entrance and kept his eyes on the ceiling. Sol Ansel stared at him for a long minute. He took in the rumpled dirty clothes, the pale face covered in pimples and the shock of red, disarrayed hair. His glance swept the room, taking in the disorder: The clothes piled in a corner, books and papers littered on the desk, a jacket flung over the chair near the bed with the gun and box of shells on the floor next to it. His gaze returned to the long, thin form of his son reclining impudently, seemingly unperturbed by his scrutiny, on the bed. *Was I ever a lazy shallow youth like him*, he asked himself?

Finally, he spoke. His voice was stern. "What's this about your playing hooky today, boy?" Stony didn't move nor take his eyes from the ceiling. "I'm talking to you, boy," Mayor Ansel said angrily. "Have you been laying out of school?"

Still looking upward, Stony drawled, "I guess Jess told on me. I wish he'd mind his own business and quit bein' a tattletale."

"You never mind how I know," his father said. "Nobody was tattling on you. The important thing is—have you been playing hooky a lot? Is that why your grades have fallen down lately?" He paused a moment and when Stony didn't answer, he added, "And, I don't want you lying to me, Stony."

Somewhat defiantly, Stony answered, "This is only the third time, Papa, and I'm studying more. My grades will be better from now on." He turned toward his father. The defiance dropped from him and his face held a pleading expression as he said earnestly, "I promise you that they will be, Papa."

A puzzled look crossed the mayor's face at his son's sudden change in attitude. "I certainly hope so, son. This is your last year of high school coming up and you've got to get those grades up if you want to get into the university." The thought of his son being old enough to leave home for college struck him fully for the first time. Stony, his face relaxed now and no longer defiant, suddenly looked very vulnerable. Mayor Ansel felt an unexpected surge of love for the forlorn figure before him. *I don't know my son very well,* he thought to himself with a feeling of dismay and shock. *With all the pressures and responsibilities of seeing after Anseltown, I haven't been able to spend too much time with my son over the years. Now, he's old enough to be going away to college in another year.* Wearily, he wiped his hand across his eyes and made a silent vow to himself. *Things are going to be different from now on—we're going to spend a lot of time together this next year. I'm going to make it all up to him—before he leaves home.*

With difficulty, he forced his mind to return to the subject at hand. "Did you see that nigger this morning at the Johnson farm?" he asked.

Stony jerked upright on the bed, his face once again showing defiance. In a strained, belligerent voice, he answered, "Yes, I saw him. I told Jess all about it—how I saw him coming out of the woods on the Johnson farm and slipping back into Mr. Jordon's field." Stony was breathing hard as the words tumbled out.

"What were you doing out there, boy?"

Avoiding his father's eyes, Stony answered, "I went squirrel hunting, Papa."

"Did Daniel see you?"

Turning his head away, Stony replied, "No, I was quite a long ways away, on the other side of a tree, watching for squirrels. Besides, he wasn't looking for nobody—he was sneaking along and acted like he was in a big hurry to get away from the woods."

"What else did you see?"

"I told Jess everything I saw!" Stony said sharply. I just saw that nigger boy come out of the woods from the direction of the Johnson's pond and go into Mr. Jordon's field."

"You couldn't have been too far away from the pond. Didn't you hear anything, Stony—any kind of struggle—any noise at all?"

Stony sat up quickly on the side of the bed and turned his back to his father. His voice was angry. "What is this anyway—the third degree?" His voice rose to an angry pitch. "No, I didn't hear anything. I told Jess and I've told you everything I saw out there and I'm getting tired of repeating it." He buried his face in his hands, his elbows resting on his knees. "Leave me alone." His voice was ragged, tortured. "Just leave me alone!"

Mayor Ansel had remained standing by the bed since entering the room. Now, something in Stony's voice made him take an involuntary step backwards. He hesitated, uncertain. Then, he walked around the foot of the bed and sat down beside Stony. He looked at the downcast head, the misery that was intensely visible on the pale face.

A great wave of pity for this defeated boy—his son—washed over him. He had an overwhelming desire to put his arms around him, to hug him as he had done when he was a child. Instead, he placed his hand awkwardly on his shoulder and his voice was gentle as he asked, "Son, do you have anything more to tell me about what happened out there on the Johnson farm today?"

Stony, his head still down, swallowed hard several times and clenched his fists, making a great effort to retain his control. At the unusual and unexpected tenderness of his father, he turned toward him, his eyes burning, tormented. His face crumpled and he burst into tears. Burying his head quickly against his father's chest, he flung his arms around his waist. He clung tightly as his entire body was racked and shaken with loud sobs, the sounds of a desolate child crying for comfort. All the while, his voice agonized, he murmured over and over, "Oh, Daddy! Oh, Daddy!"

Mayor Ansel's arms encircled his son's body, hugging him close, rocking him gently back and forth. "It is alright, son," he soothed comfortingly as he thought to himself. *He hasn't called me "Daddy" since he was just a little chap.* He felt the dampness through his thin shirt front from his son's tears and he could see only dimly through the mistiness of his own eyes. He looked at the arms clutching his waist, and then his eyes focused on the four fresh closely-spaced parallel scratch marks that he saw there.

Suddenly, Mayor Ansel jerked upright. His body stiffened, his back becoming ramrod straight. His arms dropped away from his son, hanging limply at his sides. His eyes were glazed as he stared straight ahead. Stony continued to cling to him and sob in anguish. After a long moment, he grabbed Stony's hands and pulled them from around his waist. He pushed him roughly from him. Startled, Stony ceased his sobbing and, with a bewildered expression on his tear streaked face, stared at his father.

Mayor Ansel gazed in disbelief for a long moment into his son's face. Slowly, wearily, he rubbed a trembling hand across his eyes. Then, he shook his head vigorously, as though attempting to dislodge thoughts he did not want from his mind. He looked deeply, intently into Stony's eyes. His face was determined, vehemently resolute as he shook his head firmly, unceasingly while he whispered fiercely, "No, son, you don't have anything more to tell me about what happened out there today."

Reaching out, he grasped both of Stony's arms so tightly that Stony flinched from the pain. The veins stood out, grotesquely large, on the mayor's neck. His face contained a purplish cast and his eyes bulged forth from their sockets with shock as he continued to gaze hypnotically into the eyes of his son. Punctuating each word sharply, his voice was deadly as he said, "Do you hear me, son?"

When Stony did not answer, he shook him violently and repeated the question. Stony nodded numbly. Only then did he release Stony's arms. Quickly, he rose and groped his way blindly to the door, closing it hard behind him. Trancelike, Stony stared at the door through which his father had passed.

Mayor Ansel turned the key, locking the door to his office. It was 5 o'clock Tuesday afternoon and he was leaving for the day. The insistent ringing of the phone on his desk pulled him back inside. He picked up the receiver impatiently. Chalker's voice, plainly worried, was on the line.

"Mayor, I wanted you to know that I've decided to call in the National Guard for the trial Wednesday."

"Hell, Jess!" the mayor exploded into the phone, "that ain't necessary. We can handle our own affairs."

"You must not have seen that crowd at the courthouse today, Mayor. Things could get out of hand..."

"Now, son," Mayor Ansel interrupted, his voice had become cajoling. With Jess's frame of mind, he'd better try a different tact. "They may be a trifle riled up—but what can you expect? It's justifiable under the circumstances. But they're not going to cause any trouble!"

"The hell they ain't, Mayor. I just got back from the jail. The leaders of the mob..."

"What do you mean—*mob*?" Mayor Ansel interrupted.

"Well, that's what I'd call it. You'd better get down to

the courthouse, Mayor, and have a look. It's completely surrounded by people. And, the sheriff had a run in a little while ago with the leaders. They came to the jail and demanded that he let them have the nigger." Chalker paused.

Mayor Ansel asked impatiently, "Well? What the hell happened?"

"Sheriff Hardy finally convinced them that he wasn't in the jail—that we'd moved him out of town."

"Damn it all, boy!" the mayor yelled angrily into the phone, "have you moved him out of town?"

Chalker was taken aback by the unconcealed fury in the mayor's voice. Puzzled, he hesitated momentarily.

"Well, damn it all, boy," Mayor Ansel repeated, "have you moved the son-of-a-bitch?"

Chalker felt his face flush with anger, he could put up with the mayor's wrath and his superior pompous manner but he couldn't stand his condescending attitude, the way he had of calling him "boy" when he was irritated at him. "No, Mayor, we haven't moved him," he finally replied, coldly. "And, I very much doubt if we could move him now past those idiots, with the mood they're in. But, we may be forced to get him out of Anseltown if things don't cool down." He hesitated a moment, then continued in a defiant tone, "A lot of threats have been made so I'm going to request that National Guard troops be sent in for the trial."

Chalker jerked the receiver away from his ear as the mayor shouted, "What the hell for?"

"Because that crowd is getting bigger all the time and their mood is getting worse by the hour." Jess shouted back. "Why the hell do you object to the Guard being here, Mayor?"

Mayor Ansel made an effort to bring his rage under control. He lowered his voice, saying, "We don't need any

outside help, Jess. We can take care of our own affairs in
Anseltown. The people in this town are good people, son.
They're not going to interfere with the law. Aw, there may
be a few rowdies—young 'uns who are full of vinegar and
feel like cuttin' up a little but you know how to handle
them, Jess." His voice dropped lower and, in a confidential
manner, he continued, "Now, you don't want the rest of the
state and the governor thinking that Anseltown doesn't
have law and order—that you, as our Chief of Police, can't
do the job and take care of the town, do you?"

Chalker was incensed. *Damn you, Mayor,* he thought.
He spoke sharply into the phone, emphasizing each word
clearly and slowly, "The National Guard will be here for
the trial."

Mayor Ansel's voice, no longer cajoling, was deadly,
"Damn it all , boy, don't you dare take that nigger out of this
town!" He slammed the receiver down on the hook.

CHAPTER 15

It was Wednesday morning and at 8 o'clock, the sun was already casting warm rays from its position well above the horizon, promising yet another sweltering day of August heat. The small knots of people who had gathered around the courthouse to stand and talk of the tragedy were growing each minute into ever larger clusters. The benches around the square had been rapidly filled by those who sought their comfort. Since the murder of Alicia Johnson on Friday, the numbers had grown proportionately each day. And, each day, the rumblings and mutterings had become more sinister and ominous.

Mr. Rogers, standing in front of his shoe shop with the *Closed* sign on the door, observed the scene across the street. He pulled his watch from his pocket. It would soon be time to start to the Lone Star Cafe for the customary morning rendezvous with the Mayor. He glanced up the street in the direction of Mayor Ansel's office, expecting to see him coming down the walk. He was not in sight. His attention returned once again to the people across the street on the courthouse lawn. With surprise, he recognized Mayor Ansel in one of the groups. Surrounded by a circle of young men, the mayor was talking vigorously. He was receiving the rapt attention of all, accompanied by emphatic nods of apparent and enthusiastic agreement with his words. Astounded, Mr. Rogers watched as Mayor Ansel, after several minutes of animated conversation, took his leave of this group, shaking hands with each man. Then, moving to another small cluster of men, the mayor repeated the same procedure. Mr. Rogers' mouth dropped open in puzzled astonishment at the mayor's strange behavior. He had always been adverse to fraternizing with the proletarian on the street. Rooted to the spot, Mr. Rogers observed the mayor's unusual and odd activity for a time. Finally, with a quizzical expression on his face, he turned and walked toward the Lone Star Cafe. The other councilmen, already in their usual chairs, were absorbed in a discussion of the murder. Walter Anderson glanced up at him as he entered the door and spoke. Then, looking at the mayor's empty chair, he pulled out his pocket watch, saying, "Where's the Mayor, Lonnie?" Not waiting for an answer, he added, "First time in twenty years I've known him to be late." Mr. Rogers opened his mouth to speak but, before he could say anything, Anderson had rejoined the conversation with those around him. Mr. Rogers sat in silence, frowned in contemplation and gazed perplexedly at the mayor's vacant chair at the head of the table.

Outside the courthouse, Mayor Ansel continued to move from group to group, subtly promoting and directing brief conversations with each assemblage before moving to another. He spoke emotionally, expressing shock and bombasting the horrendous nature of the crime. Response came in angry words through clenched teeth, "The bastard ought to be strung up...he doesn't need a trial...everyone knows he's guilty. No white woman's going to be safe to walk on our streets."

Mayor Ansel punctured each enraged statement with "you're right," "exactly," "now, you're talking" ingeniously injecting words and phrases, fielding them as expertly as a general might maneuver his troops into the most appropriate spots to produce the greatest effect. Sympathetically nodding in agreement with each new pronouncement of outrage, he unobtrusively departed as talk and gestures became increasingly agitated within a circle. He slipped quietly from one aggregation to the next, repeating this procedure until he had joined and spoken with each cluster gathered around the square.

In the pressing throng, no one paid any attention to him as he finally withdrew. Slowly, he crossed the street. He stopped to look back at the angry crowd milling about, their voices growing louder, more belligerent. With a trembling hand, he pulled his handkerchief from a pocket. Wearily, he wiped it across his face, mopping away the beads of perspiration. For a long moment, he watched the incensed populace, buzzing together like aroused bees. Then, leaning heavily on his cane and limping noticeably, he walked down the street in the direction of the cafe.

The rumble of heavy trucks outside the police station roused Chalker. He must have dozed only momentarily, he thought, for a small vapor of smoke was still rising from the cup of coffee on the desk. He looked at the clock on the wall. It was 8 o'clock. Leaning back wearily in his chair, he rubbed his hand across his eyes from lack of sleep. He had been up since 2 a.m. He and Sheriff Hardy had taken advantage of the darkness and isolation to secrete the accused murderer from the jail to the courthouse. They locked him inside the court room with the sheriff, his deputy and two policemen standing guard. The trial would not commence until the afternoon session at 1 o'clock in Judge Wheelus' court.

Chalker rose wearily. Going outside, he saw two trucks containing the contingency of 50 National Guard troops. A Texas Ranger disembarked from the cab of the first truck. As Chalker emerged through the door of the police station, the Ranger studied him from cold, gray eyes. Then, he stepped forward briskly and thrust out his hand.

"I'm Captain Frank Boggs," he introduced himself. "I'm in charge of the Guard. This is Johnson, Calhoun and Yates." He motioned to the three Rangers who had walked up beside him. The three men shook hands with Chalker silently, without speaking.

Chalker disliked Boggs on sight. His self-assurance, plainly apparent, bordered on arrogance. It annoyed Chalker. He figured that Boggs must be in the neighborhood of 40. He looked younger but the tinge of gray through his side burns and in the edge of his hair betrayed his strong youthful face. He looked as if he had been born in a Texas Ranger uniform. He would have appeared alien in any other apparel. With lean hips and wide muscular shoulders, the uniform suited him perfectly. Exuding confidence, he gave the impression of being much taller than his medium height. Possessing a strong belief in his own self-reliance and capabilities had resulted, for the most part, from his 15 years of service with the Rangers, an experience that had served him well.

Aware that Boggs had been sizing him up, Chalker was irked at his scrutiny. He flushed angrily as the Ranger's thoughts were revealed through the steely glinting eyes that compelled attention with their bold, direct gaze. To Boggs, he was just a young punk who couldn't handle the situation.

In a voice that was sharp and abrupt, Chalker explained the circumstances briefly. "The crowd is getting bigger and their mood is getting worse. There's a lot of outsiders coming in too—a lot of trouble makers from nearby communities. I don't have enough policemen to take care of a mob if they start something." He paused, then added, "Otherwise, we wouldn't have needed any outside help." He emphasized the word *outside*.

Boggs looked at him piercingly. *Why does a man always find an excuse to blame someone else when he isn't able to do his job,* he thought to himself. He said nothing but turned to give instructions to his men.

Chalker stood aside as Captain Boggs ordered the troops into formation. At his command, the five rows of soldiers, ten abreast and with rifles at right shoulder arms, began the march down the main street to the courthouse, three blocks away. The sound of their marching boots against the concrete pavement echoed hollowly through the quiet, relatively empty street. The crowd was stationed, once again, on the courthouse lawn, anticipating the National Guard's arrival. The people had arrived even earlier today and in greater numbers than yesterday. At the sound of the approaching soldiers, a hush fell over the aggregation, replacing the air of excitement that had prevailed. The continual milling about had halted. Instead, the people remained stationary and quiet and stared in silent hostility at the soldiers, shouldering guns and marching in the distance toward them.

The troops turned smartly from the street into the wide cement walkway leading to the courthouse steps. Marching between the crowd that lined each side of the walk, the soldiers were close enough now so that the people could see their youthfulness. The detachment consisted mostly of fresh-faced freckled boys who were clearly still in their teens. Immediately, the crowd came to life. An angry atmospheric wave swept over it. Mockery grew tantamount as abusive taunts were hurled at the miniature army. "You kids better go home to your mama!"

Several of the men moved closer to the walk and shook their fists in front of their faces. Many of the younger guardsmen, glancing nervously out of the corners of their eyes at the threatening gestures, appeared visibly pale and shaken. Captain Boggs, riding in the police car with

Chalker behind the troops, exploded with obscenities. He jumped out of the car. Angrily, he strode masterfully and confidently up the walk after his men. His gray eyes were deadly, stabbing burningly into and locking with the eyes of those who had harassed the soldiers. His gaze raked like hot coals over them. Under it, the men involuntarily stepped back and grew silent once again.

His back was straight, his stride steady and sure, as Captain Boggs proceeded up the courthouse steps where his men had already entered the building. At the top, he turned to face the crowd. With cold stern features, he looked directly into faces, as if memorizing them. They gazed back at him quietly, faltering under his probing stare. Several long minutes passed, finally, Captain Boggs, abruptly and disdainfully turned his back on them and walked through the door.

The crowd had thinned considerably around the courthouse by 10 o'clock. Only a few stragglers, consisting mostly of noncitizens of Anseltown, could be seen. Now, in contrast to the rambunctious noisiness and clamor of the previous participants, they sat quietly on the grass, talking in subdued hushed tones. For this was the hour that Alicia Johnson's funeral was being conducted at the Baptist church. It accounted for the small gathering at the courthouse. The townsfolk were in mass at the funeral service.

At half past 11 o'clock, the exodus from the church and the cemetery began, joining those who had remained on the courthouse lawn. Within minutes, the numbers swelled until the building was almost completely surrounded by a milling, surging, sullen throng whose revulsion at a white girl's ravishing murder by a Negro had been even more intensely inflamed by the Johnsons' sorrowing agony.

Mayor Ansel stood on the walk on the east side of the courthouse and watched the growing populace. His face was anxious, strained. Scanning the faces of the crowd, he recognized Tom Cooper, a young reporter representing the Duganville Daily News from the small nearby town of Duganville. He was circulating among the people, talking, listening and sensing their mood.

Mayor Ansel became aware of angry comments coming from several men near him, "Why did the governor have to send in the National Guard—that's an insult—why, they're just a bunch of snot-nosed kids! We can handle our own affairs. We don't need any outside help." The others nodded assent, making heated, scathing and obscene remarks on the mentality and ancestry of the governor. The most strident raucous voice came from an overall clad, gangly youth who stood at the outer edge of the circle, ignored by the others. Mayor Ansel recognized him as Willie Dawkins, a member of the large Dawkins clan that lived in a rundown shack by the cottonseed mill. A harmless retardant, Willie had been unkindly dubbed the "village idiot."

Mayor Ansel's eyes narrowed suddenly as he studied Willie's vacuous expressionless features. Then, purposefully, he made his way around the circle to Willie's side. Taking hold of his arm, the mayor unobtrusively drew Willie aside. Guided by his hand, Willie followed meekly, staring blankly all the while at this man that he had seen but never talked to before. When they were out of hearing distance of the others, the Mayor leaned toward Willie and, looking directly into the vapid eyes, said slowly in a low confidential voice, "I hear that the governor told that Texas Ranger not to shoot anybody over that murdering black nigger. The governor says he ain't worth it."

Willie stared dully at him for a minute before comprehending the meaning of the words. He did not answer. Instead, he turned and trotted back toward the people that he knew, yelling to them as he went, "Hey, fellows, did you hear what the governor told that smart-ass Ranger?" Not waiting for a reply, he went on. "He told him not to shoot anybody over that nigger—he ain't worth it!"

As Willie ran to rejoin his circle, Mayor Ansel, unnoticed in the teeming throng, moved swiftly away, melting into the middle of the swarming crowd. Making his way back to the walk, he halted to observe the effects of Willie's announcement. A cheer went up from those within earshot and exclamations of approval for the governor were heard. Willie, surprised at the happy reaction to his words, was elated to be the center of attention for once. Leaping foolishly in the air, he ran excitedly about, eager to spread the news—news that evidently pleased his friends very much and caused them to focus their eyes on him.

Mayor Ansel, standing on the perimeter of the people, searched the crowd until he had located Cooper, the Duganville reporter once more. He kept his eyes glued upon him. He didn't have long to wait. He saw Cooper leave hurriedly and walk rapidly down the street a short distance where he got into his car. He heard the gears grind as Cooper impatiently drove away. He watched anxiously until the car disappeared from his view. Then, without glancing at the crowd again, he turned his back to it and walked away,

Jon drummed his fingers against the steering wheel of the truck as he drove. He was anxious to reach Anseltown and get this long grueling run over and done with. His first truck run in over two months, he had inherited it only because of Bob Hardy's illness. *It's a sad state,* he thought derisively, *when you are almost happy that your friend falls ill so you can grab his job.*

The unusual arduous driving and the sticky, sapping heat that had drained his strength, totally devitalized him. This had been the long haul—swinging around by Abilene, down through San Antonio and on to Houston before returning by way of Austin, Waco and Fort Worth. He had left Anseltown early last Friday morning and this was Thursday. He'd been driving for almost a week. I'd have been home yesterday, he thought disgustedly, if this damn truck hadn't broken down in that hell-forsaken place in central Texas. And, it is always my luck to come across some Jake-leg mechanic that's as slow as the seven-day itch. Wearily slumped in his seat, he rubbed a hand, grimy with dust, across his reddened eyes. He had been on the road since 5 o'clock this morning.

He blinked dully as he looked through the windshield at the mirage of shimmering water, created by the early afternoon sun that blazed down on the crests and falls of the highway ahead. The images did not afford any relief from the heat nor lend credence to the dryness of the land that lay, brown and dead from the dearth of the Texas summer drought, on both sides of the road. Jon had both windows of the truck lowered to take full advantage of any slight breeze, but the dry, hot air hung heavily, surrounded him suffocatingly. He felt as though he were sitting in the inside of an oven and someone had turned the heat up. Reaching for the towel that he kept on the seat beside him, he mopped the sweat from his face and forehead. It felt hard and stiff against his skin and he smelled the rancid odor of stale sweat on it. He usually kept the towel wet, for the cool dampness helped a little to moisten his arms and face when the heat became unbearable. But he had forgotten to dampen it at his last stop. He felt numb, mechanical— like a robot that was controlled by another entity—one who was forcing him through the motions of driving, automatically. He longed for the moment when he would be allowed to slow to a halt and turn the key that would, at last, shut off both the truck motor—and his own.

He shook his head vigorously, attempting to disengage his mind from the lethargy that seeped over him, stupefying his senses. He forced himself to visualize the cold lengthy bath with which he would reward his tired body before climbing between the cool smooth sheets of the bed. He jammed his foot hard against the gas pedal.

He did not reduce his speed until he reached the city limits of Anseltown. The tree lined shady streets offered a cool respite from the bareness of the highway's blistering concrete as he drove toward the center of town. As he turned the corner three blocks from the heart of town, he could see the courthouse etched against the hot Texas sky. But Jon wasn't looking at the courthouse. Instead, his vision was focused on the mass of humanity that covered the lawn around it, overflowing onto the sidewalk and spilling into the streets. For a moment, he wondered if there were some sort of celebration going on but that thought was immediately canceled from his mind. He knew the only large festivity was held once a year in the fall. It consisted of the Harvest Fair and Settler's Picnic that combined frivolity and thanksgiving for another harvest which had been brought to fruition. The mood of the fair depended on the failure or success of the county's current crop that year, with a spirit of gaiety or somberness reflecting the results of this autumn harvest.

Drawing closer now, he could hear the noise of the crowd. From the sounds, he could distinguish what were obviously angry overtones. "What the hell's going on?" he muttered aloud.

Scanning the street ahead quickly, he noted that there were no parking places in the block before reaching the courthouse. So, at the last moment, he turned the corner and parked his truck before a house in the residential section nearest town. The vehicle hardly came to a stop before he had jumped from the cab, slammed the door and loped toward the hubbub of activity.

Approaching the rear of the throng, he heard yelling coming from those nearest the front of the courthouse but he was unable to decipher the words. "What's going on?" he asked several times of men standing nearby. They didn't even glance at him. He didn't know whether they had heard him over the noise or were too intent on the action going on to answer.

Craning to see over the heads, Jon saw a man, whom he did not recognize, in a strange uniform at the top of the courthouse steps surveying the crowd. Sheriff Hardy was beside him. A row of soldiers behind them stood, rigid and determined, in a line before the door, blocking the entrance.

Jon turned to the man next to him, demanding, "What's going on here anyway?" But the man continued to stare straight ahead, never diverting his gaze from the building. Jon suddenly realized that the man was a stranger to him.

Looking around, he saw many unfamiliar faces. His eyes stopped on a well-known one. It was old man Parkinson, who at 89, was one of Anseltown's oldest residents. He was standing at the curb across the street, slightly apart from others.

Pushing through the people, Jon reached his side and took hold of his arm. "Mr. Parkinson, what in hell's going on?" The old man would have ignored him but Jon shook his arm until he turned to blink at him through pale watery eyes set in his wrinkled weather-beaten face. Traces of dried snuff were on the corners of his mouth and imbedded in the lines of his chin. He raised a shaking hand and feebly cupped his right ear. "Aye? What's that?"

Damn it all, Jon thought, *I forgot that he's hard of hearing.* He leaned close to Mr. Parkinson's cupped ear, shouting, "What's going on here?"

Drawing back, Mr. Parkinson looked at Jon in astonishment. "Where you been, son? Don't you know what's been goin' on here the past few days?"

"If I did, I wouldn't be asking you!" Jon said angrily. His sarcasm was lost on the old man.

"Aye? What's that?" he asked

Jon took a deep breath and yelled once more in his ear, "What's happening?"

Finally, Mr. Parkinson said haltingly, "The trial's just starting and the crowd wants to get that nigger out of the courthouse and hang him—that's what's happening." And, with that, he effected a glob of chocolate spit from his mouth into the dirt at their feet and turned his attention back to the courthouse.

Frustrated, Jon gave him a look of disgust. He walked quickly back across the street where he elbowed his way through the multitude until he was midway to the building. The crowd was pressed tightly together at this point and it was extremely difficult to make progress but Jon continued to push his way through, squeezing past one by one until he found himself near the steps. He was astounded to see a sizeable sprinkling of women, mostly middle-aged, among the crush of people nearest the front. Until now, he had been aware of only men in the crowd. He recognized the majority of the women.

As Jon struggled to get through the crowd, the man in the strange uniform on the courthouse steps was trying to address the crowd. His voice was immediately drowned out by the people who jostled each other and screamed "Let us have him. He deserves to hang! The dirty black bastard!" After each pronounced outburst, screams from others became louder and more wildly abandoned in agreement while clenched fists were thrust into the air and waved menacingly.

The man next to Jon yelled hoarsely, "We ought to hang the bastards that are protecting that black son-of-a-bitch. They're worse than he is!" The crowd roared its affirmation and surged forward. Jon almost lost his footing but managed to catch himself against the man who had yelled. Aghast, he found himself looking into the face of Jim Sanders. He had not recognized his voice, strong with emotion. The frenzied face of his lifelong friend was equally unfamiliar. The features ware contorted, the eyes ablaze with a strange glow, revealing the inner fire burning within.

Jim looked right through Jon without seeing him. He appeared to be under a hypnotic spell. Jon grabbed both his arms and shook him roughly. "Jim, for God's sake, tell me what's happening."

Jim, shaking his head, blinked his eyes rapidly. For the first time, he looked at Jon with recognition. "Hell, don't you know man that a black bastard raped and killed the Johnson girl?" His voice rose in fury as he continued. "And, now these bastards," he waved his hands toward the soldiers, "want him to have a fair trial."

Jon stared at Jim in stunned silence. He couldn't believe it. Not Alicia Johnson. Alicia couldn't be dead. She was so young, so alive, so pretty. Why, he had taken Elisabeth and the kids to visit the Johnsons only a couple of weeks ago. Suddenly, the vision of Alicia and Larry— together that day—flashed before his eyes. They had all noticed, but pretended not to, how the two had paired off. He remembered the way that Larry had looked at her.

His thoughts were harshly interrupted by the strident shout of a man who was standing nearby, "You interfering bastards! Get out of here and stop butting into our affairs! We can take care of law and order in our town!"

Jon stared blankly at the man who had his arm raised in the air and was shaking his fist at the soldiers. It was Tad Sloane. He recognized Pete Jackson next to him. Pete was yelling also. Jon could not make out Pete's words above the noise of the crowd which was shouting in unison once again, punctuating Tad's hysterical demands.

Jon mopped at the sweat trickling down his face with his handkerchief. The heat was stifling in the press of packed bodies but the crowd was oblivious to the sun beating dawn mercilessly upon it. He rubbed at his eyes, as if to wipe away the images of the people before hire. *He must be dreaming,* he thought. *Everything was so unreal.*

A roar went up and Jon's eyes focused with difficulty on the Texas Ranger who had been standing for some time with his arms crossed, staring stolidly over the people. He had tried repeatedly to speak but it had been in vain. The crowd had refused to listen, drowning him out with their cries. Now, he had raised his arms once again for silence. As usual, the noise grew even louder.

Sheriff Hardy shouted loudly, "Quiet! Let Captain Boggs speak." Protests vociferously followed briefly before diminishing.

Then, several voices called out, siding with the sheriff, "Let's hear what Boggs has to say!" Others joined in and an uneasy quiet fell over the people as Captain Boggs commenced to speak.

"Judge Wheelus has opened court and the trial has just begun."

His words were hailed with boos, catcalls and cries of "Hang the nigger! The black bastard don't need no trial, we'll take care of him."

Captain Boggs raised his arms again for silence. The noise finally abated somewhat and, in the ensuing turbulent lull, he continued, "According to the laws of our land and our state, everyone is entitled to a fair trial regardless..."

That was as far as he got before a voice, screaming hysterically, interrupted, "That don't mean no black son-of-a-bitch that has raped and killed a white woman." The crowd became as one, a chorus of voices, screeching in agreement. The people pushed angrily forward until the front line was forced up on the bottom step. The soldiers stepped forward quickly and stood in a row on each side of Captain Boggs. At the same time, they had removed their guns that rested against their shoulders and held them at fixed bayonets, pointed at the crowd.

Suddenly, an excited flurry came from midway of the crowd. Captain Boggs, from his vantage position atop the steps, could see a man, waving a piece of paper in his hand high above his head, pushing his way through the crush. Sheriff Hardy, noting Captain Boggs' puzzled expression, said, "That's Bob Simms, a reporter for the Anseltown Times."

Simms was near enough now so that they were able to hear his voice, excitedly calling to them, "We just received a message off the A. P. wire saying that the governor has already sent an order to you." As his words became audible to those surrounding him, a path was opened for him to get through. He walked swiftly up the steps and handed Boggs the piece of paper.

"I haven't received any message like this from the governor!" Captain Boggs barked, after reading it.

Sheriff Hardy scanned the paper hurriedly. He moved close to Captain Boggs and said in a low voice, "Well, you'd better get hold of him and find out what he expects you to do about them." His glance swept over the crowd. "In the meantime, we'd better keep this quiet."

"I'll get to the phone," Captain Boggs said tersely as he strode swiftly toward the door.

Sheriff Hardy turned to caution the reporter not to reveal the contents of the message nor release it for publication. But he was too late. Simms was already making his way back through the people, asking as he passed, "What did the governor say, Bob?"

"Governor Franklin ordered Captain Boggs to 'protect the Negro, if possible, but not to shoot anyone'," Simms' voice was clearly audible to all those surrounding him. Roars of approval greeted his words. Simms repeated the message all along the way, leaving sounds of endorsement in his wake until the multitude of voices merged together, almost as one, swelling in pleased unison by the time he emerged from the throng.

"At least Governor Franklin's got some sense," Jon heard Jim shout.

"They can't shoot us," another man yelled, "the governor won't let 'em."

"Now," a voice screamed hysterically, "let's go get that son-of-a-bitch."

Voices rose to a frenzied pitch and the crowd, as if on command, surged toward the courthouse. Jon was hit with such force by the first impact of bodies that the breath was knocked from him. Unable to catch it momentarily in the crush against him, he felt dizzy and faint. Desperately he clawed at the back of the man in front of him. He felt himself being lifted up by those behind until his feet were no longer touching the ground. He was swept along on the crest of the human wave. Head and shoulders above the others, he saw the soldiers advancing down the steps, their guns at bayonet and pointed at the oncoming mob. The crowd shifted back in retreat from the sharp bayonets. Jon found himself released from his precarious position. His feet touched the ground. Losing his footing, he would have fallen to be subsequently crushed underneath the feet of the retreating horde, had not the tight enclosure of the surrounding mass of bodies prevented it.

The regression was only momentary. Regaining its angry momentum, the crowd rushed forward once more. The agitated pushing and shoving that came from the middle and rear of the throng forced those in the front lines to advance. The soldiers stepped backwards up the steps until they stood in front of the door. Suddenly, a soldier, his youthful face registering fear, raised his gun over the heads of the menacing mob and fired a shot.

Captain Boggs, attempting to reach Governor Franklin on the phone in the county attorney's office, threw the instrument on the desk at the sound of the shot and ran into the hall. He saw Sheriff Hardy and the soldiers backed against the glass door outside with the maddened mass moving toward them. Sheriff Hardy grasped the handle of the door in a futile attempt to open it. Several of the soldiers were pressed against it, thwarting his efforts. Captain Boggs ran to the door and pushed against it with all his might. It didn't budge. In desperation, Sheriff Hardy fired a shot from his pistol into the air. Instantaneously, the mob fell back and gave ground. But only for a moment. Then, they rushed forward once again. The momentary recession was all that Captain Boggs and Sheriff Hardy needed to succeed in opening the door. The sheriff ran through, along with the soldiers, pushing and shoving each other. They managed to squeeze inside just in time to escape the crazed mob that howled and clutched at them from behind.

Captain Boggs had been pushed away from the door by the incoming men. He struggled to reach it again, shouting over and over all the while, "Lock the door!" just as the last soldier came through. Captain Boggs had fought his way near enough to grab the handle. Hands grasped at the handles from both sides of the door, pulling and pushing, straining for supremacy against their opponents. Captain Boggs found himself looking into a beefy red, hate-filled face intruding inside the opened crack of the door. He pounded his fist into the face repeatedly until it withdrew. He tugged at the handle, pulling with all the strength that he could muster. Other hands aided him. Those who couldn't reach the handle, grasped his arms from behind. The door closed sharply against several restraining hands that gripped its edge from the outside. The stubbornly clinging fingers were quickly jerked away by the pain that ensued. Captain Boggs swiftly turned the lock.

He heard cries of "Get to the other door!" And he saw the mob, almost as one, turn to run to the opposite side of the courthouse to the other entrance. It had already been locked. He barked orders to Ranger Yates to station the soldiers evenly at the two entrances. Hurriedly, he instructed the sheriff to put a call through to the National Guard Headquarters in Dallas and to Governor Franklin while he went to talk to Judge Wheelus. Then, he raced down the hall to the courtroom.

The bailiff at the door attempted to block his entrance but Captain Boggs brushed past his restraining hand and burst inside. Officer Johnny Payne, who had assisted Chalker in Daniel's arrest, had just been sworn as the first witness and was beginning his testimony. All heads swiveled simultaneously at the noisy entrance of Captain Boggs. A tense uneasy atmosphere hung over the room. Daniel, cowering in his chair with his hands manacled in his lap, sat next to Chief Chalker. His eyes rolled in fright as he looked at Captain Boggs.

"Judge Wheelus, you've got to halt the trial!" Captain Boggs shouted as he entered the rear of the room. "The mob is trying to break in."

At his words, a moan like that of a wounded animal rose from Daniel. In a single motion, everyone in the room, with the exception of Judge Wheelus, jumped to his feet.

The few spectators started to move from their seats while the jurors stood, confused and uncertain, in the jury box. Banging the gavel loudly, Judge Wheelus spoke angrily, "Everyone will be seated immediately," he commanded. "No one will leave this courtroom until I order it cleared." The Judge's face was red and his jowls shook vigorously as he spoke. He was a man, short in stature with an enormous girth; nevertheless, his physical appearance did not deter from the dignity of his position in life. The high moral ethics with which he conducted both his office and himself commanded the respect of all.

There were muttered objections as the people hesitated, still standing, and looked at him. He stared back at them steadily, coldly. "I will order anyone, who leaves this courtroom without my permission, to be arrested," he said sternly. "Now, be seated." The people returned to their seats.

Turning to Captain Boggs, Judge Wheelus said, "Would you come forward, Captain? I'd like to speak to you." Captain Boggs advanced and they spoke together in low tones.

"Judge Wheelus, you've got to stop the trial," Captain Boggs said. "That mob out there is determined to get in here. I don't know how much longer we're going to be able to hold them off. I've got a call into headquarters for more reinforcements."

"It's going to take awhile for them to get to Anseltown," the Judge said worriedly, "and the prisoner is certainly in jeopardy here in the courthouse."

"There's nothing else we can do, Judge," Captain Boggs said tersely. "We have no choice! We're going to have to keep him here; it would be impossible to get him through that mob."

Judge Wheelus was thoughtful for a minute; then, he turned and called Chalker to the bench. "Jess, I've decided to stop the trial," he said. "Captain Boggs has called for more troops. In the meantime, we've got to keep the prisoner in the courthouse." He rubbed his hand across his bald moist crown, silently contemplating. Finally, he spoke. "I was thinking about that locked vault upstairs in the records room. Seems to me, it ought to be the safest place to put the prisoner, in case that mob does get in. What do you think?"

Chalker nodded in agreement. "I can't think of a safer place than that, Judge Wheelus."

At that moment, the bailiff called from the doorway, "Captain Boggs, the sheriff has the National Guard Headquarters on the phone." Captain Boggs ran from the courtroom.

Outside the courthouse, the frustrated mob milled about angrily. Jon was able to disengage himself from it when the people ran from the south entrance of the building to the door on the opposite side. Now, standing well back near the edge of the street, he watched in stunned disbelief, mentally rejecting the actions of these people he knew—or thought that he had known so well. He listened to their voices, voices he no longer recognized, uttering curses and obscenities that were strange and alien to their nature. Unlike himself, he knew that most of them were churchgoing, God-fearing folk. Over masculine shouts, he detected the shrill cries of the women who were at the front near the building.

Jon saw a flurry of commotion at the east side of the building. Windows lined the width of the courthouse on both floors. The people had congregated beneath those of Judge Wheelus' courtroom. Stepping onto a bench by the walk at the edge of the street, Jon could see over the heads of the throng. At the front of the crowd were several boys, apparently in their late teens, encircling two that were holding large brown paper sacks. One of the boys extracted the contents of one. With some difficulty, Jon made out a fruit jar that was filled with a clear liquid.

"What the hell are we waiting for?" someone shouted. "Let's go get him!"

The crowd screamed in approval. Jon saw a woman pick up a rock and throw it violently against a window. Straining his eyes, he recognized her. She was Tad Sloane's sister. Almost 50, she was one of the older ones in the group of women near the front of the throng. The sound of shattering glass echoed through the mob and, simultaneously, released the pent-up fury of their emotions. Following the woman's lead, the men and other women frantically hurled rocks at the windows which crashed splinteringly. None were spared, as the missiles were sailed determinedly through each one. All the while, the tumultuous cries mounted in chorus, rising to a high-pitched hysterical crescendo. Finally, as it reached its peak, one of the boys holding a fruit jar of liquid, ran toward a window. He raised it above his head to throw it through a gaping hole, left by the rocks.

Suddenly, a figure darted from the crowd, shouting, "Stop it! Stop this madness!" Startled, the boy hesitated. It was long enough for the man to grab the jar from his grasp. Instantly, men closed in, howling with rage, lashing out furiously with their fists. Jon gazed incredulously at the distorted, almost unrecognizable, features of Jim Sanders, Pete Jackson and Tad Sloane who were among those shoving each other in their avid zeal to get at, to strike and kick this intruder that dared to interfere.

Jon did not yet recognize the man in the obscurity of the surrounding press. But he recognized that he was making no effort to defend himself. Instead, he was attempting to reason with the others, pleading with them. Jon's mind churned angrily. *Fight back! Knock hell out of them! You can't reason with the sons-a-bitches!*

But, the man did not retaliate. He was buffeted about, helpless under the viciousness of the onslaught. Suddenly, a mighty fist crashed into his face, sending him down heavily. Falling backwards to the ground, his head struck the edge of the concrete walk. He lay very still.

Jon saw the boy, whom the man had intercepted, grab the jar once again. And, this time, without interference, he sprinted to the building where he tossed it through a broken window. Another boy followed him and threw a lighted match after it. Instantaneously, a blinding flash erupted.

Jon tried to step from the bench to get to the fallen man, but the people had retreated hastily from the building when the gasoline exploded inside the window and were pressed so tightly around him that he was unable to descend. With relief, he saw someone bending over the still prone figure on the ground. Grasping him under the arms, he pulled him toward the street. Another man moved in to lift his feet so that he was being carried bodily now.

The crowd gave way and let them through. They hurried past the bench on which he stood. Jon heard someone say, "You'd better get him to Doc Martin quick." Jon stared down into the upturned face of Wayne Winslow. He was shucked by the deathly gray pallor of his skin. He wondered if it wasn't already too late.

CHAPTER 16

Captain Boggs ran from the courtroom to the county attorney's office where the telephone call to Guard Headquarters awaited him. The jurors and spectators were filing from the courtroom and hurrying toward the north door after Judge Wheelus' dismissal. "Don't open that door for anyone!" he snapped at the soldiers standing guard before it. The troops had been divided and stationed at the two entrances. The group, startled at his command, stared resentfully at him.

"I want to get out of here!" a spectator called out in an angry tone.

"You can't keep us locked up in here!" a juror objected. "We're not prisoners!"

Captain Boggs turned around only long enough to say in a harsh voice, "Ranger Yates, you have my orders! Don't open that door for anyone."

Reaching Jones' office, he picked up the telephone from the desk, barking into it, "Get some more troops here on the double! We've got a mob trying to break into the courthouse and get the prisoner!" Just as the voice on the other end of the line started to speak, a rock crashed through the window and fell near the desk.

Captain Boggs heard the sound of a sharp explosion in the building. Immediately, someone in the hall began screaming, "Fire! Fire!" Captain Boggs shouted into the instrument, "Did you understand what I said? We need more troops—quick!" Then, not waiting for an answer, he slammed the phone down and ran for the door.

The hallway was a bedlam of confusion. People were running in all directions. In a brief instant, Captain Boggs noted the group of jurors and spectators who had remained standing near the north entrance shove the soldiers aside, unlock the door and rush in panic to the outside. The nucleus of the mob, preoccupied with breaking windows on the east side, were unaware of this exodus.

"Get that damn door locked and keep it locked, Yates!" Captain Boggs shouted as he ran toward the room from which smoke was pouring into the hall.

Through the thick haze he could see the drapes flaming at the window. The fire had grown by leaps and bounds, spreading rapidly along the gasoline soaked floor to the desk, chairs and walls. He stood momentarily transfixed, staring at the inferno. The spontaneous combustion of the gasoline had spewed the flames forth at such lightning-like speed that, although the time since its inception had been brief, already the fire had progressed too far to be brought under control by one man.

Realizing the futility of any attempt on his part to extinguish it, he ran back to Jones' office and grabbed the phone, "Operator! Operator!" he shouted, "get the fire department—the courthouse is on fire!" There was no sound. The line was dead. Someone outside had cut the wires. He flung the instrument to the desk. A sudden movement at the window caught his attention. A hand reached inside the broken jagged hole and unlocked the catch.

Captain Boggs ran into the hallway, shouting, "Yates, get some soldiers over here—quick! Hurry up, damn it! They're coming in the window!" There were shouts, sounds

of running feet and noisy chaos. Barking orders all the
while, Captain Boggs ran to several boxes against the wall
of the hall. They contained tear gas bombs that had been
placed there early that morning as a precautionary measure
when he had brought the prisoner from the jail.

Grabbing two of the bombs from a box, he ran back to
the doorway of Jones' office. Looking inside, he saw a man
with one foot and leg over the window sill. He was supported
by hands that were lifting him up to boost him through.
Quickly, Captain Boggs heaved both bombs inside and
slammed the door.

"Yates!" he yelled, "get all these office doors locked in
case anyone else gets through the windows!" Relieved, he
heard the wail of a siren. He knew the fire truck was on its
way. His relief was short lived when he heard Chalker
calling to him as he rushed down the stairs.

"Captain Boggs, we've got to get out of here while we
can! The smoke is pouring upstairs. It ain't safe up there!"

"Well, it damn well sure ain't safe down here!" Captain
Boggs retorted. "That mob's broke the windows and they're
trying to get in!"

"How the hell are we going to get Daniel past them out
there?" Chalker asked.

Captain Boggs' mind raced. "Chalker, where is your
car parked?"

"On the west side of the square."

"I want you to get that police car and drive it to the
north entrance. The crowd is on the east side of the
building. We'll be waiting just inside for you. Maybe—just
maybe—we'll be able to get Daniel into the car before
those mad dogs can reach us!"

Without a word, Chalker turned and started for the
door. Captain Boggs called after him, "Once we get in the
car—you drive like hell!"

"Captain Boggs! Look!" Ranger Yates yelled from

down the hall near the south door. Captain Boggs saw
flames licking their way through the door of the office
where the fire had started, into the hallway. He shouted to
Yates to keep the soldiers at the two entrances until he
gave orders to leave as he ran up the stairs.

The door to the records room where Sheriff Hardy, his
two deputies and Ranger Calhoun were guarding the
prisoner was locked. Captain Boggs pounded on it. Calhoun
opened the door cautiously. The sheriff was standing by
the window peering carefully through the drapes, staring
intently at the mob below. His hands manacled before him,
Daniel sat stiff and straight, as though paralyzed. His only
movement was from his glazed fear-filled eyes that followed
the men about him. His nose, swollen grotesquely, was
twice its normal size and numerous angry half-healed cuts
marred his face.

"We're going to have to make a run for it, Sheriff,"
Captain Boggs said, "this place is going up soon! Chalker
is bringing the police car to the north door. Let's get the
prisoner down there!"

"We're not going to be able to get him through,
Captain," Sheriff Hardy stated in a low voice, glancing in
Daniel's direction, "unless we shoot some of those men in
that mob! They've gone completely crazy. They mean to
have him and nothing's going to stop them..." he paused,
"except bullets!"

"Hell, man, that's the trouble! We can't use our guns!
That damn governor ordered us not to!"

"Did you talk to him?" the sheriff asked.

"No, I couldn't get through to him!" Captain Boggs
replied.

"Are you sure he sent that order?" the sheriff persisted.

"Hell, I don't know, Sheriff. I never got the message
myself..." he hesitated, uncertainly then, he said firmly,
"but he must have sent it—it came over the A. P. wires. We

can't use guns—we can't take a chance! We can't defy the governor's order!"

"Well, what the shit are we supposed to do, Captain?" the sheriff exploded angrily. "Get ourselves killed over this damn nigger?" Daniel's eyes, wide with terror, were fastened on his face.

"Damn it all, Sheriff..." Captain Boggs began furiously. He was interrupted by a hoarse rasping whisper coming from Daniel. Still petrified and unable to move, his voice quavered. It was plainly apparent that he spoke with great difficulty, forcing the words from his throat.

"Let me stay in here, Mr. Policeman!"

"We can't do that, Daniel," Sheriff Hardy said, tartly. "This place is going to burn up. We've got to get out of here!"

"Captain Boggs! Captain Boggs!" a voice yelled from outside the door. The Captain ran into the hall and looked down to the lower level where Ranger Yates stood. "You've got to come down before the stairway goes," he shouted.

Captain Boggs saw that the flames were already greedily eating their way underneath and through several steps. He knew that it was only a matter of minutes before the stairway, the only one connecting the two floors, would become impassable. Running back to the door of the records room, he shouted, "Come on! Let's get out of here!"

The two deputies already had Daniel by the arms, dragging and half-carrying him to the door. He was pulling back against them, resisting. In a panic-stricken voice, he cried out, "Please, Mr. Policeman, let me stay here!" Continuing to pull him along, they had almost reached the door when Daniel suddenly wrenched from their grasp. He sank to his knees and his whole body shook violently as he pleaded pitifully over and over, "Please don't take me out there! Don't let them get me! Please don't take me out there!"

Captain Boggs looked at him, then turned to Sheriff Hardy and asked hurriedly, "What about the vault, Sheriff? It's steel—it won't burn!" Even under the stress of the moment, he recognized the expression of relief that passed over the sheriff's face.

His face red, Sheriff Hardy shouted excitedly, "If they put the fire out in time, he'll be all right in there. If they don't, the heat will fry him like a chicken!" His face grew wary as he added, "But he sure as hell ain't gonna make it outside, Captain! None of us are gonna make it through that mob—not with him." His eyes grew crafty as he looked at Daniel. "He has some chance in that vault and if that's the way he wants it..." His voice trailed off.

"Come on, Daniel," Captain Boggs took hold of his arm and helped him to his feet and, now, Daniel went willingly. The door of the vault, unlocked previously by Sheriff Hardy, was standing ajar. Captain Boggs quickly swung its heavy weight wide and Daniel started inside. Captain Boggs grasped his arm and turned him to face him. He looked into the horror-stricken, tear-streaked, mutilated face. "Are you sure this is what you want, Daniel?" he asked.

Daniel nodded his head, gulped and whispered faintly, "Yas-suh!"

Captain Boggs took hold of the door to close it but Sheriff Hardy suddenly reached out, restraining it. Quickly taking the keys from his belt, he unlocked the handcuffs and pulled them from Daniel's wrists. He looked closely into Daniel's face and opened his mouth to speak but no words came. He swallowed and remained silent. Then, he grabbed Daniel's hand and shook it. He stepped backwards away from him. Captain Boggs swung the door shut on Daniel who stood still, rooted to the spot, and stared back at them with wide, numbly desperate eyes. The door slammed and clicked loudly. Captain Boggs turned the combination lock and the five of them ran for the stairs.

Tad Sloane jumped to the ground from the window of the courthouse. He was sputtering and choking as he retreated from the fumes of the bomb that Captain Boggs had thrown when he saw the man entering the room. The windows were a good six feet above the ground and Tad twisted an ankle in his awkward exit and descent. Rolling and groaning on the grass, he alternated between rubbing his painfully injured leg and his streaming burning eyes. The crowd, frustrated and furious at both the thwarted attempt to get at the prisoner and the bomb counterattack, shouted obscenities.

Their attention was diverted from Tad to the fire truck, which, with its siren screaming, had screeched to a halt in the street. Momentarily taken aback, the people parted slightly, making a narrow gap through which the firemen ran clumsily, pulling the wieldy heavy hoses.

A man yelled and pointed to a second story window. The crowd gazed upward. Two men with handkerchiefs held over their noses were waving and shouting to the firemen. A fireman ran with a ladder toward the building. He was aided by several men in the crowd. The throng purged forward behind them, wildly excited, anticipating the descent of the Negro. When the ladder was in place, a fireman ascended and reached the room where the men waited. It was Judge Wheelus' office situated over his courtroom on the lower floor. The men were Judge Wheelus and the bailiff who had gone to his office in an attempt to retrieve some of his important papers. Not realizing the imminence of the fire, they had lingered too long. Opening the door to leave, they had been driven back by the flames and almost overcome by the smoke before prying the window open to seek help. They descended, coughing and choking, with the aid of the fireman and made their way through the crowd who made no covert threat toward them. Disappointed instead, they showed no further interest and backed off, turning their attention once more to the firemen who were pouring water into the building. Fire could be seen chewing its way through the high ceiling into the floor above. Soon, the water began to quench some of the flames. A surge of renewed rage swept through the mob. Shouts and cries rose afresh! "Stop them! Stop those firemen!"

A woman, screaming hysterically, pushed at one of them, trying to disengage him from the hose which he aimed through the window. Men followed suit, shoving at them, grabbing at the hoses. In desperation, the firemen turned the hoses on their attackers. Water gushed into faces. Opened mouths, gasping for air, were filled with water instead. Screams, coughs and curses rent the air. The ones directly in front fell back under the heavy pressure of water against them, forcing those behind to retreat. In the clamor, they clawed each other in panic to get away from the water's painful force. Many went down. Others trampled over them or tripped to fall alongside.

Suddenly, the water stopped slamming into the crowd. Several men had grabbed axes from the fire truck and cut the hoses into. The firemen looked in astonishment at the sterile weapons in their hands. The drenched, disheveled throng, temporarily stunned by the water, was dazed but only momentarily. Seeing their tormentors now disarmed, their fury mounted even greater and swept anew over them. The astonished expressions of the firemen changed quickly to fear as they felt the murderous hostile intent of the angry horde advancing on them. Throwing down their useless hoses, they turned and ran from this mob gone mad.

Chalker drove roughly over the curb and gunned the car across the grass toward the north door of the courthouse. With the nucleus of the mob congregated on the opposite side, there were only a few stragglers on this west lawn, watching the activity. The car was halfway across when those on the edges of the crowd spotted it, yelled and pointed to alert the others. Howling like a pack of wolves after prey, they swooped in unison toward it. The cries became a chorus of triumphant harmony when they saw Captain Boggs, Sheriff Hardy, the deputies and Rangers exit and run between two protective lines formed by the soldiers from the entrance to the waiting police car by the bottom step. The troops held their guns with fixed bayonets toward the oncoming mob.

Chalker had locked all the doors. Reaching the steps, he unlocked the two on the side next to them. Sheriff Hardy was the first man to reach the car. He jumped into the front seat beside Chalker and pulled a deputy in next to him. "Get in! Get in!" he yelled at the others who were scrambling and pushing their way into the back seat. Captain Boggs groaned and cursed when Ranger Yates ground a heel into his foot, then fell clumsily into his lap as he was forced into the tight limited space, which was now occupied by eight men.

"Shut that damn door and lock it!" Sheriff Hardy yelled. Ranger Calhoun, the last one inside, closed and locked it with difficulty.

A barrage of rocks pelted the hood of the car. The mob, not to be stopped, was viciously hurling rocks, sticks and anything they could lay hands on at the soldiers and the car. Captain Boggs saw a rock catch a soldier, standing near the car, on the forehead. He staggered backwards. Blood streamed profusely down his young bewildered face as he fell to the ground.

"The sons-of-bitches!" Captain Boggs exploded. Reaching across Calhoun, he rolled the window halfway down and yelled through the opening, "Get back to the jail, men!"

At that moment, several men from the crowd had managed to get through the soldiers to the car and were pounding on it with their fists, screaming and cursing its occupants.

"Get out of here, Chalker!" Sheriff Hardy shouted. Chalker turned the car away from the oncoming numbers, forcing those in its way relentlessly aside. When it faced the west side of the square, the path ahead was clear. With the siren screaming full blast, Chalker stepped on the gas pedal. The car careened across the lawn and bounced wildly over the curb. He slowed momentarily to regain control of the vehicle, turned the wheel sharply and raced down the street, leaving the fighting fracas behind them.

The rock-throwing battle continued. The soldiers, many of whom were wounded, were frustrated at the order prohibiting their self-defense and resorted just as viciously, hurling missiles in retaliation. But, tremendously outnumbered, they were chased swiftly from the lawn of the courthouse into the street and forced to retreat under the heavy barrage until they were a block away. Here, new projectiles were added to the ammunition by the crowd. From a small soft drink stand near the edge of the street, soda pop bottles, both empty and filled, were grabbed from their cases and flung at the chaotically disorganized troops. Cries of those that were hit and sounds of glass splintering rent the air. Many fell on both sides with blood flowing from heads, noses and bodies.

A truce was finally called when the crowd lost interest in pursuing the defeated bewildered boys and backed away, "Get back to the courthouse—the prisoner's still in there!" someone commanded. They hurried back toward the burning structure. The bedraggled soldiers dragged their injured comrades from the scene and made their way dejectedly down the three blocks to the town jail to await further instructions from Captain Boggs.

Speculating that the prisoner must be confined in the steel vault, the only feasible place for safeguarding that the courthouse afforded, the mob thronged quickly once again to the east side of the building underneath the records room. Several men entered the broken windows but the devastating smoke and fire aborted them, spewing them outside choking and gasping for air. Encouraged by the ancient dry wood of the building that was over 50 years old, the blaze appeased its consuming cavernous craving by devouring the structure voraciously. The fire truck from the Duganville Department reached the scene at this moment. It was much too late. The crowd warily scrutinized the firemen, but they made no attempt to combat the blaze. A roar of intoxicated approval went up when the truck drove away after lingering only a short time.

The mob was ecstatic as the flames hungrily consumed the second floor and climbed through the roof. And there they stayed, raptly watching, as their courthouse burned.

Arriving at the police station from the courthouse, Chalker and Captain Boggs entered Chalker's office. The phone was ringing. Chalker answered then handed the phone to Captain Boggs. He took it, listened for a minute and then slammed the receiver on the hook. "Another damn threat!" he said. "Their words are getting choicer all the time about what they're going to do to me if I don't stop interfering and get out of town!" His voice was shaking with rage. "This bastard said I'd be the first one he'd shoot if I come back to the courthouse!"

He sat down at the desk and picked up the receiver again. "Operator," he said, "did you ever get my call through to the governor? This is Captain Boggs." And, after a pause, "Well, try again now, will you? And hurry!" A few moments later, he exploded, "Yes, I'll talk to the lieutenant governor!" When he answered, Captain Boggs said angrily, "Well, where the hell is the governor?"

Chalker had taken a cigar from the box of Havanas on his desk and was puffing hard on it to get it lit. With a sense of satisfaction, he saw Captain Boggs' discomfiture. *The Captain is not so smug and sure of himself now*, he thought, as he listened to him continue in a cold voice.

"I want you to get in touch with Governor Franklin and..." Evidently interrupted, he stopped momentarily before sayings "I don't give a damn how you do it—just do it! Tell him that I said to either change that order or take me off this damn case. He can take his choice!" He listened a moment, then said tersely, "I'm in a hell of a fix! Right now, the Negro is locked in the vault at the courthouse and a mob has set fire to the courthouse and there's not a damn thing my troops or I can do about it without guns to back us up! I've got fifty men and there's got to be almost five thousand people in that mob! Now, you tell the governor to change that order or free me from this case! And, at this point, as far as I'm concerned, I don't feel this damn place is worth saving—the town and the nigger deserve each other!" With that, he slammed the receiver down once more.

Turning to Chalker, he said, "I hope that son-of-a-bitch is having a nice vacation! He's on his way to south Texas for a rest after dumping this shit in my lap!" He slammed his fist against the desk. "Why the hell did he tie my hands on this thing for?" He looked at Chalker, his face contorted with fury and frustration. It was a statement rather than a question. Chalker slowly, deliberately puffed on his cigar without answering. "There's no way to stop mad men without using guns!" Captain Boggs continued, more to himself than to Chalker. "How the hell does he expect me to handle this mob with a handful of men if I can't threaten to use bullets?" He was silent a moment, thoughtful. "Almost five thousand of them and I've got fifty soldiers!" He snorted derisively. "Some odds! Hell, that's just plain suicide!"

Chalker was pleased to see him sweating. *Let him sweat,* he thought. *He didn't think I could handle it—that I was too young and inexperienced—still wet behind the ears. He was so sure that it would be a pushover for him—the big Texas Ranger!* Chalker almost chuckled aloud. *Well, even with all his little tin soldiers, he still can't cut the mustard!*

Suddenly, Captain Boggs jumped up, pushing his chair back so hard that it toppled over and crashed to the floor. Pounding the desk furiously with his fist, he said, "Well, damn it all, I'm not going to tie the hands of my troops!"

"What do you plan to do?" Chalker asked in concealed disdain.

"Well, I don't plan to have any of those kids killed—not if I can help it. They don't stand a chance against that bunch of mad dogs!"

Chalker looked at him apprehensively, puffing warily on the cigar. "Just what are you going to do, Captain?"

"I'll tell you what I'm going to do, Chief!" Captain Boggs replied arrogantly. "I'm going to order my troops to stay at the jail away from those lunatics. I'm not about to send them up against that mob again since they can't defend themselves with guns. And, thanks to your loud mouth reporter, everybody knows it!"

Chalker, trying to keep his voice calm, said, "We've got to get the prisoner out of that vault when the firemen put that fire out. We've got to send those soldiers back to the courthouse..."

"Damn it all, Chalker—don't you tell me what to do with my men!" Captain Boggs interrupted him angrily, his face red. His voice held contempt as he added, "I sure as hell don't see your policemen in front of that mob. In fact, they've made themselves scarce as hens' teeth!"

"Aw, shit, Captain, you know better'n that..." Chalker

commenced but Captain Boggs interrupted him again.

Leaning over the desk, he glared into Chalker's face. "We were supposed to be in this thing together, Chalker," he said, "but ever since we arrived, you've just let my men take over all the duties of your policemen."

Enraged, Chalker clenched the cigar tightly between his teeth. "Boggs," he did not call him *Captain Boggs*, "you let me know right off the bat that the governor had put you in charge of law and order here! So don't go trying to throw the blame on my shoulders now that you don't know what the hell to do!"

Their loud tirade was abruptly silenced by the ringing of the phone. "Hello!" Chalker shouted into it. He listened for a minute; then, without saying a word, he hung the receiver back on the hook. Glancing up at Captain Boggs briefly, his eyes returned to the desk as he said, "The fire chief says the courthouse is burning to the ground. The mob wouldn't let them put the fire out."

Captain Boggs, still leaning over the desk, pounded his fist against it. Then, straightening, he rubbed a hand wearily over his face. Chalker, his voice placating now, said, "When those reinforcements get here, will there be enough of them to get Daniel from the vault?" Then, he added, "providing he's still alive."

His face stormy, Captain Boggs glowered at Chalker. "I don't give a damn how many reinforcements we get. Until that order from the governor is changed, I'm not sending my men against that mob again!" He pointed a finger at Chalker. "If you want someone to confront it, you can just round up your men from wherever they're hiding and send them!" He strode toward the door, calling back, "After all, the governor's order only referred to the National Guard—it didn't say a damn thing about your policemen not shootin'!"

"Now look here, Boggs," Chalker said, rising angrily

from his chair, "if you're trying to force me to give orders to my policemen to shoot to kill—just forget it! My men are friends and neighbors of those people in that crowd and they're not about to let me persuade them to kill any of them over some black bastard rapist!"

"Then that's your problem, Chief!" Captain Boggs retorted. Opening the door, he turned. They spent a long moment, staring steadily into each other's eyes, sizing each other up. Finally, Captain Boggs shrugged his shoulders slightly and said sharply, "I'm going over to the jail with the Guard. And that's where we're going to stay until the governor changes that order!" He stalked out, slamming the door behind him.

"Shit!" Chalker spat out.

CHAPTER 17

It was late evening now. Long shadows, cast by the setting sun, fell across the crowd. Although the searing heat from the sun's rays had dissipated somewhat, enough lingered to last through the night and keep the air stiflingly oppressive.

The crowd of approximately five thousand people was rapidly swelling even larger. Word of the attack on the courthouse had spread like wildfire through Anseltown and to the outlying communities. The mass of humanity spilled into the streets surrounding the square, blocking cars already parked and preventing more from entering. Curiosity seekers and calmer minded citizens gathered and stood apart, well back, at the outer fringes of the mob. Flasks of whiskey, concealed in pockets, were clandestinely but generously passed. With prohibition in effect in the county, some of it was homemade, some bootlegged from Oklahoma or Dallas. When emptied, the flasks were taken to be replenished from hidden caches in cars. The odor of whiskey, blending with the fetid stench of perspiration that emanated from the sticky heat of human bodies to which clothes clung damply and uncomfortably, floated through the air.

Women with children in arms, men and boys crowded as close to the burning courthouse as the heat would permit. Blazing fingers of fire chewed at and devoured the entrails of the structure. The dancing flames, leaping obscenely, were matched by equally frenzied dancing movements of the mob below. The holocaust, like a cancerous disease eating wildly at its victim, gutted the building and left gaping holes that resembled open sores in the sides of the empty shell. The steel vault could now be seen through a smoldering, festering slash in the second story room.

"Let's get him!" a voice screamed hysterically.

A ladder, abandoned by the firemen, was quickly hoisted against the structural skeleton. The flames had died down inside now and could be seen only here and there in the roof. A youth eagerly ascended the ladder. Placing a foot through the charred opening onto the floor, he gingerly tested its strength and the heat of it. He turned to yell down, "I can make it to the vault!" A roar of anticipation went up from the crowd below as he stepped inside.

"Get that nigger!" someone yelled. The chant was taken up until the sound was that of one single gigantic voice, reverberating through the still, hot night.

Miraculously, the vault appeared to still stand solidly on the fire blackened floor. The boy worked his way cautiously, testing the strength of the surface at each step until he stood near the vault. Reaching out, he grabbed the handle of the door. He jerked his hand from it. It was too hot to touch. He took his handkerchief from his packet and jerked at the handle again through its protection but the door held fast, "It's locked!" he yelled, "I can't get it open!" He kicked at the door in frustration. The mob, growing increasingly impatient now, with the prize seemingly to be theirs at last, screamed in frenzy, "Open the door! Get that nigger!" One of the men who had climbed the ladder behind the youth shouted down, "Give me the dynamite!

We'll blow the bastard out!" A stick of dynamite was quickly passed up the ladder. A long fuse attached to it was deftly affixed to the door. As the men made their way down the ladder, the crowd, anticipating the explosion, flowed backward in a single wave. The man who had attached the fuse to the vault's door was the last to descend. He took a match from his pocket and lit the fuse that he had carried in his hand, stretching it along carefully. As it commenced sputtering, he jumped from the ladder and ran.

The lighted fuse, hissing, continued its snakelike slither upwards toward the second story. The crowd, watching in breathless fascination, became suddenly quiet for the first time during this long afternoon. As the fuse spit its way through the gargantuan hole and disappeared, the silence was almost unbearable. The stillness was abruptly pierced by an ear-shattering explosion that sent people scattering in every direction. Pieces of wood, debris and steel flew outward, hurtling forcefully through the air and digging holes in the earth with their impact. Dust and smoke poured through the structure's gnawing apertures and filled the atmosphere with dirt, sparks and cinders.

As the noise of the blast died, the crowd, like soldiers on command, did an about face. They turned, almost as one, and ran back to the courthouse, screaming with pleasure. There was a stampede to reach the ladder that had been blown to the ground. It was raised amid delirious cries of "Hurry! Hurry! Hurry!" Men shoved and pushed each other, racing to be the first to ascend the ladder and claim the long awaited reward in the opened vault. The first man to gain a footing had climbed half way up when he was suddenly grabbed and jerked from the ladder by those under him. He fell to the ground and lay moaning, holding his broken arm. The next man to begin an ascent was punched viciously in the face and knocked from the rungs. Blood poured from his nose. Men encircled the ladder, exchanging violent blows and clawing at each other in their irascible passion to reach it. Those who could not attain the proximity of the ladder crowded close to the smoldering hull of the building and began, in violent agitation, to pull down portions of the burned crumbling walls even at a distance from the vault.

When one man, in the midst of the melee, finally succeeded in scaling the ladder, the fighting ceased. Others quickly followed while the crowd roared assent. As the first man went through the opening of the records room, a rush fell over the mob as they waited in trembling anticipation. Suddenly, one of the men stuck his head through the opening and yelled frenziedly, "He's dead—the black bastard's dead!" The cry echoed through the throng. Frustrated curses and obscenities were shouted against this outrage by the mob that felt cheated of its revenge.

The body, found sprawled in a grotesque position, was carried from the vault. It was nude. The victim had evidently clawed away his clothes in a desperate effort to alleviate the suffocating heat emanating from the fire outside his sealed tomb. A deep wound on one side of the head lay open to reveal a piece of steel from the dynamite blast imbedded in the skull. The eyes, wide open, were fixed, staring in horror. The horribly parched skin was drawn and wrinkled.

The men held the body aloft at the opening for everyone to see. The people surged forward, screaming hungrily, "Let us have him!" Those holding it swung and heaved the corpse. It hit the ground with a dull revolting thud. Eager willing hands claimed the body. It was lifted and carried through the crowd toward the street. Plans that had been plotted well in advance for a living victim were not to be thwarted—not even for a dead one. A chain, taken from a car, was hastily fastened around the body and the other end was linked to the rear bumper. Men jumped into the automobile, filling it to capacity, and the motor started. Thus, the grisly procession began, with the car dragging the corpse behind it, moving slowly so the people of the mob could view their prize—this animal—this object of their hatred. As the macabre parade proceeded down Texas Street, men and women swarmed around the body, spitting upon it, throwing rocks and striking out with sticks at it. Many, taking turns, jumped on top of it to ride before being shoved off by new riders.

"Let's take the bastard to 'nigger row' and show them what we do in this town with niggers like him!" someone cried. The crowd roared in unison with approval and they made their way down the main street to the outskirts of town. The Anseltown policemen made no attempt to interfere with or stop the ghastly cavalcade. With the courthouse smoldering in ruins behind them and the mob stampeding deliriously down the streets, they simply directed the traffic, the legion of cars that had swarmed to town like bees to a honey hive, away from the hubbub of activity. And, at the same time, Captain Boggs and his National Guardsmen remained isolated at the jail.

At every desecration thought up, at each fresh atrocity perpetrated against the corpse along the way, enthusiastic cries of endorsement came from the mad frothing throng. Though death had already claimed the maimed mutilated victim being dragged through the streets, still, the people defiled and beat him.

CHAPTER 18

Mayor Ansel parked his car on the dark street, some distance from the heart of town. With the aid of his cane, he walked through the deserted side streets, avoiding the ones nearest town. Surrounding streets for four blocks on each side of the town's center had been cordoned off by the police to prevent further entrance into the area by vehicles. The streets of this outside perimeter on which the mayor now walked, were eerily empty and quiet. Faintly, he heard cries; then, the noise of a sharp explosion splitting the air came from the direction of the courthouse. Angry sparks, flitting like fireflies high in the sky, illuminated the horizon brightly.

By the time the mayor reached the alleyway that led to the back entrance of his office, he was breathing hard from the unusual exertion. He fumbled with the ring of keys in the darkness. Finally, locating the right one, he opened the door and stepped inside, making sure that it locked behind him. He did not turn on a light. The office, in total darkness, was so familiar that he moved about in complete ease, avoiding bumping into any of its furnishings.

Although this was the first time that Mayor Ansel had been in his office today, he had followed the day's events closely. After attending Alicia Johnson's funeral, he had viewed the large congregation at the courthouse from a distance, then went home. He kept in contact with Jess all afternoon. When Jess informed him that the mob was storming and setting fire to the courthouse, he overrode his wife's protests and drove to town.

Suddenly, the cries of the crowd grew louder, nearer. He heard the sound of a car, approaching in his direction. He hurried to the window. Carefully parting a small slit between the drapes, he peered through it down Texas Street. He saw the car drawing near, with the dancing, screaming people behind it. When the vehicle was even with his position by the window, he could see the chain, dangling from the rear bumper and dragging the corpse over the concrete pavement. A wave of horror swept over him as a man jumped on the body, balancing himself on it as it bumped along. He recoiled in revulsion.

He felt nauseated. He limped slowly from the window, groping blindly for his desk. Holding on to it for support, he felt his way around the massive piece of furniture. Exhausted and drained, he sank weakly into his deeply upholstered chair. Mayor Ansel sat, slumped and staring into the black void of the room, long after the noise had died in the distance and the town was vacant and silent at last.

The crowd shrieked with renewed cries of outrage when the car crossed the railroad track and reached the first shack of the Negro community on the dark narrow dirt road. The broken down ramshackle shanties stood in a row, starkly bleak in the pale moonlight, making ghostly shapes against the backdrop of woods behind them.

"Get some of those black bastards!" a voice shouted angrily.

Several men ran toward the cabin. Slamming their shoulders against the door, which yielded easily, they burst inside. It was pitch black. Someone lit a match. A candle stood in the center of the wooden table in the kitchen. One of the men lit it and made a thorough search of the four small rooms, desolate in their bareness. Running outside, they yelled to the crowds, "The bastards ain't here! They must have left town!"

A man standing near the corpse tied behind the car, shouted, "That's the place where this black bastard lived!" He kicked the body viciously.

"Burn it down! Burn all the shacks to the ground!" a woman's voice screamed hysterically. "We don't want the niggers coming back!"

Exultant, men hurriedly lit scraps of paper and applied them to the rotted wood of the shanty. It literally exploded into flames which shot skyward as the tarpaper and wood spontaneously ignited. In a matter of minutes, it was only a rubble of glowing ashes.

Jon had been transfixed all afternoon, watching the drama before him in dazed disbelief. He moved, as though in a trance, hypnotically following at a distance behind the gruesome march of the mob. He gazed in numb disbelief at familiar faces that were familiar to him no longer; faces transformed today into those of twisted ugly strangers.

Now, the sight of the men setting fire to Glo-ree's house shattered his mesmerized state. Jon raced to the hut but, by the time he reached it, the flames were already leaping wildly. He tried to enter the kitchen and reach the water faucet but, when he opened the door, the intense heat and black smoke that poured forth forced him backwards. In desperation, he began to scoop up handfulls of dirt from the ground and throw it on the flaming walls. The fire licked out at him, singeing his hair. A large burning ember from the tarpaper roof flew at his face and clung to his forehead. He knocked the glowing piece away and retreated from the shack, now a roaring inferno. His skin was stinging painfully. Shaking in rage, he stared helplessly at the fire, cursing.

Suddenly, a scream of terror nearby jolted him from his fury. In the brightness of the blaze, Jon saw a man chasing a slight fleeing figure. He overtook the thin Negro youth, about 15 years of age, and grabbed him roughly. At that moment, the man, whose back had been toward Jon, turned and the light from the fire caught his face, revealing it vividly.

My God, it's Harley Potter, Jon thought. He rubbed his eyes. They must be playing tricks on him. *It can't be him— not Harley!* His mind refused to accept the image that his vision had flashed to his brain. His thoughts were in a state of jumbled confusion. He had not seen Harley in the crowd today. Harley would be the one sane person who would not be caught up in this madness. He shook his head as if he could erase Harley's face before him. *But it is Harley! He's here, a part of the insanity that is running rampant through Anseltown.*

Jon saw Harley infuriatedly clutching the boy's throat and shaking him violently. Still, Jon stood, statue-like, unable to move. His brain was playing tricks on him. Attempting to straighten his muddled thoughts, he could not clearly grasp what was happening around him. The boy clawed wildly at his captor's hands. Jon, seeing him grow limp under the powerful hands that were choking the life from him, finally came to life.

"Turn him loose, Potter!" he shouted.

There was no response. For, in his madness, Harley did not even hear Jon. Jon swung his arm with all his strength and crashed his fist into Harley's face. His hands released their grip on the boy as Harley flew backwards from the force of Jon's blow. He fell heavily to the ground. The Negro boy streaked across the road at the back of the house into the darkness of the woods beyond.

"Damn you, Jon!" Harley shouted his fury as he rose to his feet. A group of men quickly encircled them. His face contorted, Harley rushed at him but Jon deftly stepped aside, avoiding the onslaught. Instinctively, Jon felt the movement behind him. In that brief instant before the blow fell, out of the corner of his eye, he glimpsed Jim Sanders as he swung a club at his head. The board crashed against his skull and blackness engulfed him.

The men did not so much as cast a backward glance at Jon who lay deathly still on the ground. Instead, they raced eagerly to catch up with the others who were speeding to be first in setting the torch to the remaining dozen or so huts. None of the shacks escaped. The conflagration lit up the night sky brilliantly, but briefly, as the flames exploded upward, then settled into smoldering piles of embers and ashes.

Jon stirred slowly and opened his eyes. He saw the faint glimmer of the stars overhead and wondered vaguely why he was lying on the ground. His head throbbed painfully. Lifting his hand, he touched the huge lump behind his ear gingerly. It felt warm and sticky. He raised himself on his elbows, then sat up slowly. His head spun dizzily as he tried to focus his eyes to the black strangeness of the night surrounding him and vainly attempted to determine where he was and what had happened.

Suddenly, his eyes caught sight of and lingered on several huge black mounds, lined evenly in a row, flecked with bits of red glowing coals, "Damn them!" he cursed aloud as memory came flooding back, memory of the mob igniting the cabin homes of the Negroes.

He sat and stared long moments at the rubbled havoc, while anguish and anger rose almost unbearably within him. His mind brooded on the familiar, yet totally strange faces of the people who had so ardently and feverishly perpetrated this devastation.

"Damn them!" he shouted as his feelings surfaced and burst forth. His cry startled the uncanny mysterious quietness and echoed eerily in the stillness of the night.

His anger vent, Jon felt weak. He sat very still for a
long while. His eyes riveted on a small fire, which was
burning down in the meadow beyond the last mound.
Other objects were near the fire but he could not identify
them in the distance. His eyes were blurry, fuzzy. They
hurt when he tried to focus them too closely on any one
thing. And his head ached horribly. Groaning, he lay back
on the ground again. After a time—he didn't know for how
long or whether he passed out again—he opened his eyes.
He got up with difficulty. He had to stand still for a while
to stop his head from spinning.

Involuntarily, his eyes gravitated once more to the
fire in the meadow. Without consciously willing it, Jon
found himself walking toward the spot that was pulling
him, drawing him like a magnet. Passing through what
were once the yards of the cabins, he could make out a few
flowers, incongruous looking now with their blooms
surrounding the smoking piles of rubble.

As he neared the meadow, he stopped abruptly, rooted
to the spot. He stared at the now distinguishable objects.
Suspended at the end of a rope thrown over a limb of a huge
cottonwood tree were the remains of the Negro. It hung
directly over a small mound of still glowing ashes. A large
fire had been built underneath the body by the mob that
wildly fed the flames with the shabby furniture they
carted from the huts before igniting them. The blazing
holocaust had eaten ravenously at the corpse, consuming
the flesh from it, until only an ivory boned skeleton,
bleached white, remained dangling in midair. Jon gasped
at the spectacle of bones, its stark whiteness etched sharply
against the surrounding blackness of the night, swinging
alone in the stillness.

Against his will, he walked hesitantly, trancelike,
toward it. He felt compelled to draw close to the grisly

scene. An invisible entity seemed to be forcing him to view clearly the last act of this prolonged drama that had unfolded in front of him these past hours, before the final curtain fell, exhorting him to drink the bitter dregs from this day's galling cup of insanity to the last drop.

Mesmerized, Jon gazed upward at the skeleton. His thoughts dwelled bitterly on the mob, long since gone, and this result of vengeance that culminated their lustful satisfaction. The realization of the cold-blooded and businesslike precision in which retribution was purposely perpetrated and methodically carried out by the people against their victim numbed him both mentally and physically. The mob, thinking as one, had a definite aim in mind and understood the need of keeping at the task until it was finished. So, they had worked together to achieve their ultimate goal.

Hypnotically, Jon viewed the pendulous vertebrae, this final evidence before him, this climactic act performed by the crazed crowd. His consciousness lingered on the people who, though separate beings, had united to create one body—the body of a mob. His mind brought each face in focus before him, faces of those that he had loved so much and had known, or believed he had known, so well.

"Do we ever really know anyone?" he demanded of himself, speaking the words aloud. For him, the answer came swiftly, clearly and simply. He had been mistaken. He had been horribly mistaken all his life for he had never really known these people at all.

His eyes remained fixed on the skeleton. His thoughts reverted to Glo-ree. This was all that remained of her son—this pile of bones hanging from a rope. For the first time, he thought of Daniel. He had not associated this specter with Daniel before. He felt nauseated. Savagely, he kicked at the small pile of smoldering embers. Fagots and bits of broken up furniture, converted into flames by willing eager hands applying matches, had formed both bier and pyre for Daniel.

Thrusting the toe of his shoe into the loose dirt, Jon, furious, propelled it violently, time and again, onto the coals until they were covered completely, and all illumination smothered leaving the night in total darkness. He trembled, breathing hard from emotion and exertion, but he felt an overwhelming sense of relief. It was as if by extinguishing the light from the fire, he could blot out the existence of the skeleton and all that had gone before. He could no longer see the macabre specter suspended in the air.

Suddenly, something cold, clammy touched his arm. The skeleton, in its slow oscillating motion, had swung against him. Repulsed and flinching in horror, he turned and ran blindly across the meadow to the dirt road. He stumbled and fell several times in the darkness but he was oblivious to the pain. Each time, he jumped up and staggered on. He had one desire at the moment and that was to get away from this place—from the corpse tied to the end of that rope.

"Oh, God, how I wish I'd never seen it!" he moaned. It was almost a prayer. His chest hurt so, he could hardly breathe. His head throbbed painfully. If only he could blot the memory of the scene from his mind and erase the faces of the mob. If only he could wipe this whole ugly day out of his life.

Jon ran on wildly, sightlessly through the blackness of the night. The moon had gone behind a cloud, withdrawing and hiding its face, as though it refused to shine on the ghastly scene below.

The narrow road that Jon had taken from the meadow was the one that lay at the edge of the woods behind his home. As he passed the place where he had lived for so many years, he did not even glance at it. Instead, he sped swiftly by, never once looking back at his house.

Finally, panting and gasping for air, he reached his truck. He had run all the way from the outskirts of Anseltown to its center. His chest was on fire. His lungs felt as if they would burst but he couldn't force himself to stop running until he reached the truck. His whole being was riveted on his one consuming desire. He had to get out of this God-forsaken, damnable place—or die. He couldn't stay in it another minute. He knew that he would die if he stayed or, even worse, lose his sanity like the rest of the lunatics in that mob.

It was 4 o'clock in the morning. Jon rubbed at his eyes in an effort to obliterate the drowsiness that kept pressing down on him, endeavoring to conquer his senses. He suddenly realized that he had not slept in almost 24 hours. He had driven woodenly, like a robot, since he raced out of Anseltown. He had not stopped once and, only now, was just beginning to overcome the numbness which had engulfed him, holding him in a viselike grip, since yesterday. Now, at last, he could feel again, but utter exhaustion threatened to overpower him. Though bone weary, he couldn't stop yet. He wouldn't allow himself to stop. Not yet. The events of yesterday kept staring him in the face, compelling him to look again at them, to relive each sordid act. He tried to eradicate them from his consciousness, but his mind would not cooperate. It refused to blank them out and grant him peace. All he wanted to do was forget, to leave the whole stinking town and its hateful memories behind him—forever.

He pressed the accelerator to the floor as he passed the *End of City Limits* sign. He had just passed through Amarillo. The town was asleep at this hour. Now, in the western outskirts on Highway 66, he headed toward New Mexico. Easing the pressure of his foot slightly on the gas pedal, he focused his attention on lighting a cigarette. Then he pushed the peddle to the floor once more. In an effort to combat his weariness, he forced his mind to concentrate on what lay ahead for him—California, the Golden State, the land of milk and honey, that veritable pot of gold at the end of the rainbow which promised bountiful riches!

He flipped his half-smoked cigarette through the open window. It contributed to the heat, made him more uncomfortable. Even at this hour of the morning, the west Texas heat was oppressive. His clothes clung clammily to his body and, in the confined space of the cab, he could smell the odor of his stale sweat. Once again, he directed his thoughts to return to California and to the stories he had heard of it: The cool waters of the ocean, the balmy breezes and the mountains topped with snow. His imagination ran rampant envisioning himself swimming in the Pacific and lying in the cold downy mattress of snow on a white-capped peak. At last, he was going to do all the things that he had always wanted to do and see all the places he had dreamed about. *I'm going to see that whole state, every inch of it,* he promised himself fiercely. *And I won't stop there! I'm going to travel around this entire country—inch by inch!* His body relaxed at the pleasant prospect. Abruptly, he jerked himself upright. He had almost fallen asleep.

He rubbed his eyes again and peered into the moonless night. It wouldn't be long now. He would soon be at the border of New Mexico. Slowing the truck, he stared intently into the darkness at the flat land that stretched, seemingly endless, until it blended as one with the sky. He was unable to determine where the land ended and the horizon of the sky began.

In the inky blackness and the desolate bleakness of this barren corner of the earth, he felt strangely detached.

He had the eerie sensation of being the only human mortal in the world. He had passed no traffic, had seen no signs of life for hours. An old saying of his mother's ran through his mind, "the night is always darkest just before the dawn." *Well, the night is over for me,* he thought, *my dawn is just beginning.* Contentment filled his being.

Suddenly, Jon slammed his foot against the brake. The heavy truck swayed back and forth across the road from the friction of the abrupt retarding motion and slowed to a halt. An appropriate place, for which he had been searching, had just passed the periphery of his vision. And, it was time now. He was approaching the border of New Mexico. Wide awake now, his mind was alert with a jumble of thoughts as his plans neared fruition. He would not take the truck across the state line. It would be too easy to spot. He'd be picked up quickly. And he wasn't about to be taken back to that damn town.

Jerking the gears in reverse, he backed down the deserted highway a quarter of a mile before reaching the road that led to the right which he had passed. Twisting the wheel, he turned the truck so that the headlights would shine down the narrow country lane. He stopped to gaze down the thin dirt strip as far as he could see in the beam's reflectors. It appeared lonely and abandoned as if it were rarely, if ever, traveled.

Well, this is it, he thought. His face broke into a wide grin. *This is the place. From here, he could hitchhike on to California. Or he could hop a freight. What the hell! He could do as he damn well pleased from now on!* He was light-headed with jubilation as he jammed his foot down hard on the accelerator, racing the truck motor noisily while he sped crazily down the road. Purposefully, he guided the wheels through the numerous deep chug holes, laughing wildly as he bounced roughly along.

Halting a half mile from the highway, he switched off

the headlights and got out. He made a complete circle of the vehicle with *Blossom's Flour & Grain Company* emblazoned in bold red letters on each side. He looked carefully in all directions. Then, satisfied that there were no farm houses in sight, he opened the doors at the back and lifted out the can of gasoline. Twisting the lid from its top, he sloshed half the contents over the inside of the empty van.

"I wish it was full of that son-of-a-bitch's flour!" he muttered. He carried the can to the cab where he threw the remainder into its interior, thoroughly saturating the seat and the space behind it that served as a bed. He tossed the can on the floor. Then, taking his wallet from his back pocket, he removed all of his identification cards. Replacing the wallet, he extricated a match from the pocket of his shirt. He scraped it on the side of the truck door and, when it flared, he held his identification papers over it until they began to burn. He stared at them intently for a long moment as they flamed and, when the fire crept close to his fingers, he moved quickly. Vehemently, almost violently, he flung the incendiary fragments, the remains of his past, into the open window of the cab. He jumped back as the spontaneous combustion of the fire and gasoline exploded with a loud *whoosh*, splitting the silence.

Jon stood at a safe distance from the truck, absorbed in the burning spectacle. He was breathing hard. Though his body trembled with emotion, his mind was clear and sharp. He had never been more in control, more aware of what he was doing, more certain than he was at this moment of what he wanted.

Then, after long moments, an exaggerated sense of satisfaction flooded through him. *There's one damn truck that Barney won't haul flour in anymore! Some other poor bastard won't have to work his tail off driving for him and working for peanuts—like I did.* He laughed bitterly.

The blaze quickly expanded, reaching long crimson squid-like tentacles toward the sky. The fiery redness of the inferno was accentuated sharply against the pitch black sky. As the fingers of fire leaped and danced frenziedly in wild unabated abandon, his own sublime feeling of freedom was magnified, matching the uninhibited movement of the flames. A great wave of exultation washed over him. His spirits soared. He felt as free as a bird.

No longer able to contain his intoxicating exuberance, Jon turned and ran, jumping about in his excitement, vaulting high in the air, rejoicing in the culmination of this long awaited dream—a dream he had feared would never become a reality. He was no longer fatigued. He felt as light as a feather, as if a tremendous weight had been lifted from him. The horrid taste of Anseltown in his mouth, indeed, in his very soul had been purged from him, cauterized by the fire's searing purity. The putrid galling memories of the town—and his past—were going up in smoke behind him.

Retreating, Jon could see the glow from the fire reflecting in the darkness about him. He did not look back once as he ran. This time, in direct contrast to his earlier race from horror, he was running from the sheer exhilarated joy that possessed him. Speeding across the fields toward Highway 66, he did not feel the earth beneath his feet. He had a heady stimulating sensation of weightlessness as though he were flying, floating through the air. All the while, wildly jumbled impetuous thoughts and plans flashed frantically through his head. But, despite all the mass confusion going on inside his brain, one word predominated. One word that stood out vividly, starkly sharp and distinct. And, racing through the night, he shouted jubilantly to the skies, his voice ringing triumphantly through the stillness, "Spain! Spain! Spain!"

CHAPTER 19

It was morning. The pale light of dawn heralded the end of the long night. It was over at last. The black charred hulk of the courthouse stood gloomily in the grayness, a stark reminder of the preceding day's event.

Sam sat in his Anseltown Times office on the second floor on the southeast corner across from the courthouse. He slumped in the heavily upholstered huge old chair which he had drug to the window overlooking the street last evening—the spot where he had spent the night. Emotionally spent and drained, he had been totally unable to muster the strength to go home after watching, in horrified disbelief, the actions of a town gone mad. A town that, by choice, he had adopted for his own, twenty years ago. A town that he had loved.

Sam removed the small round rimmed glasses from his nose. His sensitive brown eyes were still brightly alert in the intelligent and finely chiseled features. He possessed a thatch of thick unruly hair, one lock of which still persisted in falling forward over his forehead. His body, obviously still in good condition, was straight, with only the slightest paunch that continued to defy his diligence in maintaining a trim figure.

Wiping his glasses on his handkerchief, Sam leaned forward dejectedly in his chair. His shoulders were stooped as he peered through the misty early morning light at the dimly outlined bones of the burned building across the way. His thoughts drifted back over the years when he had first come as a young man to Anseltown.

He had found out soon enough about the unwritten law of the town: One had to get along with Mayor Ansel and the only way to do that was to do as he said. As a lowly reporter the first few years, he had no reason for a confrontation with the mayor. But, it was a different story after he managed to buy out the paper from Mr. Trumbull when he retired. From that, came his first run-in with Mayor Ansel. Determined that he would not be intimidated, Sam let him know, right from the start, that it was his paper and he would run it his way without any interference or help from the mayor. They had never got along from that day on. Mayor Ansel, outraged at his refusal to buckle under, was vindictive. Sam was slighted and overlooked in civic affairs and was not asked to be a member of the city council, as was Mr. Trumbull before him.

Deeply opposing the mayor's strategy of prohibiting outside industries into Anseltown which would have propelled its growth and prospered its people, Sam spoke out strongly against his policies. A compassionate man, he was wounded deeply by the suffering of the poor of Anseltown who were sorely deprived by the mayor's selfish greed. He respected the good, honest, genuinely "real" people who frequented his market and he recognized this hard-working class as the "salt of the earth." For, along with millions of others like them across the land, it was they who, through their backbreaking labor and adversity, had lain the foundation of this nation. They were the backbone, the spinal structure, that had supported and perpetuated the country's continuity. They had made great wealth possible for men like Mayor Ansel who, for their own parsimonious gain, shamelessly and ruthlessly exploited these benefactors by avaricious extortion.

Over the years, Lila, with Sam's help, had devoted her time and energy to children, her first love and priority. In addition, they both aided causes and contributed to many other areas, wherever people had need of them. Giving of themselves had brought deep satisfaction and happiness to their lives. And, they had been loved in return. For them, that had been reward enough. Because of the town's high regard and esteem for them, Mayor Ansel had finally, though reluctantly, called a truce and halted his harassment of the "upstart outsider" as he had called Sam. From then on, he had merely ignored him.

Well, Sam thought wryly, *that had been perfectly alright with him.* His thoughts were startled back to the present by the scuffing of marching feet echoing through the empty silent street. For the first time in hours, he stirred from the chair. He rose slowly, stiff and cramped, from his prolonged position. He looked up Texas Street through the window in the direction from which the sound came. But he already knew what he would see. For he had heard the news over the wire during the night. Nevertheless, he watched the unit of 100 additional National Guardsmen that had just arrived from Dallas while they marched past him below. His face was gray and grieved as he heavyheartedly looked after the uniformed soldiers departing down the quiet, deserted street. The scene was a radical contrast now from the overflowing deranged throng of only a few hours ago. The troops passed the square, going on to the jail to join the 150 men who had preceded them last night, arriving after the mob had taken the Negro from the vault.

Anseltown was now under martial rule. The military had come to enforce the law in a town that had been, supposedly, a good town, a civilized town, until its citizens had, for a few hours, gone mad. Sam's shoulders drooped

despondently as he gazed sadly over the rim of his glasses
at the blackened ruins across the way. He suddenly felt
very tired and very old. With a heavy heart, he sighed
wearily, "They've burned our temple of justice."

The secretary ushered Sam into Mayor Ansel's office
that afternoon, shortly before 1 o'clock. Her voice was
coldly efficient, "Have a seat, The mayor will be in shortly."
Then she turned and left hurriedly for her outer office,
leaving Sam standing uncertainly inside the door. He felt
strange in the unfamiliar room that he'd never entered
before. It was the first time in twenty years that he had
been invited to the mayor's office.

He looked around, taking in the luxurious
spaciousness of the mayor's inner sanctum and reflected
wryly that it spoke eloquent volumes of its occupant. Of
course, the mayor would have nothing but the very finest
for himself; while, on the other hand, he felt that those who
worked for him deserved nothing more than the least
amount of miserly wages that he could squeeze by with
paying them.

Sam walked to a chair, richly upholstered. He sat
down, sinking deeply into its plush thick downy interior.
He studied the extravagantly expensive furnishings about
him, and he couldn't help but compare them with the
poverty that plagued the town's poor, most of whom were
employed by the mayor. *No wonder he's such a rich man,* he
thought dourly, bitterly. Then, still thinking, he muttered
aloud, "money-wise." Images of deprivation and squalor
that he had seen over the years as he and Lila delivered
baskets of food at Christmas time to the underprivileged,
both white and black, ran through his head. The abundantly
sumptuous surroundings faded until they were, finally,
totally obliterated from his mind. They were replaced,
instead, by scenes that appeared vividly before him of
children, skimpily dressed and shivering with cold, playing

on bare damp floors both winter and summer, sleeping on piles of rags in a corner.

Disconsolately, Sam rubbed his hand across his eyes, trying to dispel the depressing mental visions. He was very tired. He had had only two hours sleep this morning after finally going home from the long night in his office. He stirred restlessly in his chair, took his watch from his pocket and glanced at it. It was five minutes until one. He was early as usual. It was a habit that he had been unable to break himself of. And, he had never figured out whether it was a vice or a virtue.

This was the first time he had been invited to the mayor's office since he had taken over the newspaper. Mayor Ansel had called a meeting of the councilmen and those prominent in the town's affairs to discuss the present situation. Sam knew how it must have galled the mayor to include him. He also knew that the only reason he did so was to attempt to gain his cooperation and present a unified front for the town, to aid in bailing it and the mayor out of the current tragic mess. Mayor Ansel was aware that speculation would run rife among the out-of-town reporters from Dallas and Fort Worth, as well as several nearby towns, if there were no representatives from Anseltown's own newspaper. And, he wanted no hint of inner conflict. Above all, he wanted no more publicity, in state or out, for his town in addition to the bizarre news that had placed Anseltown, for the first time in its history, prominently on the world map.

His thoughts were interrupted by the appearance of Mr. Rogers and Walter Anderson at the door, followed by Barney Blossom and other notables of Anseltown. They were busily engaged in conversation but they stopped abruptly when they saw him.

"No, Gentlemen, you're not seeing a ghost," he said, dryly, "it's Sam Britton in the flesh—and in the good mayor's office through courtesy of the mayor's personal invitation..." he paused before adding, "*not* the other way around."

Embarrassed laughter followed and no one spoke as they found seats. Art Jensen and Judge Wheelus entered, trailed by Chief Chalker, Sheriff Hardy and Captain Boggs. The newspaper reporters were the last to enter. They walked to the rear of the room and sat together, behind the others. Bob Simms, his reporter for the Anseltown Times, had not been included in Sam's invitation from the mayor. In the phone call that morning, the secretary had formally specified that Mayor Ansel requested Mr. Britton's presence at the meeting.

Everyone had arrived now except the mayor himself. Grumpily impatient, Sam looked at his watch again. It showed half-past one. He grunted. *Wasn't it just like him to keep everyone waiting?* he thought. The mayor never missed an opportunity to emphasize his primate superiority, to stress that he was in complete authority and was running the show.

Sam's chair at one side of the room against the wall gave him a full view of the others and, in turn, placed him in theirs. Now, he made a close scrutiny of the men, studying each face, the faces of those who, under Mayor Ansel's guiding hand, had command of Anseltown and its citizens. They dominated the purse strings that manipulated and controlled the population. These men held the power in their hands—power that decided and determined the economic status of the people. Sam felt his anger rising. He wandered if they fully comprehended the roles they played in the lives and destiny of so many. *Why?* he asked himself, *did they just plain not give a damn?*

Abruptly, Mayor Ansel walked through the door. He glanced around the room, as if making sure that everyone had preceded him. Then, seemingly satisfied that each was in his proper place, he nodded curtly. The audience immediately fell silent at his appearance. They sat quietly now, motionless and restrained, watching him and waiting for him to speak. Leaning heavily on his cane, he walked to his huge and heavily polished mahogany desk and sat down. His body was stooped and his face sagged, lined with fatigue and worry. Despite his feelings toward him, Sam felt a twinge of pity.

"Before we get underway with the meeting," the mayor began, "I would like to make a report on Wayne Winslow's condition. I'm sure that you all know about him being injured yesterday when he tried to stop those who were setting fire to the courthouse. I talked to the doctor this morning. He told me that Mr. Winslow is completely paralyzed and will remain so the rest of his life." He hesitated, looking down at his desk. He cleared his throat then, raising his eyes again, continued, "The doctor said his brain was damaged so badly that he will never be rational again."

No one spoke. There was complete silence in the room. Sam saw Barney Blossom shaking his head sadly. Finally, the mayor spoke again. His voice was brusque, vehement. "What a disgrace for our town—to have something like this happen here!"

Murmurs of assent swept through the room. Sam looked at the men about him, but said nothing. He had the distinct impression that Mayor Ansel was speaking more of the violation and dishonor on his town rather than the tragedy that had befallen Winslow. He couldn't help wondering just how long the mayor would remember Winslow—or even be able to recall the name of the man who had tried to save his courthouse, a man who had lost himself in the process.

With a resigned businesslike manner, Mayor Ansel turned toward Judge Wheelus. "Judge, I know you have been conferring with the military provost marshal and can explain to us about the martial rule we're under."

"The town is under martial law indefinitely, Mayor," Judge Wheelus said, "and the troops have been ordered to remain here until everything returns to normal. Some arrests have already been made and there is, of course, a military court of inquiry. Colonel Dawes assures me that, although the military rule will be supreme over the constituted civil authorities, none of the civil governmental agencies will be set aside."

The Judge removed his glasses and paused, searching his pockets for his handkerchief. Finding it, he sat back again and proceeded to clean them. Everyone, intent on his words, sat silent, waiting for him to continue. Finally, he went on. "The declaration of martial law does not supersede or suspend the constitution or the statute laws of Texas, but it does recognize that the enforcement of these laws by our peace officers has been rendered inoperative and powerless by existing conditions. The purpose of declaring martial law and placing the control of the town in the hands of National Guard troops is to reestablish the constitutional and civil government and to restore law and order."

He paused again to replace his glasses on his nose, then added firmly, "What they want—what we all want— is arrests. And, with martial law in effect, suspects can be picked up and held where, without martial law, the process would be much slower. The mission of the National Guard is to arrest all persons guilty of acts of violence before and after martial law was declared and to present these violators to civil courts for trial."

"Well, we certainly all agree on one thing: We want to get this thing cleared up as quickly as possible and get our town back to normal." Mayor Ansel said. There were emphatic nods of agreement and the room hummed with conversation. The voices quietened again when the mayor asked, "Captain Boggs, will you fill us in on the details of the troops and their operation?"

Captain Boggs, sitting in the front, stood up and faced the audience before beginning to speak. "As you already know, 100 additional troops came in early this morning. With the 150 that came last night and the 50 already here from the first contingent, this makes a total of 300 troops. They are headquartered at the jail and the majority will stay there indefinitely. Threats have been made against the Negro prisoners there—threats that the jail will be broken into and the Negro prisoners taken out and lynched. So, we are guarding it closely to protect them. A unit was sent out this morning to cut down the body of the Negro from the tree and it was turned over to the Negro undertaker in Duganville since the Negro undertaker's house here in Anseltown was burned last night. Also," he nodded in Chalker's direction, "in cooperation with Chief Chalker, the troops have made several arrests today. We have witnesses who have identified some of the instigators of the mob. We've placed the two women under arrest who were the first ones to throw rocks and break windows of the courthouse. One man was arrested this morning in town and we found several sticks of dynamite in his car. We arrested two other men at home who had been identified as leaders of the mob and we found dynamite on their premises."

Chief Chalker interrupted at this point to add, "We have witnesses who will identify the leaders so we should be able to arrest all those who were behind the whole thing!"

Captain Boggs continued, "We have placed a unit of the troops at the Negro school and our military headquarters has direct telephone connection with the school. It has been reported to us that threats have been made to burn it down!" He paused a moment, scanning the audience. His voice was sharp, insolent as he went on! "Our hands aren't going to be tied anymore. My men have been ordered to shoot if necessary!"

Watching him, Chalker hated him more than ever now with his swaggering self-assured cockiness. With loathing, he noted the smug expression on Bogg's face as he went on arrogantly, "Four machine guns have been set up to cover the approach streets to the jail and automatic rifles are all in place on the lawn. Crowds have been prohibited from congregating. No firearms, ammunition or explosives of any character will be sold, bartered, exchanged or given away within the affected precinct. Nor will any such be transported into it, except with the permission and under the direction and control of the provost marshal. All military officers, soldiers, Texas Rangers and other persons on duty with the military will be treated with respect and their orders will be promptly complied with." Captain Boggs stopped momentarily. He looked around triumphantly, before continuing, "There isn't going to be anymore looting and burning of the Negro homes. Many have been threatened if they don't get out of town. Signs have been found posted in their area, instructing them to leave—or else. But our soldiers are now patrolling their neighborhood and will stay there to protect them as long as is necessary. We have also heard rumors that white employers of Negroes have been warned to fire them or..."

"I got a call this morning," Ned Hilton interrupted. "A man told me I'd better fire my janitor that cleans my drug store if I knew what was good for me. He said there were plenty of white men who could use that job rather than a nigger. He called me a filthy name and said no decent white man would want to keep a nigger employed after what one did to the Johnson girl."

"Did you recognize—do you have any idea whose voice

it could have been?" Chalker asked.

"None at all. It was very muffled. He must have had a rag or something over the phone."

"Well, we've talked to the phone company," Chalker said, "and we have their full cooperation. If any of you get any calls like that, just as soon as they hang up, ask the operator to trace the call. The switchboard isn't very big and they can usually do it—provided you ask them to do so immediately after the call while the connection is still up on the board."

Captain Boggs, who was still standing, said, "What we haven't been able to do is find out who was responsible for spreading the rumor of the nonexistent message from Governor Franklin to me to 'protect the Negro if possible but not to shoot anyone'!" His voice had turned hard, sarcastic. His eyes moved about the room and rested on Sam as he said, "I talked to the governor this morning and he told me that no such message was sent by him!" An expectant hush fell over the audience. Anger was visibly evident on his face and in his voice as he addressed Sam, "Mr. Britton, maybe you can explain just how and where your reporter got news of a message that was never sent out by the governor!"

Sam, conscious of all eyes focused on him now, replied distinctly and evenly, "I'll be glad to explain how our newspaper got the news, Captain Boggs. We got it from no less than the Associated Press!"

"Well, where in hell did they get it?" Chalker exploded. "I checked with the Dallas office today when Judge Wheelus called and told me that Governor Franklin denied sending the message."

Sam replied, "A. P. told me that they got the news from the Duganville office yesterday morning. They said that, up until now, it had always been a reliable source, so they ran it. When the news about the governor's message came across the wires yesterday from the Associated Press—that's when my reporter, Bob Simms, brought it to you at the courthouse, Captain."

"He picked a helluva time to deliver it!" Boggs said, heatedly. "Right in the middle of that mob that was already worked up—it was all they needed to set them off! He might as well have struck a match and held it to a stick of dynamite!"

Sam broke in quickly, his voice sharp now, "Captain, I did not authorize Simms to relay that A. P. report to you. I did not know that he had done so until afterwards." He paused and, in a tightly controlled voice, continued, "It seems to me that the guilt lies with the person who started the lie and perpetuated it until it was printed as the truth!"

"Gentlemen, that seems impossible to determine..." Mayor Ansel began.

But Captain Boggs, interrupted, confronting Sam again, "Getting back to the Duganville paper, Britton, how come they printed the rumor?"

"Don Hughes—he's the Editor of the Duganville Daily News—said he got the story from Tom Cooper, one of his reporters who called it in from Anseltown yesterday morning. Cooper told Hughes that he had just come from the courthouse and that was the word there. Hughes thought that his reporter had gotten it from an official in the courthouse, so he printed it."

"You mean he didn't double check with some official?" Mayor Ansel asked indignantly.

"When Cooper told him the message came from the courthouse, Hughes took it for granted that he had got the word from an official." Sam answered.

"That reporter ought to be arrested!" Mayor Ansel said. "There's no doubt about it—he was the one who started the rumor!"

"Mayor, he didn't start it. He was only reporting what he heard—what everyone of us here heard all over town yesterday—and believed!" Sam said dryly. "We need to find out who thought up and started this diabolical thing!"

"Well, if it wasn't Cooper, it was probably another outsider!" Mayor Ansel said contemptuously, looking directly at Sam. The others missed the mayor's barbed implication.

"It's just a damn shame that this whole mess had to happen in our town!" Barney Blossom said, mopping at his moist florid face with his handkerchief.

"It sure is," Walter Anderson added, "why, it will probably set Anseltown back fifty years!"

"Not to mention that a man was murdered without having a trial!" Sam interjected heatedly.

"You mean you think he was innocent?" Mayor Ansel asked angrily.

"I don't know. I can't say whether he was guilty or innocent," Sam replied. "All I know is that he didn't get a trial and he denied committing the crime—he said he wasn't guilty."

"Did you think the bastard would admit it?" the mayor retorted, infuriated.

"It's not a question of what I think—or you—or anybody," Sam spoke in a determinedly calm tone. "We'll never get the chance to find out now, will we? Because the man didn't get his chance for a trial—a trial that is supposed to be guaranteed by our system of government to prove whether a person is guilty or innocent."

"If it hadn't been for your damn reporter broadcasting that 'so called' message from the governor, we would have been able to see that the Negro did get a trial!" Captain Boggs said, bitingly.

Sam looked at him coldly, "Every effort should be made to find the person responsible for starting that rumor," he said. "Perhaps, the military court of inquiry will have more success than you have had with this whole affair!"

Captain Boggs' face flushed with anger.

Before he could retort, Mayor Ansel quickly cut in. "I don't think anyone needs to tell Captain Boggs or our police chief how to run their investigation," he said, "especially outsiders! It seems to me that's been the crux of our problem. I'm sure it was outsiders who caused most of this trouble. And, because of them," he was looking at Sam, addressing his remarks directly to him, "our town is being made the scapegoat of the whole state and country— even the world."

"In the light of what's happened, it will take two or three generations for Anseltown to outlive this scandal," Art Jensen said accusingly.

"Our town's growth will come to a standstill," Barney Blossom stated.

"What growth, Barney?" Sam roared, rising halfway out of his chair in his rage. He was seething with fury. Mayor Ansel's words had broken the dam holding the reservoir of anger in check within him. Startled at the intensity and volume of his voice, all eyes focused upon him. Aware of their scrutiny, Sam made a tremendous effort to bring his passionate emotions under control. He fastened his eyes on Mayor Ansel and, although he felt like exploding, his words were spoken evenly, deadly. He kept them lucid and clear for he wanted them to be plainly understood. His tone of voice commanded attention and a hush fell over the room as everyone listened attentively.

"Mayor, you call me an *outsider*, yet, I have lived in Anseltown for twenty years. I have been a part of it and have loved most of its people all these years. The majority of them are plain good hard-working, God-fearing, honest folks who have been maligned, taken advantage of, exploited in every way imaginable by a few who have the audacity to call themselves *human beings*! All of you!" Sam pointed his finger at the men who were the merchants, the mill and factory owners. They stared at him with surprised, shocked expressions, their mouths agape, stunned into silence by his impassioned words, "All of you so called *leaders* of Anseltown," he continued, "attained this position, this title of *leader* solely because you were fortunate enough to have money. You have the audacity to think," Sam's voice rose in his emotion, "that this money gives you the power—yes, even the God-given right—to control, dictate and manipulate the lives and destinies of the poor in this town! These people who did not have the good fortune to be born with the proverbial silver spoon in their mouths as most of you were! You *leaders*, and especially you, Mayor," Sam turned accusingly toward Mayor Ansel. His mouth was open, his jaw slack, and his eyes glowered at this unexpected tirade that had left him speechless. "Mayor Ansel, you have controlled the very standards under which these people live! You have determined the types—yes, even the amounts of food most of them can eat because of the pecuniary pittance of pay that you dole out to them for their slave labor to you! You," Sam's hand swept the room, "all of you, have eaten cake by the sweat of the other fellow's brow!"

"Now you listen..." Mayor Ansel roared, finally able to speak, but he was interrupted sharply by Sam's angry, equally explosive voice.

"No!" he shouted, jumping to his feet and pointing his finger at him. "You listen to me!" The mayor, shocked at the fury and determination in Sam's tone, sank back in his chair, electrified into silence by this audacious unaccustomed assault.

Sam remained standing and continued in an emotion-filled voice, "Have any of you ever opened your eyes and *really* looked at these people—*your* people—in this town? Can't you see their deplorable plight, their underfed children, their poverty? Are you so apathetic, so..." he hesitated, searching for the word he wanted, then added, "phlegmatic? How can you be so unresponsive to the deprivation of your people?" He paused, examining their faces. Then, softly, he asked, "Are you completely blind?"

No one spoke. A deep silence prevailed over the room. Sam became aware that his body was trembling. His legs felt weak. He breathed deeply in an effort to regain control of himself. Slowly, he turned and faced Mayor Ansel at his desk and addressed him personally. His voice was lower, calmer, "If *outsider* means that one has the capabilities to see and object to the malice, the wrongdoing, the injustices perpetrated by the affluent, more fortunate class of people on the less fortunate ones, then, thank God, Mayor, I am truly—and, hopefully, I will always remain—an *outsider!*"

His anger which had momentarily subsided flared anew as he went on, speaking to the room as a whole again, "This could have been a good town. It could have been a great town. Everyone could have lived decently and well if a few hadn't been so damn greedy!"

He focused his gaze on Barney. "You speak of growth, Barney, but you don't mean it! If this town had been allowed to grow—if new industries had been allowed in, you wouldn't be able to work men who are forced to underbid each other. Indeed, they are forced to underbid their good friends and neighbors, in order to get your jobs! You didn't want Anseltown to grow." Sam's voice was scornful, filled with contempt. "If it had, you couldn't have worked men for five cents an hour—or for only a sack of flour!" Barney's face flushed red, grew even more crimson than its usual hue. He was sweating profusely. His bald head glistened in its customary sheen of wetness. He kept his eyes fastened on the floor and said nothing.

Sam turned away from him. His eyes moved from face to face, lingering briefly, searchingly on each one as he spoke, "You all know what has held this town down and eroded its growth. None of you wanted any new outside interests to be established here. You were opposed to them for they would compete with you for labor and provide other employment for the people. You were smug and complacent for you already had your wealth! So you wanted to keep things just the way they were! And you didn't want to lose your power, your hold on the people. You wanted to keep them right under your thumbs where you'd always forced them, where you could squeeze them, tighter and tighter! You didn't want them to be able to crawl out! You drained them of their labor, their energies, of every human dignity that man possesses. But, worst of all, you drained them of hope!" He paused and peered at his audience over the rim of his glasses. His eyes were penetrating. He shook his head sadly as he said, "And the pity of it all is that you actually thought you had the right to do so!"

He thrust his hands in his pants pockets to still their shaking. The magnitude of his feelings had engulfed him, overpowered him. He was exhausted. Obstinately resolved to finish what he had to say, he straightened his shoulders and stood his ground as he went on in a determinedly firm and distinct voice, "Anseltown was founded on the exploitation of the poor. That has been its code from the beginning. They have borne the brunt of this shameless, merciless exploitation, this ruthless greed and suffered terribly from it. They have been the scapegoats. They finally had all they could stand and, yesterday, they reached the breaking point! You have no one—*no one*—but yourselves to blame for the situation that you find yourselves in at this moment!"

He stopped now. In the tense electric quietness, he

gazed steadily, solemnly into the still dazed faces, into the eyes that were glued on him. After a long moment, he said softly, "You begetted your harvest in greed and it has returned to consume you with violence." He paused briefly. His eyes were somber. He said gravely, sadly, "Gentlemen, you have sown your seeds and reaped your harvest—your harvest of tears!"

Then, amid the silence that gripped the room, he turned away from them. He walked slowly, wearily to the door and disappeared through it.

CHAPTER 20

Elisabeth vigorously dug the weeds from around the rose bush in the beds at the front of the house. It was early morning. The flowers were just beginning to awaken along with the sun. The rose petals, sprinkled with the night's dew, yet undried, were waxy, almost artificial looking.

Elisabeth had already cut a half dozen of the long stemmed roses and plunged them into luke-warm water to seal the stems and preserve their fragrant freshness. From the first new buds in the rebirth of spring until the last blooms slowly faded in the frosty chill of autumn, she adorned her kitchen with their splendor. She did not own a vase and the thought never crossed Elisabeth's mind to spend the money—precious money that could be used for food for her children—to buy one. But, even the fruit jar in which they rested could not detract from their majestic nobility. To Elisabeth, the magnitude of their beauty surpassed that of anything else on earth. The presence of roses around her, being able to see, to touch and smell them, gave her an inner feeling of peace and tranquility. Their beauty gave her a sense of security in the knowledge that a Supreme Being existed. For, couldn't only God create something so magnificently lovely, so perfect? And, during each long winter, she waited impatiently for the first hint of spring that was necessary to initiate the appearance of her beloved roses once again.

She was very tired. She had spent an almost sleepless night again last night. It had been two weeks now since Jon left—the same day the town had gone crazy. She shuddered. Maybe the whole world had gone insane. It had fallen apart around her. Elisabeth's face was creased with worry and lined with fatigue. Her green eyes, emphasized by the dark circles that lay beneath them, appeared even larger in the thinness of her face. She had lost weight. The thin cotton dress hung loosely on her.

She had learned that Jon had been in Anseltown that day—the day the courthouse was burned. It was the day he was supposed to get back from his truck run and she had reports from several who had seen him in town. Then two days later, Mr. Blossom from the mill, had come to see her to tell her about the charred wreckage of the truck that had been found in west Texas which they thought might be theirs. It had been too badly destroyed to identify positively. He had assured her that no body had been found in it so, if it were theirs, Jon had apparently escaped. Although she didn't say anything to Mr. Blossom, in her heart, she knew that it was Jon's truck. She was certain, too, that he had set it afire, for she knew Jon and his overwhelming desire to escape from Anseltown, the place he had hated so much. Yes, Jon had set the fire and burned the truck. That was like Jon, to burn his bridges behind him, to sever the final link that would connect him to the past.

Until now, she had refused to accept the fact that it had been over between them for a long time; at least, it had been on Jon's part. Her refusal to agree to his acceptance of the baseball contract years ago had been the beginning— and the end of their marriage. And she knew that Jon would not be coming home again.

Elisabeth shook herself mentally. She had taken stock and come to terms with herself last night as she lay awake.

She was not going to brood and make life miserable for herself and the children—most of all, not for the children.

She could and would stand on her own two feet. Glo-ree's face flashed before her. She would be strong—like Glo-ree. She would be alright if she could emulate the courage and fortitude that Glo-ree possessed. She would make the best of things, for it must be the Lord's will. And, who was she to fight against Him?

Elisabeth's face clouded as her thoughts turned to Larry. If only I could reach him, she thought. She had always been so close to her eldest son, but now he was a stranger to her. He hadn't spoken except to answer a question and had hardly eaten since the brutal shock of Alicia's death. He had grown pale, thin and listless. He only came out of his room when it was necessary to do his chores, returning to it immediately afterwards. He had shown no emotion, at least not visibly, when she told him gently about Jon's going away. He had only listened quietly; then, without a word, he went back to his room.

Her glance strayed far up the street past the railroad track where Glo-ree had lived. She had avoided looking in that direction this past two weeks. It pained her to see the black mounds of rubble piled forlornly in the distance, the only evidence remaining of the small shanty homes of the Negroes. Now, something that moved by one of the charred heaps caught her attention.

"Oh, my God, it's Glo-ree!" Elisabeth whispered. She dropped the hoe that she was holding and began to run up the street. She had not seen Glo-ree since Alicia's murder. She and her daughters, along with the rest of Anseltown's Negroes, had disappeared quickly, hiding in the woods or leaving town completely. She did not know what had happened to her.

When she was halfway up the street, Glo-ree saw her. She stood still as Elisabeth approached and rushed to her with opened arms. She was shocked at Glo-ree's appearance. She had lost so much weight that her dress and customary white apron hung loosely, shapelessly on her thin, gaunt body.

Her eyes, sunken, wore a haunted expression. With arms entwined, they clung together, crying, saying nothing for long minutes. Then Elisabeth whispered over and over, "I'm so sorry, Glo-ree." Finally, purged of some of their grief, they parted.

"Oh, Miz Elisabeth, he didn't do it! Daniel never done it!" Glo-ree sobbed. Elisabeth held Glo-ree's hand and let her talk. "A mother knows her young 'uns. She can tell when they's lyin'. And Daniel tole' me he never done it! He tole' me he never done anything to that Miss Alicia!"

Elisabeth was at a loss for words. She did not know how to comfort her friend. She stood, patting Glo-ree's hand all the while, rendered helpless by the sorrow confronting her.

"I only got to see Daniel one time, Miz Elisabeth, after they locked him up in that jail," Glo-ree went on. "And they let me see him then for only five minutes." Tears streamed down her face. Her shoulders shook. Elisabeth's face was wet. "He tole' me, 'Mama, I didn't never kill nobody or do anything to that girl!' And he said, 'Mama, you know I wouldn't lie to you. You taught us kids not to lie and I ain't lyin' to you now'!" Glo-ree put her hands over her face while loud groans racked her body.

Elisabeth placed her arms around her, patting her comfortingly, until her sobs subsided. Finally, Glo-ree wiped at her eyes with her apron. "Jes' before they tole' me I had to leave, I put my arms through the bars and hugged Daniel. He kissed me on the cheek and he had tears in his eyes," Glo-ree's voice broke again, but she went on. "I ain't never seen Daniel cry since he grown into a man. He had tears in his eyes and he tole' me, 'Mama, no matter what anybody says or what happens to me, you always remember that I didn't kill nobody or do anything to that girl'!" Sobs engulfed her again as she whispered in anguish, "Then, them policemens—they made me leave my boy—my baby!" She lifted her face to the sky. Tears rained down her cheeks as, in a loud agonizing voice, she pleaded, "Oh, dear Lawd, take care of my baby for me."

Elisabeth placed her arm about Glo-ree's shoulders. Side by side with her, she looked upwards through her own tears into the heavens. "He will, Glo-ree," she said softly, "He will!"

After a long moment, she took hold of Glo-ree's arms and turned her, gently but firmly, until she could look into her eyes. "Now, Glo-ree, you are not to cry anymore. You have cried enough. And you know that Daniel loved you and he wouldn't want you to cry!" Glo-ree dropped her head but Elisabeth made her look up again by demanding, "Now, would he, Glo-ree?"

She answered weakly, "No, Miz Elisabeth."

"Well, now, that should settle it," Elisabeth said trying to force a smile, "no more tears!"

She was silent while Glo-ree lifted the end of her apron and wiped her face with it. Then, she asked, "Where are you living, Glo-ree?"

"I'ze been stayin' with Pastor Williams and his wife—me and the chillun'—that is, since last Sunday when we came out of the woods. We stayed hid out there with Pastor and his missus and the others till we knowed it was safe to come back to town. The policemens found us and promised that the soldier boys was goin' to stay and protect us. So, then, we come back to town."

"Are you going to stay with the Reverend?"

"Oh, no, Miz Elisabeth, me and the girls are leavin' today on the train for Chicago!"

Elisabeth's eyes widened in surprise. "Chicago? But,

why?"

"Mayor Ansel done give us the tickets to go on the train—and fifty dollars besides!" Glo-ree said. "We'ze goin' stay with my cousin till I finds me a job."

"I don't understand..." Elisabeth began.

Glo-ree interrupted. "Well, the Mayor came to see me, soon as we done come back to town last Sunday. He said he'd been tryin' to fin' me. He tole' me he wanted to help us, seein' as how I have no boy to help out at home no mo'. He said that the way I works so good that I won't have no trouble gettin' work in Chicago. He says it will be better for me up north—that I'ze goin' get mo' work and make mo' money there too."

Glo-ree turned to look at the devastation around her. "I done come back here today to see it one mo' time." Her voice broke as she gazed despairingly at the debris that was once her home. "But now I wish I didn't." Her lips trembled.

Elisabeth said quickly, "Now, Glo-ree, remember—no more tears!"

Glo-ree swallowed hard, fighting for control, before speaking, "I wanted to see if anything was left. I wished I could fin' my Bible. It was my Grandmama's. It had names of our family and dates—you know, dates of birthin's and dyin's and things like that."

"Yes, Glo-ree, I know," Elisabeth said, "well, now, let's get busy and look around and see what we can find." They busied themselves, searching around the area, scanning the ground, not talking now. Elisabeth noticed that Glo-ree, from time to time, picked up small objects. Even though they were scorched badly, she knew that they were meaningful mementos to her, reminders of days gone by. Elisabeth saw Glo-ree place them carefully, lovingly in the large pocket of her apron.

Suddenly, she heard Glo-ree give a little cry of pleasure.

She hurried to her side. She was holding a Bible that she had picked up from the dirt where it had apparently lain since the fire. Glo-ree examined it reverently. It was in surprisingly good condition. Some of the pages had been singed but, otherwise, it appeared intact. Glo-ree hurriedly turned to the family history, exclaiming joyfully when she saw that these pages had escaped damage. She smiled for the first time. Elisabeth hugged her happily.

"I'd best be gettin' back to Pastor William's house, Miz Elisabeth," Glo-ree said, "the train leaves at 3 o'clock this afternoon. I got to get the girls ready and tell everybody good-bye." There was a note of pride in her voice as she added, "Everybody is meetin' at the church at 1 o'clock to tell us good-bye."

"Then, we'd better get going." Elisabeth said, forcing her voice to sound cheerful.

Respectfully standing a short distance away, she waited quietly as Glo-ree took one more long look, silently drinking in the remains and the memories of her former home. Here in this home she had lived for so many years and raised her children. Then, without speaking, they turned together and walked slowly down the road. Elisabeth did not speak of what had happened to her family within the past two weeks—about Jon leaving her and the children. She did not want to add still another burden to her friend. She knew that it would hurt Glo-ree to learn of her troubles. And Glo-ree had already endured too much pain for one lifetime.

They stopped in front of Elisabeth's house. She clasped Glo-ree's hand, saying, "Oh, Glo-ree, I'm going to miss you! I'm going to miss you so much!" Her eyes misted over and she saw tears well up in Glo-ree's eyes as well.

"And I'ze goin' to miss you, Miz Elisabeth!" she whispered huskily, "and I'll never forget you—never, as long as I live!"

Elisabeth reached out her arms and they clung together once more for a long moment. Suddenly, Elisabeth pushed her away gently, saying brokenly, "You'd better get along now, Glo-ree, before you miss your train." Elisabeth made a brave attempt to smile, "And before we both start crying again! And, we both agreed there will be no more tears!"

"Yessum, Miz Elisabeth," Glo-ree smiled wanly back at her.

Elisabeth quickly kissed her cheek. "I'll never forget you either, Glo-ree—my friend."

Glo-ree turned away quickly. She walked swiftly down the street, her back straight, her head held high. She did not look back.

Sadly, Elisabeth watched her go, hugging her Bible in her arms. Tears that brimmed anew blurred her vision and Glo-ree's figure disappearing in the distance. Elisabeth whispered fiercely to herself, "Remember—no more tears!"

That night Elisabeth turned down the covers on her bed. She sighed wearily as she sat down on one side. She picked up her sewing basket and Roscoe's overalls from the nearby chair where she had placed them while she undressed. The knee was in need of patching again. *Roscoe is so hard on his clothes,* she thought. She pulled the oil lamp nearer the edge of the table in order to see better by its dim light as she sewed. *She had to keep her hands busy. Maybe it would occupy her mind, prevent her from thinking. She wished that she could sleep but, as tired as she was, she knew that she couldn't.*

She tried to concentrate on her needle and thread as she moved them nimbly in and out of the material, but her mind refused to blank out the vision of Glo-ree standing beside the rubbled ruins of her home this morning, crying for her son. The patch blurred in her hands. She ceased sewing and wiped at the tears coursing down her cheeks. She recalled her words, *no more tears,* that she had repeated to Glo-ree. They seemed so empty, so meaningless now. Abruptly, she buried her face in her hands while loud wrenching sobs racked her being. She was unable to stop. The emotional strain of seeing Glo-ree today for the last time, culminating the events of the past two weeks, had been the breaking point.

Suddenly, she felt a hand on her arm and she looked up into Larry's pained distraught face. Sitting down, he put his arms around her and buried his head on her shoulder. They held each other tightly as they cried together. His reserve that had been dammed up inside him finally broke at the sight of his mother's tears and gushed forth in a torrent of release. His body trembled violently. Her own suffering superseded by her son's distress, Elisabeth patted him soothingly, rocking him back and forth while she whispered over and over, "Everything's alright now, son." His body slowly relaxed. A tremendous sense of relief washed over her.

After a long while, Larry gradually grew quiet as his emotional anguish subsided. Visibly relieved, he began to talk, hesitantly at first. Then, his words that had been held in check for so long rushed out, tumbling over each other in his desire to release them. He related the events that had happened on the day of the picnic at the Johnsons' farm: Of Stony's attempted attack on Alicia at the swimming pond, his fight with Stony, and how Daniel intervened for him and saved his life. Shocked, Elisabeth listened without interruptions, without questions. When he had finished, he was so emotionally spent and exhausted that she made him lay back while she got a wet cloth and bathed his flushed tear-stained face. He fell asleep immediately.

Elisabeth gazed on her son's sleeping countenance, now peaceful and free of tension. A wave of tender pathos engulfed her. He was so young, so sensitive. He had carried such a heavy burden alone. He had told her of his promise to Alicia, his promise not to reveal their encounter with Stony. Torn apart by his grief for his first love and the vow that he made to her had proved almost too much for him. She looked once more on Larry's tranquil face before blowing out the lamp and lying down beside him. This was the first time that he had slept in her bed since he was a small boy.

She lay still so as not to disturb him, but she was wide awake as thoughts plagued her mind, nagged at her relentlessly. *What shall I do and who shall I go to?* she asked herself anxiously. *One thing is certain—I must tell someone about Stony's previous attack on Alicia. Did Stony do this terrible thing? He was the one who claimed to have seen Daniel coming from the woods on the day of Alicia's murder. Oh, God—poor, poor Daniel! Poor Glo-ree! Daniel told Glo-ree that he didn't do it—and I believe him. I've got to clear his name if I can. It's too late for poor Daniel but I've got to do it for Glo-ree. I want her and everyone to know how Daniel saved my son's life. I must go to someone and tell them about Stony. But who? How can I go to Chief Chalker? He's Mayor Ansel's son-in-law. It would be my word against the mayor's son. And, who would believe me? Should I go to that Texas Ranger and tell him?*

Elisabeth communed with herself, deliberating, reflecting, arguing. She turned ideas over in her mind until her head, confused and chaotic, felt as though it would burst. Suddenly, the solution came to her. It was so simple, so obvious that she was angry with herself for not thinking of it immediately—Sam Britton! *Of course, she thought. I'll talk to Sam. He will know what to do. I'll go see him first thing in the morning.*

With her mind free and clear at last, Elisabeth's body relaxed. She was almost asleep when she heard the faint wail of a siren in the distance. It was the second siren that she'd heard today. Strange, she thought, her mind fogged by her half-conscious state, it doesn't sound as ominous and despairing as the one which she heard earlier while preparing supper.

A slight smile played about her mouth as a last thought penetrated the misty perceptiveness of her mind. Her son, sleeping deeply beside her, had been given back to her today. He was no longer a stranger. Everything was going to be alright now. She would talk to Sam in the morning. For the first time in two weeks, Elisabeth slept soundly.

CHAPTER 21

On the afternoon of the same day that Elisabeth bid Glo-ree good bye, Sam Britton was in his newspaper office. He was seated at his desk, reading a compilation of articles concerning Anseltown which had suddenly become the world's target of dart-throwing editorials. Fingers of scorn were pointed. Floods of condemnation continued to pour in upon them. The town was being castigated by the pens and consciences of civilized men everywhere.

Thumbing through the pile of papers on his desk, Sam read excerpts from several of the editorials:

Anseltown's name has been dishonored by her own people. It will take a generation to outlive the stain on her honor if it can ever be done. The Negro who was accused of this dastardly crime is dead but this is poor pay for the loss of reputation, financial loss and the act of lawlessness that the act has set before the world.

Rain that has fallen on Anseltown since the riot doubtless will wash away the blood stains left by the raging mob, but nothing short of a baptism of hell-hot fire could remove the ghastly disfiguration left upon the character of the town.

Did this really happen in Texas? He would have been hung under Texas law. Where were Crockett, Bowie, Houston, Lamar, Throckmorton, Travis and Bonham? Dead and forgotten! It is unfortunate that the spirit that guided them and Texas to independence in 1836 could not have risen in this crucial hour and saved Anseltown from itself!

No crime that Santa Anna or Jose Urrea committed at the Alamo, Refugio or Goliad was more heinous in proportion. Has Anseltown forgotten so soon that a Negro slave was among the 144 who fought till the last drop of blood was drained in the massacre of the Alamo?

What will Texas do about Anseltown? Governor Franklin has declared martial law and says that every power in the state will be used to find and punish those responsible. But we seriously doubt if the governor will be able to do more than issue the order. Because it is nearly impossible to make a city answer for a crime of this sort. But Anseltown eventually must answer to herself. What will she say then?

Indeed, what will Anseltown say? Sam wondered, looking up from his desk and settling back in his chair. He removed his glasses and closed his eyes momentarily, resting them as his thoughts continued. Mayor Ansel had already retaliated with a typical "Mayor Ansel Declaration" saying that Anseltown was the victim of circumstances and was more deserving of sympathy than censure. He conceded that it was a great stain on their honor but, in time, it would be forgotten and the town would "return to normal." Sam wondered if Anseltown would ever again be the same, or "normal" as the mayor said.

"I certainly hope not!" he grunted vehemently to himself. However, he hoped that the innocent would not have to suffer and bear the brunt of the stigma for the actions of the guilty.

Without warning, a loud blast suddenly and sharply rent the air, shaking the building. Sam turned in his chair so that he was able to see through the window and across the street where dynamite was being detonated to demolish the remaining ruins of the courthouse. The noise had been deafening the past few days. Now, as the result of the blast, thick clouds of dust hung chokingly over the area, caught and held almost stationary in the hot stifling August heat. The sweating grimy workers in dirt clogged clothes piled the debris onto trucks to be hauled away, clearing the site for a new courthouse that would be built eventually when funds became available.

Sam saw several soldiers walking along the sidewalk. The street was vacant except for them and a half-dozen citizens who, no doubt, had pressing business to attend to in town. Anyone, appearing on the streets were stopped, questioned and sent home if he could provide no legitimate excuse for his presence in the business district. After two weeks, Anseltown was still under martial law and would remain so for as long as the governor felt that it was necessary.

Even at a distance, Sam could detect the youthfulness of the soldiers. Governor Franklin had commended the

National Guard Troops in a citation extolling "their self-contained behavior in such a splendid manner during the mob riot. They exercised great remarkable self-restraint and control in the face of danger from the mob confronting them." *The plaudits and praise for these young men were justifiably earned and richly deserved,* Sam thought. *Had they acted otherwise, panicked and used their guns, many in the crowd which included women and young children would undoubtedly have been killed.*

Sam reflected on the events of the past two weeks as he gazed through the window at the workmen across the street who were endeavoring to erase the evil evidence of that infamous day in Anseltown's history. With determined efficiency, a military court of inquiry had been set up to insure that justice was meted out to the guilty. Court sessions were convened in a room of the jail. A total of 32 witnesses had been called before the court and questioned concerning the identification and actions of those in the riot. Examination of these witnesses had resulted in the arrest of 38 men and boys and two women within two days after the mob action. With the addition of these to the prisoners already incarcerated, the total population of the jail swelled to 65, the record number ever occupying it at one time.

The court of inquiry hearings had been thorough and swift. Both the federal and the state court grand juries convened five days after the courthouse was burned. Of the total 40 persons arrested, indictments were returned against 14 men. The two women and younger boys were freed. Each man was charged with rioting, riot with intent to murder, burglary by explosives to commit arson, two charges of arson and three were charged with national prohibition law violations.

The men were promptly deported to the Fort Worth county jail and the cases were transferred to the Criminal

District Court in Fort Worth on change of venue. The military court recommended that the cases be transferred from Anseltown on the premise that fair trials would not be forthcoming from the jurors, made up of the town's citizens, who would not be in favor of convicting their friends and neighbors. The Judge of the Criminal Court in Fort Worth had already announced that the trials would most probably be delayed until September because of the crowded docket for the next month, the court vacations and the custom of slowing up jury service during the summer months to favor farmers.

Bonds for each man had been set at five thousand dollars by the Anseltown County District Court. Sam shook his head dejectedly as he recalled that, within two days after the men were indicted, a committee had been formed in Anseltown to raise funds for their bonds. And, now, the latest word was that the money was being raised rapidly and it was anticipated that the men would be released soon, pending trial.

After the riot, the Negro section of town had been placed under heavy guard by the troops who were instructed to shoot anyone caught attempting to set fire to or damage in any way the property owned by blacks. The heaviest contingent of soldiers had been placed around the school which had been verbosely threatened. The black population remained solely and restrictively in their section. Those who found it necessary to enter the white areas of town were escorted by soldiers. An investigation was being made of persons suspected to be responsible for placards that were tacked up in the black district, warning of serious consequences unless the Negroes left Anseltown. Efforts were also made to apprehend those sending decrees to white employers using black labor, ordering that they be discharged within 36 hours and whites be employed in their stead.

Abruptly, Sam's thoughts turned to Wayne Winslow, lingering sadly on him. There was no evidence against anyone for the vicious attack on him and none admitted their crime. Winslow was unable to identify his assassins who had, for all intent and purposes, murdered him, destroying him both physically and mentally, rendering him totally helpless for life.

What a tragic waste, Sam thought sorrowfully. *Winslow was so young. His life had only just begun.* His mind dwelled drearily on the aftermath of the riot. The bizarre events that had unfolded day by day were as shockingly unpredictable as the murder and the mob action had been—events that had nakedly revealed the true nature and character of men, both good and bad.

The military court had also conducted a painstaking check of the Western Union office and the telephone company in an effort to ascertain any communication from Governor Franklin to Captain Boggs prior to the burning of the courthouse. No records of any messages whatever between the two could be found. Captain Boggs testified of his thwarted and vain attempts to reach the governor after receiving the mysterious "order." The court had been equally unsuccessful in tracing down the source of the rumor.

Sam sighed. Leaning his head back against his chair, he closed his eyes and sat quietly, engrossed in deep contemplation. *He was still bewildered, puzzled by, this aspect—by this mythical fictitious command of the governor. The inconsistencies, the incongruity of the whole story concerning the legendary message perplexed and bothered him.* The curiosity that made him a good newspaper man would not leave this issue alone. *Something just didn't add up.*

Immersed in enigmatic circumspection, he did not hear the knock on his door. It was repeated, louder this time. Sam reverted his pensive attention to the present with difficulty. "Come in," he called. Looking up, he saw an overall-clad, skinny youth, whom he did not recognize at first, standing timidly in the doorway. Then, noting the blank expression on the boy's face, he realized that it was Willie, the retarded son of Jess and Bertie Dawkins. He was the eldest of their sizeable brood of children. The Dawkins' name, along with the majority of families living near the cotton mill where the men worked, came up each Christmas on the needy list for baskets of food and toys, a program that he and Lila solicited and sponsored. These families occupied the rows of "shotgun" shacks, so called because of their construction: Four rooms, one directly behind the other, which extended, narrowly long and straight, from the front to the rear.

Gangly and awkward, Willie remained standing in the doorway holding his battered cap in his hands and looking at Sam nervously. "Come on in, son," Sam said kindly, motioning him to the chair opposite his desk. Willie walked hesitantly to the chair, fingering his cap self-consciously. He sat down and kept his eyes fastened on the cap in his hands.

He must be at least 18 or 19 now, Sam thought, although his childlike and vacantly innocent features denied the chronological years. It didn't seem possible that it had been that long since Lila, delivering Christmas baskets, had advised Jess and Bertie to take him to a specialist in Dallas. He was not developing nor advancing normally for a baby his age. He and Lila had great compassion for the Dawkins and even greater admiration when Jess and Bertie, upon learning that Willie was incurably retarded, would not allow him to be institutionalized. He was their child and they wanted him.

Finally, after a long pause, Sam asked, "What can I do for you, Willie?"

Looking up at last, Willie licked his lips. He gulped noisily and, speaking in a fast jerky manner, he plunged in. "I gotta talk to somebody about it, Mr. Britton, and I knowed you could tell me what to do. I'm skeered to tell the police—afeared they might put me in jail, too—like they was doing with all them others!"

"What are you talking about, Willie?" Sam asked. Then, noting that Willie's hands were shaking and his face was red from heat and agitation, he added soothingly, "Now, just slow down, Willie, and don't be afraid. Would you like a glass of water?" Without waiting for an answer, he poured water from the ice filled pitcher on his desk and handed the glass to Willie. He drank it quickly, thirstily.

When he had finished, Sam asked gently, "Now, what is it that you want to talk to me about, Willie?"

"Well," Willie began again, "the police and them soldiers been asking around all over town about the message from the governor to that Texas Ranger feller. I been feeling awful bad about it but I was scared to say anything 'cause I didn't want to get locked up in no jail!"

"Hold on a minute, Willie!" Sam interjected. "Are you talking about the rumor regarding the message that Governor Franklin was supposed to have sent to Captain Boggs, telling him to protected the Negro if possible but not to shoot anyone?"

"Yes-sir!"

"Well, what do you know about it, Willie?" Sam asked impatiently, leaning forward anxiously in his chair. "Do you know who started it?"

Willie's lip quivered and, for a minute, Sam thought he was going to burst into tears. He gulped again several times. Finally, in a low voice that was barely above a whisper, he said, "I did, Mr. Britton!"

"You started it, Willie?" Sam shouted, incredulous. He had jumped from his chair. He towered over his desk, glaring at Willie, as he asked angrily, "Why, for God's sake?"

Willie cowered back in his chair and looked fearfully up at Sam, "Are you mad at me, Mr. Britton? Are you going to let them put me in that jail?" His lips trembled.

Sam was breathing hard. With difficulty, he gained control of himself. Willie was scared. He had frightened him. And he couldn't afford to frighten him. He had to find out what Willie had to say. After a moment, he lowered his voice deliberately, saying, "No, Willie, no one is going to put you in jail. And I'm not mad at you, son. Now, you just tell me, slow and easy, why you started that rumor."

Willie, relieved that the anger was gone from Sam's voice, relaxed a little. "Well, I was just standing there listening to everyone talking..."

"Standing where, Willie?" Sam interrupted.

"Right over yonder on the square by the courthouse," he answered, pointing out the window. "I was listening to everyone talk about the trial and that nigger."

"When was this, Willie?"

"It was the morning on the day that that nigger was going to have his trial—the day the courthouse burned."

"Well, why did you say such a thing, Willie?" Sam asked. His voice was sharp despite his attempt to control it. Willie's lip started trembling again. Sam said hurriedly, "It's alright, Willie. I'm not mad at you. Just tell me why you said it."

"I just said what I heard him say. He tole' me about the message that the governor sent to that Ranger feller."

"Who, Willie? Who told you?" Sam demanded.

"Mayor Ansel tole' me." Willie answered.

Sam's eyes widened. "Mayor Ansel? Are you sure he was the one who told you, Willie? What did he say?"

Willie, confused by Sam's rapid-fire questions, hesitated. Sam asked impatiently, "Are you sure Mayor

Ansel told you, Willie?"

"Yes-sir, Mr. Britton, that was where I heard it. I was just standing there and he come up to me and tole' me about the governor sending a message to that Ranger feller telling him not to shoot nobody."

Sam, who had remained standing, sank down now into his chair. He sat still a long moment, saying nothing. Willie watched him anxiously. Finally, Sam spoke again, "What did you do when he told you, Willie?"

"Well, I just went around telling everybody else about it," he replied. "They all seemed real happy to hear about it." Remembering, Willie grinned foolishly.

Sam straightened in his chair and leaned across his desk, looking closely into Willie's face as he asked earnestly, "Are you absolutely sure, Willie, that Mayor Ansel was the first one you heard it from?"

"Oh, yes-sir, Mr. Britton!" Willie replied eagerly. "Cross my heart and hope to die!" With a forefinger, he solemnly made an imaginary cross on his chest before going on, "I never heard it before, from nobody, until he came up to me and tole' me about it."

"Did you hear the mayor tell anyone else, Willie?"

"No-sir, Mr. Britton."

"Where was Mayor Ansel, Willie, when everyone started talking about the governor's message?"

"I saw him leaving. He was going across the street. I never seen him no more."

"You didn't see him in the crowd again?" Sam asked.

"No-sir," Willie answered, "I never seen him no more."

Sam was silent for a long time. He was so absorbed in his thoughts that he was totally unaware any longer of Willie's presence. Willie fidgeted in his chair, turning his cap around in his hands uneasily. At last, he stood up and looked down at Sam, asking fearfully, "Mr. Britton, are them soldiers going to put me in that jail?"

Startled by the sound of his voice, Sam looked up. Rising, he put his arm about his shoulders and led him toward the door. "No, Willie," he said quietly, "no one is going to put you in jail."

Willie's vacuous features lit up now in a wide smile. "I knowed you'd make everything alright, Mr. Britton!" he said, happily. "You was always good to us—you and Miz Lila—bringing my ma and pa and us kids baskets at Christmas." Sam opened the door. Willie put his cap on his head, adding, "I knowed you'd help me. I've been mighty scared. I couldn't hardly sleep nights thinking about being locked up in that jail!" He self-consciously grabbed Sam's hand and shook it awkwardly as he said again, "I knowed you'd make everything alright, Mr. Britton!"

Sam watched his gangly figure bound joyfully down the stairs. He walked slowly, heavily back to his chair.

His mind was a total disarrayed jumble of chaos and turmoil. A multitude of questions tumbled around in his head. *Why did Mayor Ansel tell Willie about the governor's message? Could Willie be lying? Or did he make it up?* His mind discarded the ideas. *The boy may not be very bright but there's one thing he's got going for him—he's truthful. And, besides, he's not smart enough to fabricate a story or make anything up.*

Sam sighed. He was confused and tired and sick at heart. So much had happened in such a short time to the town, his town, and its people—to those he loved and to those whom he could not bring himself to love. He slouched in his chair dejectedly, almost defensively, as though to ward any further blows of despair away from his weary body, mind and soul. Tumultuous questions pounded and hammered through his head, demanding that his brain search for and find the answers—answers that eluded him.

The puzzle bits were askew and just wouldn't match up.

He recalled how, at the town meeting, Mayor Ansel had been so ready and eager to place the blame for the rumor on Tom Cooper, the reporter from the Duganville paper. Also, he had been perplexed when Glo-ree informed him that the mayor had paid the train fare to Chicago for her and her daughters, even gave her extra money. Frowning, Sam leaned his head against the back of the chair. *One question persisted and stood out clearly above all the others: Why would Mayor Ansel want to tell Willie about the governor's message to Captain Boggs?* He pounded his fist against the arm of his chair in agitated frustration. *Damn! The only logical answer that he could possibly come up with was that the mayor, knowing Willie would repeat whatever he was told, wanted the rumor spread. But, why?*

An expression of fierce determination settled on his face. He rose quickly to his feet and, in a decidedly resolute voice, said aloud, "There's one thing for sure—I'm going to see Mayor Ansel and find out!"

He reached for his hat from the rack hanging on the wall at the side of his desk. The large clock chimed. Glancing at it, he was surprised to see that it was 5:30 p.m. He had lost complete track of the time. It had been over an hour since Willie left. Placing his hat on his head, he walked purposefully toward the door. At that moment, the mournful sound of a siren rent the air outside. He paused at the window and saw an ambulance race past. Once again, he started to the door. He hesitated, undecided, then turned back to his desk. Without removing his hat, he picked up the telephone and, after a slight pause, said, "Winifred, ring the Funeral Home for me, please."

"Jed, who's going to the hospital?" he asked when the voice answered on the other end of the line.

"Bad news, Sam," Jed Ellis, owner of the Funeral Home, replied, "It's Stony Ansel..." his voice trailed off.

"What's the matter with him, Jed?"

"He was found a little while ago in the woods on the Johnson farm," he answered. "He committed suicide! From the looks of things, he stuck a rifle in his mouth and blew his head off!"

Sam sank down into his chair. Shocked, he was unable to say a word. After all that had happened in Anseltown the past two weeks, he had believed himself to be immune to further shock. A long silence followed.

"Are you alright, Sam?" Jed asked anxiously. "Are you still there?"

"Yes, I'm here, Jed," Sam said, at last, weakly. "I just find it hard to believe."

"I know," Jed said sadly. "I just got back. I drove out to the Johnson farm in my car behind the ambulance when we got the call. Mr. Johnson had called Chief Chalker and he brought Mayor Ansel out with him." He paused, then added, "The mayor's in awful bad shape. It's understandable. He insisted that we get Stony to the hospital. He wouldn't accept that he was dead. So, we did as he wished." Another silence ensued.

Finally, Sam, still unable to find any words, said simply, "Thanks, Jed." Slowly, he hung the receiver back on the hook.

That dark, moonless night, Sam and Lila sat on the porch. They did not talk. It wasn't necessary. Mother and son, they could communicate in silence. They could not see the shimmering lake in the darkness but they felt the gentle breeze that wafted from the water's coolness. Beyond the lake, the lights of Anseltown glimmered dimly, twinkling softly in the distant valley. A siren moaned faintly, seemingly from a long way off, in the still night. They looked at each other, still did not speak but continued to sit, contented.

Later, the phone rang in the hallway. Lila answered, talked briefly and hung up. She returned to the porch, walking slowly. She looked disconsolately at Sam and said quietly, sadly, "It was Mary Rogers. She said that Mayor Ansel is in the hospital. He had a stroke two hours ago. The doctor says he's dying."

The next morning dawned cool and fresh. The sun, not fully visible yet, promised a new day. Sam, already up, was deep in thought. He had neglected his store with all the activity at the newspaper. So he arrived early this morning, opened up and started stocking shelves. The physical activity occupied his hands and felt good. But his mind still dwelt on the events of the past weeks. They had taken their toll on everyone. *Everyone was asking "Why?" So far there were clues but no answers.*

He thought of his life also. And he thought of Elizabeth. *What would she do now that Jon was gone and, clearly, was not coming back?* He had waited too long when she was a girl. *I'm not going to make that mistake again,* he thought. *Why had life led him through this circuitous path? Alone?*

He looked up from the ever-depleting potato bin, seeing the outline of Elisabeth's familiar form in the doorway. The rigors of motherhood, Jon's leaving and the toils of daily routine had not taken from her beauty—the beauty he remembered as a youngster on the farm next door.

"Elizabeth, what are you doing here so early this morning?"

"I need to talk to you. I need someone to know." At this Elizabeth, poured out the story that Larry had related to her, the story of Stony's attack on Alicia, Daniel intervening and Stony's words "I'll get you for this!"

Sam's mind absorbed the information and, like the spoke of a wheel, this piece of information made all the pieces fit together. He smiled for first time in a long while.

Elizabeth, unburdened, was quiet. Then her thoughts went back to Larry and she told Sam how apathetic and silent he had been since Alicia's death.

"Maybe he would like to work at the newspaper office a few hours a week and get a taste of what being a reporter is like," he had stated. "Of course, he will be doing all sorts of odd jobs—running errands and such—but he will have the opportunity to see, first hand, what it's like to write for a newspaper. It might get his mind off this tragedy."

"Sam, what a wonderful opportunity for him. He'll be overjoyed!

"Thank you. Thank you for everything you do for my children, and for me. If there is anything I can do for you, please tell me." She studied him as he worked at the menial task; his desk in the corner was piled high.

"You know, Sam, you really work way too hard."

"There's lots to do," he replied, looking toward his guest and folding the now-empty sack of Number One Idaho potatoes. "But, you're right. I could always use some help. Mom has all she can handle and she's getting a little frailer with each passing day. Then, there's the newspaper..." his voice trailed off.

Sam reached deep. Screwed up his courage and waited for the words to come. Words he had practiced dozens of times over the years—but, till now, had never been uttered.

"Elisabeth," his voice drained of its vigor trailed off again. He could take on the entire city council, but now, he looked at the floor, shuffling his feet like a schoolboy in the principal's office.

"Yes, Sam," Elisabeth said, almost coyly, sensing the burden that Sam was carrying.

"Elisabeth...I really need you," Sam finally blurted out. "What I mean is, I could use your help."

"Sam, I..." Elisabeth started to speak.

"No, let me finish," Sam interjected. "I mean with all we have here to do. And I know you could use some extra money. I've been searching for someone to help Mother with the housework and cooking. Glo-ree worked for us for a few hours every week while she was employed by Mayor Ansel's wife. Now that she's gone...well, you'd be great help to Mother. You are a great cook, keep a wonderful house and Mom thinks the world of you." Sam stopped selling.

The years were melting away. Elisabeth knew it.

"Why, Sam," Elisabeth said, a smile erupting across her face. "That would be new beginning, a second chance for me." She, too, felt like a school girl again, blushing and smiling up at him, "A second chance for both of us."

They agreed that she would start on Monday. She wanted to get her own house and yard in order the remainder of this week before she started to work for Sam and Lila.

She hurried home. Elizabeth was overjoyed at this chance for Larry, and this new turn in her own life. She had cleaning, mending, weeding to do. She needed to prepare the children. She'd never worked for anyone before—what would she wear? She laughed at the excitement of it all. As she approached her home, she was pleased at the neat appearance presented by the flowerbeds and well-kept front lawn. Her eyes rested on her beautiful roses blooming beside the doorway. *God's gift to me,* she thought *His assurance that somehow everything will work out.*

That night, long after Lila had gone to bed, Sam found himself in a reflective mood on the front porch of his home. He stared sightlessly into the darkness of the night. Thoughts came to him randomly; thoughts that had no meaning, it seemed—at least no meaning he could wrap his hands around. The burning of the courthouse...the lynching of Daniel...and finally the death of Mayor Ansel. *How do you put all these things together? Or, do you?* As he set his mind adrift and stared at the darkening sky, speckled with an array of stars, he suddenly took notice of the crescent-shaped sliver of moon shimmering over the lake and town in the distance. The crescent held promise...promise of a full moon in the days to come— lighting the night sky with her brilliance. He thought again of Elisabeth and the hopes he had there. He thought of Anseltown and the possibilities that could be. Then, somehow, it all seemed right. The dark, moonless night of yesterday, but tonight, a crescent moon that promised a waxing to full...a promise of a new and much fuller life for himself ...a promise of a new way of life and a renewed love affair for the town he'd adopted and come to call home.

THE AUTHOR

Betty Pelley Smith
was born on
March 24, 1924 in
Sherman, Texas.
She graduated from
Sherman High School and
Draughons Business
College in Dallas, Texas.
During World War II, she married Jack Gordon Smith
from Cincinnati, Ohio who was stationed with the Tenth
Army Corps in Sherman. While Jack was in the military,
they lived in a number of states and in Paris, France.
Returning to the U.S. in 1966 after 22 years in the military,
they moved to Gardena, CA. In 1988 after the death of her
husband, she returned to Sherman, the Pelley family home.

Betty writes, "I was 5 years old when I saw the
Sherman courthouse burn and saw a body hanging from a
tree. In my 5-year-old mind, I remember thinking, 'I
thought he was black. All I see is white,' as only white bones
were hanging there. I was haunted all my life by this sight.
I could not understand how anyone could do such a horrible
thing. I promised myself someday to write a book about it. I
kept that promise and, in 1971, I began to write this book. I
finished it in two and a half years, before my 50th birthday!
It was a form of therapy.

"Even now, 75 years later, I am so emotional about this
that I shake as I write."

Printed in the United States
43753LVS00006B/1-72